# INTROVERTED ME

Kevin Martz

Copyright © 2020 Kevin Alan Martínez Reyna

All rights reserved

The characters and events portrayed in this book are fictitious. Any similarity to real persons, living or dead, is coincidental and not intended by the author.

No part of this book may be reproduced, or stored in a retrieval system, or transmitted in any form or by any means, electronic, mechanical, photocopying, recording, or otherwise, without express written permission of the publisher.

ISBN-13: 9798668760435

Cover image credit: Rachael Crowe (@hellorachaelcrowe)
Back cover image credit: Renee Fisher (@reneefisherandco)
Library of Congress Control Number: 2018675309
Printed in the United States of America

*To my mom and dad
for everything
and more*

# CONTENTS

| | |
|---|---|
| Title Page | 1 |
| Copyright | 2 |
| Dedication | 3 |
| Chapter One | 9 |
| Chapter Two | 18 |
| Chapter Three | 23 |
| Chapter Four | 28 |
| Chapter Five | 34 |
| Chapter Six | 39 |
| Chapter Seven | 44 |
| Chapter Eight | 53 |
| Chapter Nine | 60 |
| Chapter Ten | 67 |
| Chapter Eleven | 73 |
| Chapter Twelve | 78 |
| Chapter Thirteen | 86 |
| Chapter Fourteen | 90 |
| Chapter Fifteen | 101 |
| Chapter Sixteen | 104 |
| Chapter Seventeen | 109 |

| | |
|---|---|
| Chapter Eighteen | 112 |
| Chapter Nineteen | 124 |
| Chapter Twenty | 129 |
| Chapter Twenty-One | 134 |
| Chapter Twenty-Two | 137 |
| Chapter Twenty-Three | 145 |
| Chapter Twenty-Four | 149 |
| Chapter Twenty-Five | 154 |
| Chapter Twenty-Six | 162 |
| Chapter Twenty-Seven | 168 |
| Chapter Twenty-Eight | 180 |
| Chapter Twenty-Nine | 191 |
| Chapter Thirty | 200 |
| Chapter Thirty-One | 205 |
| Chapter Thirty-Two | 211 |
| Chapter Thirty-Three | 221 |
| Chapter Thirty-Four | 227 |
| Chapter Thirty-Five | 235 |
| Chapter Thirty-Six | 244 |
| Chapter Thirty-Seven | 251 |
| Chapter Thirty-Eight | 257 |
| Chapter Thirty-Nine | 261 |
| Chapter Forty | 270 |
| Chapter Forty-One | 275 |
| Chapter Forty-Two | 279 |
| Chapter Forty-Three | 287 |
| Chapter Forty-Four | 295 |
| Chapter Forty-Five | 300 |

| | |
|---|---|
| Chapter Forty-Six | 312 |
| Chapter Forty-Seven | 321 |
| Chapter Forty-Eight | 324 |
| Chapter Forty-Nine | 333 |
| Chapter Fifty | 336 |
| Chapter Fifty-One | 347 |
| Chapter Fifty-Two | 354 |
| Chapter Fifty-Three | 358 |
| Chapter Fifty-Four | 364 |
| Chapter Fifty-Five | 371 |
| Chapter Fifty-Six | 384 |
| Epilogue | 394 |
| Acknowledgments | 402 |
| Author's Note | 405 |

# CHAPTER ONE

"Okay, you can do this. It's just a couple of hours." I've been repeating this to myself for the last 5 minutes.

I should be out there with my family "having fun," but instead, I'm standing in front of a mirror watching a 14-year-old skinny brown-haired boy wrestling with himself. He's hiding in his aunt's bathroom because he doesn't want to go outside and face the sea of people that he calls family. He's like a little deer lost in the wilderness. I feel sorry for him and I am ashamed of him—or, well, of me.

This might sound stupid, but I'm terrified of large family meetings. I don't know why, but they always make me uncomfortable.

Okay, I do know why. It's the endless questions, the forced small talk, and the fact that there are SO MANY PEOPLE. Seriously, I don't understand how I'm supposed to be related to every single one of the people out there.

If it were up to me, I would've stayed in the bathroom the whole night, but I had already been there 15 minutes and my mom was probably starting to wonder where I was, so I washed my face one more time, took a deep breath, and braced myself for a long night.

As soon as I left the bathroom, the questions began. My aunt Ophelia intercepted me on my way to the living room and started asking me questions about school. She's a nice lady, but she's also a bit nosy and judgmental. I tried to be polite and answer her many questions while also trying not to mention anything that might lead to more questions. I didn't want to be rude, but I also didn't want to be there, so I tried my best to bore her with dull answers so the conversation could wrap up quickly.

She didn't get the message I was trying to send with my one-word answers, though, because she proceeded to talk extensively about how her kids were doing in school. It was my fault, really. I might not be a great talker, but I am a great listener. There's something about me that makes people want to tell me their whole life story. Maybe it's because, unlike a lot of people I know, I never try to hijack the conversation and make it all about myself. However, just because I'm a good listener doesn't mean that I'm interested in everything that comes out of someone else's mouth. Still, I pretended to care about the lives of my cousins to keep my aunt happy. I'm not very close with them, but apparently, Rita is getting straight A's and Rony was selected to be on the basketball team. She sounded so proud of them. I liked that. I wonder if my mom talks about me with such pride to other people.

She then proceeded to mention how handsome I was getting. "You look just like your father," she said, grabbing my face. If there's one thing I really hate, is people grabbing my face. My de facto response is to immediately push their hands away from me, but I didn't want to cause a scene, so I controlled myself and I just smiled—though it's hard to put on a fake smile when all you want to do is run away.

She then asked me if I had a girlfriend and, to me, that meant that it was finally time to stop being polite and escape. I know she means well, but I don't enjoy sharing details about my personal life with anyone, much less with an aunt I only see three times a year, so if that was where the conversation was headed, then I couldn't get out of there fast enough.

"No, not at the moment," I answered. "Aunt Ophelia, do you know where my mom is?"

"In the living room, sweetie," she answered.

I already knew that, of course, but it was the quickest way I could think of to get out of the conversation without being overly rude.

I entered the living room and saw my mother and my little sister sitting on one of the couches, talking to a bunch of my aunts. They were all proudly boasting about their children, trying to upstage one another. I knew some of them were lying, though. I'm pretty sure my cousin Mark, who still has trouble knowing what's 8 times 8, is not "on the fast lane to be valedictorian," or that my cousin Yara, who once asked me why do meteorites always land on craters, is not "definitely going to Harvard next year," but for some reason, they feel better about themselves when they boast about their children. In their eyes, the achievements of their kids are directly proportional to their proficiency as mothers, even when that's not always the case.

They were also criticizing and gossiping about the family members that didn't come to the reunion. They talked about my cousin Jackie's new tattoo and they blamed her mother for letting her get it—even though Jackie's already 22. They also discussed my uncle Ned's new girlfriend, who, according to them, "was probably just a gold digger," but to me she seemed really nice.

As usual, there were only women in the living room. It was the unspoken rule of my family: in family reunions, the women were supposed to be in the living room or the kitchen and the men were supposed to be in the backyard. I hated that rule. Between being with the women and being with the men, I preferred being with the women. I don't really get along with my cousins and most of my uncles annoy me. But, of course, if I stayed in the living room all night, the men would be calling me a girl in no time. I wonder if it's different in other families.

Before I inevitably had to go outside to be with the men, I decided to enjoy the little time I could spend there, so I sat on the arm of one of the couches, next to my mother.

"Where have you been, Hunter?" My mom asked.

"I was just talking to my aunt Ophelia," I answered.

She stared at me for a few seconds, like trying to figure out if I was lying or not and then she smiled, so I guess she realized that I was telling the truth.

"Go talk to your cousins," she said. "They've been asking about you."

I knew that wasn't true, but I decided that it was better to listen to her and go with my cousins than contradicting her and having an argument in front of so many people.

I went to the backyard, where there were approximately 21 people: 7 men and 14 boys of all ages. I wanted to get out of there as soon as I put a foot in there, but there was no going back now, so I reminded myself that it was all going to be over in a few hours and I forced myself to keep walking. I sat with the boys that were closer to my age, including my big brother Axel. He was only sixteen, but he was already drinking a beer and boasting about all the times he has gone to third base with a girl. For some reason, the teenage boys of my family have the brains of a 3-year-old and the libido of a sex-crazed monkey.

I didn't join the conversation, I just half-listened to what they were saying and I faked a smile once in a while. But they were talking about girls in such a derogatory way that I decided to stop paying attention to them altogether. I wonder if I'll ever be like them. I hope not. Then I watched my little cousins running around the backyard like crazy and I wondered if I ever was like them. I don't remember ever being like that. My mom says that when she used to pick me up from kindergarten, instead of running and playing with the other boys, I was playing alone with Legos on a corner or organizing the mess the kids left behind. Maybe I was never a normal kid and maybe I will never be a normal teenager, maybe I was born being an adult.

After my cousins listed all the girls they would like to have sex with and rated actresses from 1 to 10, I decided that I'd had enough of stupid teenagers for one night and I went to sit with the adults. But that wasn't the huge improvement that I was expecting. Even the adults acted like teenagers here. Some people never truly grow up. Or maybe I didn't know what growing up was. Maybe I was not normal, period.

The men were watching football and drinking. That's what all men in this town do. Watch football and drink. As soon as I sat down, my uncle Harold asked me if I wanted a beer.

"I'm fourteen," I said.

"So?" He asked.

"It's illegal," I said.

"Who's gonna tell? You're with family!" He said, handing me a beer.

"No, thanks," I said, refusing to grab it.

"Come on, it's better that you drink with us than with some strangers in a parking lot. Besides, I was 13 when my father gave me my first beer and so was your dad," he said.

He tried to give me the beer one more time.

"I don't want it," I said with a firmer tone this time. "But thanks."

"All right, suit yourself," he said as if I had just rejected the opportunity of a lifetime.

They were all watching the game, so they were less talkative than my cousins, but their conversations weren't exactly better. Their exchanges basically centered around three topics: the football season, the government's incompetence, and casual misogyny. I now know where my cousins' respect for women comes from. Not only were they talking about how much they would like to have an affair with their secretaries or with a co-worker, but they also made casual jokes about domestic violence. I couldn't believe I was related to these people. We're in the year 2003 and they still talk about women as if they were objects. It was despicable. The worst thing was that these were the adults, they were supposed to be better, but they were worse. My dad didn't say anything about these topics, of course, but I wonder what he says when I'm not around.

At one point, they also started to criticize the financial and work decisions of my uncle Phil, who didn't come to the reunion. That's something that the women and the men in this family had in common: they both loved to criticize other family members behind their backs.

I was about to get back to my cousins when my uncle Jack said, "What's wrong, Hunter? Look alive!" after I didn't laugh at one of his stupid jokes.

"It's because he's not drinking. Stop being a killjoy and grab a beer," my uncle Harold said with a smug smile.

Then my uncle Larry decided to join the fun. "Yeah, you've been awfully quiet, Hunter, do we bore you?"

I hate it when they do that. My cousins were already used to my quietness, but my uncles always felt the completely unnecessary urge to point it out. I still don't get why they do it. Is it to try to change me? To try to make me more like them? Because that wasn't going to happen. Or was it just because they felt the need to share every little thought that went through their heads, even when no one asked them to do it? I desperately wanted to inform them that not talking was an option and that not everyone needed to open their mouths all the time, especially if, like them, you don't have anything worthwhile to add. But I feared that my well-meaning PSA would only make this night even more unbearable.

"I just don't have anything to say," I answered.

Then, of course, my uncle Richard weighed in. I don't like most of my uncles, but I can stand them. But him? I really hate him. He is the worst. But don't just take my word for it, his kids hate him too and his ex-wife divorced him because he used to hit her. She even sued him, but he got away with it with just a light slap on the hand. Why, you may ask? Because he is a man and he is white. And the worst part was that the entire family rallied to his side. No one believed his ex-wife's accusations and some even went as far as blaming her. They decided to support him, even though he was obviously guilty. I mean, you don't have to be Sherlock Holmes to recognize a piece of crap when you see it. But he is "family," and to some people, blood is thicker than justice.

I really loathe Richard and I despise the fact that I have to call him uncle. Not only is he a woman hitter, but he is also racist, sexist, and homophobe, really an all-around scum. And I hate that I'm related to him.

"Why are you always such a party pooper, Hunter?" Richard asked. "You must not be getting laid."

I didn't say anything, but fury was starting to build inside of me.

"Yeah, that's the problem," he continued, "you should get a girl to turn that frown upside down."

Some of my uncles laughed and I hated them for that. I turned my eyes to my father, looking for a kind of support I knew he wasn't going to give me. He just smiled and gave me an "ignore him" look. He was the youngest one in his family, so he never stood up to his brothers, he always just advised my brother and me to laughed it off and ignored them because that's what he had been doing his entire life. He put on a fake smile whenever they teased him, but I never could. My smiles are not for everyone. Instead, I looked at that bastard Richard straight to his face, with fury in my eyes and not the slightest sign of a smile on my mouth.

"I'm just messing with you, kid," he said, laughing. "But seriously, you should hurry up and get a girl before people start to think that you're a pansy."

That's what women were to him, just a reflection of a man's "masculinity." He was absolute trash.

I wanted to answer him. I wanted to tell him that he is the worst person I have ever met, that I was ashamed of being related to him, and that he should be in jail. I wanted to say to him that his children hated him and that he was so loathsome and deplorable that he was probably going to die alone. But I didn't. That would only make things worse and get me into deep trouble with my parents, so I just bit my tongue. Luckily, someone scored a touchdown, and, as soon as the men turned around to celebrate, I was out of there.

I thought about going back to my cousins, but I really didn't want to keep listening to any more stupid men that night, so I decided to go to the rooftop. It was a bit tricky to get there without being seen, but at that point, I would've climbed Mount Everest to get away from my family.

I found a relatively clean spot and I laid down to watch the stars. I love starry nights. There's something so beautiful and peaceful about watching the endlessness of space. I could've stayed there forever, but suddenly, a drunken voice interrupted my thoughts and I noticed that I was right above the kitchen.

"Hey, where's your son, the stick-in-the-mud?" Asked a drunken male voice.

"Richard!" Answered my aunt Mary.

"What? Oh, sorry, ladies. I'll let you finish washing the dishes in peace, I'm just here to get more beer," said the same male voice, which now I identified as being Richard.

"Don't listen to him," my aunt Mary said. "He can be an asshole when he's drunk."

"Yeah, I know," I heard my mom said. "But can I tell you a little secret?"

"Of course," said my aunt Mary.

"I do worry about Hunter sometimes," my mom said.

"Why? Because he's quiet?" Aunt Mary asked.

"Yeah, he's way too quiet and he always wants to be alone in his room," answered my mom.

"I'm sure it's just a stage, Alice. Don't worry about it, he's a teenager, he'll grow out of it," Aunt Mary said.

"I really hope so because I don't know how to help him. He doesn't have a lot of friends in school, you know. When Axel was his age, he was on every sports team possible and he used to bring home a new friend practically every other day. And Hunter's just not like that. He's so… different. But maybe you're right. Maybe it's just a stage and he'll grow out of it soon."

"I'm sure he will," said my aunt Mary.

Well, I guess that's how my mom talks about me with other people.

After that punch in the gut, I decided to stop listening. Thankfully, I brought the new iPod my dad gave me on my birthday, so I put my headphones on, turned the volume up, and tried to forget what I had just heard by focusing on the relaxing notes of the music and the beautiful stars of the night sky. But, out of nowhere, a flow of tears started to run down my face.

One would think that I'm used to dealing with this by now. After all, I've heard this kind of stuff my entire life. But apparently I'm not.

Boys don't cry, I remember my dad once told me.

Boys don't cry, I repeat to myself.

Well, this one does.

I knew I should've stayed in the bathroom.

# CHAPTER TWO

My name is Hunter Grayson. I'm 14 years old. I like reading, swimming, and playing with my dog. I also like being alone and I don't know why so many people seem to have a problem with that. My family gets upset when I want to be alone, my classmates pick on me because sometimes I like to be by myself during recess, and my teachers always try to get me to socialize, even when I don't want to. I don't get why it bothers them so much that sometimes I prefer to be by myself. If I don't have a problem with it, why do they?

I like being alone because it's relaxing and it gives me time to think. Being with other people sometimes can be exhausting. People can be exhausting. When I spend too much time with a lot of people, I always end up feeling overwhelmed. I always end up feeling like a fish that desperately needs to get back to the water.

For me, it's completely normal to do some things by myself, like eating, playing, and going to the movies, but for others, it's an undeniable fact that there's something wrong with me. And sometimes I think that they might be right. But I don't fully understand why. I don't get why wanting to be by myself from time to time is so frowned upon. I understand that it's not considered something "normal," but I don't get why.

When I go to the movies and the cashier hears "One ticket, please" it's as if I had confessed that I murdered several people. "Just one?" the cashier asks with a perplexed face. I hate it when people do that. I hate the pity in their voices. Yeah, just one, what's so weird about that? You have to be quiet in the movies anyway, why do you need company for that? Sometimes I don't get this world and that annoys me.

I also like being alone because it gives me time to unwind. My brother would sooner die than having to spend a whole weekend stuck in his bedroom, but honestly, I love it. Getting to spend two entire days in my room reading books, watching movies, and listening to music is usually the best part of my week, especially after five busy days of school.

However, contrary to what some people might think, just because I like being alone from time to time doesn't mean that I hate people. I mean, I hate some people, but not all people, and I like being alone, but not all the time. I also enjoy spending time with my friends (yes, I do have friends, just not a lot of them) and with my family (well, with some of my family), but sometimes I need a break. And sometimes I have a better time when I'm by myself than when I'm with people.

I know that probably makes me sound like I'm a few years away from moving to the attic of a big cathedral and spending the rest of my life alone, but I swear that I'm not. I'm just pretty happy by myself... although I'd be lying if I said that sometimes I wouldn't like to be more like my brother. I know my parents would definitely want me to be more like him. They probably still hope that someday I will wake up and magically be more like him. And I won't lie, sometimes I wish that would happen too. But I know that's not going to happen. It's not just a stage, I've been like this my entire life. There's something inside of me that prevents me from being like him, like them, but I don't know what it is. I don't know what's wrong with me. Maybe my mom drank when she was pregnant or maybe someone dropped me when I was a baby. Whatever it was, I can't seem to change it.

Sometimes I feel like a broken machine. Like a computer that was not properly connected or a toaster that softens the bread instead of toasting it. I wish I could find my user's manual to find out what went wrong so I can fix it or at least to try to understand what's the problem. But humans are more complicated than machines. We don't have a reset button that can fix us. We have to live with our glitches.

There have been times when I've tried to explain to my parents why I prefer to spend my Friday nights locked up in my bedroom with a good book instead of out with friends or why I rather go to the movies alone than to a crowded birthday party, but I haven't been very successful. It's hard to explain something you can't understand. I mean, how do you say "sometimes I'm happier when I'm alone" without sounding like an absolute weirdo?

My inability to put into words how I feel and their reluctance to accept as normal something different than what they know is a bad combination. Although I would say that the fact that they can't seem to accept that I'm not like them is not entirely their fault, I blame this town for that. I live in a small town in Texas named Mountdale and in small towns like this you're supposed to be like everyone else. Difference is frowned upon.

I think that normally in a big city, a quiet kid like me would go unnoticed because everyone minds their own business, but in this town, I stand out like a sore thumb because everyone's so chatty, friendly, and outgoing and I'm not. Everywhere you go, you can find someone that will talk your ear off, even if you don't even know them. Many people think that I'm rude because I can't hold a conversation with a stranger as easily as they can, but I'm not trying to be rude, it's just that it doesn't come naturally to me. I don't know what you're supposed to say when someone tells you that the weather is nice or that last night's game was a nail-biter.

Small talk is the cornerstone of small towns and I'm terrible at it. It's one of the many reasons that I want to get out of this town. I can't wait to grow up and move to a big city. Cities are where the future is created and little towns like this are where the past refuses to die.

In a city, everyone can be whoever they want and do whatever they want, but in a small town like this everyone is supposed to do the same as everyone else. Almost everyone here follows the same path of life: they're married with children by the time they're 25, they buy a house a few blocks away from where they grew up, and they get a job that doesn't fulfill them but that pays the bills. I'm terrified of following the same blueprint as everyone else here and ending up like that, trapped in this town for the rest of my life.

The biggest employers in town are all industries, like Telai (a car manufacturer), Sourst (a beer producer), and Sterra (a steel producer), which means that the most valued professions and occupations here are those related to industrial work like engineers, mechanics, and administrators, while professions related to other areas like humanities and the arts are usually looked down on. That's kind of a bummer because, while I still don't know what I want to be when I grow up, I lean more towards the latter areas than the former.

As for leisure, the primary source of entertainment here is sports. This town has basically two main religions: Christianity and sports. Specifically football. On Sundays, almost everyone goes to church in the morning and then watches a game at night. In here, high school football games are a massive event that paralyzes the entire town, the Super Bowl is practically a national holiday, and the only thing that boys my age know how to do for fun is play sports.

But if you don't really like sports like me, living in this town can be pretty dull. There are not a lot of other things you can do here. There are only two museums (one of art and one of history), three malls and a few movie theaters. The public library is quite small and there are only a handful of public swimming pools around town. There's a zoo and an amusement park downtown, but they get quite boring after a couple of times. There are no attractions to visit, no theaters for plays, and no venues for concerts. Basically, the only significant events we ever get here are sports-related events.

I'm only 14, but I'm already pretty bored of this town.

To be honest, Mountdale has never really felt like home to me. I don't belong here. And this town has always made sure to remind me that I don't. I want to get out of here. But since that's not going to happen anytime soon, all I can do for now is suck it up.

# CHAPTER THREE

After a long summer of reading and swimming, it was finally time to go back to school.
Ugh.
And not only that, it was my first day of high school.
Double ugh.

I had such a good summer that I didn't want it to end, but nothing lasts forever, so this morning I had to summon all my strength to drag myself out of bed and get ready. I gotta say that waking up at 7am after two months of waking up at noon was even harder than I expected, especially because the prospect of leaving the comfort of my bed to go to my first day of high school was so unappealing, but if I missed the bus, my mom would never let me hear the end of it and that frightened me even more than whatever was waiting for me at school.

When I finally made it downstairs for breakfast, everyone was already at the table except for my little sister Ashley. I'm the middle child of the family and I actually kinda like it. I know what everyone says about being a middle child: that they're left out, ignored, and even neglected. And I can attest that all of that is true, but I kinda like it. I can't imagine the kind of pressure and attention I would receive if I was the oldest or the youngest. What I get is already more than enough. It's safe and simple in the middle.

When I sat at the table, my mom was finishing our lunches while dad and Axel were talking about his upcoming junior year of high school. I'm always amazed by how similar they are. My dad is a successful engineer and my brother is a mini-copy of him. They both have black hair, blue eyes, and a big nose, and they both love sports, cars, technology, and action movies. Dad is even teaching Axel basic engineering so he can work for the same car manufacturing company as him when he graduates from school. It's seriously freaky how similar they are. Right now, I have the theory that Axel wasn't born naturally, he was just cloned from a strand of hair of my dad, but I haven't gathered enough evidence to prove this.

My mom, on the other hand, is a big shot real estate agent and I can't think of a better job for her. She loves talking and convincing people to do things that they don't want to do. Seriously, she always has a story at hand and she could convince a blind person of buying a 60-inch TV. If you don't believe me, just ask the three 'Realtor of the Year' awards she has in her office.

She's also really outgoing. I've always heard that it's difficult for adults to make friends, but whoever said that never met my mom. She can talk to people with such ease that, frankly, I envy her. I mean, she has more friends than I do and she's 40—but that probably says more about me than about her. Physically, I'm more similar to her than to my dad. I got her brown hair and her big brown eyes. Too bad I didn't get her social skills too.

"Are you excited for your first day of high school?" My mom asked me.

"Thrilled," I answered, trying as hard as possible not to sound sarcastic. Fortunately, it worked and she smiled at me. I like her smile, it's so full and warm.

"Where did you go last night, Hunter?" My dad asked. "The Pats scored an incredible final touchdown and you missed it."

I didn't even know The Patriots were playing, I only sat with them because I wanted to get away from my cousins. But I was not going to tell that to my dad. He still hoped that someday I would magically start to love football like him and my brother, but that was like hoping to see a unicorn in the middle of an

Interstate Highway.

"Oh, sorry," I said. "I went... to the porch, I was sick of Uncle Richard."

"What happened with Richard?" My mom asked.

"Nothing, he's just a jackass," I answered.

"Hey!" My mom said with a firm tone. "What have I told you, young man? We don't talk about family that way. You should respect your uncle."

"Why?" I asked.

"Because he's your uncle," she answered.

"So?" I asked.

"So? He's your family!" She said.

"Mom, you're not giving me a reason, you're just stating facts," I said.

"Oh, am I? Well, how about because I'm your mother and I'm telling you to do it. Is that a good enough reason for you?" She asked.

"Fine, sorry," I said. Although I still don't get mom's logic. Just because you're related to someone doesn't mean that you have to like them, much less respect them. Uncle Richard can have my respect when he has earned it, although I don't think that'll ever happen. However, I do respect my mom, and I was not going to ruin her morning by getting into an argument with her. Besides, there was no point in arguing with her because she would rather jump off an airplane without a parachute than to ever admit that she's wrong.

"God, please give me the strength to deal with two teenage sons," my mom said.

"Hey! What did I do?" Axel asked.

"Nothing yet... and you better keep it that way!" Mom said.

Dad tried to break the tension by talking to Axel about last night's game. I pretended to be interested in their conversation to avoid looking at my mom, who surely didn't believe my apology. Luckily, a few seconds later, Ashley finally came downstairs dressed in head-to-toe pink and with a big red bow in her long, blonde hair. She started telling mom how excited she was about seeing her school friends again, and this allowed me to stop pretending to care about football and get back to eating my breakfast in peace because I no longer felt the stare of my mom on me.

As I watched my mom talking to my sister and my dad talking to my brother, I was hit by a strong feeling of happiness and sadness. On the one hand, I really *really* love them and I'm very thankful that I have them. Almost half of my middle school classmates had divorced parents. I don't know what that must be like, but I'm guessing it's not easy. I can see that my parents still love each other and that they really love us, and unfortunately, not every kid can say that.

But, on the other hand, I feel like I don't belong with them. I'm nothing like them. I've always felt like I'm an alien and my spaceship just happened to land in their backyard, so they had no choice but to adopt me. My siblings are the perfect combination of the best of my parents, while I feel like I'm from an entirely different species. I watch them, and I want to be like them, but I'm not. I'm something else. I wonder if they think I'm an anomaly too. I wonder if they like me.

I mean, parents HAVE to love their children, but do they have to like them?

I'm not entirely sure if my dad likes me. He loves me, alright, I'm sure of that. I know he would do anything for me, but I'm not sure if he likes me. I like to believe that he does, but we don't have many things in common, so we don't spend much time together. I wish I could be closer to him, but I don't know how to do that. I know he wishes I could be different, even if he never says it aloud. He doesn't have to. I know he wishes I was more like him, but I don't know how to do that either.

My mother, on the other hand, is more difficult to read. I know she definitely loves me, but I'm not sure if she likes me either. I think she does, but sometimes I don't get her. But then again, maybe that's the problem. I don't get her and she doesn't get me.

When the bus arrived, Axel and I grabbed our backpacks and

ran outside. Before we left, my mom gave us a kiss goodbye and my dad wished us good luck.

"Remember the rule," my brother whispered to me when we walked to the bus. "You don't know me."

I just nodded.

When my brother found out that I was going to attend the same high school as him, he made me promise that I was not going to talk to him. I actually had no problem with that. We hardly ever talk at home anyway, so I doubt that I would suddenly want to talk to him at school.

When we boarded the bus, Axel immediately sat with his friends and they loudly started to laugh and talk about their vacations. Most of the front half of the bus was already full, so I looked for an empty seat in the back and I put my headphones on. I gotta say that when my dad first gave me my iPod, I didn't really like it. He always gets so excited about the latest technological gadgets and I simply don't get it. But it was the best gift he could've given me. That little device was slowly becoming my best friend. Music and looking out the window were now one of my favorite combinations, along with reading a book on a rainy day.

I've always loved looking out the window. There's just something so peaceful about watching things go by so fast. Add music to it and you have the perfect catalyst for imagination. Unfortunately, my house is pretty close to the school, so we arrived in less than three songs.

As soon as I saw the school building, I felt a giant hole appear on my stomach and the air in my lungs started to disappear. This happened to me every first day of school, but this was way worse because it was high school, a whole new territory. I took a couple of deep breaths and reminded myself that it was just school and that everybody was probably just as nervous as I was.

I got off the bus, repeated to myself that, no matter what, everything was going to be okay, and I braced myself for my first day of high school.

# CHAPTER FOUR

When I entered the building, I was amazed by how many people there were. I had already visited the school before to familiarize myself with the building, but seeing it full of students was a completely different experience.

Everyone was walking around, talking to new people, and catching up with old friends. It was a little overwhelming, so I decided to go to the restroom to kill some time before my first class began. I washed my face and imagined myself going back home in a few hours to give me strength. "You can do this," I whispered to myself when I heard the first bell rang.

My first class was Math, which was *just* what my sleep-deprived brain needed at 8am. Luckily, I already knew where the classroom was, so I didn't have to ask for directions like many other freshmen were doing.

When I entered the classroom, it was already full of students eager to socialize and get to know each other. I didn't even have the energy to kneel down to tie my shoe, but somehow all my classmates were already learning each other's names and making small talk about their summer. To be honest, I've never understood how everyone's so good at making friends and talking to new people. It has never been one of my strong suits. I feel like everyone went to a 'How to Socialize' class that I wasn't invited to. Sometimes I wish I was more like my mom or like my brother so that I could talk to anyone, anywhere, anytime, just like them. I mean, I can talk to people, but sometimes I don't want to… and sometimes I can't. It's a weird duality.

Thankfully, like a light among darkness, I saw two familiar faces in that sea of unknown people. Rachel and Suzie, two friends from middle school, were sitting together in the middle of the classroom. I walked towards them like a moth to a flame and, as soon as they saw me, they stood up and hugged me. I'm not a big fan of hugs, but I allowed it this time because it was a special occasion.

I wouldn't consider them *close* friends, but I did like them, and it was very nice to see them in this new uncharted environment. I sat behind them and we talked extensively about our vacations. I could notice that they were also kind of nervous about the first day of high school, which was comforting because at least now I was sure that I wasn't the only one.

I was also delighted that they decided to sit in the middle because I've never liked sitting in the front. I don't like all the attention the front-seat students get. I prefer the middle, where I can just blend in. Where I can just disappear. And that is precisely what I want to do in high school. I don't want to be the troublemaker, the class clown, the nerd, the teacher's pet, the jock, the outcast, or the geek. I don't want to be the protagonist of this particular high school movie. I don't want all eyes on me. I don't want expectations. I just want the freedom to be myself and do whatever I want without pressure from external forces.

And it's not like I'm a bad student, I'm actually pretty good. I was in the top five of my generation in middle school. My teachers used to tell my mom that I could've easily been number one, but there was one thing holding me back: class participation. It was very important to some teachers and, since I didn't really like participating in class, my grades took a hit in those particular subjects.

I've never really understood the importance of class

participation. If I have the knowledge and I can prove that I have it in a test or in some homework, then why do I have to show it off in front of the whole classroom to get the grade? Or worse, if I don't know the answer, why do I have to humiliate myself in front of the entire classroom just for some points? I just don't get it. All I can say is that I definitely didn't want that top spot hard enough to participate daily in every class.

Although I gotta say that sometimes I was tempted to force myself to participate just so I could get the teachers off my back. "You have to learn to come out of your shell," "Don't be shy, we don't bite," "You're never going to make it in the real world if you don't talk." They always used the same old, tired phrases.

I knew some of them had good intentions, and maybe they were right, maybe I needed to speak up and participate more, but why did they think it was a good idea to motivate me like that? I'm sure there are other ways to promote class participation without being so aggressive or rude. Public humiliation was not going to magically transform me into someone outgoing like my brother, my parents had already tried that for years with no results.

It is the teachers' job to create a safe space for students to grow and develop, not a safe space for mocking and bullying. By singling me out as the "quiet one," the teachers basically put a target on my back and gave my classmates permission to mock me for the same reason. And they took that permission by heart. All through middle school, many kids enjoyed bullying me for being quiet—and for other things, like preferring to read during recess instead of playing sports and for my short stature, but mostly it was for being quiet, which is something that I've never fully understood. Why did being quiet make me stand out? Shouldn't it have been the other way around?

I used to try to not pay attention to the bullies, but when so many people—including some of the teachers—tell you that there's something wrong with you, you can't help but start to wonder if they're right.

The Math teacher arrived just after Suzie finished telling us all the fun things she did in Canada this summer. She introduced herself as Mrs. Sawyer and informed us that she had been a teacher for more than 30 years. She seemed very strict, but I felt like there was a lot of kindness behind that cold exterior. To the surprise of the classroom, after she introduced herself, she went straight to explaining the syllabus of the course, without asking us to introduce ourselves first. This was a great relief to me because I really hate first-day introductions, but a devastating blow to some of the other students who were hoping to do nothing that first day.

I did my best to try to pay attention to her, but when she started to list all the topics we were going to cover, my mind immediately started to wander. I looked at the empty chair beside me and I couldn't decide if that was a good thing or a bad thing. It was one of those classrooms where there are two chairs per table, so it kind of bothered me that I was sitting by myself. But not because I was alone—I actually liked that—it was because of the image that that empty chair sent to the rest of the classroom. I don't want people to look at me like I'm the "quiet kid" anymore, I'm sick of being singled out. But being one of the only students sitting by themselves didn't help. The other kids were probably already thinking that I was a lonely loser. It was something that made me stand out, and that was the last thing I wanted.

But, at the same time, I kinda liked that it was empty. That way I didn't feel forced to make small talk at 8am with a complete stranger. God knows that if someone were sitting next to me, I would spend the whole class thinking about what to say and how to say it and I hated that kind of pressure.

Then I started to think about Ben.

Ben was my best friend in elementary school and middle school. I really *really* liked him. We could talk for hours and hours about anything and about everything. He was not like the other boys our age; he was funny, kind, and very mature for his age. I don't think I would've been able to survive school without him. He had been my best friend since we were both 6, but then his father got a job offer in London and he had to move.

It's so weird how someone else's decisions can impact your life so much; how someone else's life can totally change yours. I don't know how to feel about that, I don't like the idea of not having total control over my life. But I'm really happy for Ben, he finally got out of this town. We used to talk all the time about how we were going to grow up and move to a big city someday.

I wonder if he's happy. I really hope he is.

I do miss him terribly, though. If he were here right now, he would be sitting right next to me, and I wouldn't be worrying about stupid things like what an empty chair represents for my future in high school.

We were about 20 minutes into the class when a knock on the door interrupted Mrs. Sawyer.

"Come in," the teacher said, and a girl with chestnut hair and colorful clothes entered the classroom.

I liked her clothes, they were pretty original and eye-catching, especially her bright red jacket, but I could hear how some of the girls and boys behind me were whispering mean things about her. That really annoyed me. I hate it when people think they have to be mean to be cool.

"Are you a student in this class?" Mrs. Sawyer asked.

"Yes, I'm terribly sorry for being late," the girl answered.

"What's your name, miss?" The teacher asked.

"Ariana Matthys," the girl said.

"Well, miss Matthys, I don't know if you are aware of this, but school starts at 8 o'clock," Mrs. Sawyer said.

"Yeah, I know," Ariana said. "I'm so sorry, but on my way here, I saw a bird playing with a squirrel, and how often does one get to see something like that? I just *had* to stop and take a photo for my collection, I'm sure you understand. But I promise that tomorrow I'll be here extra-early to compensate for today."

That made the whole classroom laugh, including myself. I didn't know this girl, but I already liked her.

"That's not how things work, miss Matthys, but come on in," said Mrs. Sawyer.

"Thank you," Ariana answered.

She stopped for a second to decide where she was going to sit. There were still some empty chairs in the front and the back of the classroom, but she decided to walk towards the middle and sat next to me.

"Hi, I'm Ariana," she said with one of the friendliest smiles I've ever seen in my entire life.

"Hello," I clumsily responded. "I'm Hunter."

# CHAPTER FIVE

Ariana was just as lively and unique as her clothes. We had to do a couple of math problems together, and she spent the whole time telling me in great detail about how she spent more than 20 minutes quietly chasing a bird and a squirrel to get a perfect shot. She was so effortlessly funny that the teacher had to tell us to be quiet a couple of times. Needless to say, that doesn't happen to me very often, but it was so easy to talk to Ariana that it was almost impossible to stop doing it.

Unfortunately, she wasn't in any of my next classes, but Suzie and Rachel were in two of them. We talked about what we thought of high school so far, and they asked me about Ben. I told them that I hadn't spoken to him since he left, but that I missed him a lot.

We ran out of conversation topics pretty quickly, so I didn't look for them in the cafeteria when the lunch break arrived. I wasn't really in the mood for forced conversations. After four classes and a couple of first-day introductions, all I wanted to do was to go to the safety of my bed and take a 3-day nap. But since I couldn't do that, I decided to eat by myself.

At first, I thought about going to the library to eat my lunch there, but I was told that the library didn't open during the lunch periods, so I ended up going to the cafeteria, and I sat at an empty table near the exit.

I could see almost all of the cafeteria from there, all

the tables full of people and all those people talking. Every freshman had used their socialization power to the maximum during the crucial first hours of high school for this moment and this moment alone, to have someone to sit with at lunchtime so they wouldn't end up being the weirdos who eat alone. So they wouldn't end up like me.

I didn't mind eating alone, but I did mind all the weird, pitiful looks I was receiving. I could only imagine what they must've been thinking: "Poor lonely boy, he has no one to eat with," "Why is he alone? Is there something wrong with him?" "First day of school and he has no friends. So sad."

I hate the pressure there is in high school to belong. Everyone has to belong to a group, and those who don't are social outcasts. It was only the first day of school, but everybody had already desperately looked for a group they could belong to. It was only the first day of school and I was already the social outcast.

I couldn't stand the glances anymore. I know I shouldn't care because I don't even know them, but I do care, and I hate it. I decided to look for Rachel and Suzie to make the glances go away, but three tall, muscular boys sat in front of me before I could get up.

"Hey Blunter, why so lonely?" Asked the boy in the middle.

Shoot. I knew this would eventually happen, but I didn't expect it to happen so fast.

The boy in the middle was Tony, he was in the same middle school as me, and he loved picking on me. I didn't know the other two, but I guess they were Tony's new friends who wanted to join the fun. I've never understood why some boys like Tony liked to pick on me. They were usually kids I had never spoken to, so I don't know why they felt the need to pick on me. Once, I read that bullies typically go for the kids they see as defenseless. I really hate that. I hate to be seen as weak. I am *not* weak—but someone had to tell that to my body.

"Hi, Tony," I said, hoping this wouldn't take too long.

"I heard your boyfriend moved to London," Tony said. "I

can't say I blame him, he probably wanted to escape the stink of your nerdiness, that's why he moved to the other side of the Atlantic."

His new friends started to laugh idiotically like the hyenas in *The Lion King*. I didn't say anything. But my silence, instead of making him go away, was fueling him.

"Is that why you're all alone? Are you going through your mourning period? Or is it just your regular period?" Tony said.

His friends laughed again, and the people nearby started to look at us.

"What's going on? A cat got your tongue? Why are you always so quiet, Blunter? Say something!" He said. For some reason, it had always bothered him how quiet I was. In middle school, he pointed it out every time he could.

"Hey, stereotypical 80's bully," a voice behind me said. I turned around and saw Ariana standing behind me with an assertive pose and a bold look in her eyes. "I don't know you, but I'm guessing your name's something like Buster or Butch. Have you finished bothering my friend, Buster? Do you feel more like a man now? You do know that acting like a dick won't make yours any bigger, right?"

This took Tony by surprise, and the students on the tables nearby were trying to hold their laughs. Tony's face started to turn red from anger and embarrassment.

"Who's this, Blunter? You hired Mary Poppins to protect you?" Tony said, and his two friends started to laugh hysterically.

"No, Hunter has a nice personality, Butch," Ariana said, "not a garbage one like yours, so he doesn't need to pay people to pretend to like him. But hey, can I give you a piece of advice? Leave my friend alone and grow up. You're in high school now, please stop making a fool of yourself by trying to be the tough guy because it doesn't make you look cool, it makes you look like a sad loser that doesn't have anything better to do with his miserable life."

After hearing this, the students close to us started to

turn around to see who had said those words and, more importantly, who she was talking to.

Tony was speechless and red like a tomato. He seemed like he wanted to say something, but the many eyes that were now on him must've intimidated him because, after a few seconds, he whispered "Let's go" to his friends, and they followed him out of the cafeteria.

"Wow," I said to Ariana when she sat in front of me. "Thank you."

"No problem," she answered with a smile. "I've always heard that high school is a dog-eat-dog world, so I'm always ready to put a bully in his place."

"That's a pretty useful skill to have," I said. "But I don't like that phrase. Dogs are way too nice to eat each other."

"I know, right? I love dogs," she said. "I don't know why people say that."

"Oh, do you have a dog?" I asked.

"No, my mom's allergic, but I've always wanted one. What about you? Do you have any dogs?" She asked.

"Yeah, one," I said. "His name's Rufus. He's the best, I would literally die for him."

"I believe you. I don't even know him, but I would die for him too."

I laughed. There was something special about this girl. I barely knew her, but it felt like we had already been friends for years.

"Do you have any pets?" I asked.

"Yeah, I have two chickens and a parrot," she answered.

I tried to react as if that was something normal, but I think I didn't do a good job because Ariana immediately added: "I swear I'm not crazy, it's just that chickens are some of the most lovable animals on this planet."

"Really? I didn't know that," I said. "What are their names?"

"Hennifer Aniston, Chick Jagger, and Polly Parton," she answered.

Okay, this girl might be crazy.

But I like her.

# CHAPTER SIX

The first couple of weeks of high school were better than I expected. The classes were interesting and relatively easy, I was already getting used to the giant crowds—they still bothered me, but I was getting used to them—and Ariana and I were becoming really good friends.

She's very talkative, which is great because I'm more of a listener anyway. She always has something interesting to say and she's not afraid to speak her mind, especially about topics she really cares about, like nature and gender equality.

She's also quite unique, she loves to wear colorful clothes, and she doesn't care about what other people think of them. So far, out of all the clothes she has worn, I think her red jacket is still my favorite because it's both quirky and badass, just like her. But she also has an eye-catching green scarf that looks like something out of a movie.

She's not a big fan of literature, which is a bummer, but she does love another form of art: photography. Taking pictures is her favorite thing to do and she's always looking for unique things to capture on her digital camera. Once, we went to the park after school and she spent 20 minutes chasing a yellow butterfly with green dots just so she could take a photo of it to show it to her mom because those were her favorite colors.

"It's just a butterfly, Ari," I said when she was climbing a tree to follow the winged insect. "I'm sure that if you look for that species in a book about butterflies, you'll find a great picture of it."

"I'm sorry, Hunter, but we're gonna need to get a translator if you're gonna continue to talk like that because I don't speak quitter," she said from the top of the tree.

She was really something else. I'm very glad I found her—or, well, that she found me. I don't think the first weeks of high school would've been nearly as good without her. However, there are also other things that I'm enjoying about school. The high school library is much bigger than the one in middle school, and the classes are way more challenging, which is something I enjoy. I really like Biology and Social Studies because they're interesting and thought-provoking, and solving the algebra problems we're seeing in Math is weirdly amusing, but so far, my favorite subject is definitely English.

My English teacher is named Dan Brooks. He's only 24, but he looks and acts older. It's his first time teaching, but I can safely say that he's one of the best teachers I've ever had. I've never met any other teacher like him before. It's hard to explain, but you can feel that he really *cares.* He cares about the students, he cares about teaching, and he cares about leaving a positive mark on us.

Maybe it's because of his age, perhaps with time people just stop caring. Or maybe it's because it's his first time teaching and he hasn't learned yet that not all teachers care. Whatever it is, I'm really happy that I have a teacher like him.

Unfortunately, we're only reading three books this semester: *Lord of the Flies*, *The Catcher in the Rye*, and *To Kill a Mockingbird*. Don't get me wrong, those books are great, but I think three are way too few for a whole semester, especially since I already read those. Luckily, Mr. Brooks told us that if we ever want to read more books, we can look for him in the library and he would be delighted to recommend us something else to read. Apparently, he's in there every day after school because he was tasked with modernizing and expanding the library.

As soon as I learned that *Lord of the Flies* was going to be the first book we were going to read, I started re-reading it. I liked it the first time I read it, but I didn't love it. However, now that I was reading it for the second time, I was appreciating it more. That's why I love re-reading books, because I can get more out of them the second time. I can discover new things that I hadn't noticed before. It's not that the book has changed, it's just that I've changed and I'm able to see and understand things differently. I really like that because it reaffirms to me that time is not passing in vain, that I'm learning more and more every year and that—hopefully—I'm becoming a better version of myself.

Oh, and I almost forget to mention, I also love English because it's the only class so far where I feel comfortable raising my hand and participating. I know I said that I don't like participating—and I don't—but it all started on the second day of school. Mr. Brooks asked if someone knew what *Lord of the Flies* was about. Of course I knew what it was about, but I didn't want to answer, so I waited for someone else to take the spotlight and answer the question. However, nobody did.

"Come on, it's one of the most famous books in the world," Mr. Brooks said. "Nobody?"

He seemed really disappointed. I thought that he would eventually give up and answer the question himself as any other teacher would, but he didn't, he kept asking. I felt so sorry for him that after two minutes I finally raised my hand and said that the book was about a group of British boys stranded on a desert island who are torn between living in order and living in chaos.

"Excellent!" Mr. Brooks said. "Thank you. What's your name?"

"Hunter," I answered.

After that, things spiraled out of control fairly quickly. Mr. Brooks rapidly learned my name and whenever he asked a question that no one wanted to answer, he looked at me, hoping that I could answer it. Most of the times, I could and, after the first three or four times, I started to really like answering his questions. Maybe it was because they were not textbook questions, they were deeper, almost philosophical questions that didn't have just one right answer. We had to come up with our own personal answer and convince him that it was the correct one. We had to stand our ground and defend our posture against his counterarguments because he liked to question our logic to make it stronger. It was like being in a friendly debate. It was quite challenging and I really liked that. Apparently I'm a quiet kid who loves to debate. I'm a walking contradiction.

For years, teachers have tried to make me "come out of my shell" by trying to shame me into participating—with very poor results, I might add—but Mr. Brooks managed to do it without really trying. Talk about teacher of the year.

In the third week of school, I decided to go to the library to get another book because I had already finished re-reading *Lord of the Flies*.

"Hello, Hunter!" Mr. Brooks said when I entered the library. "What brings you here?"

"Hi, Mr. Brooks," I answered. "I wanted to ask you for a book recommendation. I already finished *Lord of the Flies* and I don't know what to read next."

He then stared at me for a few seconds, like trying to figure me out. I don't like looking at people in the eye for too long, so I looked away and centered my attention on the bookshelves behind him. After a few seconds, he went to his desk to grab a book and gave it to me. It was called *The Curious Incident of the Dog in the Night-Time*.

"This one just came out," he said. "I read it over the summer, and I really liked it. I think you're going to like it too."

"Thanks, Mr. Brooks," I said.

And he was right. I liked it so much that I finished it in just two days. It was a serious page-turner. The mystery was addictive and being inside the mind of this boy really opened up my perspective.

When I went to the library to return it to Mr. Brooks, we discussed it for about an hour and a half. It was great to be able to talk about books with someone else again. I hadn't been able to do it since Ben moved away. I think being able to share your thoughts and feelings about a book with someone else enriches the experience exponentially. It helps you express your ideas, consider different perspectives, and have a healthy debate about the book's themes and characters. It's genuinely one of my favorite things to do, and I'm glad that I finally found someone to share this experience again.

# CHAPTER SEVEN

"Are you going out this weekend?" My mom asked me on Friday while we were having dinner.

"Why do you ask?" I answered. That was my automatic response to most of my mom's questions because I knew that, more often than not, the information she wanted could be used against me.

"Because tomorrow's your cousin Matt's birthday and he's having a party," she said.

"Another family party?" I asked. "We just went to one a couple of weeks ago."

"So?" She asked with a defiant tone. With just one word, she was challenging me to explain what was so wrong about spending time with family.

"Nothing… it's just that I can't go… I have a lot of homework to do," I lied.

She stared at me for a couple of seconds and then said: "Fine, you can stay here. But we won't bring you any cake. That's only for the people that go to the party."

Damn, I love cake, so that was a low blow. But if that was the price that I had to pay to miss the party, then I was more than willing to pay it.

I feel like I need to clarify that I don't hate family parties. What I hate is being told about them at the last minute. If I'm going to go to another family party, I need at least a 3-day notice to mentally prepare myself for it.

And it's not like I had plans or something—I didn't even have homework—but I had already pictured a quiet Saturday at home and it was hard for me to let that go. It's weird, I cannot put into words why, but I *really* hate last-minute changes to my plans, even if those plans are doing nothing all day. If I already made up my mind about what I'm going to do, I hate to change it, especially at the last minute. Unfortunately, my mom has the habit of always telling me about family events at the last minute. I've gotten into several arguments with her over this, but they always go like this:

"The party's tomorrow?" I usually ask. "You know I hate being told about plans at the last minute. Why didn't you tell me before?"

"Why? Do you have other plans?" She usually asks.

"No."

"Then what's the problem?"

And that's the thing. To her, it's not enough that I explicitly tell her that I hate it when she does that, she needs a reason as to why I hate it. She needs to know what's the problem because she doesn't mind being told about plans at the last minute —especially if she doesn't have anything else to do—so she doesn't understand why I do. And since I cannot explain why I have a problem with it, she keeps doing it.

I spent the whole dinner thinking about giving in and telling my mom that I could go to my cousin Matt's party after all, mainly because I was already picturing the many things my aunts, uncles, and cousins would be saying about me if I skipped the party: "Why didn't he come? That's so rude," "He wanted to stay home instead of coming to the party? What a weird boy," "He has always thought that he's better than us." But, then again, it was better for me to imagine those comments from the comfort of my bedroom than to hear them straight to my face—or to my back. So, in the end, I decided to keep quiet and rejoice in the prospect of having the whole house to myself.

By the way, have I mentioned that I love my bedroom?

Because I LOVE my bedroom. It's hands down my favorite place in the whole wide world. It's not very big, but it has everything I need. My bed is twin size, but it's as comfortable as a cloud. I have three pillows because, for some reason, I can't sleep with just one. I have a desk for doing homework and a comfy chair for reading. I also have a TV, a DVD player and three big bookshelves that contain all of my books and DVDs. If I had a fridge and a bathroom, I wouldn't leave my bedroom for days. Why would I? I could spend all day reading, watching movies, and sleeping.

My dad might not share my passion for books and movies, but he has always fomented it by buying me any book or DVD I want. I really appreciate that, I know not all dads can or would do that.

Oh, and next to my bed, it's Rufus' little dog bed. I had to fight my mom to let me have Rufus inside the house. Initially, she wanted him to be in the backyard, but I used my superb arguing skills to convince her otherwise. Rufus's small size and cuteness also helped a little.

Fortunately, when my little sister was born, we moved from our previous two-bedroom house to a four-bedroom, so now I don't have to share a room with my brother like I did when I was little. I don't know what I would do if I had to share a bedroom with him now. I probably would've moved out already. His room is always filthy and dark, it's like it belongs to a sports-loving troll instead of a human. I mean, I'm willing to admit that I'm not the most organized person ever, but even I have my limits—he doesn't.

As soon as my family left for the party on Saturday, I took Rufus on a little trip around the house. I love walking around the house when it's empty. Sometimes, when I wake up in the middle of the night and I can't go back to sleep, I go downstairs, pour myself a glass of chocolate milk, and sit in the living room to contemplate the peacefulness of the night. I know it sounds weird, but I swear I'm not crazy, it's just very peaceful.

The first stop on my little tour with Rufus was my parents'

bedroom. It's by far the biggest bedroom in the house, and it's filled with pictures, souvenirs, and memories. Every time we go on vacation, my mom loves to frame a photo from our trip and hang it in the bedroom, and my dad loves to collect things from the places we visit. They complement each other pretty nicely in that sense.

Their bed is huge, so the first thing I did was jump on top of it, with Rufus following shortly after. My mom hates it when Rufus jumps into her bed, but Rufus loves it, so I let him.

We stayed on the bed for a while, just listening to music. I love listening to music with Rufus by my side. If I could only do a limited set of things for the rest of my life, this would definitely be on the list.

After an hour or so, I stood up and started to look around my parents' bedroom. They have pictures and souvenirs of every place we've ever been: Orlando, Canada, Los Angeles, Cancun, Yosemite, the Grand Canyon, and Honolulu. We go on a family vacation almost every summer. It's our little family tradition.

My favorite pictures are the ones from our first couple of trips. I've really enjoyed our last trips too, but nothing will ever top those first ones. They were peak fun and happiness.

This year we went to Honolulu, Hawaii. It was good, but it could've been better. I got into a couple of arguments with my mom because all I wanted to do was swim in the ocean and sit on the beach to read, but she had made a tight schedule filled with tours, shopping, and tourist attractions. I ended up so tired from that trip that I slept like 14 hours when we returned home. The picture my mom framed from that trip was one of the whole family in front of the beach, and my dad bought a tiki shot glass as a souvenir.

I think my favorite trip so far has been the one to Canada five years ago. I like beaches because I love to swim, but I'm not a big fan of warm temperatures. I prefer the cold and Canada was as cold as it can be. We went to a ski resort in the north of Quebec. It was the first time I had seen so much snow and it was a blast to learn how to ski. We spent the whole trip drinking hot chocolate, going on sleigh rides, and playing in the snow. It was absolutely the best.

Axel and I used to have ski races every day to determine who was the ski master. Unsurprisingly, he won every time, but I had a lot of fun nonetheless. It was one of the last times I remember Axel and I getting along. That was before he hit puberty and became the insufferable jerk he is right now. That trip, my dad bought a little moose statue and the picture my mom framed is of us next to a snowman we built.

Next to the picture of our best trip was the picture of our worst trip so far: Cancun. There's nothing wrong with Cancun itself, it's actually quite beautiful, but a category five hurricane unexpectedly hit the coast when we got there and it forced us to stay inside the hotel for four days. Four days of the whole family locked down in a relatively small hotel room.

FOUR DAYS.

At first it was fine, we were really grateful that we were inside and not outside—and we were also a little annoyed with my dad for not checking the weather before he booked the tickets—but then it became increasingly clear that there were not many things we could do inside. The TV had no signal, we got bored of the board games pretty quickly and I finished the book I brought to the trip on the first day—it was a long plane ride. By the second day, everyone was stressed out and bored as hell. Every conversation turned into a fight and every meal was an uncomfortable mess. As I mentioned before, the room was relatively small, so we were forced to be together practically 24/7, which made the fights even worse. Seriously, I don't know how we survived those days without killing each other. At one point, I began to think that I had died and gone to hell without anyone telling me.

At first, I believed that I was going to be fine, after all, I don't need TV or big tourist attractions to have a good time, and I certainly don't need anyone to entertain me. I thought that there was nothing I *absolutely* needed from the outside to have a good time—or at least to survive a couple of days—

but it turned out that there was something I really needed that I couldn't get in that room: some alone time. There was no privacy anywhere, nowhere I could just be alone for a couple of hours. I was locked up and there was no escape. At one point, I even started to shower twice a day just so I could have some extra minutes by myself.

That was always a problem with me and vacations. I mean, I love going out to other places and I love spending time with my family in different settings, but the trips always wore me down. I don't know why, but spending that much uninterrupted time with people is exhausting for me. It always makes me cranky, even when those people are my family.

Ever since I was a child, I discovered that I could improve my mood by swimming by myself in the hotel pool or taking a long walk around the hotel gardens, but since at that time there was nowhere I could be alone, I started to get really irritated. Everything bothered me: the rain, the discussions, the games, even the regular conversations. I couldn't stand any of it, the mere presence of my family bothered me. I was mad all the time, I just wanted to go home and be alone in my room.

After the hurricane dissipated, my mom arranged a trip to go to a nearby island for the day, but I begged her to let me stay in the hotel by myself. She didn't understand why I wanted to stay in there after four whole days stuck in that room and I didn't know how to explain it to her either, but after much insistence, she ended up letting me stay there and I spent the whole day swimming in the pool and relaxing by the beach. It was glorious. After that, I was in a much better mood and I was able to properly enjoy the few days we had left in there.

However, even though I had a good time at the end, when I think about that trip, the first thing that comes to my mind are the four horrible days trapped in that hotel room. I still don't know how I survived them. After it was all over, I was expecting a call from the president to congratulate me for such a feat.

The picture my mom framed of that trip is beautiful, of

course. It's a picture of the whole family playing cards the first day we were trapped in that room. Anyone that looked at that picture would probably think, "Wow, what a beautiful family," but there was a lot of yelling, stress, and fighting behind that picture. There's always more behind a picture than what meets the eye.

When I look at all the other pictures my mom has framed, all I can see is a beautiful family, and all I can think of are the happy memories of those vacations, but I'm sure that those trips also had their fair share of bad things, it's just that I have forgotten about them. I've only kept the good things and my brain has decided to gradually forget about the bad things.

Were the first couple of trips really the best ones, or did my mind trick me into believing that? The trip to Cancun was only a year ago, that's why I remember the bad stuff so vividly. I wonder if all the other trips were as great as I remember. I wonder if I felt the same level of happiness then as when I look at the pictures now. I wonder how much effect time has had on my memories and feelings.

Vacations are stressful and loud and complicated, but when I look at the pictures and the souvenirs now, all I can think of is the happiness I experienced during those trips. Maybe someday I will look at the Cancun picture and all I will be able to remember is that mom was so happy that she won that game that she decided to take a family picture to remember how much fun we were all having and how good it felt to finally beat dad in a cards game.

Maybe that's why mom loves to hang pictures and dad loves to buy souvenirs. To only remember the good things. Who wants to remember the bad things anyway?

After a significant amount of time in my parents' bedroom, the next stop on my little trip around the house was the office downstairs. I never go to my siblings' bedrooms when I walk around the house. Ashley's room is so pink that it hurts my eyes, and I'm scared that if I open Axel's room a roach will jump at me or something.

My parents' home office is a big room with three desks and some cabinets with work stuff. Mom and dad go in there when they need to work from home or make phone calls without being interrupted. Technically, I'm not supposed to be there without their permission, but I doubt they'll notice.

I sat in my dad's chair and spun it around like I used to do when I was a kid. Dad's chair is more comfortable than mom's, but her desk is bigger than his and it has more things on it. That's because dad doesn't do a lot of work at home, but mom does. On her desk, she has a lot of pens, a stapler, a couple of notebooks, a ton of paperwork, and a framed picture of Axel, Ashley, and me, while my dad only has a lamp, a swiss army knife, a little flashlight, and a Newton's cradle.

There's also a big desktop computer on the third desk. My dad loves that thing. When he bought it, he couldn't stop talking about it. As I said, I'm not such a big fan of technology, so I didn't really understand what all the fuss was about. To me, it was just a big box. He was so happy that, honestly, I would've liked to share his excitement, but I just didn't.

I still remember when he first brought it home, he was telling us about all the features it had and all the fantastic things we could do on the internet.

"This is the next big revolution," he said.

He told my mom that she could read all the latest celebrity gossips and promote her business, he told Axel that he could play video games and search for interesting sports trivia, and he told Ashley that she could play dress up games online and make colorful drawings with Microsoft Paint.

"And Hunter," he said when he finally got to me. "You can… um, read and stuff."

He wanted me to get excited, but it didn't work. Why would I want to read on a computer? I have books for that. But he looked so happy that I just smiled and told him that I couldn't wait to use it. I have used it a couple of times since then, but I don't love it. And I didn't want to use it right now, so I decided that it was time to go to the backyard.

As soon as I opened the door to go outside, Rufus started to run around on the grass like crazy. He loves to run, but he also gets tired really fast, so he lay down on the floor after only a couple of minutes to play with his chewing toy.

I decided to sit on the old tree swing and watch the stars. Every time I swung, a couple of leaves fell off the tree and into the trampoline that nobody used anymore. I remember that when we were little, Axel and I used to jump on it all day long. We used to have competitions to see who could jump higher or who could do a better somersault. But then Axel started to bring his friends home to play on it and I felt a little left out.

After that, I only used it when my brother wasn't around, and incredibly, I found out that jumping on it by myself was just as fun as jumping on it with him. I didn't need him to have a good time. I could jump as high as the springs of the trampoline allowed me and pretend that I was touching the sky or imagine that I was flying from world to world, saving people who were in trouble. I was perfectly happy on my own, imagining a new adventure every day.

I was starting to consider jumping on the trampoline again when I heard the garage door open, so I rapidly grabbed Rufus and ran back to my room to pretend that I was finishing a big stack of homework.

As promised, my mom didn't bring me any cake, but I was fine with it. She tried to make me feel bad for skipping the party by saying that everybody asked about me—which I'm pretty sure wasn't true—and by exaggeratedly describing it as "the party of the year." But none of that made me regret staying home. I was very glad that I didn't go to the party because, even though I did "nothing" all day, I had a great time.

# CHAPTER EIGHT

On Sunday, I accompanied my dad and my brother to a football game. I didn't want to go, but when my mom asked me if I had already finished all my non-existent homework, I foolishly said yes, so I didn't have any excuse not to go anymore. Besides, I couldn't say no to my family two days in a row. I would never hear the end of it if I did.

Even though we don't talk a lot, I like spending time with my dad. When we go out just the two of us, there are a lot of silent moments, but they're not uncomfortable. At least not for me, anyway. I enjoy those quiet moments in the company of my father, unlike my mother, who feels the need to fill every second with a conversation whenever I go out with her. She even asks me what's wrong if I spend more than 5 minutes without saying anything. Not that she needs me to keep the conversation going, she could spend hours and hours giving a monologue about her day, about the latest family gossip, or even about the weather. And don't get me wrong, I love spending time with my mom too, but sometimes all I need is a quiet car ride.

Unfortunately, this isn't what I got this time because Axel was in the car. He and dad spent the whole ride to the stadium talking about which team they thought would win the game and what that meant for the rest of the season. Fortunately, I remembered to bring my iPod, so I sat comfortably in the back, listening to music and looking out the window while they talked about sports.

I don't usually go with them to the games. The noise, the ridiculous amount of people, and the fact that I don't understand half of what's going on keep me away from them. But a friend of Axel canceled at the last minute and my dad insisted that I joined them. I don't know why, though. When it came down to sports, there was not a lot of difference between me and an empty seat in the stadium. Whenever I go with them to a football game it's like I don't even exist.

When I was little, I used to get very jealous of my brother. Not because he spent more time with dad or because I thought that he was his favorite, it was because I didn't have that kind of relationship with my father and I would probably never have one like it.

I wanted to be able to talk to him about sports too. I wanted him to be able to talk to me about books and movies. I wanted to be able to talk to his friends and spend time with them without feeling embarrassed or uncomfortable. I wanted to be able to talk to him about how I feel and about what I think, and I wanted him to be able to do the same thing. I wanted to go on a car ride with him and not be able to stop talking. I wanted to have the same kind of relationship that he had with Axel. But I couldn't. There was an invisible barrier between us that neither of us was able to break.

That still made me a little sad, but I was not jealous of my brother anymore, I had already accepted that things were like that and that there wasn't much I could do to change them. I couldn't change him and I couldn't change myself. I just had to live with it.

I know that everyone says that people can change, but I don't believe that. I think that people don't really change, they just evolve. They can evolve into better or worse versions of themselves, but they can't change who they are, they can't become someone else entirely, at their core, they're still the same.

I believe this because I was raised in the same way that

Axel was and that did not stop us from being totally different. We were born different and we're still different. When I was little, my parents wanted me and my brother to do everything together. My dad always pointed out how lucky we were that we had each other because all of his brothers were way older than him, so he didn't have anyone to play with when he was a kid. But pretty early on, it became increasingly clear that we were very different. My parents wanted me to be like them or like my brother, but I was born being me.

When I was 5, they even sent me to the same football club for kids that my brother was in. They didn't even ask me if I wanted to go—I didn't—they just enrolled me in. Needless to say, I didn't like it at all. I've never liked team sports. I don't exactly know why, but I guess it's because I don't like to depend on others and I definitely don't like it when others depend on me. I hate the idea that other people count on me not to mess up in order to win. What if I miss and we lose because of it? I don't like that kind of pressure. I don't like disappointing people. And I didn't want to disappoint my parents, but I didn't want to play either, so after a couple of weeks, I begged them to get me out of there, and they did.

My dad was kind of bummed out that I didn't love football like him and my brother, but he didn't give up. He was convinced that I was a born athlete like Axel, but I just hadn't found the right sport yet, so over the next few years I tried them all: basketball, softball, soccer, volleyball, and even tennis. And I sucked at all of them. But we were kids, everybody sucked. The reason I quit them all was not because I sucked at them, it was because I didn't like them. It wasn't a matter of talent, it was a matter of preference.

But finally, when I was 7, my parents enrolled me in a swim school, and I immediately fell in love with it. I had always loved swimming, but I never really saw it as a sport, to me, it was just something you did for fun. But my parents did see it as a sport, and I'm very glad that they did because it was the perfect one for me. I loved the soothing nature of the water, the peacefulness of floating, and the flying-like sensation of swimming. It's so relaxing. When I'm in the water, all the worries of the world disappear and my mind starts to think and reflect more clearly. I'm ashamed to admit that I have bumped into the walls of the swimming pool *several* times because I was so concentrated on my own thoughts. It's like meditating but in 100,000 gallons of water instead of in a mat.

And I was good at it. I was faster than most of the other kids my age and I even won a couple of bronze and silver medals in local competitions. I mean, I wasn't the next Mark Spitz, but I was relatively good. However, I never did it for the trophies or the medals, I did it for fun. And my parents were happy that I had finally found a sport that I liked, so it was a win-win situation.

I also made a few new friends, but I loved that there was no pressure to do it. Unlike the other sports that I had tried, there was no pressure to be constantly talking and getting along with everyone. Once we were in the water, everybody was on their own. If I failed, it only affected me and, if I wanted, I could swim the whole hour by myself and not interact with anyone else, just me and the water. I'm not saying that I hated talking to the boys on the other teams that I was, because I didn't, what I hated was the constant pressure to do it.

I've never liked feeling pressured to socialize. The idea of talking to strangers and creating an immediate bond with them has always been a little intimidating to me. I need time to get comfortable with someone, I can't do it right away like so many other people can. Add the pressure of an external party to it and it becomes downright terrifying and unbearable.

I remember that when I was little, my mom used to take my brother and me to the park as one of her efforts to create a closer relationship between us, but it never really worked. As soon as we arrived at the park, Axel used to run to the basketball court to play with the other boys while I stayed in the swings and the sandbox to play by myself.

I didn't like playing basketball, but thankfully I didn't need to play with the other boys to have fun. I was good on my own. When other kids approached me while I was in the sandbox, I played with them, but sometimes what I wanted was to play alone. I wanted to create a new world or a new adventure in my mind and lose myself in it without the pressure of having to entertain someone else.

However, what my mother wanted was for me to play with Axel and the other boys, so she always insisted that I join them. "Don't be shy," she used to say. "Go play with your brother," "You'll have more fun there, just talk to the other boys," "It's just a game, you'll be okay."

I tried joining my brother and playing with them a couple of times to get my mom off my back, but I always ended up having a horrible time. I was not the best at basketball, so the other boys used to mock me. It was a playful mock, but it still bothered me because I didn't know them. And, unlike Axel, I didn't know how to talk to them, it was like they spoke an entirely different language. I have never felt comfortable in that type of environment or with that type of boys. When I was with them, I felt like I didn't belong there. I didn't know how to be like them, and I didn't know how to be myself around them, so I stopped trying to join them, but that prompted my mother to insist even harder that I play with them, and I hated that too. So, at the end of the day, one way or another, I always ended up having a horrible time at the park.

Luckily, when my sister was born, my mom was so busy that the regular visits to the park ceased. And not only that, but she also stopped trying to force a relationship between my brother and me. Ironically, I have a better relationship with my sister than with my brother. But to be fair, I have a better relationship with almost anyone than with my brother. Our relationship basically consists of him ignoring me and me staying out of his way.

But I have a warmer relationship with my sister. There is a 4-year gap between us, so we don't have many things in common, but she loves Rufus almost as much as I do, and when I take him to the park, she always wants to join us.

However, she's ten now, and she has started to change her Barbie dolls for secret diaries and her stuffed bears for makeup kits for girls. Unfortunately, she's also starting to leave her sweet personality behind and adopting a new brattier one. It's kind of hard to see her grow. Sometimes I still see her as the 4-year-old who used to beg me to read her a bedtime story when mom and dad were too busy to read her one. But that girl is gone now and has been replaced by a new one that talks back to mom and dad, is rude and interrupts others when they're talking, and throws tantrums when she doesn't get what she wants.

I think she's now like this because she wants to be like her ballet friends. Mom loves ballet, and she used to practice it when she was younger, so when Ashley was 6, mom immediately enrolled her in a ballet school and Ashley loved it. She felt like she was a dancing princess, and she loved to see all the family at her recitals. But she was recently transferred to the class for girls of 10 to 15, and I think that's why she now thinks that being bratty is cool, she wants to be like the older girls. Mom says that it's normal for a girl her age to behave like that, but she only says that because Ashley is her favorite and she hates to scold her.

Mom always says that she doesn't have favorites, but it's pretty obvious that it's Ashley. Just as it's obvious that dad's favorite is Axel. I know that I'm no one's favorite, and I try not to be bothered by it, but I'd be lying if I said that it doesn't make me sad sometimes. I know my parents love me, but sometimes I do feel a little left out.

Sometimes I wish I was more like them. I wish I were more like my mom so that I could have a better relationship with her. I wish I were more like my dad so that I could talk to him about anything. Sometimes I even wish that I was more like Axel so that I could know how it feels like to have the kind of strong brotherly relationship that I've read so much about in books.

Sometimes I wish I could change and not just evolve.

# CHAPTER NINE

Ariana has officially become my best female friend. It's not like there was a lot of competition, but I take titles seriously, and to make it official, it's a big deal for me.

We have sat together in the cafeteria every day since I met her and we always sit together in Math and Social Studies, the only two classes we have together, which is a shame because she always makes me laugh in class. Unlike me, she has no problem participating. She's always raising her hand, even if she doesn't have anything particularly worthwhile to add. She just likes to be part of the conversation. That's something I cannot relate to. I don't like to participate just for the sake of participating. I need something important to add to the conversation, otherwise, why bother? But Ariana doesn't see it that way. If she has something in her mind that she wants to share, then she does it, it doesn't matter if it's relevant or not. But she doesn't do it for the points, as other students do, she just does it because she wants to.

And she always asks the most ridiculous questions that make the whole classroom laugh. I never know if they're laughing with her or laughing at her, but I don't think that she cares. She doesn't let shame get in the way of her curiosity, which is something I cannot say about myself. Sometimes, even when I do have an important question or something meaningful to add, I don't do it because I take too long formulating what I'm going to say to not sound stupid. Unfortunately, time doesn't stop when you're overthinking, so while I carefully put together the words that I want to say and study every possible scenario that could result from my participation, the moment passes or the class ends.

I'm ashamed to say it, but sometimes I let the fear of what other people might think of me control my life. That's something I like about Ariana, she really doesn't care what anyone thinks of her. Sometimes I wish I was more like her, and not just in that regard. Besides her confidence, I would also like to have her social skills. She's one of the most outgoing and friendly people I've ever met. She gets along great with everyone she talks to, which is why I don't understand why she decided to be friends with me in the first place.

Why would such an outgoing and charismatic girl want to be friends with someone like me? I just hope it's because we get along great and she actually likes me and not because it's part of an elaborate plan à la Stephen King's *Carrie* because I don't think I could survive high school without her—and I'm pretty sure that I don't have telekinetic powers to carry out an act of revenge in case someone bathe me in pig blood.

Another great trait I've noticed about Ariana is that she's quite adventurous. She's always looking for something fun to do and she can't sit still for too long. She has even suggested a couple of times that we should skip Math and go to the mall or something, but honestly, I'm too scared to do it. I think she's like that because she's a city girl. She and her family moved here only a month ago, just before school started. I don't know why someone would like to leave the city and move to a small town like this, that's bonkers, but when I asked her why they moved here, she didn't answer nor did she seemed like she wanted to, so I didn't insist.

Fortunately, they moved only a couple of blocks away from my house, so sometimes Ariana and I walk home after school instead of taking the bus. I love walking home with her because it gives us time to chat. Sometimes we even go to the nearby park, which is really fun. When we ride the seesaw or the swings, people always stare at us, obviously thinking that we're too old to be doing that, but Ariana doesn't care, so I don't care either—okay, I do care a little, but most of the times the fun outweighs the shame. Ariana even insisted on teaching me how to hang upside down from the monkey bars after I told her that, when I was a child, I always wanted to learn how to do it, but I was too afraid to try it.

"Come on, Hunter," she said before I tried it for the first time. "Just remember to hold on tight with your legs, take a deep breath and let the wind catch you."

She then hung upside down to show me how to do it. She had a big smile on her face and hair flowing all around her. Somehow that image gave me the confidence boost I needed to try it. And it worked. Before I realized it, I was hanging upside down next to her, feeling the wind hit my face and my hands fall down below my head due to the gravity. It sounds like a minor and even childish achievement, but it was something that I've always wanted to do, and I was so happy that I could finally do it.

When she saw me smiling, she rapidly got off the monkey bars, grabbed the camera inside her backpack, and took a picture of me. I was caught off guard by this, but you couldn't tell that by the picture she managed to take. In the photo, I was smiling so much that my eyes were practically closed. My arms were down, floating in the air, and the sun was shining bright behind me. It looked like one of those too-good-to-be-true pictures that came in brand-new photo frames.

She was great at capturing small moments like this. I don't know how she does it, but that camera is like an extra limb to her, she has excellent control over it and is able to make even the mundane look amazing. Whether it was a cloud with a weird shape or a father playing catch with his son, Ariana was able to take anything and turn it into a picture worth framing.

But what she loved photographing the most were animals, and she went through any means to do it. It didn't matter if it was climbing a tree or running down a hill, Ariana did anything to take a perfect shot. She loves nature, and nothing brings more joy to her than to capture an animal in its native state with her camera. I have a feeling that she will be a wildlife photographer when she grows up. I can totally see her working for *National Geographic* or something like that. It would be perfect for her because I don't think she would be happy with a 9 to 5 office job.

I don't know if I would be happy with an office job either. In fact, I have no idea what I want to be when I grow up, but I've always wanted to do three things: I want to do something important, I want to help people, and I want to get out of this town. I'm not sure what I want to do yet, but I know that it has to include those three things. I'm terrified of waking up in 20 years and still be in this town with a boring, dead-end job. I'm not sure of what I want, but I do know that I don't want that. I want something else. Something better. Something *more*.

I've talked about this with Ariana a couple of times and she understands it, she's not too happy with this town either, but she has warned me that I should not wish my life away and that I should try to enjoy every step of the way.

"Who says that things are gonna be better in another city?" She told me. "Or that life is gonna be easier when we're older? You may wake up in 20 years on a hideous 500 square feet apartment in Reno with a huge debt, a divorce in process, and three illegitimate children. So, if I were you, I would enjoy my life now before you have to give all your salary to your bookie, your ex-wife, and those three poor kids."

That made me laugh a lot. She never fails to make me laugh, even when we're talking about something serious. I once told her that she was really funny and her answer made me laugh even more.

"I get that a lot," she said. "But I'm actually not, I'm just way too honest and people always think that I'm kidding."

I knew she said that as a joke, but she was actually pretty honest. But the good kind of honest, not the mean kind of honest. She was the kind of person that would always tell you her honest opinion if you asked for it, but she would never tell you out of the blue that you look "fat" or that you're "annoying." People who do that are just rude, not honest.

Once, in middle school, a boy that I wanted to be friends with told me that he didn't want to talk to me anymore because I was "too boring." What a rude thing to say! I didn't know what to do with that information, what was I supposed to answer? "Thank you for pointing that out, I'll try to be more interesting next time."?

When we were first starting to know each other, Ariana told me that I was very quiet. Of course, this wasn't the first time that I'd heard that, but to hear it from her was kind of a bummer because all my life the word "quiet" has been used with a negative connotation. When people used it, it was to point out something negative in me, something that I should change. So to hear it from her scared me because I thought that maybe that meant that she didn't want to talk to me anymore, just like that boy a couple of years ago.

"Oh… sorry," was the only thing I could utter.

"What?" She asked before I could say anything else. "No! I didn't mean it as something bad. I meant it as a compliment. I like it, it means that you're a great listener, most people never stop talking and just listen to you to reply with a shallow comment or with a story of their own, but you listen to understand. And when you talk, you always have something interesting to say. I like that."

To hear that coming from her meant a lot. It was the first time in my life that someone described my quietness as a strength and not as a weakness. At that moment, I knew Ariana and I were going to be very good friends. And I was right.

I usually take my time before I can consider someone a *friend*, but it was almost immediately with Ariana. I loved how, from the very first moment, we were able to talk about silly and superficial stuff just as easily as we could discuss deep and serious topics. The day we met, we talked about our pets, our hobbies, the movies we liked, the plausibility of time travel, the purpose of institutional education, and what we wanted to do when we grew up.

I guess I can say that we hit it off right away, which was surprising because I'm usually not very good with first meetings. I was not born with my mom's ability to just go to someone new and start talking. I can't just naturally charm strangers with small talk like her. When I try doing it, I feel uncomfortable, anxious, and fake. And, unfortunately, it's no better when other people try making small talk with me. I never know what to say, my mind just goes blank and I inevitably lead the conversation down a path of uncomfortable silence. It's like the little speaking part of me gets locked up in a big, impenetrable cage. But with Ariana it was different. With her, I was able to get out of that cage pretty quickly. With her, talking was easy.

She has actually been helping me socialize in school without even knowing. She's so charming, quirky, and outgoing that people are naturally drawn to her, and since we spend most of our time in school together we also meet new people together.

Now, when I meet someone new, I don't feel pressured to be talking all the time to keep the conversation flowing. Ariana gladly takes on that responsibility. I can just listen and chime in when I'm ready, when I actually have something to say, not just talk for the sake of talking. And she makes me feel safe because, no matter what, they always love her. It is a brand-new world.

We've actually started sitting in the cafeteria with some of the people we've met. There's Leo from my Spanish class, who's kind of a jokester. He's funny, but sometimes he's a bit too much or gets too familiar, which is something I don't like, but overall I like him—in small doses. There are Lizzie and Margo, two girls from our Social Studies class that are obsessed with *Smallville*. I like them, they're cheerful and friendly. And finally, there's Jake from our Math class. He's kind of geeky and nerdy, which is something I like about him.

I don't know if I would call them all *friends* yet, but I'm glad that I met them, we're an interesting cafeteria table. We're not really "popular," but we're not "losers" either, we're in a nice middle and that's where I want to stay. I have never really cared about popularity, I don't like that kind of attention. Thankfully, Ariana feels the same way.

"Caring about popularity is pretty stupid," she said when I asked her about it. "There are far more important things in this world than that. And, believe me, I have learned that it's better to have a few good friends than having dozens of fake ones."

By the tone she said that, I knew there was something else that she wasn't telling me, but by this point I knew better than to ask. If there was something she wasn't telling me, it was because she wasn't ready to do it, and I had no problem waiting until she was. I was already used to it because there had been other times when I had asked her about some personal stuff —like her life before she moved here—and she had just stayed quiet or said that she didn't want to talk about it. I never insisted because I understand that there are some things that are hard to share even with your closest friends.

# CHAPTER TEN

Ever since Mr. Brooks recommended The Curious Incident of the Dog in the Night-Time to me, I have continued to go to the library almost every day after school. At first, Ariana and I considered joining an after-school club, but the options were pretty awful, so in the end, she decided to enroll in an after-school photography class. She asked me to enroll in the class with her so we could walk home together, but I don't like photography as much as she does, so I told her that I would wait for her in the library.

I have no problem with this because the library is actually my favorite place in school, and since there isn't a book club for students, going to the library every day after classes is the next best thing.

Mr. Brooks has continued to recommend me books, and I seriously couldn't be more grateful. Not only has this given me a chance to discover a few unknown gems, but now I have someone I can discuss them with, so in a sense, we do have a little book club of our own. I've always loved books, but he has made me love them even more, which I didn't think was possible.

At first, I feared that maybe spending 2 hours in the library every day would get boring, but apparently, I could spend hours and hours discussing the characters, themes, and ideas of the books I had read. It turns out that conversations like that not only fueled my soul, they also made the time fly by because every time Ariana returned from her 2-hour photography class, it felt like only 15 minutes had passed.

After a couple of weeks, Mr. Brooks told me that I could call him Dan outside of class because hearing "Mister" so many times a day made him feel old.

"Oh, thanks," I said. "But no, thank you."

I couldn't call a teacher by his first name, even if that teacher was only ten years older than me. But he insisted, so eventually, we came to an agreement, and now I call him Mr. Dan when we're not in class. He laughed a lot when I first suggested calling him that, but he agreed that it was the most logical compromise.

"You're really something else, Hunter, do you know that?" Mr. Dan said, laughing.

I just smiled. I've heard that kind of thing my entire life, but it was nice that this time it meant something good for a change.

And he was really something else too. I have never met a teacher like him before. He's young, but very wise and he really wants to make a difference in this school and in the students' lives. Most teachers just go to school, teach their class, and go home, but he wants to do more than that, he wants to make a lasting impact. He doesn't want students to just learn his subject like parrots, he doesn't want them to memorize what he's teaching them without really understanding it, he wants them to really learn and grow, to think on their own and construct their own knowledge instead of just repeating someone else's ideas.

And it's weird that I'm talking about it as if he was some kind of radical revolutionary because, when you think about it, that's how every teacher should be. But they're not. I mean, what's the point of having a good grade if we don't actually learn? A student with a good memory can get an A+ on every test but forget everything after a week because he had no significant learning, he just memorized the stuff that was going to be on the test.

But Mr. Dan doesn't want students to do that, he doesn't want them just to repeat what he says or what's in the book, he wants us to think by ourselves, to form our own ideas and question the established ones. He wants us to apply the knowledge he teaches us beyond the classroom, and he wants us to grow not just as students but as human beings as well.

I have never had a teacher like him before. He had the knowledge and skills to be teaching in an elite private school somewhere in a big city, but by some weird twist of fate, he ended up in this high school, and I couldn't be more thankful that that happened.

When he first told us that he would be in charge of the library, I thought that it was because he was very well-prepared and had a drive that I had not seen in other teachers, but the reality was much grimmer. It turns out that he was in charge of the library because the school had some financial cuts, and the first thing to go was the librarian.

"What?!" I asked when he first told me this. "How could that happen? Is that even allowed?"

"Yes, it actually is, because it is not a statutory requirement for a school to have a library, much less a librarian," Mr. Dan answered. "And in this school, less than 10% of the students use the library, so when the cuts came in, it was apparently clear for the administration who had to go."

"That is outrageous," I said.

"Yes, yes it is," he answered. "Did you know, Hunter, that it is not mandatory for a school to have a library, but it is for a prison? That's pretty interesting."

Some teachers protested the firing of the librarian, Mr. Dan included, but after it became clear that the administration was not going to rehire her, he asked to be put in charge of the library. The principal agreed to this and gave the job to Mr. Dan because he's young, new, and he could pay him less than what he deserved. This, of course, is unfair, but apparently, Mr. Dan doesn't care about the money.

"If I cared about it, I wouldn't be a teacher," he said.

He didn't ask for the job for the extra money, he did it to transform the library and to improve the student's academic experience. But still, there's something really wrong with society when those in charge of imparting education to the next generations have some of the lowest salaries in the country. I couldn't help but wonder how many people that could've been excellent teachers were discouraged from that profession because they did care about the money? Or how many teachers that decided to chase their passion lived from paycheck to paycheck because their salary was a joke? Just imagining the answers to those questions made me extremely sad.

The world is unfair in many ways, but to know that I can't do anything to change things like that really bothers me. That's why I admire Mr. Dan's quest to improve the library. He's trying to make the world a better place from his own little corner. He wants to instill in students a love of reading because he knows that it can help their intellectual and personal development and increase their empathy. And to teach empathy to students means creating a better future society. It's a tough goal to achieve, but I think that if anyone can do it, it's him.

So far, he has been busy updating the databases, but he already has some ideas in mind on how to achieve his goal, including rearranging the space to make it more accessible to students and increasing the book collection.

After the first couple of weeks of visiting him after classes, I started to feel guilty because I was taking up a significant amount of Mr. Dan's time and not letting him move along with his plan more quickly, so I started to help him. At first, I only helped him move stuff around and capture information on the computer, but then I started helping him with ideas too.

I proposed that he could select a book of the week and display it in the library or write engaging reviews of books students might be interested in and paste them around the school. He actually liked those ideas a lot, and I was thrilled that I could contribute to his project, but I could never have imagined what happened next.

"Hunter," he said one day after we finished reorganizing a bookshelf. "I want to offer you a job."

"Excuse me?" I answered, not understanding what was happening.

"Well, since you're here helping me pretty much every day, I want to make it official. I want you to be my library assistant. Unfortunately, I'm not able to pay you very much, but you can put it in your résumé, and I can even talk to the principal to see if he would be willing to give you school credit for it. What do you think? Do you want to be the new library assistant?"

I couldn't believe what was going on. Was he really offering me a job? I was waiting for him to say "gotcha!" and laugh at me, but he didn't say anything, he was waiting for my answer.

"Ye-yeah," I said. "Of course! I would love to!"

"Great! I'm very happy to hear that, Hunter, I'm sure we'll be able to do great things together. Now, I expect commitment, but I don't want this to interfere with your academic or personal life. If at any point you think that this is taking up too much of your time, don't be afraid to tell me, the most important thing is that you can get some benefit out of this and that you feel comfortable. Regarding the salary, I can offer you $6.50 per hour, I know this isn't much but…"

I know I should've been listening to what he was saying because it was important, but I couldn't believe that this was happening. My mind was racing. I mean, to officially work in the library with Mr. Dan? To get the chance to help him in his quest to improve the library and contribute to the students' integral development while getting paid for it? It was a dream come true. A dream I didn't even know I had.

When I saw Ariana after her photography class, I couldn't contain my excitement and I immediately told her the good news.

"That's great! I'm so happy for you, Hunter," she said, hugging me.

We spent the whole way home talking about school and my new job, but I couldn't concentrate on our conversation because I was too busy trying to come up with new ways to get students into reading.

"Is there something wrong, Hunter?" Ariana asked after she noticed that I was a little distracted. "You are even quieter than usual."

"No, there's nothing wrong," I answered. "I'm just happy."

# CHAPTER ELEVEN

When I got home, I began to write down all the ideas I had for the library and I started to make a list of all the books I thought were essential for students to read. I hoped it wouldn't take me too long because I also had some homework to do, but before I knew it, my mom was calling me to go downstairs for dinner. Three hours had passed since I got home and I was so focused on what I was doing that I didn't even notice when the sun set.

Before I went downstairs to have dinner with my family, I thought long and hard about what exactly I was going to tell them about the job. But in the end, I decided that I was not going to tell them anything. At least not yet. I didn't know what they were going to think about it and I didn't know how to explain it to them yet, so I decided that first I was going to find out exactly what my job was going to be and, after a few weeks, I would tell them.

But you know what they say, you want to make God laugh? Tell him about your plans.

"Hunter, remember that you have to come home early tomorrow," my mom said during dinner. "You have a dental appointment at 5:30pm."

I had totally forgotten about that. I couldn't get home early because I couldn't miss my first day at work, and I couldn't ask my mom to reschedule the appointment without giving her a valid reason. My plan was already falling apart.

"Mom, can you pick me up at school? I can't take the 3:00pm bus, I have to stay in school until 5," I told her.

"Why?" She asked.

I could've lied and said that I had to stay in school for a project or that I had homework to do, but I decided not to, I knew she would just keep asking me questions until my story fell apart. And I guess that, deep down, the part of me that makes rushed decisions wanted me to tell my parents the news because I didn't even hesitate when I answered.

"Because I got offered a job and I accepted it," I said.

"What?" The whole family asked at the same time.

"Yeah, I am the new library assistant and I have to stay until 5," I said.

"Oh my god, I didn't think you could get even nerdier," my brother said.

"Why did you get a job? Are we poor?" My sister asked.

"Is that really what you want to do with your free time, Hunter?" My dad asked.

"Why didn't you tell us?" My mom asked.

Those were a lot of questions to get in five seconds, but I decided to only answer my mom's and ignore the other ones.

"It was offered to me today, I was going to tell you tonight, I promise," I lied. "Look, it's a great honor that I got offered this job, okay? And it's something that I really want to do. Mr. Brooks has a great plan to modernize the library and I think that I can really make a difference in school."

"As a library assistant, honey? If you want to make an impact at school, why don't you find something else?" My mom asked.

"Because I don't want to do something else, I want to do this," I said. "It's something that I believe in. I actually already have some ideas on how to get more students into reading. I think that–"

"But you're a kid, Hunter," my mom interrupted me. "You're only 14 years old. You should be doing other things, not worrying about stuff like that. You should be enjoying high school, not spending your afternoons in a library."

"But I enjoy being in the library," I responded. "And if we can get more students to use it, we could potentially be creating a more empathetic future society. Studies show that–"

"Nobody goes to libraries anymore, doofus," my brother interrupted me.

"I didn't even know they still existed," my sister added.

This was one of the things that bothered me the most about my family. They're always complaining that I'm too quiet, but when I actually have something to say, they don't listen.

"Are you at least going to get paid?" My dad asked.

"Yes, $6.50 an hour," I answered.

"Just that? You could be earning more flipping burgers," my dad said.

"I'm not doing it for the money," I answered.

"Clearly," he said sarcastically.

I knew they wouldn't get it. *I knew it*. Ever since I was a child, I learned not to expect my family to get excited about the same things that excited me, but a little part of me thought that maybe this time would be different. What a fool.

"To me, it sounds like this teacher wants to take advantage of you," my dad added. "He wants you to do all his work for him and pay you peanuts in return. You're a smart kid, Hunter, don't let him fool you into believing that this is a great opportunity, because it's not."

I was starting to get *really* angry, I was not going to let them dampen my enthusiasm. My mother must've noticed this in my face because she immediately tried to lighten the mood. But instead of lightening it by supporting me and my choice, she decided to offer me advice I didn't ask for.

"Honey, I think what your father is trying to say is that you're in high school, you should be dedicating your time to something else, you know, you should be going out with your friends, maybe have a girlfriend, you don't want to miss out on the high school experience. Why don't you better join a club or try out for a sports team?"

"Yeah, right. As if Hunter could be selected for one of the school teams," my brother said.

"Don't say that, Axel," my mom said. "Your brother is very good when he wants to be. And he's a very good swimmer, why don't you try out for the swimming team, Hunter?"

"I don't want to be on a sports team, mom. I want to do this," I answered.

"But honey…," my mom started.

"Mom, just leave him alone," Axel interrupted her.

Wait, was my brother defending me?

"If he wants to be a weirdo, then let him be a weirdo," he said.

Ouch. But it was the nicest thing anyone had said to me at the table all night, so I'll take it.

"Don't talk to your mother like that," my dad said to Axel. "Hunter, we just want you to think things through."

"Yeah," my mom added. "We just want you to realize that this might not be the best thing you should be doing with your time."

I wanted to answer them. I wanted to tell them that I was not asking for their opinion or their permission. I wanted them to tell me that they respected and supported my choice. I wanted them to be happy for me just because I was happy, but apparently that was too much to ask for in this family.

I wanted to get out of there.

I wanted to run to my room.

I wanted to yell and I wanted to cry.

But I didn't.

All I could say was: "Mom, can you pick me up or not?"

"Of course I can, honey," she answered.

And then we went back to eating dinner as if nothing had happened. My mom and my sister talked about her ballet class, my dad and brother discussed how things were going with his girlfriend and I just sat there, trying to pretend that I was listening and that I was fine, but in reality, I just wanted to get out of there. I was emotionally drained and exhausted. I just wanted to go to sleep so I could stop thinking about what happened. I just wanted to get their words out of my head.

    I can't believe that just a few hours ago I was happy.

# CHAPTER TWELVE

The next day Ariana accompanied me to the library after class. She was jokingly acting like she was a proud mom dropping off her son on his first day of work.

"It's true what they say," she said while trying to comb my hair with her fingers. "Kids *do* grow up fast."

"Stop it," I said, laughing.

Mr. Dan got out of his office to receive us when he heard the door.

"Hi, Mr. Dan," I said.

"Good afternoon, Hunter. Hello, Ariana," he said, smiling at us.

"Hey, Dan," Ariana said with a slight nod of her head.

Unlike me, Ariana had no problem calling him Dan outside the classroom, probably because she didn't have a class with him, but most likely because she was Ariana and respect for authority was not one of her strongest suits.

"Have fun and don't work too hard, okay?" She said to me.

"Okay," I answered with a chuckle.

"And you better not use your paychecks for drugs and alcohol, young man," she said.

"Mom!" I said.

She laughed and then hugged me.

"Good luck," she said.

"Thanks," I answered.

"Bye, Dan!," she said to Mr. Dan.

"See you later, Ariana," he answered. "Are you excited for your first day of work, Hunter?"

"Absolutely. What's my first task?" I asked.

"Get a pen and paper because we got some planning to do."

We went to his office, which was a small room in the corner of the library. He had a ton of organized paperwork on his desk, along with some lists and sketches of what I assumed were plans for the library. He took a seat behind his desk and sat in one of the two chairs in front of it.

"As you know, I want to modernize the library and make it more accessible to students. I want them to take advantage of all the books and resources that are offered to them for free and I want them to not only read but also to enjoy reading. One of the reasons I decided to hire you is because I want to have a student's perspective. So first I have to ask you, why do you like reading so much?"

Oh boy, that was a difficult question. I mean, why do I like cheesecake? I don't know, I just love the taste of it. It's the same thing with reading, I just love it, but I'm guessing that Mr. Dan was looking for a more in-depth answer, so I tried my best to come up with a coherent explanation.

"Well... I think it's because reading can transport you to different worlds and realities, you know? I can open a book and forget about my life for a couple of hours. I can meet new people and explore other cities or planets without leaving my room. I can discover what it's like to be inside someone else's mind or live in a different place just by the magic of reading. So yeah... I guess that's why I love it. I've had so many adventures and I've learned so much from reading that I really can't imagine what my life would be like without books."

"That's great, Hunter. That's exactly how I want other kids to feel about reading. Did your family environment contribute to this? Did your parents instill in you your love for reading?"

"God, no, my parents don't like to read and my siblings mock me for reading too much. It was definitely not my family environment. My mom even used to reprimand me for staying up too late reading, so I got a flashlight to read at night without her noticing."

"I used to do the same!" Mr. Dan said, laughing. "Then how did you first get into reading?"

"Well," I said. "My grandpa was a renowned scholar, and when my brother Axel was born, he hoped that he might follow in his footsteps. So, when Axel turned six, my grandpa gave him a huge collection of children's books so he could start developing a love for reading. But my brother hated it, he wanted a Game Boy, not schoolwork, so he abandoned them in our closet. I discovered them when I was seven and I immediately fell in love with them. With these new treasures, I could travel to a faraway land or the deepest parts of the ocean from the comfort of my bed. I didn't get to spend much time with my grandpa because he died when I was five, but I've always been thankful for that indirect hand-me-down gift that practically changed my life."

"That's amazing. Do you remember the books or the authors?"

"Of course, I probably still got them somewhere in my room. They were mostly books by Mark Twain, Hans Christian Andersen, A. A. Milne, Dr. Seuss, and Jules Verne."

"Wow, that's a pretty great collection. You know, I've always loved children's books and young adult literature, even now. I think they're highly unappreciated. People in literary circles always disregard them, but they are essential. Some of the best books in literature started off as children's books. *The Lord of the Rings, The Chronicles of Narnia, Adventures of Huckleberry Finn, The Little Prince, Alice in Wonderland,* even *Harry Potter*. The really great ones can transmit complex ideas in simple ways, and that's a huge accomplishment. That's why I think these kinds of books deserve way more respect. Besides, how else are you supposed to get children and teenagers interested in literature? I love Faulkner and Dostoyevsky, but *Crime and Punishment* will hardly get a teenager into reading."

"Yeah, I totally know what you mean!" I said. "When I

was younger, I started to read *The Iliad* because I love Greek mythology and it's supposedly one of the greatest adventure stories ever told, but I couldn't get past page 20 because it was way too complex."

"Exactly!" He said. "When you start hiking, you don't start with Mount Everest. The students have to read the classics and I have to teach them, but a regular teenager is rarely going to develop the habit of reading for pleasure by reading *To Kill a Mockingbird* because it feels more like a chore than something you do for fun."

"Yeah, as a student, sometimes the pressure to read can overshadow the fun and that's really disappointing. I think reading should be a fun experience and reduce the stress of students, not add to it. Maybe that's why kids my age don't like reading. It is not perceived as a 'cool' activity, it's something the school forces us to do."

"That's exactly right, Hunter. And that's why I want to modernize this library. I want students to think that reading is more like watching a movie and less like solving a math problem. I want them to know that there is a world outside the mandatory schoolbooks and that somewhere in here there is a perfect story for them just waiting to be discovered. That somewhere in this library there is a perfect book for them, one that will get them into the amazing world of reading."

I really loved his commitment and enthusiasm. What he wanted to do was harder than taming a white shark. He wanted a whole generation of teenage students to read for fun, yet somehow he talked about it like it was just a simple walk in the park, and more astonishingly, he made me believe that it was possible.

I'd be lying if I said that my family didn't get into my head last night, but Mr. Dan's passion helped me forget about that. I was now 100% committed to this idea and this project, no matter how unattainable it was.

"Where do we start?" I asked.

"I have a couple of ideas," he said. "I'm going to run them by you and if you have any comment or any ideas of your own, please, I'm all ears."

He started off by emphasizing the importance of a good marketing strategy. He wanted to reinvent the library's image around the concept of escapism. He wanted students to see the library as a place where you could escape from the pressure of school and life in general for a couple of hours. He showed me some pretty great preliminary posters he made that conveyed this feeling.

He also wanted to make recommendation charts, which I thought was a pretty interesting idea. Basically, he wanted to make charts that could recommend a book based on a couple of variables, like mood or interests. The recommendations were going to be like 'Read *The Alchemist* if you feel stressed,' or 'Read *Hoops* if you like basketball,' or 'Read *Neuromancer* if you liked *The Matrix*.'

He also wanted to establish a 'Book of the Week,' an idea we had previously discussed. It basically consisted of selecting a book that appealed to teens each week and writing a short review about it, along with bullet point reasons of why they should read it. I showed him the list I made of books I thought every student should read, which I made based on this idea, and he loved it.

"Do you want to write the reviews?" He asked.

"Me?" I said. "I have never written a review before."

"Don't worry, I would help you, of course, but I think it would mean more if it comes from you. From a student to other students."

I agreed to write the reviews, but I was utterly terrified of it. It was a huge responsibility, one that I didn't know if I could handle, but I was so inspired by Mr. Dan that at that moment I couldn't possibly say no.

We decided that it was best to do a calendar and set realistic goals we wanted to achieve from here until the end of the school year. Or at least what Mr. Dan considered to be 'realistic,' because getting more than three-quarters of the school to rent at least a book not related to their classes by the end of the school year was pretty far-fetched. But aim high, right?

"I also want to expand the catalog," he said. "I want more modern and youth-oriented books, but that's going to be a bit hard because we have no money. However, I already started to talk with some institutions and friends that can donate us some books and I will also contribute with a few books from my own personal collection."

"I can donate some books too," I said.

"No, Hunter. Thank you, but that's not necessary. I will take care of that."

"I really don't mind. Besides, I have to make room for new ones. If I don't let some of them go, pretty soon there won't be any space left for me in my own room."

"Okay, if you really don't have a problem with it, then great. Sounds like we have a plan. This is really starting to take shape. But I think that, before anything else, we have to make this place look less like Mordor and more like Hogwarts."

Mr. Dan grabbed one of the sketches on his desk and showed me what he wanted the library to look like. He wanted to move all the bookshelves and computers to the sides so the books were more easily accessible and there was more space in the middle for tables and chairs.

"I want to create a safe and social space for students," he said. "I want them to be able to come here and not only read, but also work, study, discuss, and even play together. I was even thinking of buying some board games so students can take a break when they're working or just to relax after a hard day."

He also wanted to divide the literature books from the reference and study materials and give more promotion to the former.

"If a student wants a book for class, they're going to find it no matter what, because they'll come here looking for it," he said. "But I've learned that with students and literature books, it's usually the other way around. Among so many books, a good literature book has to stand out for a student to pick it. Of course, there are exceptions like you, but for the most part, the book has to find the student."

All in all, I liked his proposal, but he wasn't kidding when he said he wanted to create a social space. The library was now designed for people to go there in groups. There were only tables and chairs for a minimum of four people and a maximum of eight. Gone were the spaces behind or in between bookshelves where you could hide and read in peace. Now you could see every corner of the library from any place and if you wanted to go alone you'd have to share a table with someone else.

"What do you think?" he asked.

"It looks great," I answered. "But what if someone wants to come here to read alone?"

"What?"

"Yeah, I mean, I think that what you're proposing is great and I know that the space is limited, but I think there should also be a place where you can just sit alone to read without having to share a space with someone else."

He stared at me for a few seconds without saying a word.

Oh god, he probably was thinking that I was some loner weirdo with a pathological desire to be alone or something. Why else would someone refuse to share a space with someone else? I shouldn't have said anything. Me and my big mouth.

"You're right," he said. "I was so focused on creating a social space for students that I forgot one of the main purposes of libraries."

Then he grabbed another sheet of paper and started sketching a new design. There was still a lot of room in the middle for chairs and tables for groups, but now there were two bookshelves separating a corner of the library from the rest.

"We can put some individual couches and carrel desks in there," he said. "This will be our 'quiet' zone. What do you think?"

"I think it's perfect," I answered.

"So it's settled then, I'm going to talk to the principal to see if I can get some help from maintenance over the weekend, and hopefully, we can start seeing some changes by next week."

"Sounds great."

"Shoot," he said, looking at the wall clock. "I didn't realize it was so late. You can go now, Hunter, you did an amazing job, thank you for your help."

It was already 5:05pm, my mom was going to kill me if I wasn't outside when she arrived.

"Thank you, Mr. Dan," I said, grabbing my backpack. "See you tomorrow."

And as soon as I was out of the library, I ran as fast as my legs allowed me.

# CHAPTER THIRTEEN

My mom was going to pick me up in front of the football field, which was fairly close to the library, so I didn't have to run very fast to get there quickly.

When I got there, she hadn't arrived yet, so I sat on the sidewalk to wait for her. Thankfully, the junior varsity team was the one training on the field and my brother was on the varsity team, so I didn't have to watch him train. However, I totally forgot that there was someone on the junior varsity team that I wanted to avoid even more than my brother: Tony.

He hadn't picked on me a lot since Ariana defended me in the cafeteria—probably because he was scared of her and I spent most of my time with her—but sometimes he still called me names in PE and Spanish, two of the classes we have together. We also have English together, but he never picked on me there because Mr. Dan has a zero-tolerance policy on bullying—something that, for some reason, not all teachers have.

I stared at him for only a second, but that second was enough for him to stare back at me. I quickly turned around, but I knew it was too late, he had already seen me. Damn it, I would've preferred to lock eyes with my brother than with him. I still don't know why Tony hates me. I haven't–

PUM!

I felt a huge blow on my back that made me fall forward. I managed to break the fall with my hands and my backpack absorbed most of the blow from the football, but it still shocked me to my core.

"Dude! What the hell's wrong with you?" Said a voice running towards me.

When I looked up, Ty Johnson was in front of me, lending me a hand to help me stand up. He was Tony's cousin. I had never actually talked to him, but everybody knew that they were cousins because they were the up and coming stars of the football team. And because they pretty much looked the same, except that Tony was white and Ty was Black.

"Are you okay?" He asked as he helped me stand up.

"Yeah, thanks. But I think I flattened your ball," I joked.

"That's a good one," he said, laughing, then he turned to his cousin, who was still on the field. "Don't you have something to say?"

"What? It was an accident," Tony said, laughing.

His teammates were laughing too, but they tried to hide it when they saw how angry Ty was.

"Come on, man, he's fine, get back to the game," said one of the other players.

Ty angrily threw the ball back at them, but he didn't get back to the field.

"Sorry about that, my cousin can be a real jerk sometimes," he said to me.

"It's okay," I answered. "It's not your fault."

"Are you sure you're okay? I can take you to the nurse's office if you want," he said.

"No, yeah, I'm fine, thanks," I said.

"Hey, you're in my Biology and English classes, right? Hunter, is it?" He asked.

I was surprised that he knew my name. Although I never stopped talking in English, so I shouldn't have been so surprised.

"Yeah, and in Painting too," I said. "You're really good, by the way. One of the best, I would say."

"Thanks. But come on, it's just painting, it's like the easiest subject ever," he said.

"Oh yeah? Tell that to my B- on last week's project," I said.

He laughed.

I wasn't just saying that to be nice, Painting was way more challenging than I thought it would be. I only chose that subject because the school didn't have a Film course and because I thought that it would be easier than Sculpture. But the teacher turned out to be very strict and demanding. It was the class where I was struggling the most, but Ty made it look so easy.

"But seriously, you have a real talent," I added.

"Thanks, man," he answered with a big smile. "So, what are you doing here?"

"I'm just waiting for my mom," I said.

"Are you in a club or something?" He asked.

"No," I answered.

"Then why are you here so late?" He asked.

"I was in the library… I kinda work there," I said.

"Really? Doing what?" He asked.

"I'm a Library Assistant," I said.

"Whoa. And what do you do?" He asked.

"I'm not sure yet, I just started today, but I'll get back to you when I know what I'm doing," I said.

Ty laughed.

"I've never been to the library, is it dope?" He asked.

"It's okay, I guess, but soon we're going to remodel it, and dope is exactly what we're shooting for," I said.

He laughed again. He was way nicer than I thought he would be. He was in a different middle school than Tony and me, so I didn't know him before high school, but I thought that, in terms of personality, he would be more like his cousin. I was gladly surprised that he wasn't. There are already way too many Tonys in this world, it's nice to see that someone that looks so much like him doesn't share his more unpleasant characteristics.

"Cool, maybe I'll go visit someday," he said.

"Great," I answered. "We'll be waiting."

Then my mom's car parked right in front of us. She arrived just in time because I didn't know what else to say to Ty.

"Oh, that's my mom," I said. "I gotta go, but thanks for picking me up the floor."

"No problem," he said with a chuckle. "I'm just happy you weren't hurt."

He smiled and I waved goodbye.

I entered the car feeling pretty good about that interaction, but then I realized that now I was doomed to awkwardly say hello to him every time I saw him in school. I mean, what else could I do? We could never be friends, he was the cousin of my personal bully and he only hung out with football players. But I couldn't totally ignore him either because he behaved very kindly with me, if I did, I would look like a total jerk.

Damn it, maybe if I hadn't run from the library, I would've gotten to the football field right when my mom was arriving and none of this would've happened.

# CHAPTER FOURTEEN

The next day I couldn't wait to tell Ariana how my first day of work went, but she didn't come to school. It was odd because she didn't seem sick the day before and she didn't tell me she had any plans of skipping school.

I spent the entire first period worrying that something bad might've happened to her, but then I realized that the Math teacher didn't receive any notice from the school administration, which meant that it probably wasn't anything serious. I bet she just didn't feel like going to school that day.

My day without Ariana was pretty dull. There was no one to make funny remarks on Social Studies, no one to make Math more bearable, and no one to *really* talk to during lunch break. I even thought about not going to the cafeteria and spend my lunch break somewhere else, but that would've been seen as rude, so I sat at my regular table and listened to Lizzie and Margo discuss the latest episode of *Smallville* while Leo tried to make everything into a joke.

I couldn't skip the lunch break altogether, but I did manage to leave early to go find Ariana's teachers and ask for the homework of the day. They didn't know why she missed school either, but they told me to send her their regards.

In English class, Ty said hi to me before the class started and I awkwardly nodded at him. Thankfully, he sits in the back and I sit in the front, so we didn't have to make any awkward small talk.

When the last bell rang, I couldn't wait to go to the library. It was my reward after a dull day at school. Fortunately, I was not going to start writing the reviews for the Book of the Week until the library was rearranged, so I still had about a week to prepare.

Instead, that day Mr. Dan taught me how to check-in and check-out books, how to find and shelve them, and basically how the library system worked. He also started to teach me how to make book recommendations in case someone didn't entirely know what they were looking for, but he told me that I should only do that when I felt comfortable doing it and that I should hand over the more challenging cases to him.

He had a lot of work to do, so he spent the last hour of my shift in his office while I was at the librarian's desk reading book reviews from old newspapers to start trying to understand how to write one. They weren't very helpful, though, because they were all very different from one another.

No one came to the library all day, so I was pretty surprised when I heard the door open almost at the end of my shift. I was excited and terrified at the same time. What would my first "library patron" want? To check out a book? To return one? A recommendation? Was I ready for it? But all those questions were replaced by new ones when I saw Ty Johnson enter. Why was he here? What could he possibly want? Was he lost? Maybe he did was like his cousin and he came to mock me. No, he didn't seem like that kind of person, it had to be something else.

"So this is the library, huh?" Asked Ty.

"Ty? What are you doing here?" I asked.

"I said that I'd come to visit, remember?"

"Yes, you did…"

I didn't think that he was serious when he said that. After all, he didn't seem like a bookworm. But who knows? Maybe he was.

"Well…," I said. "Welcome to my book kingdom, where you can travel to a million different worlds, from a land ruled by a wizard to a world with six suns. Sunscreen's not included."

It was a very lame joke, but it made Ty laugh.

"So, do you like reading?" I asked.

"Not really," he answered. "I can never get past three pages at a time."

"Maybe you haven't stumbled upon the right book yet."

"Maybe... Hey, sorry again for what happened with Tony yesterday. He can be such a dick sometimes."

Oh, so this is why he was here. He felt sorry for me.

"Don't worry about it," I said. "Really. And I appreciate what you're doing, but you don't have to do it. You don't have to feel sorry for me. I would actually be offended if you did."

"What?" He asked.

"Yeah, you don't have to feel forced to make amends or talk to me just because your cousin sometimes picks on me. I'm fine."

He looked at me with a curious look on his face, like he didn't fully understand what I was saying. Then he chuckled.

"I don't feel forced to do anything," he said. "And I'm not here because I feel sorry for you."

"You're not?" I asked. "Then why are you here?"

"I don't know," he smiled. "I just wanted to talk to you."

"Why?" I asked, confused.

He laughed as if I had just told him the funniest joke ever.

"I don't know. I guess... I guess it's because I've met a lot of people since high school began, you know? I've met funny people, rude people, friendly people, cool people, fake people... but you... I don't know, you seemed different."

"Oh," was the only thing I could utter.

"I mean that in a good way. You seem nice."

I was really not expecting that. It was weird hearing those words coming from someone who looked almost exactly like Tony. I didn't know what to say, so I just smiled. Luckily, once again, someone interrupted us before he noticed that I had nothing else to say.

"You can go home now, Hunter," Mr. Dan said, getting out of

his office. "Thanks for everyth– oh, hi, Ty."

"Hi, Mister Brooks," Ty answered with a big smile.

"What brings you here? Are you looking for a book?" Mr. Dan asked.

"God, no," Ty answered.

"Excuse me?" Mr. Dan asked.

"I mean... God knows I am. I was just asking Hunter for some recommendations," Ty said.

"Good," Mr. Dan answered, obviously not believing him. "Let me know if you guys need anything."

"Thanks, Mr. Dan," I said.

"Yeah, thanks, Mr. Brooks. See you tomorrow," Ty said.

Mr. Dan waved at us with a smile and went back to his office.

"Nice save," I said, grabbing my things to go home.

"Thanks," Ty answered.

"Well, Ty, I gotta say that you seem pretty nice too."

"Cool. Then it's official, we're friends now. Expect your certificate to arrive in two to five business days."

I laughed. I knew he was joking, but it wouldn't have surprised me if making friends was really that easy for him.

"Is your mom coming for you again?" He asked.

"No, that was a one-time thing," I answered. "I usually walk home."

"Where do you live?"

"In Briarwood."

"Me too! Do you mind if I walk home with you?" He asked.

"Not at all," I said. "I just have to make a stop at a friend's house first, if you don't mind. It's just to leave her today's homework."

"No problem."

Ty talked most of the way to Ariana's house. He's really funny, he spent the whole way there telling me stories about his childhood. He had an amusing anecdote of an injury in almost every street of Briarwood. He was the kind of kid that spent most of his time playing in the streets. On the other hand, I spent most of my childhood in my house—and

I wouldn't have had it any other way—but it was fun to hear all the things that were happening just a couple of blocks from where I lived.

"Are you okay?" Ty asked about halfway to Ariana's house. "You've been really quiet."

"Yeah," I said. "Sometimes I just like to listen."

He smiled and continued to tell me stories about all of his scars. In a way, I felt like he was still that kid that spent most of his time playing in the streets. We only did about 20 minutes to Ariana's house, but that was enough time for me to notice that he has a lot of energy, a short attention span, and a very positive attitude. He reminds me of a very friendly Golden Retriever. He even kicked and played with a stone he found on the floor all the way to Ariana's house.

When we got to Ariana's home, she answered the door.

"Hunter? What are you doing here?" She asked.

"I brought you today's homework," I said, handing her the homework. "And I wanted to know if everything was fine."

"Aw, thanks. Yeah, everything's okay, I'm just a little sick. But I'll be there tomorrow, I promise."

It was weird because she seemed fine, but it was not typical for her to lie, especially not to me. I was trying to study her face to determine if she was lying, but then I remembered that I was not alone.

"Oh, by the way, this is Ty Johnson," I said, pointing to Ty.

"Hey," said Ty with the biggest smile his mouth could possibly make.

"Hi," Ariana answered with little enthusiasm. Her head was clearly somewhere else.

"Hey, you won't believe what happened today in Math," I said, trying to relieve the tension.

"Hunter, I can't wait to hear it, but I'm kind of busy right now. Do you mind if you tell me tomorrow?"

"Oh, okay. No problem."

"Thanks for coming by. See you tomorrow."

"See ya."

"Feel better," Ty said, but she had already shut the door.

"Sorry about that," I said to Ty. "She's not usually that rude, but she must be really sick."

"Was that a chicken?" He asked.

"Oh yeah, her name's Chick Jagger. She's really playful. She has another one named Hennifer Aniston, but she's more of a diva."

"Okay then," he said, laughing. "I had never met anyone who had pet chickens before. I mean, that is her pet, right? She's not gonna cook it…"

"No, no, she's not going to cook it," I said, laughing. "Those are her pets. And yeah, I had never met anyone who had pet chickens before either, but she's not just anyone. She's the coolest. You'll see when we all get together some other day."

What the hell was I doing? I just met this guy and I was already planning a get-together?

"I mean…," I added. "*If* you want to get together some other time… you don't have to… I…"

"I'm sure I'm gonna like her," he interrupted me with a smile. "So, what do you wanna do now? I don't wanna get home yet because I have a ton of homework waiting for me in there."

He still wanted to hang out with me? Even after I made a fool of myself? I was finding it harder and harder to understand him. Why would a cool and popular guy like him want to hang out with me? Did all of his other friends ditch him? Did he lose a bet? Did he feel sorry for me? Oh, right, he asked me a question.

"Um, I don't know," I said. "Not to encourage your procrastination, but maybe we can go to the park."

"Sound great," he said. "I'll race you there."

Then Ty started to run really fast. I was still thinking about the whole get-together mess, but when I realized what was going on, he was already at the corner of the street.

The park was only a couple of blocks away, but I managed to catch up with him. He was a football player, but I loved to run, so in the end, the race was pretty close. He still beat me, but not by an embarrassing margin.

"Damn, you're pretty fast," he said to me. "Have you considered joining the soccer team? They could use someone like you."

"I have," I said, trying to breathe normally.

"And?"

"I hate the idea," I said, laying down on the grass.

Ty laughed and sat next to me.

"You don't like sports?"

"No, not at all."

"Wow. I had never met a boy who didn't like sports before."

He seemed really surprised, but I don't think it was because I didn't like sports, I think it was because I was willing to admit it. Sports were kind of a religion for the men in this town. If you didn't play them, you at least had to be a fan. If you were neither, then you were weird. And I was neither. To admit that you didn't like or play sports was like heresy in this town.

When I was younger and people asked me about sports I used to lie. "Yeah, I like soccer, but I like basketball better," "Football? I don't play it, but I watch it," "Favorite player? That's a tough one, probably Peyton Manning." But I don't lie anymore. What's the point?

I ended up having a really good time with Ty. At first, I was worried because I didn't know what we were going to talk about. I barely knew him, but I could tell that we didn't have many things in common. However, my worries were completely unfounded. It turns out that talking to Ty was as easy as breathing. He's very silly, but also quite mature, a combination difficult to find. And he had the same kind of humor as me—by which I mean pretty sarcastic.

When I showed him that I could hang upside down from the monkey bars, he was expecting something more.

"That's it?" He asked. "I thought you were going to do a quadruple somersault or something."

"Are you kidding me? I think I would break my neck just by

thinking of doing that. This took me a whole day to master. It's the proudest achievement of my life," I joked.

"Oh, I'm sorry," he said, laughing. "I'll call the Olympics committee to see if they're still accepting participants for next year's games."

"Please do, I would love to go to Athens and show my talent to the world," I said while hanging upside down again and extending my arms like gymnasts do after they complete a perfect routine.

And apparently, he was still quite impressed by my speed because, after that, he challenged me to run to the other end of the park to see who was faster. To my surprise, I won, but it took a toll on me because I ended up breathing more heavily than Darth Vader while Ty didn't even break a sweat. I was faster, but he had more stamina, so when he suggested that we did it again, I immediately said no.

"I'm sorry," I said. "But if I do that again, I will probably end up throwing up, and I just don't feel like doing that today."

"All right, fair enough," he said, laughing and sitting next to me on the floor.

We stayed there for a bit while I recovered and, to spend the time, he challenged me to a thumb war that lasted for more than 10 minutes.

"Your hands are really sweaty," he said.

"Of course they are," I said, laughing. "We just ran like 2 miles."

"Those were barely 150 yards," he said with a chuckle.

"Sorry, Mr. Lengths and Measurements."

After I recovered my breath, we went back to the playground and he immediately began to climb the monkey bars again. I didn't know where all his energy came from, I was already physically exhausted but he seemed like he had just woken up. However, I was having such a good time that I fought through my weariness because I didn't want to leave yet.

Fortunately, we found an empty bench and we spent the rest of the time just talking. He told me a little about how he spent his summer vacations, I told him the terrible time I had in Cancun, and we joked about how Mr. Jones, our Biology teacher, always finds a way to tell a story about his personal life in every class.

Then a conversation about my job at the library led to one of my favorite—and least favorite—topics: the future.

"I don't know," Ty answered when I asked him what he wanted to be when he grew up. "When I was younger, I used to think that maybe I could be a professional football player, but that's a pretty long shot. I'll probably end up like my dad, inheriting the family business. What about you?"

"I don't know either," I said. "But it's definitely going to be something that gets me out of this town."

"You don't like it in here?"

"No, not at all."

"Would you rather have been born somewhere else?" He asked.

"Definitely," I answered. "I feel like I got the short end of the stick by being born here, you know? Sometimes I think that the place you're born in is part of a cosmic lottery and I just didn't get the winning ticket."

"What do you mean? It's not that bad in here."

"No, I know it's not that bad, it could've been worse. It just bothers me how unfair life can be, you know? There are people all around the world that have to work all their lives to move to a big city or to a different country looking for a better life or more opportunities, but there are also people who just had the good fortune of being born there, in a modern city or in a rich and powerful family. They entered the game ten steps ahead of everyone else. How is that fair? It feels unearned."

Ty didn't say anything. He looked like he was still processing what I'd just said.

"Sorry," I added. "Don't listen to me, I'm just thinking out loud."

"No, don't be sorry, you're right. I just never thought of it that way," he said.

"I try not to think too much about this because I know that it makes me sound like I'm an ungrateful bastard. And I swear that I'm not, I know I'm very lucky to have the life and opportunities that I have. My life could've been much worse."

"But you're saying that it also could've been better."

"Exactly… I know I'm luckier than a lot of people, yet not as lucky as some… but anyway, what about you? Would you like to stay here all your life?" I asked him.

"I don't know," he said. "I mean, of course it would be cool to live somewhere else, but I don't know if I could do it."

"Why not?"

"This is my home… I don't know if I could leave my friends and family behind. I mean, could you?" He asked.

"I don't know," I said. "I think I can."

"Wouldn't you miss your family?"

"Of course I would. I think…"

"Family problems?"

"Not really problems… it's complicated."

"I get it."

"You do?"

"Yeah, um… my relationship with my dad is… complicated too."

Wow. I would never have imagined that someone like him would have problems with his father, he's basically the son my dad would've loved to have.

"I'm sorry to hear that," I said. "Do you want to talk about it?"

"No, I don't wanna bore you," he said.

"You won't. I'm all ears."

He smiled, I don't know why.

"Maybe some other time," he said. "Now it's getting late."

He was right, the sun was already starting to set. I had to go home or my mom would start to get worried.

"Do you live close?" He asked.

"Yeah, on Maple Street," I answered. "Only a couple of blocks from here."

"Cool, I'll walk you there," he said, handing me my backpack. "I live on Pine Street."

That was only three blocks away from my house, he lived much closer to me than I thought.

That day did not go at all like I was expecting. I couldn't tell Ariana how my first day of work went, I had a mediocre day at school and I still didn't know how to write a book review, but I ended up making an unexpected friend and that more than made up for all the other crappy things.

# CHAPTER FIFTEEN

The following day I finally was able to tell Ariana how much I was loving my job. She was very happy for me and asked me to tell her all the details. We were talking so much that Mrs. Sawyer even threatened to send us to the principal's office. But it was until lunch break that I finally had the opportunity to tell her about what happened after work and why I went with Ty to her house. She was furious at Tony for what happened on the football field, but somehow she was angrier at me for spending the afternoon with Ty.

"Why are you mad about that?" I asked her.

"You know I don't trust popular kids," Ariana said.

"Hunter, are we supposed to believe that now you're friends with one of the most popular guys in school?" Lizzie said.

"Yeah, how gullible do you think we are?" Margo asked.

"I'm not trying to convince you of anything," I said. "I'm just saying what happened."

Frankly, I had forgotten that they were there, so I didn't even know that they were listening to what I was saying to Ariana.

"Yeah, right, and Jessica Alba's my wife," said Leo.

Then someone put his hand on my shoulder and I angrily turned around to see who was invading my personal space.

"Hey, Hunt!" Said Ty.

"Oh, hi, Ty," I said, turning my frown upside down.

Everybody at our table, except for Ariana, was trying to hide their surprise. I don't know why they treated popular guys like celebrities, but they did.

"And Ariana, right? Do you feel better now?" He asked Ariana.

"Yeah, thanks," she said with the coldest tone ever.

"Can I sit for a moment?" He asked.

"Of course," I answered and I looked at Ariana so she could make some room for him at her side of the table because on my side there was no more space.

"Actually, it's already a little bit crowded in here," she said.

"*Ariana*?" I said to her, reprimanding her rude tone.

"You can sit here," Margo said with a rush. She was on the other side of Ariana's side. But then the boys at the popular table started calling for Ty.

"Ty, come sit!" Said one.

"What's taking so long?" Asked another.

"Yeah, why are you wasting your time with those losers?" Tony asked.

Ty just made a hand gesture to calm them down.

"Thank you, but I actually have to go now," he said to Mago. Then he turned to me. "Hey, there's a big party this weekend at Alana Richard's place, if you wanna go."

"Um...," it's all I could say. I was frozen. I definitely did not want to go to a popular kids' party, but I did not want to reject him either.

Ty then got a pen and piece of paper out of his pocket and started writing.

"Here's my phone number," he said, handing me the piece of paper. "Call me if you wanna go so I can give you the details."

"Okay, sure, thanks," I said, awkwardly.

"Catch ya later, Hunt."

"See you, Ty."

Before anyone could say anything, I turned to Ariana.

"What the hell was that?" I asked her.

"What?" She said as if nothing had happened.

"Why were you so rude?"

"I don't trust popular guys, Hunter, and neither should you."

"Why? He's pretty cool."

"Cool? He's a jock, Hunter. And he's the cousin of that dummy over there, so he's probably a jerk too."

"At first I thought that too, but he's not. He's really nice. And you shouldn't judge a person by who they're related to. Ty's a good guy, I promise."

"Yeah? We'll see about that."

"I'm sorry to interrupt your bickering," Leo said. "But you're going to take us to that party, right, Hunter?"

Everyone was staring at me as if I had just opened a chocolate bar with a golden ticket.

"I'm not going to the party," I said.

"What?!" Leo said.

"You're kidding, right?" Asked Margo.

"You can't do that to us, Hunter," said Lizzie.

"Yeah, Hunt, you have to go and you have to take us with you," said Jake.

"Sorry, guys, but I don't like parties," I said.

But of course that wasn't the end of it. They spent the rest of the lunch break trying to convince me of going to the party —and of taking them with me. In the end, I said that I would think about it just to get them out of my back. But there was nothing to think about, my mind was already made up. I was not going to any party.

# CHAPTER SIXTEEN

The rest of the week went by really smoothly. On Thursday, Ariana visited me at work because her Photography class was canceled. No one had gone to the library yet, but she helped me practice what to do when someone actually did. We practiced everything, a check-in, a check-out, an easy recommendation, a hard recommendation, we even practiced what to do with a difficult patron.

It was fun until Mr. Dan came out of his office to watch and I got too nervous to continue. But then he started pretending that he was a patron too and my nerves went away.

On Friday, someone finally showed up at the library during my shift. It was a senior student looking for an AP Chemistry book and she asked me for help to find it. Luckily, I had memorized the location of the AP books, so I found it without using the database.

I was already very familiar with the check-out process too, so I was able to find it and check it out in less than a minute and a half. I was pretty proud of myself, especially after Mr. Dan congratulated me when the girl left. I didn't even know he was watching, but I was glad that he was content with my work.

That same Friday, Ty approached me during Painting and asked me if I was going to be able to make it to the party.

"I don't think so. I have a family thing that my mom won't let me get out of," I lied. "I'm sorry. I was really looking forward to it."

The funny thing was that I always lied and used my mother as an excuse to get out of plans that I didn't want to attend, when in reality, she would probably give me money and drive me there herself just to get me out of the house.

"Oh, that's a bummer," Ty said. "Do you want me to talk to your mom? I bet I can convince her. Parents love me."

"No!" I said, almost shouting. "It's okay, really. I already tried. She won't give in. But maybe next time."

"Okay then. Next time."

When I got home, I was exhausted because I helped Mr. Dan get most of the books off the bookshelves so the maintenance personnel could move them over the weekend. All I wanted to do was sleep until Sunday, but my mom woke me up when my dad got back from work.

"What's going on?" I asked.

"We just want to talk to you," my mom said.

Oh boy, they were getting a divorce, weren't they? I was not ready for this.

"How are you doing at school, son?" My dad asked.

"Um… pretty good, actually. I got an A+ in a surprise quiz my Math teacher applied on Monday…"

"No surprise there," he interrupted.

"Look, honey, we're asking because we're kind of worried about you," my mom said.

Worried? What could they possibly be worried about? I was doing great at school, I had a great friend, and I was loving work—not that they knew that because they hadn't even asked me how I was doing at work since I started.

But I bet they were about to give me the "you're so quiet, don't be afraid to speak up and make friends" talk again. Like I had forgotten or something. They gave it to me almost every school year, but it never really worked. Whatever was wrong with me was not going to be fixed with a simple talk. Though I had to give it to them, it was kind of admirable that they still had hope. They still thought that I was one pep talk away from magically turning into someone like my brother.

"Why are you worried?" I asked.

"Are you depressed, son?" My dad suddenly asked.

What?!

"What?!"

"Don't get mad, Hunter, we're just worried about you," my mom said.

Okay, this was new.

"What are you talking about?" I asked.

"Well… your mother and I think that maybe you should… go out more and try out new things, you know? Live the high school experience," my dad said.

"It's just that when your brother was your age, he had friends over almost every day, and he went out with them almost every weekend and you never want to go out; you just want to be in your room all day. That's the textbook definition of depression, honey," my mom said.

"I am not depressed, mom," I said.

I was actually happier than I've been in a long time, something that they would know if they asked more frequently about my life and not just to shame me and compare me to my stupid brother.

"We've always tried to support you and understand when you've wanted to be alone, when you've wanted to quit a team, or when you've wanted to miss a party. But you're in high school now, honey, and we're worried that you might be missing out on things. This is a time that doesn't come back," my mom said.

"Yeah, you should be trying out for a sport, going out with new friends, going on dates with girls, you shouldn't be wasting your time locked up in your room or with this library thing, Hunter, you're a kid, you're a teenager, have fun," my dad said.

I was starting to get really mad. They should just ask what they really wanted to know: "what's wrong with you?"

"We love that you're a great student, honey," my mom said. "But it's important to have fun too. We don't want you to feel like we're pressuring you to concentrate just on school or to spend all your time studying and reading in your room, we want you to have fun too."

Oh, I definitely felt like they were pressuring me, but it wasn't to do well at school, that pressure came from me. They were pressuring me to be someone that I'm not.

"And you certainly shouldn't have to feel pressured to work at your age, son. If you need money just ask for it," my dad said.

"I'm not working because I need money, dad, I'm doing it because I like it!" I said, angrily.

"Okay, okay," my dad said, trying to calm me down. "We just don't want you to miss out on things, Hunter. This is a wonderful time in your life and it never comes back. You know, I would've never met your mother if I hadn't joined the football team."

Yes, dad, I know, my mom had only told me that story a zillion times before. But of course that wasn't going to stop her from telling it again.

"Oh yeah," she started. "He was the captain of the football team and I was the head cheerleader. After he scored the winning touchdown in the final against Jefferson High, he finally got the courage to ask me out. We were so meant to be."

After she finished telling the story, they held hands and kissed while I just stood there, wanting to die. A divorce announcement didn't sound so bad now.

"Anyway, honey," she continued. "What we're trying to say is that we don't want you to miss out on the high experience because it's truly a magical time in your life."

Again with that "high school experience" thing, what the hell did that even mean? I am perfectly happy with *my* high school experience. But since I'm not popular and partying every weekend, then that must mean that I'm depressed and I hate my life, right?

I was so angry that I would've done anything to get them out of my room. I know that they mean well and that they're only trying to "help," but I wish they would just stop worrying about me because it was not helping at all. I wish they would just back off and leave me alone. I wanted to tell them that, and I wanted to tell them that I didn't have to be like them or like my brother to be happy. I wanted to tell them that I was perfectly happy being myself and that, for once, I wished that they were happy about that too. But, as usual, I didn't. I didn't want to fight or waste my words trying to explain something that I knew they wouldn't understand. I just wanted that conversation to end, but the words that eventually came out of my mouth surprised even myself.

"Look, I appreciate your concern, but I'm fine; I *am* living the high school experience, I *do* have friends, and I'm actually going to a party this weekend."

# CHAPTER SEVENTEEN

Great. Now I have to go to a party.

Luckily, my parents left me alone after I told them that I was going to go out this weekend. All my life I've been trying to make them proud with my grades, but it turns out that all I needed to do was go to more parties.

At least that would get them off my back for a week or two, and hopefully, they will stop criticizing my decision to work at the library, so, in the end, that excruciating talk wasn't totally useless. Well, except that now I had another problem: I had to go to a party.

The good thing was that I had saved Ty's phone number in case of an emergency. The bad thing? Now I had to call him. What was I going to say? "I know I already rejected you, but after a cringe-worthy conversation with my parents, I have decided that I do want to go to the party after all."

I spent what it felt like an eternity thinking about it in my room. What was I going to say? How was I going to say it? What was he going to respond? What if someone else answered the phone? God, there were so many variables, but it was already 8:00pm and I couldn't waste any more time, so I wrote down the best lines I had come out with on a piece of paper, I practiced them a couple of times in front of my mirror, and I went downstairs to make the call from the phone in the living room.

It started ringing, and with every ring, I doubted more and

more what I was doing, but I was determined to get it done.

"Hello?" Asked a familiar voice.

Thank god it was Ty because I was ready to hang up if someone else answered the phone.

"Hi, Ty! It's me, Hunter," I said.

"Hey Hunt, how's it going?"

"Pretty well, actually. Um, I was just calling to tell you that my mom let me go to the party after all."

"Really? That's great, man!"

"Yeah, um, great!"

"It's tomorrow at 8pm at Alana Richard's house."

"Where's that?"

"Right, the address is… #345, Oak street. It's a big white house with an American flag on the top."

"Cool, I'm looking forward to it."

"Yeah, man, it's gonna be dope."

"Hey, can I bring Ariana?"

"Um… sure, why not?" He said. He doubted for a second before answering, and for the first time, I didn't hear joy in his voice.

"Is something wrong?" I asked

"No," he answered with his characteristic positive tone. "Everything's fine."

"Are you sure?"

"Yeah… well… it's just that I'm pretty sure that she hates me."

"What? No! She doesn't hate you."

"Are you sure?"

"Yeah, I'm sure. She just… um, had a horrible headache. Yeah, that's why she was so cranky. But don't worry, she doesn't hate you."

"Really? Great! I mean, not great that she had a headache… you know what I mean."

"Yeah, don't worry," I said, laughing.

"So I guess I'll see you tomorrow then," he said.

"Yeah, thanks for inviting me. See you tomorrow."

Great, now I only needed to convince Ariana to go to the party with me. But that was like saying that all I needed to do to win a Nobel Peace Prize was put an end to all wars. Easier said than done.

I spent almost an hour on the phone with her trying to convince her. I tried everything: begging, bargaining, blackmail, I even almost cried, but in the end, I managed to convince her by saying that we could go and make fun of the popular guys while eating their food. That was all she needed to hear to say yes.

The only thing I needed to do now was convince myself that going to the party was a good idea. That and stop all wars.

# CHAPTER EIGHTEEN

I convinced Ariana to come to the party early, but knowing her, she was probably going to arrive at 10pm. If it were up to me, I would've arrived at 10 too, but my parents insisted on driving me there, even though Alana's house was only a few minutes away from mine. I guess they wanted to verify that I was not lying.

The house was so big that even my parents were impressed, and the noise of the party was so loud that it could be heard from a block away. My parents seemed strangely proud of this, but I was terrified. Before I got out of the car, my dad put his two thumbs up and told me to have fun, my mom wished me good luck with a big smile, and I prayed that someone would call the cops before 11pm so that I could be in my bed in time for the *Friends* reruns.

I spent the whole day worrying about that moment that I was already pretty exhausted before I even entered the party. I didn't know who was going to be there or what to expect and that was terrifying.

"Okay, calm down," I had to tell myself before entering Alana's house. "It's just a loud party filled with strangers, it's not the worst thing in the world… I can't think of anything more stressful or anxiety-inducing right now, but I'm sure that there are worse things, right? I mean, it's not the end of the world, kids my age do this every weekend. I'm sure I'm going to be fine… I think."

I opened the front door and saw a sea of people talking, dancing, kissing, drinking, laughing, and just having fun in general. I was wrong, this was worse than the end of the world. There were way too many people, and the noise was unbearable; I was fooling myself if I thought I could survive more than an hour in there.

I was about to turn around and get out of that house when I heard someone shouting my name.

"Hunter!" Ty said with a huge smile.

Damn it. Okay, plan B, where's the bathroom?

"I'm glad you could make it," Ty added. "Come with me, there are some friends I'd like you to meet."

He took me to a huge living room, filled with people dancing and drinking. His friends were in one of the corners, talking in a circle.

"Hey, everyone," Ty said. "This is Hunter, he's a freshman too."

I just waved and said "Hi." There were about 8 or 9 boys. I'd seen most of them in school, they were from the junior varsity football team, so most of them were sophomores.

"Here you go, man," said one of the bigger ones, handing me a beer.

"No, thanks, I don't drink," I said.

"Come on, man! No one will tell."

"No, I…"

"Come on, don't be such a pussy."

"He said he doesn't drink, man," Ty interrupted. "Just drop it."

"Okay, jeez," said the boy. "I just want him to have some fun. Hey, you actually look kind of familiar. Have we met before?"

"I don't think so," I said.

"Aren't you Axel Grayson's brother?" Asked one of the freshmen.

I nodded.

"No way! Your brother's a legend," said the big guy.

"Yeah, he's easily the best player on the varsity team right now, man!" Said the boy who was next to me while squishing my shoulders. Why the hell was he touching me?

"Are you on crack, dude?" Asked one of the other boys. "Yeah, he's good, but Michael Sawyer's way better. No offense."

"None taken," I said.

"I didn't know you were Axel's brother," Ty said to me while the rest of his friends were arguing about who was the best football player in school.

"Yeah, I am," I answered.

The next hour was a mix of loud laughs, immature jokes, and conversations centered around football, video games, and girls. I wanted to get out of there, but there was nowhere else I could go to, so I just stood there and pretended to be interested in their conversation while at the same I was constantly looking at the front door, waiting for Ariana to enter. Once in a while, Ty whispered something funny in my ear about one of the boys who was talking and I laughed, but that was the furthest my social interaction in that group went.

I tried to force myself to chime in and be part of the conversation, but I didn't have anything to add. Plus, it didn't help that the boys didn't really let each other talk. If you wanted to say something, you had to steal the spotlight from whoever was talking at the moment. They didn't wait for their turn to speak, everybody interrupted each other as if what they were going to say was infinitely more important than what the person talking was saying. It was as if something was tearing them from the inside out and they just couldn't wait another second for everyone to hear what they had to say.

I thought this was quite rude, but they didn't seem to mind. Maybe it was because they were already used to it, but I wasn't. I realized that if I wanted to be part of the conversation, forcing my way into it was the only way to do it, but I couldn't just talk over someone else like it was not a big deal, so I didn't. I felt like I was in the park with my brother again, trying to be friends with boys I didn't understand and who, quite frankly, I didn't want to be friends with. I felt like I was trying to belong somewhere I knew I didn't belong.

Fortunately, when even more people started to arrive at the party, the group began to separate, and Ty eventually told me to follow him to the kitchen, where it was less noisy and crowded.

"What do you think?" He asked. "Are you having a good time?"

"Yeah…," I said.

"Where's Ariana? I thought you said she was coming."

"Yeah, she is, she's just very unpunctual."

"Cool. Do you want something to drink?"

"Yeah, sure."

"What do you want?"

"Water is fine."

He handed me a bottle of water from the cooler and grabbed a beer for himself.

"Let's go meet some other people," he said.

We went to the dining room, which was just as big as the living room, but a little less crowded. We approached the snack table and Ty immediately started talking to a couple of sophomores while I pretended to be busy grabbing some chips from the table.

Eventually, I forced myself to join the conversation and talk to them. It was actually not that bad, they joked about Mr. Jones's almost pathological need to deviate from the class topic, and they told us which teachers we should stay away from in our sophomore year. Unfortunately, more and more people started to join the conversation and we ended up being like 9 or 10 people again, so I went back to the role of quiet listener.

The good thing was that now I was close to the snack table, so I had something to distract myself with. I wasn't even hungry, but I ended up eating more than enough chips to fill a medium-size bowl. Anything to pretend that I was doing something and not just look like the awkward, loser kid.

Then a girl invited Ty to dance, and he told me to follow

him into the living room again. I don't really like dancing, so I stayed on the periphery of the room, where I got into a few meaningless conversations with other freshmen, including a boy named Adam who loved boasting about how drunk he was, a boy named Dylan who didn't seem interested in what I had to say and instead just wanted someone to listen to him while he bragged about his apparently perfect life, and a girl named Vicky who seemed to love attention more than anything else because she managed to find a way to make every conversation revolve around her.

After about half an hour, I decided to take a break, so I verified that Ty wasn't looking my way and I got out of there. I wanted to go home, but it was not even 10pm yet, and if I returned home so early, my parents were going to bombard me with questions about what happened, so it was easier to stay at the party a little bit longer. I just needed a break from that noisy living room, so I decided to look for a quiet place I could rest for a few minutes—but a quiet place was difficult to find at a party that big. I tried the bathroom, but a couple was making out in the bathtub while a girl was throwing up in the toilet, so I went to the backyard instead.

There was a sign on the backyard door that said "DO NOT GO OUT THERE," but it was the only empty place in the house, so I decided to ignore it. The backyard was big, dark, and, most importantly, empty, so it was perfect. I closed the glass door behind me, and I leaned against it to take a deep breath. I immediately felt a little better, but then I was hit with the horrible realization that at some point I would have to get back to the party. I started to consider that maybe I could hide in there for an hour or two and then go home, but then I realized how crazy that was. Everybody in that party was having the time of their lives and I was out here, planning on hiding in a dark, empty backyard for a couple of hours? What was I doing? What was wrong with me? Why wasn't I having fun like the rest of them?

But "fun" isn't supposed to be this stressful and tiresome,

right? I was at a party, a supposedly fun event, and I hadn't felt so overwhelmed and lonely in a very long time. And I know it's stupid to feel lonely at a party filled with people, but I did. It's a contradiction that I don't even know how to put into words. I was surrounded by people, but I still felt lonely. The kind of 'lonely' that I don't feel when I'm actually alone. I like being alone, but I don't like feeling alone and, at that moment, I felt completely alone. And I hate to feel this way because it only confirms to me what I already knew: that I'm a freaking weirdo. I couldn't imagine Ty or Axel or my mom ever feeling this way. Why was I so different? How could I be at a party filled with some of the most popular kids in school and still feel so miserable? What was wrong with me?

I was embarrassed that I actually thought for a second that coming to this party would make me feel normal. That, by entering this new space, I would be magically transformed into one of them, and I would stop being me. I was a fool. I felt so stupid. I was about to start crying when I realized that there was someone in there. Three persons, actually. One boy and two girls. They were sitting by the pool, that's why I didn't see them at first, but I almost had a heart attack when I finally noticed them because they were all staring at me with curious looks in their eyes.

"Oh, sorry," I said. "I thought there was no one here. The sign…"

"Oh, yeah," said one of the girls. "We put that in there. We didn't want to be disturbed."

"Sorry," I said.

"It's okay," the boy said when I was about to leave. "You can stay."

"Are you sure?" I asked.

"Yeah, we're just talking," the boy said. "Come join us."

I agreed, but only because I didn't want to go back to the party yet.

"Hey, you're the boy that's working with Mister Brooks in the library, right?" Asked one of the girls. I didn't notice it at first, but she was the senior girl that came to the library looking for the AP Chemistry book.

"Yeah, that's me," I answered.

"He's the boy I told you about, the mini-librarian," the girl said to her other two friends.

I laughed.

"Actually, I'm a library assistant," I corrected her. "I don't think 'mini-librarian' would look very good on my résumé."

They laughed.

"What's your name, library assistant?" Asked the boy.

"I'm Hunter Grayson," I said. "And you?"

"I'm Gabe," said the boy.

"I'm Nina," said one of the girls.

"I'm Betty," said the other girl.

"Nice to meet you," I said. "So, what are you doing out here? Why aren't you at the party?"

"Nah, that's just for freshmen and sophomores," said Nina.

"We're having our own party out here," said Betty, raising her beer.

"Oh, so how do you know Alana?" I asked.

"She's my sister," Gabe answered. "What about you? How do you know her?"

"I don't, actually…," I said. "I was invited by a friend."

"And where's your friend?" Betty asked.

"He's dancing in the living room," I answered.

"And why aren't you dancing in the living room with him?" Nina asked.

"I don't really like dancing and that's… that's not really my kind of environment," I answered.

"Why not?" Gabe asked.

"I don't know… I don't like all the noise… or all the people… or all the small talk. I don't feel comfortable in there. I… I don't know how to act like them. I feel like a weirdo."

"So why did you come?" Gabe asked.

"Honestly, because my parents are always on my case saying that I should go out more and live the 'high school experience,' whatever that means, so I hope that this will get them off my back for a while. And also... I don't know, I guess I came because I thought that it would make me feel normal... but it has had the opposite effect."

Huh, so apparently I have trouble talking about my feelings with my friends and family, but I have no problem oversharing with complete strangers that are mildly kind to me. Interesting.

"Hunter, there's no such thing as normal," Nina said.

"Yeah, don't let anyone tell you what you should or shouldn't do or what you should or shouldn't be. Just be whoever you want... or whoever you are," said Betty.

"They're right," Gabe said. "Look, you're obviously not a party guy, otherwise you would not be here with us, so don't try to force yourself to be one. It's okay if you're not. The question now is: who are you?"

"I... I don't know," I answered.

"That's okay," Betty said. "That's what high school is for. You'll end up learning more about yourself than about algebra or trigonometry."

"And you'll learn to accept that you don't need to force yourself to do things that you don't want just to keep others happy," Nina said.

"And don't worry, we all feel like weirdos sometimes," Gabe said. "I, personally, know exactly how you feel. My sister's always been the social butterfly, while I've always been the wallflower. I've always been the 'different one.' One way or another, all my life people have been telling me to be more 'normal' too, but you eventually learn to ignore them, you know? You learn to stop caring about what they say, and those words, designed to make you feel bad about yourself, lose their power over you. It's funny, everybody wants you to be your real and authentic self as long as that real and authentic self is similar to everyone else's. But fuck 'em, you be whoever you want."

"Thanks, guys," I said. They were being very kind to me

and they genuinely made me feel a lot better. I hadn't felt so understood in a very long time, but all the attention was starting to make me feel a little bit uncomfortable, so I decided to shift the focus of the conversation away from me for a bit. "So, you're all seniors?"

"Yeah, we're finally on our way out of high school," Betty said.

"And on our way out of this town," Gabe said, raising his beer.

"Really?" I asked. "Where are you going?"

"I'm going to NYU," Gabe answered.

"I'm going to UCLA," Beth said.

"And I'm going to the University of Chicago," Nina said.

"Wow, that's amazing!" I said. "Congratulations! Do you know what you're going to major in?"

"Nope," Gabe said. "No idea, but probably something related to Biology or Chemistry."

"I want to major in political science," Beth said. "And then go to Yale Law School."

"Yeah, Beth's going to be the first female President," Gabe said.

"Hopefully, there will be another one before me," Beth said. "But if not, I'll be happy to break that glass ceiling."

"That's great, I promise I'll vote for you," I said with a chuckle. "And what about you, Nina? Do you know what you're going to major in?"

"No, not yet. But I like Design, so probably something related to it, like Architecture."

"That's amazing," I said.

"What about you, Hunter?" Beth asked. "Do you know what you want to be when you grow up?"

"Of course he doesn't," Gabe said. "He's still a child."

"So what?" Beth answered. "I knew that I wanted to be in politics when I was 14."

"Yeah, but that doesn't count," Nina said. "You've been planning your presidential campaign since you were in your mother's womb."

Beth flipped her off and Nina laughed.

"That's not very presidential," Gabe said.

"Anyway," Beth said, trying not to laugh. "Do you know what you want to be when you grow up, Hunter?"

"Not yet," Hunter said. "But it definitely has to be something that gets me out of this town."

"Ohh," Gabe said. "You don't like Mountdale either?"

"No, not really," I said.

"Welcome to the club!" Gabe said, putting his hand up in the air so I could high-five him and then Beth and Nina did the same thing.

"It's weird," I said, "I haven't met many people who also want to get out of this town. Even those who go to college somewhere else always come back, you know? For some reason, everyone that's born here stays here. And I'm not saying that's a bad thing… it's just not me. That's not what I want."

"We certainly feel you," Beth said.

Over the next hour, we talked extensively about the future and our dreams. It was certainly not the kind of conversation that I expected to have that night, but it was a very pleasant surprise. I was so invested in our talk that I had even forgotten that there was a party on the other side of the glass door. Well, that is until that door suddenly opened right when we were preparing to play cards.

"There you are!" Ariana said, entering the backyard.

"Ari! You made it!" I said, standing up to hug her.

"What are you doing here, Hunt?" Ty asked, entering behind Ariana. "We've been looking all over the house for you. I didn't even notice when you left the living room."

"Oh, yeah, sorry," I said. "I wanted to get some fresh air, so I decided to come out here for a bit. By the way, this is Gabe, Alana's brother, and these are Beth and Nina."

"Hi!" They all said.

"We were about to play cards, do you want to join us?" Nina

asked.

"Sure," Ariana said.

"Umm...," Ty said, looking back at the glass door. Behind it, the party was still going strong. "Okay, why not?"

Gabe dealt the cards and we played a bunch of different card games until 1am. I didn't win once, but I enjoyed every single game because we talked about everything and anything while we played, from our favorite food to the role that popular culture plays in our perception of the world. It was awesome. I wanted to freeze time and stay in that moment forever. Everything was so simple, so fun, so nice. But everything must come to an end, so when Ty won his 15th game, we started to wrap things up.

We stood up and started to say goodbye because it was already pretty late, but then Gabe accidentally slipped into the pool and Nina and Beth decided to follow him to the water. They started to throw water at each other and then they invited us to join them.

"That sounds like fun," I said. "But I didn't bring a swimsuit with me."

"So?" Ariana asked and then she took off her shoes and jumped into the pool fully clothed. "Oh my god, it's freezing," she said, laughing. "Come on, last one in is a rotten egg!" She said to Ty and me.

I looked at Ty, hoping he wouldn't follow in Ariana's footsteps, but I hoped in vain.

"Sure, why not?" He said, taking off his shoes and jumping into the pool fully clothed too.

Now all eyes were on me, waiting for me to do the same thing. I doubted for a few seconds, but Ty was right: sure, why not? I took my shoes off and I jumped into the pool with them. Ariana was also right, the water was freezing, but I didn't mind, I've always felt right at home in the water.

We spent the next hour swimming, playing Marco Polo, and having swim races. It was so much fun. I didn't even notice that it was already past 2am until I saw my fingers wrinkled like old raisins. But no one else seemed to notice that it was that late either—or they didn't care—because they all looked like they could stay there all night long.

I sat at the edge of the pool for a bit and I tried to force my brain to make a permanent memory of that scene. Of that summer night and that freezing water; of those three kind strangers with wise words and bright futures; and of those two great friends that I still couldn't believe that I had the good fortune of meeting. I wanted to hold that moment in my brain forever because, at that moment, everything felt right. At that moment, I felt absolutely happy. At that moment, I felt completely normal.

## CHAPTER NINETEEN

To my surprise, I ended up having a really good time at the party—though it was when I wasn't actually at the party—but still, when my parent asked me at breakfast how was it, I didn't have to lie, I just confidently said that I had a great time.

And I did have a great time, but last night had completely drained me out. Who knew being 'normal' was so exhausting? After breakfast, I immediately went back to my bedroom because I wanted to stay in my bed all day, just reading and sleeping and reading and sleeping. But I guess God wanted to have a laugh because my mom woke me up at around noon when I was taking my first nap of the day.

"Hunter, you have a call," my mom yelled from the first floor.

I was very confused. Who could be possibly calling at that hour? And why? I got out of bed and went downstairs to find out.

"Hello?" I asked.

"Hey Hunt, it's me, Ty."

"Oh, hi, Ty. Is everything fine?"

"Yeah, everything's great. I was just calling to thank you for going to the party last night. I hope you had a good time."

"Yeah, I had a great time, thanks for inviting me."

"Oh good, I'm glad to hear that because there's another party tonight if you want to go. There's this girl Susan, a sophomore I met last night, who's having a–"

"Oh, thanks, but no," I interrupted him.

"What?" He asked.

"Sorry, Ty, I had a great time last night, but I'm exhausted. I don't know how people go out for two, three, or even four nights in a row. I went out one night and all I want to do now is crawl up to my bed and wake up in April."

He laughed.

"I'm really sorry," I continued. "Maybe next time."

"Don't worry, I understand. I hope you enjoy your day. Guess I'll see you in April then," he joked.

"Yeah, I promise I'll better by Easter."

He laughed again.

"See you tomorrow, Hunt."

"Bye, Ty."

I was about to go back to my room to take my second nap of the day when my mom intercepted me on my way to the stairs.

"Who was that?" She asked.

"It was just a friend," I answered.

"What did he want?"

"Nothing, he was just calling to invite me to another party."

"Really? That's great! So are you going out tonight too? Do you want us to give you a ride?"

"Umm…," I was about to say no, but she seemed so excited and impressed that I didn't want to erase that look of happiness from her face. "Yeah… and no! The party is only a couple of blocks away. I can walk."

"Oh, okay. What time are you leaving?"

"Umm… 7pm."

"Okay, your brother's also going out and your father and I are going to a business dinner party and we're taking your sister with us, so don't forget your keys. Oh, and ask your father for some money."

"Okay, thanks, mom."

Shoot. I could've had the house all for myself and now I was stuck with going out again. But there was no way I was going out with people, much less to a party. If I were going to leave my bed that day, it would be to go read alone somewhere else. So, at 7pm, I hid in my jacket the book that I rented about how to write book reviews and I managed to get out of the house without too many questions. The good thing was that it was Sunday, so it wouldn't be suspicious or unusual for me to come home early. The bad thing was that there were not a lot of places that I could go to on a Sunday night. Well, not a lot of places I liked.

I couldn't go to the mall because I might run into someone I know and I couldn't go to a museum or the public library because they all closed at 6pm, so, in the end, I decided to go to the old movie theater near my house.

I bought a ticket for the 8:20pm screening of *Freaky Friday* so I could have an hour to read my book in peace before the movie started. As usual, the cashier looked at me with pity when I asked for just one ticket, but I was too tired to care. Although I think I will never understand what's so wrong or weird about going out alone.

Maybe I'm wrong, but I honestly think that it's worse not to know how to be alone than to want to be alone from time to time. I mean, my mom would never in a million years go out to eat by herself and my dad would rather die than go to a football game alone, but why? If they are going for the food or for the game, why do they desperately need company? I get that going with someone can sometimes improve the experience, but it's not something absolutely necessary for the enjoyment of it.

It's sad to think that they may have missed out on trying a new restaurant or going to an awesome game just because they couldn't find someone to go with them. How many people miss out on great experiences just because they're afraid to do them alone? Or because they're scared of what other people might think of them when they see them alone? I really wished that doing things by yourself was seen as something normal, so that people could see how enjoyable and peaceful being alone can be.

Although the truth is that I'm a total phony because I think and say things like these, but sometimes I'm also afraid of going out alone. But not because I need company or because I don't know how to be by myself, it's because sometimes I'm too afraid of what other people might think of me. I love going out alone, but I hate that people make me feel like a weirdo for doing it. That's why when I go out alone, I always go to places that are practically deserted, like the old movie theater or the public library. I'm too afraid that if I go somewhere else, the people won't be able to stop looking at me and feeling sorry for me. And I know I shouldn't care because I don't know them, but sometimes I do care, and I hate it. I hate letting fear and insecurity stop me from doing something that I want to do. I hate letting those horrible feelings control me.

Just last month, a new Italian restaurant called *Il Pagliaccio* opened near my house, and I've been dying to try it, but I haven't gone yet. The weekend it opened, I invited Ariana to go with me, but sadly she couldn't go, so I lied to my parents and said that I was going out with her when in reality I was going out alone. I still wanted to try it, and I thought it would be fine since I love doing things by myself anyway, but when I got to the restaurant, the place was packed and I froze. I didn't even enter, I just saw a lot of people and I left.

I was afraid that when the hostess heard that I wanted a table for one, she would burst into laughter and make fun of me; I was afraid that when I sat alone, the rest of the customers would point their fingers at me and laugh at the lonely loser that was bumming everybody out with his presence; I was afraid that the waiter would ask if I was waiting for more people to join me, and when I said no, he would think that I was the most pathetic human being ever; I was afraid that the following day the story of a solitary boy who ate alone in a restaurant full of people would spread around town and everybody would immediately know that it was me and start looking at me with even more pity.

So I left. I missed out on trying a new restaurant because I was too afraid of what others might think of me. And I know this doesn't make any sense. I know I shouldn't care what other people think of me, especially strangers, but sometimes I can't help it. I'm smart enough to know I shouldn't care, but not smart enough to know how to do it. Lucky me.

Sometimes I try to convince myself that I don't care about what others think and that the only opinion I care about is mine, but I know that I'm lying. Even now, sitting alone at a table in front of the snack bar of an almost deserted movie theater, I worry about what the employees or the couple at the table next to mine must be thinking of me. I act like I don't care, but I do. I want to stand up and say that I'm alone by choice, that I do have friends, but that I enjoy spending time by myself. I don't know why, but I feel like I have to explain myself to people I don't even know. I shouldn't care, but I do.

In times like these, I wish I could have an invisibility cloak so I could disappear and make all eyes go away. Or better yet, I wish I could have the confidence not to care. For once, I would like to know what it feels like to be strong and unbothered by what other people might think, instead of just faking it.

I'm not quite there yet, but I think I'm making some progress, and I'm glad that once in a while, I force myself to go out alone like today because I had a great time. I finished my book, I had a delicious hot dog, and the movie was better than I expected. Plus, when I got home, my parents still couldn't believe that I had "gone out" two days in a row, so I'm gonna count this as a win.

# CHAPTER TWENTY

The library was unrecognizable after the renovation. Mr. Dan came to the school over the weekend to make sure that everything turned out as he wanted. And it did. The library now looked exactly like he had planned: it looked more spacious, more modern, and, overall, more welcoming.

Now it was time for us to start implementing the first steps of his plan to get more students into reading. First, we started by pasting the posters Mr. Dan designed all over the school and I'm proud to say that the students only vandalized 6 out of 30, which is a pretty good number considering that almost 40% of the posters in this school get vandalized.

The next step was something that I had been preparing for almost a week now: write the first review of the Book of the Week. I was scared because it was a lot of responsibility, but after a lot of preparation, I felt like I was ready for it. I decided to write about *The Giver* by Lois Lowry because it was entertaining, accessible, and it had an important message. Plus, we had four copies of the book, so it was possible for multiple students to rent it at the same time. It took me a whole day to write the review, but I was pretty happy with the end result. And, thankfully, so was Mr. Dan.

"This is great, Hunter," he said after he read it. "I have nothing else to add to it. You're a natural."

I wouldn't exactly call hours of research and preparation

"natural," but I was happy that the effort paid off and that he liked the review. We decided that the best way to reach the maximum number of students was to paste a bunch of copies around the school, send it to the school paper for printing, and publish it on the library web page.

I knew that students weren't going to turn into avid readers overnight or come in herds to the library to leave the bookshelves empty, but it was still kind of disappointing that a whole week passed by and no one came to the library to rent one of the copies of *The Giver*.

When I was writing the review, I promised myself that I wasn't going to let things like this affect me. After all, this was a long-term goal that was going to take a lot of time to achieve, but it still made me really sad when, at the end of my shift on Friday, I realized that I hadn't been able to convince one single student with my words.

I tried hiding my disappointment, but Ariana noticed it right away and she invited me to Jambo's, a new burger restaurant across the school, to cheer me up. We also invited Ty, who had been walking home with us every other day that week. He and Ariana were not best friends yet, but they had been getting along better and better since the party.

At first, I rejected the invitation. I didn't want to go eat burgers, all I wanted to do was lie down in my bed and listen to sad songs for the rest of the day while I questioned the purpose of life, but I changed my mind after listening to Ariana and Ty argue about whether hamburgers, pizza or ice cream were the best food to cheer someone up. At that moment, I felt incredibly lucky to have them, and maybe a little cheering up wasn't so bad after all.

"To Hunter!" Ariana said, raising her milkshake at the restaurant. "It might not feel like it right now, but I can guarantee you that this is just the beginning, not the end, and that you and Dan will achieve every single one of your goals because you're super talented, incredibly determined, and very caring people."

"Yeah, to Hunter!" Ty said, raising his glass too.

"Thank you so much, guys," I said. "It really means a lot."

"That's what we're here for," Ariana said with a smile.

"Yeah, don't worry about it, that library will be full of people in no time," Ty said with a big smile. "I'll be right back, I have to go to the restroom, but if the waitress comes back to take our order, I want a triple monster burger with extra fries on the side."

"Just that?" Ariana asked sarcastically.

"Yeah, I have to leave some space for dessert," Ty joked.

I was so happy to finally see them get along. Ty made a great addition to our little group.

"So, are you finally willing to admit that Ty's nothing like his cousin?" I asked Ariana.

"Fine," she said. "You were right, he's actually pretty nice. But I still don't fully trust him."

"Oh, come on," I said.

"Uh-oh," she said, looking at the front door. "Speaking of the devil."

Tony and two of his friends had just walked in and I made the terrible mistake of making eye contact with him again.

"Well, well, well," he said, getting closer to us. "If it isn't Mr. and Mrs. Dork."

"Look, Biff, we're kind of busy, so can we ignore you some other time?" Ariana said.

"Don't try to get smart with me, you freak. It's not going to work this time," Tony said.

"Oh, am I getting smart with you?" Ariana said. "How would you know?"

"Listen up, you freaking weirdo…," Tony said, putting his hands on the table.

"What's going on?" Ty asked when he returned from the restroom.

"Nothing," Ariana answered. "It's just that your stupid cousin here lost his pacifier and decided to pick on us while he waits for his nap."

"Ty? What are you doing here?" Tony asked.

"I'm with them. Is there a problem here, Tony?" Ty asked.

"Wow," Tony said. "You know, I heard that you spent most of Alana's party with these losers, but I refused to believe it. 'My cousin?' I said. 'No, he's not dumb enough to do that.' But I see that you are dumb enough."

Ty didn't say anything. He wasn't ready for this.

"What happened to you, Ty? Is this really how you want to spend your high school years? With losers and weirdos?" Tony said, pointing at us.

"Leave them alone," Ty finally said.

Tony got closer to me.

"I care about you, cousin, so I suggest that you stop doing charity work by hanging out with these losers before your reputation takes a big hit. You're too much to be friends with a teacher's pet," Tony said, placing his hand on my head.

Ariana was about to stand up, but Ty was faster and he pushed Tony away from me.

"I told you to leave them alone," Ty said.

"Or what?" Tony asked.

"Or I'll tell your mother that you use her precious, hand-made Egyptian cotton towels to jerk off," Ty said.

Everybody in the restaurant started laughing, including Tony's goons.

"You're gonna regret this," Tony said.

"Am I?" Ty asked fearlessly.

Tony looked at me one more time and then left with his friends.

"Are you okay, Hunt?" Ty asked.

"Yeah, I'm fine," I answered. "Thanks for having our backs."

"No problem," he said with a big smile. But I could see the worry in his eyes.

We had just caused a family dispute that could have ripples in his personal life, not to mention in his school image. And I felt terrible because it happened just because he was hanging out with us.

"To Ty!" Ariana suddenly said, raising her glass.

"To Ty!" I repeated.

"To Ty!" He said after we stared at him for not raising his glass. He was smiling for real again.

# CHAPTER TWENTY-ONE

After the burger place incident, everything changed. Ty began to sit with me in class, and he started walking home with Ariana and me every day. He still sat with his football friends in the cafeteria, but he started spending more and more time with us at school. At first, I was worried that Ty's popularity might suffer because of it, but if anything, he got even more popular because word got around about what happened at Jambo's and how he humiliated his cousin.

Ty told me that he and Tony worked things out, but everybody could see that there was now a clear breach between them. They still got along, but it was different now. They weren't inseparable anymore, and Tony blamed me for that, I could feel it. Now he hated me even more than before, but he didn't act on it because he knew Ty had my back. It was a weird situation.

Meanwhile, the library had a slight surge in visitors this week. We went from four visitors per week to seven. It doesn't sound like much, but Ariana was right, this was just the beginning and, hopefully, those numbers will continue to grow week by week.

For the second Book of the Week, I decided to write about a teen classic: *The Outsiders* by S. E. Hinton. It has always fascinated me how that book was written by an actual teenager instead of a grown man trying to lecture the youth, so I thought that maybe the students would be drawn to that. But I was wrong.

Two students did come by to rent the book and that made me immensely happy, but I later found out that they rented it because they were reading it in their English class and they didn't want to buy it.

I won't lie, that was a hard blow that completely broke my heart, but thankfully, I started helping Mr. Dan with other things, like making the recommendation charts and organizing some of the library paperwork, so I didn't have much time to bemoan. Also, Ariana and Ty started visiting me whenever they could, and it was literally impossible to be sad around them. Whether it was Ariana trying to find the books with the funniest titles or Ty telling me one of his thousands of humorous anecdotes, I was always laughing with those two.

Sometimes, when I didn't have a lot of work to do, we even played with some of the board games that Mr. Dan had bought for the library, like Jenga and Scrabble. Mr. Dan even played with us when it was a slow day, but he preferred to play Trivial Pursuit because he always beat us in that game.

And when we did have a lot of work, Ty helped me finish faster while Ariana helped Mr. Dan. She finally realized why I loved talking to him so much. There were just certain topics that other kids our age weren't really interested in, but we could easily discuss them with Mr. Dan. For example, her favorite issues to talk about with him were feminism, climate change, and the importance of photography in the modern world.

It killed me that sometimes I couldn't be in those conversations, but work came first. And besides, I also really liked spending time with Ty. He helped me put the books back on their bookshelves and paste the newest Book of the Week reviews all over the school. And because he was Ty, he always turned it into a fun competition to see who could finish first. I'm proud to say that we were currently tied 3-3, so he hadn't really "mop the floor with me" yet as he had jokingly promised.

"You're losing your touch, Johnson," I jokingly said when I tied the score.

"No, I'm not," Ty said. "I just didn't wanna beat you again. It was starting to get embarrassing, so I slowed down to let you win this time."

"Really? Then why are you sweating?" I asked.

He started to laugh. "That's the level of compromise I have to make this defeat look believable, man."

"How nice of you," I said with a smile. "Let's go get you some water for your compromise then."

"Thanks," he said. "By the way, do you have any plans next Saturday?"

"Why?" I asked.

That was my automatic response to questions like that so I could say yes only to the plans that I liked and come up with an excuse for the ones that I didn't. I mean, I really like Ty, but I was ready to come up with an imaginary family trip if he invited me to another "popular guys" party.

"Because it's my birthday next week and I'm going to have a party," he said.

Damn it, I couldn't say no to that one.

# CHAPTER TWENTY-TWO

I hate my birthday. There, I said it. I understand why some people love their birthdays, but I hate mine. I hate the extra attention I receive for something as trivial as turning one year older; the pressure to make it a "special day"—usually with a party—is insufferable; and I never know what to do when people sing me the Happy Birthday song. If I could, I would skip it every year.

I especially hate it when it falls on a school day. When I was younger, my mom had the tradition of bringing a cake to school so I could celebrate with my classmates during recess. It was a lovely thing to do, but I didn't like it at all because I hate being the center of attention. Every time I stood in front of a cake while my classmates sang *Happy Birthday*, I felt like a deer struck by lightning. I didn't know what to do, where to look, or which face gestures to make. I hated standing there looking like a dumbass while everybody sang what it felt like a 3-hour rendition of *Happy Birthday*.

Thankfully, when I entered junior high, she stopped doing that, but I still didn't like going to school on my birthday because the teachers still reminded my classmates that it was my birthday and some teachers even asked them to congratulate me or to write me little birthday notes. Again, this is such a nice thing to do, but—and I cannot stress this enough—I hate the attention.

On my last birthday, I even pretended to be sick so that I didn't have to go to school. I know this sounds excessive, but I didn't want my classmates to sing *Happy Birthday* to me at the beginning of every class, especially because I knew that most of them just did it to lose class time and not because they actually wanted to congratulate me. I wish I could do it again next year, but I know my mom will not fall for it two years in a row.

And speaking of my mother, I also hate my birthday because she is always pressuring me to have a party and "make a special day out of it." I think I've already established that parties are not one of my favorite things in the world, and this definitely doesn't change when the party is mine. If anything, it worsens it.

I'm not saying that I haven't enjoyed my birthday parties, because I have, but I always end up feeling anxious and worrying if everyone else is having a good time. Because it's *my* party, I feel the responsibility to be a good host and make sure that everyone's having fun, but in the process, I end up forgetting about having a good time myself.

For my 13th birthday, I finally got the courage to tell my mom that I didn't want a birthday party anymore, but naturally, she thought that I didn't mean it. She couldn't possibly believe that I didn't want a party and, instead, she thought that there was some kind of secret message behind it, so she decided to throw me a surprise party. Objectively, this was a very nice thing to do because it must've taken her weeks of preparation and dedication, but it was an absolute nightmare for me. Entering my house and seeing dozens of family members, friends, and classmates yelling "Surprise!" was like realizing that I went to school naked, except that I didn't wake up this time.

If there's anything worse than having a party, it is not having knowledge or control over your own party. When my brain first started to process that it was a surprise party, I couldn't believe that it was mine because there were so many people. Due to the fact that my mom couldn't ask me who I wanted to invite, she decided to invite EVERYONE, including classmates from middle school and boys from the swimming school that I didn't even talk to. In fact, there were some boys who probably didn't even know my name, but that gladly came to the party because my mom had promised them a water slide, a rock-climbing wall, and as many pizzas as they could eat.

Looking back now, it was actually a pretty impressive party, and it's heartwarming to think about all the effort my mom put into it, but I couldn't enjoy it properly at that time because I was extremely overwhelmed. I hadn't had a surprise party before, so I didn't know what to do. I didn't know if I should be with my friends having fun or spending time with my family or even getting to know the people that I barely knew. It was all too much for me. That's why I hate mixing family with friends. I don't like mixing different worlds. And it was even worse to mix family with friends with strangers. It got to the point where I just wanted to run to my bedroom and forget about the party, but it was *my* party, so that was not an option.

That experience was so exhausting that, for my 14th birthday, I explicitly told my mom that I didn't want a party (including a surprise one) and that I only wanted a quiet family dinner and to go to the bowling alley with Ben. She reluctantly accepted because she knew that Ben and his family were going to move at the end of the summer, but she wasn't very happy about it. Still, that turned out to be one of my best birthdays ever. I want to do something similar for my next birthday, but I know my mom won't let me get away with it so easily this time. In fact, my birthday is until May, but she has already started to pressure me to have a party.

"Honey," my mom said to me last week during a car ride. "Remember that if you want to have your birthday party in Trinox, you have to tell me now because I have to make the reservation months in advance."

Trinox was the most popular party venue for teenagers in town. It was like a nightclub, with live music and everything, but for teens. My brother had celebrated his last two birthdays there. He and my mom really liked it, but I hated that place. It's loud, it fits way too many people, and there are not a lot of things you can do there besides dancing. Needless to say, I do not want to celebrate my birthday there.

"That's okay, mom," I said, "you don't have to worry about that, I don't want a party in Trinox."

"Oh honey, don't tell me that you want another birthday party in the house because it's exhausting to clean up and decorate," she said.

"No, I don't want to have a party in the house either. I don't want a party. Period."

"What? You have to have a party, honey. It's your 15th birthday!"

"So?"

"*So?* You only turn 15 once!"

"Yeah, mom, you only turn any age once. That's how it works."

"Don't get smart with me, young man. You know what I mean. This one's important. Trust me, if you don't have a party, you're going to regret it."

"I don't think I will."

She was about to give me a speech about the importance of birthday parties, but luckily, she got distracted when a client called her on her cell phone. She hasn't mentioned anything about a party since then, but there was still a long way to go until my birthday and I knew that the war was far from over because my mom was not someone who easily accepted defeat. I knew she was going to keep insisting harder and harder, especially after hearing about how huge Ty's 15th birthday party was.

I gotta admit that I was surprised by the size of Ty's party, and I was already expecting something big. When I entered the venue, I thought that I had accidentally stepped into the high school building because more than half of our grade was there. It was intimidating. However, I did not make the same mistake as last time. This time, I went to Ariana's house before going to the party so we could arrive together.

"Holy crap," Ariana said when we entered the venue. "Is this a party or a Black Eyed Peas concert?"

"Guys! You made it!" Ty enthusiastically said when he saw us.

"Of course," I said, giving him a hug and handing him his present. "Happy birthday, Ty."

"Yeah, happy birthday, Johnson," Ariana said, hugging him too.

"Thank you," he answered. "Come, I'll show you where you can sit."

Ty took us to one of the few tables that were not full yet and sat down with us.

"You gotta try the little burgers before they run out, they're amazing," he said.

"You don't have to tell me twice," Ariana said, grabbing one from the center of the table.

"How are you doing, Ty?" I asked. "Are you enjoying your birthday?"

"Yeah, it's been great," he said. "By the way, I'm having a sleepover at my house with a few cousins and friends from school after this. You have to come."

"Oh… I don't think I can… I promised my mom that I would go with her to church tomorrow morning," I lied.

I felt bad for lying to Ty on his birthday, but I would've rather been forced to clean up my brother's messy room for a year than to go to a sleepover filled with football players and strangers.

"No, that's too bad!" Ty said. "Maybe you could–"

"Oh my god," Ariana interrupted. "Did you murder an angel and cooked him up? Because these are the best burgers I have ever tried!"

"Right?" Ty said.

"Well, now I gotta try them," I said.

"Good luck trying to take them away from me," Ariana said, grabbing the plate from the center of the table.

Ty laughed and I jokingly grabbed a fork to use as a sword.

"Ty, your mom's looking for you," said a lady with a pink coat when I finally managed to convince Ariana to give me one of the two remaining burgers.

"Thank you, auntie," Ty responded. "I'll be right back, guys, try not to murder each other in the meantime."

But he didn't come back. There were so many people at the party that he couldn't be in one place for more than 5 minutes. He was trying to spend at least a little time with everyone. I didn't know how he did it. If it were me, I would've probably given up and go hide in the restroom, but Ty was hopping from one place to another with his signature Ty smile at all times. I was happy to see him happy, he deserved it.

And even though I didn't get to spend a lot of time with the birthday boy, I ended up having a really good time. Ariana and I spent the whole night eating and talking about the rest of our classmates that were in attendance. Nothing bonds a friendship like junk food and gossip. However, when the DJ turned the music up and everybody got up to dance, we decided to go outside for a few minutes because it was way too loud inside.

"Have you ever had a birthday party this big?" I asked Ariana when I could finally hear my own thoughts again.

"Yeah, I have," she answered.

"Really? When?"

"My last birthday party before I moved here. It was pretty big."

"Did you enjoy it?"

"At the time I did, but not so much in hindsight."

"Why?"

"It's a long story."

"I got time."

"Maybe some other time. What about you? Have you ever

had a birthday party this big?"

"No, thankfully never this big."

"Not a big fan of big parties, huh?"

"Definitely not. Actually, can I tell you a secret?" I asked.

"I'm offended that you have to ask," she said.

I laughed. I'm glad she lightened up the mood because I had never said this out loud, so I didn't know how she was going to react.

"I hate my birthday," I said. "I know everyone's supposed to love their birthdays and it's everyone's favorite day of the year, but I hate mine."

"Really?" She asked. "Why?"

"I don't know. I guess I don't like the attention. Oh, and I can't stand the pressure to make a special day out of it. I mean, I get it, I was born on this day, but why does it have to be the most special day of my year? Why am I supposed to have the time of my life specifically on that day? That's just setting myself up for failure because the expectations to have a good time are way too high, you know? And don't even get me started on the stupid *Happy Birthday* song."

"Wow," she said.

"Sorry," I said. "I know. I know it makes me sound like I'm some weird hermit yelling in the middle of Times Square."

"No, it doesn't," she said with a smile. "It's totally valid that you feel like that. I don't actually like my birthday either."

"Really?" I asked.

"Yeah, everyone knows birthdays were invented by Hallmark to sell cards."

I laughed again.

"You're right," I said. "They didn't have enough with inventing Christmas to sell their movies, they also had to invent birthdays."

"Those greedy bastards," she said.

We laughed and then we heard that the DJ said that it was time for the cake, so we entered the venue again. Everyone had already surrounded the table where the cake was, so we ended up all the way back. We could barely see Ty among so many people, but we got there just in time to sing him *Happy Birthday*. If that many people were singing that song to me, I would've probably had a panic attack, but Ty had a gracious smile on his face the whole time.

The cake was super delicious and the waiters had just refilled the snacks on the tables, but it was already past midnight and our parents were going to arrive at any time, so Ariana and I said goodbye to Ty and went outside to wait for them. Ariana's parents arrived first and they offered me a ride, but I told them that it wasn't necessary because my parents were already on their way.

They arrived shortly after and I braced myself for the tons of questions I was going to receive about the party.

"Hi, honey," my mom said. "Did you have a good time?"

"Yeah," I answered. "It was pretty cool."

"I didn't know about this venue. Is it big?"

"Huge."

"Did you like it?"

"Yeah, it was nice. The food was great."

"Maybe you could have your 15th birthday party there."

"Mom, I already told you that I don't want a party."

"Come on, Hunter, you don't mean that."

"Yeah, son, you have to have a party," my dad added. "You can have it wherever you want, don't worry about the price. We will spare no expense to give you a 15th birthday party as good as your brother's."

"Thanks," I said. "But can we talk about this some other time? I'm really tired right now."

"Fine," my mom said, turning on the radio. "Get some rest. We'll talk about it later."

# CHAPTER TWENTY-THREE

The following day I woke up until noon, and not just because I was exhausted from Ty's party, but also because I was trying to avoid my parents so they couldn't keep pushing me to have a party. Fortunately, it worked, and when I finally went downstairs, they were about to leave to visit my aunt Ophelia. That meant that I was going to have the house all to myself because they were taking Ashley with them and Axel was going to go out with his girlfriend.

This made me very happy because I hadn't had the house to myself in a very long time. The first thing I did was turn up the volume of the radio to properly sing along while I cooked my belated breakfast. I decided to eat in the living room instead of the dining room because I wanted to watch a movie while I ate. My mom hates it when I do this, but unless she has secret cameras I don't know about, she wasn't going to find out about it. It took me a while to decide which movie I should watch, but when I stumbled across the DVD of *Jurassic Park*, I stopped searching. It was one of my favorite movies, and I hadn't watched it in a while, so I thought that this was the perfect opportunity to do it.

About halfway into the movie, the phone started to ring, but I ignored it because it was probably from the bank—and because I was so immersed in the movie that I didn't want to stand up. However, when the phone rang for the second time, I had to pause the movie in the middle of the T-Rex attack—my favorite scene in the whole movie—to find out who was disturbing my valuable downtime.

"Hello?" I said, slightly irritated.

"Hey, Hunt!" Ty said with a cheerful tone. "How are you?"

"Oh, hi, Ty. I'm fine, how about you? Is everything okay?"

"Yeah, everything's great. I was just calling to thank you for going to my party yesterday. I hope you had a good time, and I'm really sorry for not spending more time with you, guys."

"Don't worry about that, Ty," I said. "We had a great time and we knew that you were busy, so don't sweat it. What's important is that you had fun."

"Thanks, Hunt," he said. "So, how was church?"

"Oh… you know, great," I said. "How was the sleepover?"

"It was so dope, man! It's a shame you couldn't be here."

"Yeah, sorry, maybe next time."

"I hope that's a promise."

"It is," I lied.

"By the way, thank you so much for your present. It was amazing," Ty said. I was so glad to hear that because I put a lot of effort into finding him the perfect gift.

This is going to sound super corny, but I like giving presents more than receiving them. It's not that I hate receiving gifts, but I do dislike having to open them in front of people. I can't put on a poker face to save my life, so if I don't like something, my face won't be able to hide it. That's why I hate it when, at birthday parties, they make you open the presents in front of everyone. To me, that's one of the most anxiety-inducing things ever.

But to give someone a present is an entirely different experience. You get to make someone you care about feel special by giving them something that shows them how well you know them and how much you care. What's better than that? That's why when Ty first told me about his party, I immediately started to think about what to give him. I wanted to show him that, even though we've only been friends for a month, I consider him a very good friend. So, after much consideration, I decided to not only give him one thing but to give him three: a t-shirt of the painting *Impression, Sunrise* by Claude Monet, which he once told me was his favorite painting; a couple of rare baseball cards that I had collected when I was younger, but that I knew he would appreciate more because he also collected them when he was a kid, but he had sadly lost them in a fire; and some new acrylic paints and brushes because I knew that, even though he doesn't like to admit it, painting is one of his favorite hobbies.

"Oh, good," I said to him. "I'm glad you liked it."

"Are you kidding? I loved it! How did you know I would like all that stuff?" He asked.

"What do you mean?" I asked.

"Are you some kind of psychic? Oh my god, reading too much has opened your third eye, right? Quick, what am I thinking?"

"No!" I said, laughing. "What are you talking about, Ty? At one point or another you've told me that you like all that stuff. I just listened to you."

"Oh, right... you listen. Well, thank you again. It's one of the best gifts I've ever received."

"I'm sure you're exaggerating. You had a mountain full of presents. What else did you get?

"Mostly money, but I also got a cool skateboard, a bunch of clothes, and a couple of video games. Oh, and two basketballs, four soccer balls, five footballs, and seven different people gave me the new Dallas Cowboys jersey," he said, laughing.

"Oh my god," I said, laughing too. "That has actually happened to me before. For my 12th birthday, my aunts and uncles didn't know what to give me, so most of them bought me the newest Harry Potter book, which I already had, by the way. So I have like seven copies of *The Goblet of Fire*, if you want one."

Ty laughed.

"Yeah," he said. "I guess when many people give you the same thing that can mean one of two things: either they know you very well or not at all."

"Yeah, I guess so… but hey, at least now you have enough materials to start your own summer sports camp. I've heard those can leave you a lot of money in this town," I joked.

"You're right, I won't let this business opportunity get away."

I laughed.

"Hey," he added. "Do you wanna go to the movies tonight? My treat. Yesterday I got like $500 and I can't wait to see the new *Freddy vs. Jason* movie."

I couldn't help but laugh.

"Of course," I said. "But I think that movie is rated R."

"Don't worry, I know a guy," he said.

"Great. Then I'm on board."

"Perfect. I'll call Ariana to invite her. At 7pm is fine?"

"Sound like a plan."

"Great, see you there."

"See ya."

Well, good-bye to my plans of staying home all day watching movies. But a night out with friends didn't sound so bad. Especially with *my* friends.

# CHAPTER TWENTY-FOUR

October, my favorite month of the year, was finally here. I love it because the leaves start to fall, the temperatures start to drop, and everywhere I look there's a lovely shade of orange and yellow, which are two of my favorite colors. Unfortunately, I haven't been able to enjoy it properly because things haven't improved at the library.

It's already been a month since I started working here, but our weekly visitors haven't exactly gone through the roof yet. We have gone from four to nine visitors per week, which is arguably a step in the right direction, but not exactly something that you open the bottle of champagne for. We're already past the point where we should be receiving more than 50 visitors per week, but we still haven't even gotten to 10. My friends and Mr. Dan have told me that things will pick up soon and that I should stay positive, but it's hard to do that.

Maybe it's my fault, perhaps I let my expectations get too high, but it's difficult to lower them when I see the hard work that Mr. Dan has been putting into this project. He's been doing the hard yards to make sure that the library is an accessible, comfortable, and well-equipped space for students, all while getting paid peanuts in return—both from the administration and from the students. He deserves better than this.

At first, I was entirely sure that our work and our actions

were going to motivate at least half the student body to read, but now I'm not sure if they'll ever cause even a small change in this school. To be honest, I'm even starting to question the purpose of putting so much effort into my reviews if no one ever rents the books I recommend. Why do the work if no one appreciates it?

I've been trying to hide these feelings, but my face is the biggest snitch in the world, so when another Friday rolled around and our weekly visitors still hadn't crossed to double digits yet, Mr. Dan could clearly see the disappointment in my eyes.

"Don't worry," he said to me, "eventually more students will come."

"I know," I said. "But… what if they don't?"

"Hunter, these kinds of things take time. Rome wasn't built in a day," he said.

"Yeah, I know, I know… but what if things don't change? What if things never pick up? What if, no matter how hard we try, we just can't make a change in this school?"

"You can't think like that."

"Why?"

"Because with projects like this is important to be optimistic."

"Yeah, but it's also important to be realistic, right? Maybe we live in a society where students just aren't interested in reading anymore, and maybe no matter how hard we try, we just can't change that. Maybe the world's too hard to change."

He stopped what he was doing, took a deep breath, and put one of his hands on my shoulder.

"You're right," he said. "Maybe we do. And maybe it's my fault that you feel this way. I shouldn't have painted you a picture where we could turn the students of this school into avid readers in a matter of weeks. That's on me. I'm sorry about that. I'm idealistic, not stupid. I know it's not likely that by this time next year this library will be filled with students eager to learn beyond the classroom. I should've been more pragmatic and told you that this was a hard goal to achieve and that we were going to face many setbacks and disappointments. And I also should've told you that this was okay and that we don't need to change the life of *every* student in this school. I mean, if we do, that's great, but if the end of the school year arrives and we were only able to impact *one* life positively, then it would've been worth it. We don't need to change the whole planet or even the whole school to make a positive change in the world, Hunter. Every little action counts. If your goal is to go to Mars, then reaching the Moon will seem like a small achievement, but it's not. Those small achievements count. They're still achievements. Sometimes we forget that because we're too focused on the big picture, but it's important that we don't, because it's those small achievements that will keep us going. It will take us time, but we'll get where we want to go, Hunter. I know it. And if we don't and we only reach the Moon, well, then that's a pretty big achievement too."

"You're right. I… I don't even know what to say," was the only thing I could utter. I was speechless. I wanted to say something more deep and meaningful, but I truly didn't know what. I was still processing everything Mr. Dan had just said.

"You don't have to say anything," he said. "I know this is a lot to process and I know it's hard. Believe it or not, I know exactly what you're going through, Hunter. I've had my fair share of faith crises before."

"What do you mean?" I asked.

"Well… I haven't told you this yet, but when I was your age I also wanted to desperately change the world. But my goal was a little bit bigger. I wanted to be a lawyer and work at the United Nations to help solve the world's biggest problems…"

Wow. I would've never imagined that he wanted to be a lawyer when he was younger. To me, it seemed like he was born to be a teacher. But sometimes I forget that teachers were kids and teenagers at one point too and that they also have dreams and hopes beyond the classroom.

"And what happened?" I asked.

"Well, it's a very long story, but the bottom line is that I realized that the world is a mess and a single person can't change it... it wasn't an easy thing to accept, and when I eventually did, it sunk me into a deep depression. It left me without direction. Aimless. Lost. But I didn't give up. I took some time to think and reflect and I understood that sometimes the first step to change the world is to admit that you can't do it. Only after this, I started thinking straight. I realized that I was never going to be happy being a lawyer. I didn't want to feel powerless all my life. I didn't want to be surrounded by an environment filled with corruption and injustice and not be able to change it. I didn't want to be angry and sad for the rest of my life. So, instead, I changed my dream. I made it more grounded and attainable. I still wanted to change the world and make a positive impact on society, but I also wanted to be happy."

"Is that why you decided to be a teacher?" I asked.

"Yeah," he said. "Believing that I could solve all the world's problems was leading me down a path of unhappiness and disappointment. But when I finally was able to accept that I couldn't, I began to concentrate on finding what I was passionate about and how I could still have a reasonable positive impact with that. I thought about becoming a doctor for a while, but I'm not so good with blood and injuries. I also thought about becoming a scientist because I love biology, but I wasn't especially good at it, I was average at best, so I probably would've ended up in a lab doing meaningless research instead of discovering the cure for cancer. Finally, I realized that I loved teaching. I love encouraging students to reach their maximum potential, I love watching them grow personally and academically, and I love the smile on their faces when they learn something new. When I realized this, everything suddenly clicked. I understood that teaching was the perfect profession for me because I could contribute to making this world a little bit better by imparting knowledge to the new generations. My family begged me to choose something else, something where I could make more money, like finance or architecture. But I was not looking for money, I was looking for fulfillment. I was looking for happiness. And I was looking to improve the world, one kid at a time. It's funny, I guess sometimes you need to accept that you can't do something to actually start doing it. But look, Hunter, if this is taking an emotional toll on you, you can quit whenever you want. I don't want you to be worrying all the time. I want you to enjoy your time in high school."

"No!" I interrupted him. "I would never quit. I love my job. I really do. It's just that sometimes… I guess I feel like what I'm doing is not enough… sometimes I feel like I'm letting you down."

His face went from a smile to a frown after he heard those words.

"Don't ever say that again, Hunter," he said with a serious tone. "I am extremely proud of you, okay? Seriously. You wanna know one of the reasons I haven't given up yet? It's because of students like you, Hunter. I love teaching, but it can also be hard sometimes. It can be a thankless job. You don't know if you're actually making an impact on your students or if they're just sitting on their chairs and staring into the unknown for an hour, learning nothing from you. But, once in a while, a student like you comes along to remind us why we do this. We get proof that we're actually impacting someone else's life, hopefully for the better, and it makes it all worth it."

That was one of the nicest things I had ever heard.

"Thank you," was the only thing I could say before my voice cracked.

"Thank *you*, Hunter. Now go enjoy your weekend with your friends," he said right before Ariana and Ty entered the library. "You deserve it."

# CHAPTER TWENTY-FIVE

I wish I could've followed Mr. Dan's advice and enjoy the rest of the day with my friends, but in the morning, my mom told me that I had to be home before my father arrived because he had some big news that he wanted to share with us, so I went straight to my house after work.

It turns out that the big news was that my dad had been promoted at work, which included among its benefits a brand new luxury car that he paraded around the block.

"What do you think?" Dad asked us, getting out of the car. "It's a beauty, right?"

"Jesus Christ!" Axel said. "This is the sweetest drive I've ever seen."

"I love it, daddy!" Ashley exclaimed.

"It's beautiful, my love," my mom said.

"Congratulations on the promotion, dad," I added.

"Thanks, son. It was a surp–"

"Wait," my brother interrupted. "Does this mean…?"

"Yeah… you're getting my old car!" My dad said, throwing the keys of his old Chrysler to Axel.

"Sweet!" He exclaimed.

"Everybody, get in, we're going to celebrate," dad said.

He took us to his favorite restaurant: The Mountain Fox. I hated that place because it was always way too noisy and crowded. Thankfully, we only went there on special occasions, but since it was a Friday night, the place was even louder and more crowded than usual.

However, the noise didn't only come from the conversations of the dozens of customers, there was also a band loudly playing music in one of the restaurant's corners. I don't know how that's supposed to improve the eating experience of the customers because, to me, every beating of the drums and every blow of the trumpet felt like actual blows to my head, especially because we were seated so close to them.

I couldn't think straight with all that noise, it was way too much for me, so I decided to block it all out and focus on what was going on inside my mind instead. The only problem with this was that I also blocked out the conversation my family was having—but it's not like they needed me to keep the conversation going anyway.

At first, it worked and I was able to calm down and think normally again. However, I discovered that it was very loud inside my mind too. The conversation I had with Mr. Dan was still swirling around in my head. I hadn't been able to properly process everything he had told me yet. There was a lot to unpack. For starters, I still couldn't believe that at some point he wanted to be a lawyer, a doctor, and a biologist. This was shocking, but also strangely comforting. Lately, I've been giving myself a hard time because I have absolutely no idea what I want to do when I grow up. I know I still have a lot of time to decide, but my family's relentless criticism of my cousin Marcus' choices has not been making things any easier.

Marcus is one of the smartest people I've ever met and he's currently studying at one of the top universities in the country. However, he has changed his major a couple of times now and has "lost and wasted"—my mother's words, not mine— a couple of years as a result. It must be very hard not to be entirely sure of what you want to do with the rest of your life when you're basically an adult already, but instead of giving him support, my family always finds a way to criticize him and point out all the things he has done "wrong."

I feel terrible every time I hear one of those unfair and unnecessary attacks. It's not Marcus' fault that he's good at basically everything, nor that we're supposed to decide what we want to do with the rest of our lives when we're too young and still learning. If you make the wrong choice, it can ruin the rest of your life. Thankfully, Marcus realized this sooner than later and decided to change things. I'm proud of him because he did it even though he knew his family would disapprove. He did it because he knew it was the best thing for him. After all, he's the one that has to live with that decision, not his family, so it was a choice only he could—and should—make.

I'm already in high school, and I still don't know what I want to do with my life. But maybe that's fine. I still have a lot of things to learn and a lot of growing up to do. And even if the day comes when I have to choose a path and later on I realize that I made the wrong choice, it's nice to look at Mr. Dan and Marcus and see that there's always a chance to correct that. After all, it's better to "waste" a year than to waste the rest of your life doing something you don't like.

Out of everything we talked about, there was one thing Mr. Dan said that kept coming back to me: "Sometimes the first step to change the world is to admit that you can't do it." All this time, I had convinced myself that Mr. Dan must've been feeling pretty sad and disappointed by the results we were getting from the library. But that wasn't the case. He was fine. He was prepared for those results. I was the one who was disappointed. All this time, I had been projecting my feelings on him. I was the one who thought my hard work was being wasted. I was the one who wanted better results. But Mr. Dan was right, believing that we could change the whole school and make a reader out of every student was leading me down a path of unhappiness and disappointment.

These last couple of weeks I've been enjoying less and less my time at work because I've been so fixated on the number of students that go to the library. Instead of being happy because new people are visiting us and showing an interest in reading, I've been angry because they've only been four or five students instead of a hundred. Instead of talking to them and encouraging them to love reading as much as I do, I've been constantly looking at the door, waiting for more people to come in.

My conversation with Mr. Dan was a wake-up call. If I kept thinking like that, I would continue to be unhappy. I needed to change my attitude. I needed to start caring about the students that came to the library instead of constantly focusing on the ones that didn't.

I was starting to think about all the things that I should change when a pair of snapping fingers startled me.

"Earth calling Hunter," my mom said.

"Wh-?" I uttered.

I started to pay attention to my surroundings again and I realized that my whole family had their glasses raised in the air.

"Oh, sorry," I said, raising my glass too.

"To dad," Axel said.

"To dad," everyone repeated.

"Thank you," he said. "I love you all very much and I want you to know that everything I do, I do it for you."

"We love you too, my love," my mom said.

"So what's going on, Hunter?" my dad asked me. "Where's your head at? You seem very distracted."

"We're not interesting enough for him," Axel said.

"Shut up," I told him.

"Hunter!" My mom said to me.

"Sorry, mom," I said. "I just got a lot on my mind, dad. That's all."

"Really? Like what?" He asked.

"Nothing… just work stuff," I answered.

"Oh," was all he said.

That reaction didn't surprise me. Once in a while, my parents asked me about school and about my friends, but they never asked me about work. I guess it was their subtle way of saying that they still didn't approve that I chose to work at the library despite their very explicit objections. And this was fine with me because I didn't want to talk about work with them anyway. I mean, I did, but I knew that if I did, they would just find a way to criticize it. That's what they always did. They couldn't help it.

At that moment, I was dying to talk about some of the things I had in my mind with someone so I could sort out my thoughts better and analyze them from a different perspective, but I was almost certain that talking about them with my family would not help. It was not a good idea. I preferred waiting until Monday and talk about them with Ariana and Ty.

"What is it?" My mom asked.

"What is what?" I replied.

"What is this thing about work that you can't stop thinking about?" Mom asked.

"Oh, nothing," I answered.

"Come on, tell us," she said.

I didn't know what to do. My mom seemed genuinely interested, and I was eager to talk about it, but in my experience, this never ended well. I wanted to take some time to consider whether to tell them or not, but everyone's eyes were on me, so I ended up succumbing to the pressure and, against my better judgment, I decided to tell them. I mean, who knows? We were celebrating, so maybe this time it would be different.

"Well," I said before taking a deep breath. "One of the main reasons I decided to work at the library was to help Mr. Dan reach his goal of getting more students to read and use the literary resources that the school provides. To do this, we crafted an extensive plan that included, among other things, modernizing the library, increasing the fiction book catalog, and publishing weekly book recommendations written by me."

"You write those?" Axel asked.

"Yeah, have you read them?" I said.

"No, but my bud Jack always grabs the ones in the locker room to make paper planes. It's hilarious, one time he actually managed to get one stuck in Jimmy's afro."

"Anyway," I continued while Ashley was laughing at Axel's anecdote. "I–"

"Wait," my father interrupted. "So you're telling me that now this teacher is forcing you to write something he should be writing himself?"

"What? No, he's not forcing me to do anything, it was actually my idea to implement the Book of the Week," I said.

"Is he at least paying you more for that?" He asked.

"No, it's part of my job," I answered.

"Unbelievable," he said.

I knew this was a bad idea.

"Just forget it, okay?" I said. "Let's talk about something else."

"No, please continue, Hunter. We want to listen to you, right?" My mom said, looking sternly at my dad.

"Yeah, sorry, son. Continue," dad said.

I doubted again. Every fiber in my body was telling me to shut up and change the subject, but the look of interest in my mother's eyes convinced me to keep talking.

"All right...," I said. "We have already implemented most of our plan, but the results have not been stellar. The weekly visitors have definitely gone up, but not as much as I hoped, which has been disappointing. But tod–"

"Don't beat yourself up for that, honey," my mother interrupted. "It's not your fault. Reading is just not something that regular teenagers care about. You should've just joined a sports team as I told you, instead of wasting your time on a lost cause. But don't worry, honey, I'm sure no one will blame you for quitting if that's what you want."

Oh... so that's why my mother insisted so much that I talked about what was going on in my mind: she thought that I was considering quitting my job and she wanted to give me a little push to do it.

"Quitting?" I said. "No, I would never quit. I love my job."

"You're not quitting?" My mom asked. "Then what are you worried about?"

"I'm not worried about anything, I just got a lot of things on my mind... I mean, sure, at first I was worried that the number of students that go to the library had not increased very much, but today I had a long chat with Mr. Dan, and he made me realize that maybe those numbers don't matter. That, if at the end of the year, we were able to impact the lives of two or three students, then it would've been worth it because every little action counts. To make a positive change in society, we don't need t–"

"Wait, he really told you that?" My dad asked. "That numbers don't matter? What a small mentality."

"Small?" I said. "No, it's the furthest thing from that. I–"

"Yeah," Alex said. "That's like saying that the score doesn't matter in a game. Everyone knows that only the losers say that. Of course it matters."

"Yeah, my ballet teacher says the same thing," Ashley added. "Excuses are for losers, she always says."

I had never noticed it before, but my family did the exact same thing that the boys from Alana's party did. They constantly interrupted whoever was talking to say something themselves, even if the other person had not finished talking yet. It was so frustrating.

"Your father's right, Hunter," my mom said. "Your teacher's probably only telling you that to trick you into continuing to work for him, even when you already realized that it's a waste of time because it's impossible to turn regular teenagers into avid readers. It's not your fault, honey. No matter how hard you try, that library will never be full of students eager to read. You should just quit now before the end of the year arrives and you realize that you wasted your entire freshman year in something meaningless."

"No, you're missing the point," I said. "Let me finish. I kno–"

"Ladies and gentlemen, can I please have your attention?" Said a man in a fancy suit. "Here at The Mountain Fox, we are pleased to congratulate Andrew Grayson, one of our most loyal customers, for his very well-deserved promotion at work."

The people around us started clapping, and a waiter placed a piece of cake in front of dad.

"This one's for you, Andrew, and may the achievements continue," said the man in the fancy suit, and then the band started to play *Hotel California*, my dad's favorite song.

My mom put her head on my dad's shoulder, Ashley and Axel started to eat my father's cake, and I went back inside my mind. I wanted to be part of the celebration, but I was furious at all of them. It was always the same with my family. They loved pointing out how quiet I was, but here I was with something that I actually wanted to talk about and I couldn't because, when they were not interrupting me, they were criticizing me—or interrupting me to criticize me.

I should've just waited until Monday.

When will I learn?

# CHAPTER TWENTY-SIX

When Monday arrived, I felt a huge relief because I could finally share everything I had in my mind with my friends. Luckily, I spent all weekend sorting out my thoughts and feelings, so when I finally was able to express myself, I wasn't an unstable blob of emotions anymore, I was someone with a very specific goal: to help every student that visited the library as much as I could and to enjoy doing it.

"That's great, Hunt!" Ty said after I told them about my change in attitude.

"Yeah," Ariana added. "I'm so happy for you, Hunter."

Thankfully, I didn't have to wait very long to put my new attitude into use because, that very Monday, two sophomore students entered the library to take shelter from the rain outside.

"Hi," I said. "Are you looking for a book?"

"No," said one of the girls. "But the sky's falling outside. Can we wait for our parents here?"

"Of course," I said. "Take a seat."

They sat down at the nearest table and put their stuff down. Normally, I would've left them alone and go back to my desk, but this was my chance to try to make an impact on them.

"This is very nice," said the other girl, looking around. "I didn't know we had such a nice library. I remember it was a dump when I was a freshman."

"It was recently remodeled," I said. "I'm Hunter, by the way."
"I'm Linda."
"I'm Stacy."
"Nice to meet you," I said.
"Do you work here?" Asked Linda.
"Yeah," I answered.
"Really?" Asked Stacy. "Why?"
"Because I like it," I answered. "Do you like reading?"
"No, not really," Stacy answered.
"Yeah, me neither," Linda added. "I mean, I read when I have to for school, but I don't exactly do it for pleasure."

I was about to give a whole speech on why reading is the best and they should totally do it for pleasure, but I stopped myself at the last second and I decided to take a different approach.

"Do you like *Charmed*?" I asked after I noticed that both of them had a pin of a triquetra on their backpacks.

"Yes! It's our favorite show," said Linda.

"Do you know it?" Asked Stacy.

"Yeah, I watch it all the time with my mom," I said. "I'm a big fan too."

We spent about half an hour talking about the show and about our favorite characters (theirs was Phoebe, mine is Paige). Their parents arrived for them shortly after the rain stopped, but I managed to convince them to rent a book before they left.

"Trust me, if you love the Halliwell sisters, you're also going to love the Mayfair witches," I said, handing them both a copy of *The Witching Hour* by Anne Rice.

"All right, we're gonna trust you," said Stacy.

"Yeah, but we don't promise anything," said Linda.

Our interaction left me pretty happy, but I was even happier when they returned on Friday for the second book of the series.

"You were totally right," said Stacy. "We loved it."

"Yeah, it was awesome," said Linda. "Please tell us that you have the continuation."

"I do," I said, going to get the two copies of *Lasher* that we had. "I'm so glad you liked it."

"We're as surprised as you are," said Linda.

"Yeah, who knew reading could be so… not boring," said Stacy.

But Stacy and Linda weren't the only students I managed to convince to rent a book that week.

On Tuesday, it rained again and I saw a boy outside the library sitting on the sidewalk, using his backpack as protection against the rain.

"Are you okay?" I asked.

"What?" He said, taking his headphones off.

"I asked if you're okay," I said.

"Oh, yeah," he said. "I missed my bus, so now I'm waiting for my mom to pick me up."

"If you want, you can wait for her in here."

"That's okay," he said. "She won't take long."

"Are you sure?" I asked. "Your iPod might stop working if it gets too wet."

"Oh, damn, you're right. Fine, I'll wait inside. Thank you."

"No problem."

"Damn, this place is dope," he said when he stepped into the library.

"Thanks," I said. "Are you a freshman?"

"Yeah," he answered.

"Cool, I'm a freshman too."

"I know. I've seen you in the halls with Ty Johnson."

"Oh… well, my name's Hunter."

"I'm Scott."

"Do you like reading, Scott?"

"No."

"Oh, well, do you want to play a board game while you wait for your mom?"

"You have board games?"

"Yeah."

"All right. Yeah, sure, why not?"

We decided to play Connect 4 because it was easy and fast.

I let him win the first rounds to keep him happy and it worked.

"Man, you suck at this," he said with a smile after winning the fourth game in a row.

"Or maybe you're too good at it," I answered.

"Maybe," he said.

"Want to make this more interesting?" I asked.

"How?" He asked.

"How about if I win the next game, then I'll recommend you a book and you'll have to rent it and read it. Not just rent it and return it in a week, you'll actually have to read it. And if you win, I'll do your Math homework for a week."

"All right, sounds fair. I'm feeling pretty good about my chances, so you got yourself a deal," he said, shaking my hand.

I stopped pretending that I didn't know how to play Connect 4 and I managed to win in six moves.

"You set me up!" He said. "You pretended to be bad on the first rounds so you could easily beat me in this round and win the bet."

"No, I didn't," I lied. "Maybe you lost on purpose because you secretly wanted me to recommend you a book."

"I sure as hell didn't," he said, laughing. "But I'm a man of my word, so go ahead and give a book to read. Just please don't give me a big one."

"Don't worry," I said. "I know exactly what to give you."

I went to the graphic novels section and grabbed one of my favorites: *X-Men: God Loves, Man Kills* by Chris Claremont and Brent Anderson.

"X-Men? Man, I love their movies!" He said.

"Then I think you're going to love this one," I said, handing him the book.

I didn't feel so good about lying to him, but it was for a good cause.

Oh, and this week I also managed to convince someone to rent the book I reviewed this week. On Thursday, a junior girl with long dark hair and green eyes came to the library looking for a book for one of her classes.

"Hi," she said. "I'm looking for a book."

"Great," I said. "What's the title?"

"I don't remember," she said. "But it's a blue book."

"Oh, do you know who's the author?" I asked.

"No, but it's a big book," she said.

"Okay… is it a fiction book, a non-fiction book or a reference book?"

"What? I don't know. It's a Chemistry book and I think it has an atom on the cover," she said.

"Oh, I think I know which one you're referring to. Wait here, I'll bring it to you."

I went to fetch the book and, when I returned, the girl was reading one of the reviews for the Book of the Week that I had on the top of my desk.

"Is it this one?" I asked.

"Yes, thank you so much," she said. "What's this, by the way?"

"Oh, it's a review for a book I'm recommending this week," I said.

"What book?" She asked.

"*The Westing Game* by Ellen Raskin. Have you heard of it?" I asked.

"No," she said. "Is it good?"

"Yeah, it's like an Agatha Christie novel, but more accessible and with a lighter tone."

"Who's Agatha Christie?" She asked.

"Never mind," I said. "Have you ever played the board game Clue?"

"Yeah, I love it," she said.

"Well, the book's like a really entertaining game of Clue."

"Interesting."

"If you want, I can bring a copy so you can rent it and read it at home."

"I don't know…," she said. "I'm not much of a reader."

"I'm not either," I lied. "But I really enjoyed this one. If you like mysteries, I swear you're going to like this book. And if you don't, I promise I'll return you your money."

She laughed, but she still seemed unsure.

"Come on, it's better if you take it now because tomorrow, after I paste the reviews all over school, it'll be very hard to find," I lied again.

"All right," she finally said. "I'll take it."

"Great," I said, going to find one of the copies of *The Westing Game* so I could give it to her. "Please let me know what you think of it," I said, handing the book to her.

"I will," she said with a smile.

This week I managed to convince four different people to rent a book that was not related to school or to their classes and all it took was a brand-new positive attitude—and a little bit of lying. Sure, it may not sound like much, and sure, we still haven't received more than ten visitors per week, but that didn't matter anymore. I was proud of our small achievements. I was happy.

It's amazing what a new attitude can do.

# CHAPTER TWENTY-SEVEN

Today, our Biology teacher, Mr. Jones, didn't come to class. Apparently, he caught a stomach bug or something, which is ironic because just last week he was telling us about all the wonderful things humans can do with viruses and bacteria, like medicines and vaccines. But anyway, he sent a substitute teacher with an activity about ecosystems that we had to turn in the next class. We were supposed to do the activity in the classroom, but the sub teacher didn't even bother to stay for the whole hour. He left right after explaining the activity, so a couple of students decided to learn a little from him and they left too.

I chose to stay and finish the activity there because I didn't want to take the extra work home. I was a little behind on my Math homework, and I still hadn't finished writing the review for the Book of the Week of next week, so I had to take advantage of all the extra time I could get. However, a couple of minutes after I started working on it, someone playfully pushed my elbow, which made my hand move and ruined what I was writing. I angrily turned around to see who had done it, and I saw Ty with a big and mischievous smile on his face.

"What are you doing?" I asked.
"I'm bored," he answered.
"Did you already finish the activity?" I asked.

"Of course not. Come on, let's ditch, we can finish this later. Let's go do something fun," he said, enthusiastically.

I laughed. He seemed like a little kid that had woken up to a snow day.

"What if the sub teacher comes back?" I asked.

"Mr. Welles? Please, I bet you 10 bucks he's already taking a nap in the teacher's lounge," he answered.

Ty was probably right. Mr. Welles was famous for being one of the laziest teachers in school. But still, I didn't want to leave just like that. What if we got into trouble? Although half the classroom was already gone, so if we got into trouble we wouldn't be the only ones.

"Pleeeeeeease," Ty said with the biggest smile his face could make.

I laughed again.

"Fine," I said, picking up my stuff.

"Yes!" He yelled, grabbing his already packed backpack.

"Where do you wanna go?" I asked.

"I don't know. Let me think," he said.

"We can go to the library. Mr. Dan's probably there," I said.

"Umm…," he said, doubting.

"What?" I asked.

"I'd rather not," he said.

"Why not?" I asked. "We can play a board game and talk to Mr. Dan."

"Well, don't take this the wrong way, but I don't like talking to him as much as you and Ariana do," he said.

This caught me off guard. "You don't like Mr. Dan?" I asked.

"No, of course I do," he said. "I think he's a great teacher… but when I talk to him outside the classroom I feel kinda dumb."

"Dumb?" I asked.

"Yeah, like, he's so knowledgeable that I can't keep up… I don't know, I just feel weird talking to him," he said.

"Oh," was the only thing I could say.

I didn't know Ty felt this way. It's weird because the exact opposite happens to me. I love talking to Mr. Dan because it makes me feel smarter. But I never stopped to think about how Ty felt about spending so much time with a teacher outside of the classroom because of me. It was easier for Ariana because Mr. Dan wasn't her teacher, but he was Ty's. I just assumed that he liked it because I liked it, but that was wrong of me.

"I'm sorry, Ty," I added. "I never thought…"

"No, don't feel sorry," he interrupted me. "Look, I'm not saying that I hate talking to him. He's actually quite funny and I really like visiting you at work. It's just that I'm not really in the mood to talk to him right now, okay? Maybe we can do something else."

"Yeah, totally, I understand," I said. "We can do whatever you want. Where do you wanna go?"

"Hmm… oh, I know! Follow me," he said.

I didn't know where he was taking me, but we had to avoid like three hall monitors to get there. Ty didn't want to answer any of my questions regarding our destination, so I figured that maybe we were going to a secret classroom or an unknown hideout. However, when we finally arrived there, it was the opposite of what I was expecting.

"The basketball court, Ty?" I asked. "Really? Do you even know me?"

"Come on," he said, grabbing a ball. "It's gonna be fun. Just try to take the ball away from me."

"Are you trying to humiliate me?" I jokingly asked.

"Of course not," he answered. "I just want you to have some fun."

"All right then," I said, smiling. "I'll have fun."

I moved quickly to take the ball away from him while he was distracted and, to my surprise (and his), it worked.

"Now, that's what I'm talking about," he said with a big grin on his face. Then he easily took the ball back and scored a point.

He scored another two before I could finally take the ball from him again and score two points myself.

"I'm impressed," he said. "You could've actually had a shot at being on the basketball team. Why didn't you try out?"

"I don't play sports because I don't like them," I said, "not because I suck at them."

He just smiled and took the ball from me again.

We spent a few minutes playing and then he suddenly stopped.

"How about we make this a little more interesting?" He asked.

"Okay. But if it's something that involves taking off my shirt or my pants then I'm out," I jokingly said.

He laughed.

"No, it's nothing like that," I said. "How about when we score a point we have the right to ask the other a question?"

"All right," I said. "That could be fun."

"But you have to answer honestly, okay? No lies," he said.

"What? I never lie," I lied.

"Okay, George Washington," he said. "Here, I'll give you a head start."

He handed me the ball and left the hoop unattended.

POINT.

"You can now ask me a question," he said.

"Umm…," I said, pretending to think, but I knew exactly what I wanted to ask him. "What's your favorite subject in school?"

"Seriously, Hunter?" He said.

I had previously asked him that question several times and he always said Physical Education, but I knew that it was Painting. I could see how his eyes filled with joy every time he finished a painting, but I think that he didn't want to admit it because all the other boys thought Painting was a joke and they even mocked him sometimes for how colorful and beautiful his work was.

"No lying, remember?" I told him.

"Fine, it's Painting," he said.

"I knew it!" I said.

"Are you happy now?" He asked, turning his back at me to grab the ball from the floor. He seemed kind of mad.

"Hey, Ty, look at me," I said. "I'm not Tony, okay? And I'm not like your other friends. You don't have to lie to me about stuff like that. I think it's great that you love Painting. I've told you before how good I think your work is. You have a real talent, don't be ashamed of it."

"Thanks, Hunt."

"No problem."

POINT.

"If you could have any superpower, what would it be?" Ty asked.

"Probably the ability to stop time," I answered. "Or invisibility."

"Really? I thought you were going to say read minds," he said.

"No, thanks," I answered. "I have enough with my own thoughts."

POINT.

"What's your favorite color?" Ty asked.

"Yellow," I said.

"Really?" He asked.

"Yeah," I said. "But dark yellow, not bright yellow. I think its name's amber."

POINT.

"What's *your* favorite color?" I asked.

"Green," Ty said.

"Any particular green?" I asked.

"Nah, I like all types of green," he said.

POINT.

"What's the craziest thing you've ever done?" Ty asked.

That was a hard one since I think I have been a relatively good boy all my life. But, after a few seconds of thinking, I knew exactly what the answer to that question was.

"Well," I said. "When I was about eight years old, I went with my whole family to a couple of cabins in the woods. And I mean my WHOLE family. Aunts, uncles, cousins, grandparents. Everybody was there, so I had to share a room with like four of my cousins and every minute of the day was filled with family activities, so I didn't have any time to relax and unwind, you know? One day, I decided to take a walk in the woods to be by myself for a few minutes, but I was having such a good time that those few minutes turned into five hours. When I got back, everybody was desperately looking for me. My mom was extremely worried, my dad called the police, and even the local TV news showed up. They thought I had been eaten by a bear. I got into so much trouble that I'm surprised I'm not still grounded."

Ty laughed so hard that he was practically on the floor.

"No way! That's crazy! I didn't know somewhere in there, there was a troublemaker," he said, pointing to my chest and handing me the ball.

POINT.

"What's your favorite childhood memory?" I asked.

"Ooh, that's a tough one," he said. "I'm gonna cheat because it's not just one memory, it's a whole bunch, but I think my favorite part of my childhood was going to the stadium with my parents to watch a football game and then going to the park to have a picnic and play catch with my dad."

"That's beautiful," I said. "Do you still do that?"

"No, we haven't done that in a while," he said. "But I'll always have those memories."

"I guess that's when you started loving football, right?" I asked. "Or were you one of those kids that were born with a football under his arm?"

He laughed.

"Well, I have always liked football," he said. "But yeah, I think that's when I first started loving it."

"That's amazing," I said, wondering how different my life would've been if I had been born loving football—or at least liking it.

POINT.

"What do you like the most about yourself?" I asked.

"Damn, man!" He said, laughing. "You're coming at me with all these hard questions."

"Hey, it's your game!" I said, laughing. "Don't enter the kitchen if you can't stand the heat."

"You're right, you're right," he said with a smile. "Hmm… I don't know. I… no. Maybe… no. Ugh, why is this so hard?"

"What are you talking about, Ty?" I said. "You have like a million good qualities, just pick your favorite one."

"Okay… I… oh, I'm tall! There, I like that about myself," he said.

"Really? That's what you like the most about yourself?" I asked.

"Yeah, next question," he said, grabbing the ball.

POINT.

"Okay, I know you don't know what you wanna be when you grow up yet, but what did you wanna be when you were little?" Ty asked.

"Honestly… I wanted to be a writer," I said.

I think that was the first time I ever said that out loud. When I was little and people asked me what I wanted to be, I used to lie and say that I wanted to be an astronaut, but the truth is that I wanted to be like the authors I read. I wanted to inspire people with my words and provide comfort and adventures to children all around the world.

"Really? And what happened?" Ty asked.

"I don't know. I grew up, I guess," I said. "It's a nice dream, but a far-fetched one."

"Nonsense," he said. "I think you could totally be a writer. I've read your reviews and they're amazing."

"Really? You've read my reviews?" I asked.

"Of course," he answered.

POINT.

"Do you have any strange habits?" Ty asked.

Yes, going to the movies alone, but I wasn't going to tell him that. I didn't want to lie either, so it took me a little time to think about something that was honest, but that wasn't going to totally freak him out.

"Oh, I know," I finally said. "Sometimes I have to sleep with the TV on."

"Why?" He asked.

"Because my mind tends to overthink a lot, and sometimes this doesn't let me sleep, so I turn the TV on to concentrate on the sound instead of on my own thoughts," I said.

"Does it work?" He asked.

"Yeah, like a charm," I answered.

"Interesting," he said.

I was kind of surprised by his reaction. I was fully prepared for him to freak out or laugh, but he didn't do any of that. I wonder what his reaction would've been if I had stuck to my first option and told him that I love going to the movies alone.

POINT.

"What's something you've always wanted to do but have never done?" I asked.

"Hmm, do you know Hill Street?" He answered. "The really inclined street downtown?"

"Yeah, 'Kill' Street, of course I know it," I said.

"Well, I've always wanted to skateboard down that street, but I've never done it," he said.

"Probably a smart choice," I said. "Doing that would most likely prevent you from doing other things, like breathing or being alive."

He laughed.

"Yeah, but imagine all the dope tricks I could do," he said.

POINT.

"Why don't you like parties?" Ty asked.

I totally froze when I heard those words.

"What…?" I answered.

"Well, ever since I met you, I have invited you to at least seven parties and you have only come to two: the first one and my own. You always say that you're gonna try to go, but you never do. Why is that?" He asked.

"I… just have been very busy," I said.

"No lying, remember?" He said.

"Fine. I… just… I don't feel very comfortable at parties," I said.

"Why not?" He asked. "These are cool parties, you know? With cheerleaders, football players, and older students. Any other freshman would die to go to these parties, so why don't you wanna go? Don't you wanna have fun? Don't you wanna be popular?"

I thought a lot before answering him. I contemplated lying again, but if I was going to continue being friends with Ty, I decided that being honest was the best choice.

"I think my definition of fun is a little bit different than yours, Ty," I finally said. "To me, staying home is more fun than going to a crowded party filled with people I don't know. And no, I don't wanna be popular. I'm perfectly fine with my C-list status. I don't need everyone to know my name. I would actually hate that. I like having just a few good friends and being anonymous to the rest."

"Okay, forget the popularity thing, then," he said. "There are really cool people at these parties. I know for a fact you had fun at the first party with Alana's brother and his friends. What if there are a bunch of potential friends out there in other parties, just waiting for you to go?"

I was getting really uncomfortable with this conversation.

"I think the odds of that happening again are very low, Ty," I said. "Look, I get what you're saying, but I don't look at social life the same way that you do. I don't need to know everyone in this school and I certainly don't want everyone to know me. I'm perfectly fine with a small number of friends, I don't need more."

"Yeah, but…"

"Ty," I interrupted him, "why are you insisting so much on this?"

"Because you're one of my best friends, Hunter," he said. "I know we've only known each other for a few weeks, but you are. I have so much fun with you that I want everyone to know how cool you are. And I wish you and my other friends got along so we could go to parties together or play a friendly game of soccer or have a sleepover or just do something outside of school together, you know, like normal friends do."

I was one of his best friends? That was a very nice—and quite surprising—thing to hear.

"Ty… I… I can't promise you that I'm going to be friends with your other friends because they're not my type of friends and I'm clearly not theirs either, but you and I can always hang out outside of school whenever you want. I had a lot of fun at the movies last Sunday, we can do other things like that, we can go wherever you want… just not to parties, okay?"

"Okay… okay, I think I can live with that," he said.

"Great," I said.

"Wait, I have one more question."

Damn it, I really wanted that conversation to be over already.

"… go ahead," I said.

"Do you really prefer to stay at home instead of going out?" Ty asked.

"Um, yeah, sometimes I do," I said.

"But… don't you get bored?" He asked.

"No, I like not going out," I said. "I like being by myself. It gives me time to do a lot of things I love, I don't need anyone to entertain me. And I really love my house, you know?"

"But don't you ever get lonely?" He asked.

"No, it's peaceful," I said. "You should try it sometime. And I don't always stay home, sometimes I go to a museum or to the movies."

"Alone?" He asked.

"Yeah," I answered.

"Why?" He asked with a look on his face that I knew all too well.

That was it. I already had enough of this kind of conversations with my parents, I didn't want to have one with

Ty because he wasn't going to understand either. At first, I thought he might, but I was fooling myself. If I continued talking, he was going to think that I was crazy or weird. Just like them.

"I don't want to play this game anymore, Ty," I said, leaving the ball on the floor and walking towards the exit. He ran and placed himself in front of me.

"No, Hunter, I'm sorry," he said. "You don't have to answer, I'm sorry if that was rude. We can go if you want, but please don't be mad. Please."

He seemed really sorry.

"It's okay, Ty," I said. "I'm not mad. It's just that I don't like talking about this because I know I sound like a weirdo."

"What do you mean?" He asked.

"You know what I mean," I said with a cracking voice. "The look you gave me is the same look I've been getting all my life from my parents, my uncles, my aunts, my siblings, my cousins, my teachers, my classmates, and even my friends. The 'what's wrong with you' look. The 'why aren't you like the other kids' look. The 'why are you so weird' look."

I was about to start crying and I hated it, but then Ty unexpectedly hugged me.

"Hunt," he said. "If there's something I've learned from you is that I should not care what other people think of me, so don't."

He stopped hugging me and I managed to fight back the tears.

"And you're not weird, okay?" He continued. "I mean, sure, you're different, that's true. I had never met anyone like you before. You're not like the other boys our age, you're very smart and you like to talk about deeper stuff, like dreams and the future and the meaning of life, which always leave me with a headache, but I still love talking about that kind of stuff with you because no one else does; and you care about what I have to say, you never try to hijack the conversation and make it all about yourself, you listen and you ask and you care; and I know

I haven't known you for very long, but if I had any problem I know I would probably tell you first because I trust you and I know you would give me good advice and you wouldn't make fun of me or give me shit like some of my other friends. So yeah, you're different, but that's a good thing, Hunter, and that certainly doesn't mean that you're weird."

I was about to cry again, but for a completely different reason.

"Thanks, Ty," I said.

"You're very welcome. And sorry if this stupid game got a little bit out of hand. I didn't mean for this to happen, but I feel like I know you a little better now and I'm really happy about that," he said.

"Yeah, me too," I said.

After that, we went back to play regular basketball again. No more questions this time. He was really good, but I was in competitive mode, so the game was more even than I expected. Well, to me, 32 to 21 is almost even.

We were having so much fun that, when we remembered that the school day wasn't over yet, we were already late for our next classes. We didn't have time to shower, so we did our best to wipe the sweat off with hand paper and bathe ourselves in spray deodorant.

"What happened to you?" Ariana asked when I finally made it to Social Studies. "You look like hell."

"Nothing," I said. "I just had fun."

# CHAPTER TWENTY-EIGHT

This weekend, I planned to stay home and do nothing but finish the pile of homework I had amassed over the last couple of weeks, but a certain unexpected visitor ruined my plans.

"Hunter!" My mom yelled from downstairs. "There's someone here for you."

Those words took me by surprise because I wasn't expecting anyone. My mind started racing thinking about who it could be. Maybe I had ordered something in the mail and I'd forgotten about it, or perhaps I'd lost my wallet with my high school credential inside and someone came over to return it. Whatever it was, I was hoping that it wouldn't take too long. But when I finally went downstairs, I was surprised to see my mom cheerfully talking with Ty, who had his usual big smile on.

"Ty?" I said. "Wh-what are you doing here? Is something wrong?"

"No, not at all," he said.

"Hunter, why hadn't you told me that you were friends with such a charismatic young man?" My mom asked.

"I kinda did, mom," I said. "This is Ty. Remember that I told you that he had been walking home with Ariana and me? I also went to his birthday party a couple of weeks ago."

"Oh, right," my mom said, then she turned to Ty. "Sorry, Ty. I had imagined you completely different."

"Happens all the time," Ty said and my mom laughed.

"Mom," I said, "can you give us a minute?"

"Sure, honey," she said. "If you guys need me, I'll be in my office."

"Your mom's pretty nice," Ty said after she left.

"Yeah, I guess," I said. "Ty, what are you doing here? Wait… why do you have a sleeping bag? Did you run away from home?"

I hadn't seen them at first because they were on the floor, but he had a sleeping bag and a big green backpack with him.

"No," he said, laughing. "It's not that. Remember that you told me that you love your house and that we could hang out anytime? Well, I thought that maybe we could have a good, old-fashioned sleepover."

"Oh… I should've told you to call first too…," I said.

"Why?" Ty asked with concern. "Do you have other plans already? Sorry, I wanted to surprise you."

"You certainly did," I said.

"Do you want me to go?" He asked.

"No, of course not," I said. "Don't be silly. I'm glad you're here… yeah, this is gonna be fun. Come in, let's go to my room."

My mind absolutely hated last-minute plans, but a sleepover with Ty didn't sound so bad, so I immediately started to mentally reorganize my weekly schedule to include doing the homework that I was planning on doing today. I was going to have to sleep only 6 hours on Monday and Tuesday, but I think it was worth it.

I helped Ty with his sleeping bag and led him to my room upstairs, but before we got there, I stopped mid-stairs because I was forgetting something kind of important.

"Wait… mom, can Ty stay over?" I yelled.

"Of course, honey," she yelled back.

"Great, let's go," I said to Ty.

We entered my room and I immediately started picking up

clothes from the floor.

"Sorry," I said. "I wasn't expecting any company."

"Woah," he said. "Your room's huge."

"Yeah, my mom's a realtor, so she kept the biggest house with the smallest price for herself," I said.

"That makes sense. I like the color of th—wait, you have a dog?!" He asked after he saw Rufus' bed on the floor.

"Oh yeah," I said. "His name's Rufus. He must be with my sister."

"I can't believe that I know you had a crush on Lola Bunny, but I didn't know you had a dog," he said.

"Hey, I told you that in confidence!" I said, laughing. "Do you want to meet him?"

"Of course!" He said.

"Rufus!" I yelled and he came running to my room.

"Oh my god, he's so adorable! Who's a good boy? Who's a good boy? Who's a good boy?" He said, petting him. "Man, I love dogs, but my mom won't let me have one because she hates them."

"That sucks," I said. "My mom didn't want a dog at first either, but a few years ago I saw Rufus on the street. He was alone and cold, so I decided to take him home with me and my whole family fell in love with him right away. We tried looking for his owner, but he didn't have one, so I begged my mom to let me keep him and she eventually said yes."

"God, if I ever came home with a dog, my mom would probably kick me to the streets with him," Ty said.

"Yeah, I think it helped that I was nine when that happened and I was still kind of adorable, so she couldn't say no to both of us," I said.

"Man, I miss being adorable. I was able to get away with so much. Now I have to be responsible or whatever," he said, sitting on my reading couch so he could pet Rufus more easily.

I laughed and sat on the bed.

"By the way," Ty added. "I knew you liked your job, but I didn't know that you loved it so much that you opened your own library in your room."

He was referring to the dozens of books that filled the bookshelves in my bedroom.

"I told you I liked reading," I said.

"Yeah, Hunt, but this is not just liking, this is an obsession," he said, jokingly. "So, which one's your favorite book?"

"You can't ask that to a bibliophile," I said. "It's impossible to have just one favorite book, it's like making a parent choose a favorite child. I have many favorite books."

"All right then, which are your favorite books?" He asked.

Ty didn't know it at that moment, but he was opening Pandora's box with that question because I couldn't stop talking after that. I told him about my favorite books, what I thought of them, why there were special to me, and even why I decided to buy them. I felt kind of bad because I wasn't able to shut up, but he didn't seem to mind, he actually seemed really interested. And not just in the books, he asked me about everything in my room: the movies, the photos, the objects, everything. I don't know if he actually wanted to know or he was just being polite, but I told him things that I hadn't been able to tell anyone else before—mostly because no one in my family has any interest in what I like.

I was so invested in the conversation that I didn't even notice that the sun had already set until my mom called for us to go downstairs for dinner. To be honest, I probably didn't notice because I was scared that this would come. I didn't want to go downstairs because I was terrified of Ty meeting my family and vice versa. I even thought about having dinner in my room, but I knew my mom would never let me get away with it. And I wasn't nervous because I thought that they would not get along, I knew they were all going to like Ty, but I was not like Axel, I didn't like mixing family with friends. For me, it was very uncomfortable.

Fortunately, it went better than I expected. They not only liked Ty, they loved him. My mom and dad bombarded him with questions about his life and his likes, Axel trash-talked the football coach of the school with him, and I think Ashley even developed a little crush on him. Honestly, I was a bit jealous of how easy it was for him to fit in with them. And I think they were very impressed by the fact that someone like me had a friend like him—I mean, sometimes even I couldn't believe it.

After dinner, we played a little basketball on the front porch and then we watched a movie. I wanted to watch *The Sixth Sense*, but he insisted on watching *Scary Movie 2*, a dumb parody film that he had brought from his home. It's one of the stupidest movies I've ever seen, but he laughed so hard that it made me laugh too.

"I can't believe you forced my eyes to go through that horrible experience," I jokingly said when the movie ended. "I will never forgive you for that."

"Please, there's no need for you to thank me," he answered.

We discussed his terrible movie taste for a bit and then we decided to go to sleep so we could watch the sunrise in the morning.

But I had so much in my mind that I couldn't sleep. For starters, I still couldn't believe that Ty Johnson was now one of my best friends and that he was sleeping in my room. I had judged him so badly at first. He ended up being so much more than what I thought he would be. So different from the brainless jock I thought he was when I first saw him with Tony.

People are way more complex than what they seem at first. You can only get so much out of a first impression, after all. I was amazed by all the things I had learned about Ty in the last couple of weeks and I'm sure that there were still many more things that he hadn't shown me yet. I wonder if you can ever know another person completely. After all, the person I am with Ty and Ariana is not the same person I am with my family, or the person I am with strangers. And I bet I'm not the only one who hides or modifies certain parts of themselves with different people, even with their closest ones.

We only see what other people allow us to see about

themselves. I wonder what it would be like to be able to read minds. To be able to know anyone completely, without filters. Would it be a blessing or a curse? Probably something in between.

I wonder how well I know the people I love the most. My mom, dad, Ashley, Axel, Ariana, and Ty immediately popped into my mind. Do I really know them? Do they really know me? Do I really know myself? Do people love each other because they really know each other or because they don't really know each other? It was a scary thought. To love someone without really knowing them. But I guess it happens all the time.

My mom once told me that Aunt Rose and her husband got divorced because they were very young when they got married, and with time, they discovered that they were way more different than they thought at first. I guess that's what happens with most divorced couples. They are so blinded by the chemicals in their brains that they cannot see that they don't really know each other. I wonder if I'll ever know or love someone enough to want to spend the rest of my life with her.

My head started to hurt from overthinking. Sometimes I love it when my mind runs wild like this because it allows me to think about many things I hadn't considered before, but right now, I just wanted to sleep.

"Hunt?" Ty asked an hour after I first tried going to sleep. "Are you up?"

"Yeah," I said. "You can't sleep either?"

"Nope," he said.

I got out of bed and turned the light on.

"Do you want to do something?" I asked. "Maybe we can watch another movie—a good one this time—or maybe we can play a video game. I don't have any in here, but if you want, I can borrow my brother's PlayStation 2."

"No, that's okay," he said. "We can just talk."

"Oh, great, because I suck at video games," I said. "What do you want to talk about?"

"This may sound weird, but... how did you do on last week's

Math test?" He asked.

"Oh, pretty well," I said. "I got an A+. What about you?"

"Well, let's just say that I think I would've received a better grade if I hadn't taken the test," he said.

"Come on, it couldn't have been that bad," I said.

"No, it was worse… can I tell you a secret?" He asked.

"Of course," I answered.

"I think I'm gonna fail Math… and Biology," he said, looking at the floor.

"Ty, you're not gonna fail," I said.

"Yes, I am," he said. "High school is turning out to be way more difficult than I expected. I mean, I already knew that I was stupid, but I didn't know that I was stupid enough to fail two classes in one year."

"Hey, listen to me, you're not stupid, okay?" I said. "And you're not gonna fail. There's still plenty of time to recover."

"But what if there isn't?" He said. "I'm afraid I'm gonna get kicked out of the football team if my grades keep falling. And I've been trying to improve, I really have, I've been reading the book and doing the homework, but I just can't seem to understand it. And I feel so stupid because everyone else can, but I can't."

I'd never seen him like that, he seemed so scared, like a puppy in a thunderstorm.

"You… you're not going to fail, okay?" I said.

"But what if…," he started.

"No," I interrupted him. "There's no 'but.' You're not going to fail. Period."

"Why are you so sure?" He asked.

"Because I'm going to help you," I said.

"What?" He asked.

"Yes, I can help you study for the midterm exams after football season is over," I said. "You can come to the library after school and we can review the topics that you're struggling with."

"No, Hunt," he said, "thank you, but I can't let you do that.

You already got enough on your plate. I didn't tell you this so you would help me, I just wanted to talk about it. But this is my problem, I'll find a way to solve it."

"You don't have to do it alone, Ty," I said. "I can help you. I *will* help you."

"No, I…," he said.

"Ty," I interrupted him. "If you think I'm gonna let you fail, then you don't know me at all. I'm going to help you. End of discussion."

He looked at me and just smiled. For the first time since I'd met him, he was speechless.

"Thank you, Hunter," he finally said. "You're a great friend."

"You're a great friend too, Ty," I told him.

"You know, sometimes I wish I was as smart you," he said.

"Stop it," I said.

"No, I'm serious," he said. "I mean, you're like super wise for your age, you ace all your classes, and you read like five books a day."

I didn't know what to say, I had no idea Ty felt this way. This was all new to me and my mind was not ready to process it all.

"Grades are just a number, okay?" I said. "There are more important things than that. And if it makes you feel any better, you're kicking my ass in Painting."

"Yeah… I'm only doing well in the most useless class," he said.

"Don't say that," I said. "Don't belittle yourself or your talent, Ty. You have the kind of artistic sensibility that I can only dream of. There's more than one way to be 'intelligent,' you know? Besides, you're athletic, charismatic, and outgoing. There are people who would die to have your talents, myself included."

He was stunned by this unexpected confession—as was I.

"Look," I added, trying to break the tension. "Everyone has different strengths and weaknesses. It's how we use them and adapt to them that makes us stand out or fail. You can feel sorry for yourself because you don't have the same strengths that other people have, or you can use your own strengths to stand out and make the most of the great potential that I know you have."

He was speechless again, but this time it took longer for him to say something. I was starting to get worried. I thought that maybe I said something wrong. I was about to apologize when he finally broke his silence.

"Thank you, Hunter," he said. "You're right. And sorry for making things uncomfortable again. This was supposed to be a fun time and I ruined it, but I needed to get that out of my chest. I'm sorry."

"Stop apologizing," I said, "this is what friends are for. I'll always be here for you if you want to talk about things like this. In the good times and the bad times… do you remember the first time we went to the park? You didn't want to tell me something because you thought that it might bore me and I told you that I was all ears. Well, I meant it. I meant it then and I mean it now. You can always talk to me about anything, that is literally what friends are for… now tell me, do you want to lose in Monopoly or in Uno?"

He finally had his characteristic big smile again.

"I think I'm feeling like beating you in Uno," he said.

We spent all night playing board games, eating junk food, and talking. We did manage to watch the sunrise, but only because we didn't sleep all night. When we finally went to bed, it was already 7am. I thought that my mom wasn't going to let us sleep because she always cleans the house on Sundays, but we were so tired that not even the noise of the vacuum cleaner or the loudspeakers playing a collection of 80s hit songs managed to wake us up.

When we finally woke up, it was already 3pm and we were starving, so the first thing we did was go downstairs to have breakfast—or, well, lunch.

"Finally," my mom said when she saw us. "My sleeping beauties. I was about to go upstairs to check your pulses because I wasn't sure if you were still alive."

"I'm sorry, Mrs. Grayson," Ty said. "But your son kept me up all night because he wanted me to beat him in every one of his board games."

My mom laughed.

"Well, I'm glad you kids had fun," she said. "Hunter doesn't do this very often. You know, the last time he had a slee–"

"Where's everyone?" I interrupted her before she started oversharing personal information as usual.

"Your brother and your father went to a game, and Ashley is at a birthday party next-door," she said.

Oh, good. That meant that I didn't have to worry about any more interactions between Ty and my family. Well, except for my mom, who ironically was the one that worried me the most. But hey, glass half full, right? I just needed to get something quick to eat and then I could take Ty outside or back to my room.

"Are there still pizza leftovers from yesterday?" I asked.

"You're not gonna eat that," my mom said. "You haven't eaten anything all day. Sit down, I'll make you some pancakes."

Damn it.

"So, Ty," my mom said. "Hunter told me that you had a pretty big birthday party."

Here we go.

"Oh, yeah," Ty answered. "I don't know if I would say 'pretty big,' but yeah, it was kind of big."

"Did you enjoy it?" She asked.

"Big-time," he said. "It was awesome. One of my top 3 birthday parties for sure."

"You see, Hunter? You can have a great time if you have a party. You should learn a little from your friend," my mom said to me with an expression of victory on her face, and then she turned back to Ty. "He doesn't want a party for his 15th birthday, can you believe it? I keep insisting that this is an important age and that he should celebrate it, but he's such a party pooper. You know, for his 14th birthday he didn't want a party either, I was ready to max out the credit card to give him the party of his dreams, but he decided to go to the bowling alley with just one friend instead. Can you believe it?"

I. Was. Speechless. I truly didn't know what to say to save myself from this embarrassment. I was hoping that I would wake up from this nightmare at any time, but nothing happened, no matter how many times I pinched myself. And oh my god, I was so worried about what Ty must've been thinking of me. I was one hundred percent ready to crawl into a hole to live the rest of my days in solitude and forget everything about my life on the surface when Ty finally said something.

"Well, yeah, I can. I mean, parties are not for everyone and that's okay," Ty politely said to my mom and then he turned to me and smiled. "But hey, if you decide to do that bowling alley thing again, you better invite me because I'm a great bowler and I can't wait to beat you in that too."

I just smiled. My soul had successfully returned to my body and now my mom was the one left speechless. Her plan had backfired and, since she wasn't going to admit defeat, she quickly changed the topic to Ty's football prowess.

After that, I decided to sit back, relax, and enjoy the pancakes while my mom and Ty talked because now I knew that, no matter what my mom told him, he wasn't going to judge me or think less of me. He had my back. In the good times and the bad times. I was so happy that I had found a friend like him.

Although it was kind of surprising—and sad—that a friend I had known for less than two months was more understanding than my own mother.

# CHAPTER TWENTY-NINE

It was finally Halloween! My favorite holiday of the year. Although sometimes I don't even understand why I love it so much if I don't like going to costume parties and I'm way too old to go trick or treating, but I do. Maybe it's because I love spooky things and, on Halloween, everything is decorated with spider webs, witches, and skeletons, and the TV is filled with horror specials and scary movies.

I think my brain is not wired correctly, though, because I get scared way too easily, but I love the feeling of adrenaline that fills my body after a good scare, especially after I realize that everything is fine and that the danger was never real, that it was just a guy in a mask or a carefully directed scene or a chillingly written sentence. It's like riding a roller coaster but without the motion sickness.

Ty and Ariana know that I get scared very easily, so they spent the whole day trying to scare me. And they didn't even have to try very hard, they would just yell "Boo!" really loud and I would inevitably jump. But the joke's on them because I really enjoyed it. By the end of the school day, I counted 27 scares and three scolds from teachers telling us to stop it because we were interrupting the class.

But we were not the only ones causing mayhem that day. This year, Halloween fell on a Friday, so everyone wanted to get out of school as soon as possible. Some students didn't even go to school and some were so eager for school to be over that they started the tricking earlier this year. I heard that an entire classroom was filled with toilet paper and that someone spiked the cafeteria's apple juice.

And since it was Friday *and* Halloween, everyone was either going to a party or throwing one.

"So, what's your plan for today?" I asked Ty when he joined Ariana and me at the library after his football practice.

"I'm going to Melissa Jamerson's costume party," he said. "I heard it's gonna be dope."

"Wait… and you didn't invite me?" I asked.

"I… what…? I thought you said you didn't like parties…," he said, very confused.

"Yeah, but that doesn't mean that I don't want to be invited!" I said.

"Wh– I… what?" He asked, not knowing what to do.

"Don't worry, I'm totally kidding… kind of," I said. Ty was slowly starting to get his smile back and Ariana couldn't stop laughing. "So, what are you going as?"

"Oh, I bought a cheap monster costume at the mall," he said. "I'm not really into dressing up. What about you, guys? What's the plan for today?"

"We're going to watch some of my favorite scary movies and carve pumpkins at Ariana's," I answered.

"You're welcome to come if you want," Ariana added.

"Thanks," Ty answered. "But I think I'll stick to the party."

"Okay, it's your loss," she said. "We're also going to bake my famous burnt down cookies."

Ty laughed.

"I think I can live without them," he said. "Wait, I thought you said you didn't like scary movies."

"I don't. He's forcing me to watch them," she said, pointing at me.

Ariana didn't share my love for horror movies, she was more of a Christmas kind of girl, but I convinced her to have a marathon by saying that my favorite scary movies (*Scream, Silence of the Lambs, Alien, Nightmare on Elm Street,* and *Halloween*) all featured strong, tridimensional female characters that ultimately defeat the villain in the end.

We went to her place right after my shift was over. Her parents were going to be at her aunt's until late at night, so we decided to turn off all the outdoor lights so kids wouldn't knock on the door asking for candy because we didn't have any.

The first movie of the marathon was *Silence of the Lambs*, and just as I thought, Ariana loved it.

"Jodie Foster is my new goddess," she said after the movie was over.

"I told you you'd like it," I answered.

"Like it? I loved it!"

We spent almost 40 minutes talking about the movie while making the cookies. We talked about the feminist message of the film, about how awesome, intelligent, and badass Clarice was, and about how weird it was that a genre that has been so misogynist over the years also has some of the best female characters in all of cinema.

After we put the cookies in the oven, it was time for another one of my all-time favorites: *Scream*. I'd seen that movie at least ten times, but somehow I still jumped and got scared with the opening scene. It didn't help that the phone started ringing just after Drew Barrymore's parents discovered her body.

"Don't worry," Ariana said. "It's probably just my parents checking up on us."

She paused the movie and stood up to pick up the phone.

"Hello?" She said.

Then her face got really serious.

"What? Who is this?" Ariana asked.

"Stop it," I said, knowing that she was probably pranking me.

"Why do you wanna know my favorite scary movie?" She asked, nervously.

I was starting to get scared.

"H-how do you know my name?" She asked.

I was seriously two seconds away from either wetting my pants or running to the kitchen to grab the biggest knife I could find.

"H-he wants to talk to you," she said, handing me the phone.

I was about to answer when she yelled "Boo!" and my heart stopped for a few seconds.

"Oh my god, don't do that, man!" I said. "You know how scared I am of serial killers!"

She just laughed and grabbed the phone back.

"Yeah, everything's fine, dad. I was just scaring Hunter… okay… okay… okay… love you."

She hung up and sat back on the couch.

"My parents say hi," she said. "They're still gonna take a while. Where's the remote?"

"I don't know," I answered.

We started looking for the remote when a loud ring interrupted the silence and we both jumped and screamed.

"Oh," Ariana said, catching her breath. "It's just the cookies. I'll be right back."

"No! Don't say that! It's one of the rules!" I said.

"Don't worry," she said. "I promise that if I get murdered, I won't come back to haunt you. Unless you want me to. I mean, if you get this much scared by a kitchen timer, I would like to see how far you'd jump if you saw an actual ghost."

"Just go!" I said, laughing.

I sat on the couch to wait for her when I heard a noise at the window. It was probably nothing, but I was really nervous, so I decided to go check.

"Uh-oh," Ariana yelled from the kitchen. "I think we over-burned them."

I was about to go to the kitchen with her when a loud knock on the door startled me.

"Can you get that?" Ariana asked from the kitchen.

"Sure," I said. But there was no way in hell I was going to open that door. "Sorry. We don't have any candies," I yelled.

But the knocking kept going.

"Just open it, Hunter!" Ariana said from the kitchen.

"Fine!" I said. "But if I die, I *will* come back to haunt you."

I grabbed an umbrella that was by the door to use as a weapon and I started to turn the knob.

"Boo!" said a man with a horrible mask when I opened the door.

I screamed so loud that the kids and the parents on the street turned to verify that everything was fine.

"Calm down," the man said, removing his mask. "It's just me."

"Ty?" I asked from the floor because I got so scared that I fell back. "What are you doing here?"

"Well, if the offer still stan—Ouch!" He said.

Ariana had come running from the kitchen when she heard my scream and she threw a cookie at Ty's face when she saw me on the floor.

"What the hell?" He asked.

"Ty?" Ariana asked. "Sorry, I thought you were a serial killer."

"And you were gonna stop him with a cookie?" He asked.

"Did it hurt?" She asked.

"Yeah, kind of," he answered.

"Then yes," she said.

It turns out that Ty decided to ditch the party at the last minute and hang with us instead. He even brought his own pumpkin.

"Why the sudden change of heart?" Ariana asked.

"Well," he said. "If Hunter pees a little every time he hears the word 'boo,' I wanted to see what he does when he watches a horror movie."

"You're in for a treat, my friend," Ariana said, laughing.

We finished watching *Scream* while eating the few decent cookies that we deemed eatable. It's funny because they were supposed to be little ghosts, but ended up looking like burnt down Kirbys.

Ariana loved the movie (especially because of Sidney Prescott), but Ty thought that *Scary Movie* was better—I don't even know what to say about that… his movie taste is beyond saving.

After watching the movie, we decided to play a traditional Halloween game: doughnuts on a string. We helped Ariana hang nine doughnuts (three for each one of us) on a string across the kitchen. The rules of the game were simple: we had to stand under the doughnuts with our hands in our back and the first one to eat the three doughnuts without any of them falling to the ground won the game.

Surprisingly, Ariana won by a landslide. I finished second and Ty ended up in third place.

"Really, Ty?" Ariana asked Ty when she finished eating her third doughnut and he was still in his first one. "I once saw you eat a whole burger in three bites and now you can't even finish a doughnut?"

"It's not fair," he said with his mouth full. "It's because I'm taller than you. If this were a regular doughnut-eating contest, you guys would be so over."

He was right, the string was perfectly placed for us, but he was at least half a foot taller than us, so he had to hunch over to reach the doughnuts.

"You're right, you're right," I said when I finished and he was barely starting his second doughnut. "But I think you're really gonna like our next game."

"Yeah," Ariana said. "Stop whining because you're totally gonna kick our butts in the next one."

"Really?" Ty asked. "Are we gonna play a sport?"

"God, no," Ariana answered.

"Something better," I said.

While I waited for Ty to finish eating his third doughnut, Ariana went to her room to get a whiteboard and some markers for our next game: Halloween Pictionary.

"Oh, I hope you guys are still hungry, because you're about to eat my dust," Ty said when he realized what we were going to play.

Instead of using the traditional Pictionary cards, we decided to make our own ones with Halloween-themed things like ghosts, witches, and black cats. However, the rules stayed the same: when one of us picked a card, he or she had one minute to draw the object on the whiteboard while the others tried to guess. If they guessed the object correctly, then the person drawing won a point. The person with the most points at the end was the winner.

As we all thought at the beginning, Ty ended up being the absolute winner with 10 out of 10 points. Ariana came in second with 7 points and I ended up in last place with 5 points after no one could guess what my perfectly drawn raven was (something about it looking too much like the T-Rex from *Jurassic Park*). It's a shame, I guess they can't appreciate beautiful art when they see it—just like my Painting teacher. It's truly sad.

But anyway, after we finished playing, we decided that it was finally time to carve the pumpkins. I decided to carve a traditional jack-o-lantern, but Ariana and Ty decided to go down another route. She carved a three-eyed alien with a mullet, while he decided to carve a football. But he didn't plan it very well because, when he made the final cut, the details fell and it just looked like a giant oval.

"Oh no!" He yelled when he realized what had happened.

Ariana and I were on the floor laughing while he was trying to put the pieces back together. In the end, he decided to add little eyes above the giant oval so it at least looked like a face, but it looked hilariously ridiculous because the mouth was like ten times bigger than the eyes.

"Let's get them outside to take a photo," Ariana said. "I'll go get my camera."

Ty and I grabbed the pumpkins and lined them outside on the front stairs of the house while we waited for her.

"They look great," I said.

"Yeah, they do," Ty said. "Hey, Hunter, do you know which is the plant that likes Halloween the most?"

"I don't know, which one?" I asked.

"The bam-BOO!" He said.

I screamed, jumped, and laughed, in that order.

"Oh no," Ariana said, getting out of the house. "I heard a scream, did I miss another Hunter scare?

"I only screamed because I witnessed a crime against humor in the form of a terrible joke, not because I was scared," I said.

"Do it again so I can take a picture of it," Ariana said.

"Sorry, you had to be here," I said.

"BOO!" Ty said behind me.

I screamed and jumped again, but this time my friends were the ones laughing.

"Very funny," I said. "I hope you at least captured it."

"Of course I did," she said.

Ariana showed us the picture she took and it looked like a renaissance painting. I had an expression of terror on my face that would make Edvard Munch jealous, Ty was laughing so hard behind me, and, in the background, there were kids dressed up as monsters and superheroes that were very confused by what was going on.

"That's amazing," I said. "You can clearly see the moment my soul left my body for a few seconds."

After that, we sat on the stairs with our pumpkins and Ariana set the timer on the camera to take a photo of the three of us together.

"Everybody, say 'boo!'" Ariana said, running back to take her place on the stairs.

"Boo!" We all said at the same time.

When she showed us the picture, I teared up a little. We looked so happy. I felt so happy. I couldn't believe that three months ago I didn't know them, but now I couldn't imagine my life without them. I don't know what I would do without the girl with the colorful clothes and the electrifying personality or without the boy with a smile that was surprisingly even bigger than the one his pumpkin had.

But there's one thing I do know: October continues to be my favorite month of the year.

# CHAPTER THIRTY

November had officially arrived and, in this school, that only meant one thing: the end of the football season. The varsity team didn't do so well this season —something my brother hadn't stopped complaining about for the last two weeks—but the junior varsity team (the one Ty was on) managed to win nearly every one of its games. That meant that, when the day of the final game arrived, there was a lot of pressure on them.

Ariana and I hadn't gone to any of the previous games. This was in part because Ty said that it wasn't necessary for us to go, but mostly because we hated football. However, guilt had slowly but surely started to fill our minds because we wanted to support our friend, so when the day of the big game finally arrived, we decided to put our loathe for football aside and surprise Ty by going to the stadium to show our support.

I know this sounds like a bare minimum thing to do, but for us, it was like completing one of the twelve labors of Hercules. I don't even go to my brother's games, so it was a big deal for me to put a foot in that stadium.

"Guys? What are you doing here?" Ty asked with a big smile when we went to see him before the game started. "I thought you hated football."

"We do," Ariana said.

"But we came to support you," I added.

"Aww, thanks, that's really nice," he said. "But you shouldn't have. You're just gonna get bored."

"No, we won't," I lied.

"Yeah, we probably will," Ariana said at the same time.

"What are you doing?" I asked her.

"I'm being honest with my friend," she answered. "We will most likely die of boredom on those bleachers, Ty, but we don't care because we know this is an important game and we came here to support you. No matter how boring football is."

Ty laughed.

"Thanks, guys, but do you even know who we're playing against?" He asked.

"Of course not," I said.

"I couldn't care less," Ariana added.

"I think it starts with a P," I said.

"It's the Lincoln's Bulldogs," Ty said.

"Close enough," Ariana said.

"It doesn't matter," I added. "We're not here for the team or the school, we're here for you."

"Thanks," Ty said with a smile. "That means a lot."

"Johnson!" The coach yelled. "It's time to go."

"I gotta go," Ty said. "But thanks so much for coming."

"Good luck!" I said.

"Yeah, break a leg!" Ariana yelled while Ty was leaving.

"That's for theater," I told her.

"Man, I don't know. What am I supposed to say? Good balling?" She said.

"I think it's good ball game," I said.

"That sounds ridiculous," she said.

"Let's just go," I told her.

We went to find our seats, but the stadium was packed, so it took us like 15 minutes to finally find them. I didn't expect it to be so crowded, it was only a junior varsity game after all, but everything related to sports in this town was a huge event. When we finally sat down, the game had already started.

I usually hate going to football games because they're loud, hot, crowded, and the stadiums always smell like piss, but this time it was a little more enjoyable because I was concentrated on Ty, so for the first time I was actually excited when one of the teams scored a point—or something, I still don't quite understand how the scoring system works. The point is that this time I actually cheered when the whole stadium cheered instead of just rolling my eyes to the back of my head.

Ariana didn't have such a good time, though. She had never watched a football game before, much less went to one, so she was shocked by the loudness of the crowd and the brutality of the game.

"What the hell was that?" Ariana asked when four guys tackled Jeremy Nichols to the floor. "Why are they so aggressive?"

"That's how the game works," I answered.

"This is so barbaric. I feel like I'm in the Colosseum watching gladiators fight," she said.

"Bread and circus," I answered. "Speaking of which, you should go buy something to eat, it'll make time go faster."

She followed my advice and bought a hot dog and some nachos, which kept her happy for the first quarter of the game.

"Is it over already?" She asked when the first quarter ended. "Thank goodness! I thought it was gonna be longer."

"That was just the first 12-minute quarter," I said. "There are still three left."

"What?" She asked. "What are you talking about? First of four? Wait, did you just say 12 minutes? Those were not 12 minutes! It's already been like an hour!"

"Yeah, I don't get it either, but that's how the game works," I said.

"This is the stupidest sport ever," she said.

"I don't know about that, have you ever watched golf?" I said.

During the first two quarters of the game, our team was wiping the floor with the Lincoln's Bulldogs, but during the last two quarters, the tables turned, and the Bulldogs managed to pull a surprise victory.

"I can't believe they lost," I said when the game was over.

"What?" Ariana said. "They lost? I thought they were winning."

"That was like an hour ago," I said.

"Oh… damn, I really thought they were gonna win," she said.

"Yeah, me too. Let's go find Ty to see how he's doing," I said.

When we finally found him, he was with his family and a bunch of his football friends. They all seemed really bummed out, except for Ty, who looked strangely fine. When he saw us, he ran towards us.

"Great game, Ty," I said.

"Yeah, how are you doing?" Ariana asked.

"I'm fine," he said with a smile.

"Are you sure?" I asked.

"Yeah," he answered. "It sucks that we didn't win, but it's just a junior varsity game. There are more important things in life. And besides, we had a great season and there will still be plenty of games in the future."

I didn't expect him to react to the loss with such maturity. Not because I didn't think that Ty was capable of that, but because I know how intense some men can be about sports. I mean, the only time I've ever seen my dad cry was when the Patriots lost the Super Bowl in 1997.

"Anyway, what did you think of your first football game?" Ty asked Ariana.

"It was awesome," she answered.

"You're a terrible liar," he said.

"Fine, it was excruciating and barbaric," she said.

Ty laughed.

"But you did a great job," she added.

"Thanks. So what are you guys doing now? Are you going somewhere?" He asked.

"Yeah," Ariana answered. "We were going to get something to eat. Do you wanna come?"

"Of course. I'm starving," he said.

"Um, didn't you tell me that you always go out with your team after a game?" I asked.

"Yeah, we always go to Charlie's," he answered. "But you made the effort to come to the game, I rather go out with you."

"Are you sure?" I said. "This is the last game of the season, Ty. If you wanna go out with them, we understand."

"No, I'm sure," he said. "I rather go out with you, I'll go out with them some other time. Let me just go tell my parents."

He went back to tell his parents, who seemed to understand, but after he told his teammates, I could clearly feel the hate-filled looks they were throwing at us, especially Tony, who must've been thinking that we were stealing his cousin away from him. This was certainly not going to make me more popular with those guys, but I tried not to think about that and instead concentrate on the fact that Ty had picked us over his more popular friends two times in a row now. That was insane and it went against everything I thought I knew about high school behavior—which, to be fair, had come almost exclusively from teen books and John Hughes movies. But I guess Ty was more than a one-dimensional movie character.

# CHAPTER THIRTY-ONE

Things in the library have been going great. This week we finally crossed the double-digit barrier—we received 14 visitors, to be exact—and to celebrate this achievement, Mr. Dan bought a little chocolate cake to share with me, Ariana and Ty.

"I know this sounds like a small feat, but I can feel that it's just the beginning of something great," Mr. Dan said. "And I want to thank you, Hunter, for your amazing work these last few weeks. Many other people would've given up already, but you decided to go above and beyond to support this project, and I cannot thank you enough."

"Thank you for giving me the opportunity to be part of this," I said.

"There's nothing to thank," he said. "Now, let's eat."

"I thought we weren't supposed to eat in the library," Ty said when he received his slice.

"I won't tell if you don't," Mr. Dan answered him with a smile.

"Now, that's my kind of attitude," Ariana said with a mouth full of cake.

Also, since football season is finally over, I started tutoring Ty after work just like I promised. I had never tutored anyone before, so I decided to read a couple of books about teaching to prepare myself for it and I found some fascinating stuff. Apparently, there are many diverse theories about how humans learn, but the one that I found most interesting was the Multiple Intelligences theory. This is a theory developed by Howard Gardner to explain how humans learn differently from one another. He proposed that humans possess different types of intelligences in varying doses rather than one single type of intelligence. All humans possess the different types of intelligences, but we usually have one or a few more dominant than the others. The current school system is designed to benefit mainly the students with dominant logical-mathematical and verbal-linguistic intelligences, which I think is very unfair.

I believe that Ty's dominant intelligences are the visual-spatial one and the bodily-kinesthetic one. People with these types of intelligences tend to think in pictures rather than in words, have great body coordination, learn better with hands-on activities than listening to lectures, and have trouble understanding abstract concepts. This would explain why he's having such a hard time with Math and Biology, as well as why he's such a great painter and athlete.

In hindsight, I think it should've been obvious to me that Ty learned in a different way than me. Our Biology classes consist mainly of Mr. Jones talking and writing complicated words on the board, which is kind of boring, but I have no problem learning this way. However, whenever I look at Ty, he's always distracted, playing drums with his pencils, looking at the pictures in the book, or drawing in his notebook. I don't have Math with him, but I imagine the same thing happens there too. Contrarily, during Painting he rarely seems distracted because he always has something to do, it's more of a hands-on class than a listening class.

It's worth noting that the Multiple Intelligences theory hasn't been definitely proven and it has its fair share of detractors, but it made sense to me, so I decided to use it as a basis for my tutoring sessions with Ty. Instead of trying to teach him the concepts in the same way that the teachers had already tried to, I decided to focus on Ty's strengths and come up with new alternatives. For our first couple of weeks of tutoring, I chose to concentrate on Math because it was the subject that Ty was struggling with the most.

"Are you sure you don't want to join our little study group?" I asked Ariana on the day of the first tutoring session because I knew that her grades in Math could also improve.

"Nah, I'm fine with my B-," she said. "A grade doesn't define me… unless it's a 100. Let me know when you're ready to go home. If you need me, I'll be in the quiet section finishing my book."

I know, I'm as impressed as anyone that Ariana was reading a book. And a book I recommended, no less. So far, I had restrained myself from recommending her any books because I feared that she might not like them (she hadn't even read the books she was supposed to read for her English class), but these last couple of weeks in the library gave me the confidence to finally do it. All the students I had recommended a book to had loved—or at least liked—my recommendations, and if I could recommend a book to someone I barely knew, I could definitely recommend a book to my best friend.

I thought long and hard about which book to give her, but as soon as I started to think about all the things that she liked, the answer became clear. I recommended her *Alanna: The First Adventure*, the first book of *The Song of the Lioness*, a fantasy book series about an adventurous girl who trades places with her twin brother in order to become a knight. So far, Ariana had loved the book, which made me both happy for her and proud of myself.

But back to Ty, on the first day of tutoring, I decided to give him a diagnostic test with a bunch of problems of varying difficulty so I could identify the things that he was struggling with the most.

"What if I don't know how to solve some of the problems?" He asked.

"That's okay," I said. "If you don't know how to solve something, just leave it blank. I'm trying to help you, not grade you. This test is just to have an idea of where to start."

"Oh good," he said, "because I'm not really sure of what I'm doing, but I'm pretty sure that I'm doing it wrong."

The test result was very informative because I could notice that Ty had difficulty understanding the basic concepts of algebra and that had a domino effect on everything else. After all, if you don't understand the foundations, then you can't understand the rest, so that is where we had to start.

I didn't want to use the textbook that we used in class to explain these concepts to Ty because it only provided cold, rational descriptions with words that sometimes even I couldn't understand. It was like it written for someone who already had a PhD and not for an average high school student. So instead, I found a couple of great books that explained basic algebra with images and real-life examples.

I really liked these books because the problems in them were pretty amusing and imaginative, unlike the problems we saw in class, which were mostly just equations we had to solve. The teachers didn't give us any type of explanation as to why we needed to solve them or how we could apply that knowledge in real life. Everything was pretty abstract. They were just random numbers and letters that somehow we had to solve. I could definitely understand why Ty had a hard time solving these problems if he couldn't even properly visualize them to begin with, so I hoped that these books would help him with that. The only problem was that they were aimed at a slightly younger audience and it was fairly noticeable because some of the images were way too childish and colorful. I was worried that Ty would be offended when he saw them, but fortunately, that wasn't the case.

"I know these books look kind of childish," I said. "But I already read them and they're pretty good. The authors do a great job explaining the meaning and purpose of algebra and its concepts. They even helped me understand some things that I had not been able to understand in class, so please don't be offended if they look kind of childish. It's just something to begin with to solidify your bases."

"Don't worry, Hunter," he said, laughing. "Oh my god, you look so scared. I'm not offended, I swear. If you think it's a good idea, then I'm totally down for it. I trust your judgment completely. Besides, I'm in no position to be picky. I still can't believe that you're doing this."

"Okay, great," I said. "Then let's begin."

We spent a whole week reviewing the basic concepts, like what was an equation, a variable, a function, etcetera. It was tedious work, but it was totally worth it because once he understood those concepts, how they related to each other, and what was the purpose of it all, it was so much easier for him to understand how to solve the problems.

In the second week, we started solving equations, but first, we assigned a different color to each of the different types of variables so he could visualize and identify them better on paper. We also did this with the positive and negative signs so he wouldn't confuse them or forget about them, which is one of the main types of mistakes students make in Math tests.

And speaking of mistakes, we also made a list of recurring mistakes that he made when solving problems so he could avoid them in the future, as well as a list of different types of equations and problems with instructions on how to solve each different type. We color-coded and assigned an image to each of the items on these lists so Ty could remember them more easily. Mr. Dan was so impressed with the work that we were doing that he even lend us a whiteboard and some markers so Ty could stand up and move around when he was trying to solve the math problems and not just hunch over a notebook.

Frankly, I was very impressed with Ty's progress. At the end of the second week, I applied the same diagnostic test to him again and he went from being able to solve only two out of ten problems to being able to solve eight out of ten correctly.

"Is it correct?" He asked when he finished solving the last problem of the test on the whiteboard.

"It is correct," I said.

"Hell yeah!" He said with a jump. "Who knew kicking Math's butt was so satisfying?"

At the end of the day, it turned out that Ty wasn't really bad at math, he just needed someone to explain it to him differently. This made me kind of sad because it made me think about all the students that are left behind or that feel stupid because they don't have dominant logical-mathematical and verbal-linguistic intelligences. If scholars have known for years that people have different ways of learning, then I don't understand why we're still being taught with an archaic model that doesn't take this into consideration. I'm lucky because the system benefits me, but other students like Ty have to suffer because the people in charge of education refuse to evolve and adapt to the diversity in the classroom. It's not fair. After all, you can't judge a fish by its ability to fly.

# CHAPTER THIRTY-TWO

On Veterans Day weekend, Ariana invited me to go camping with her and her dad and I said yes faster than a speeding bullet for three reasons: 1) I love nature, 2) I love spending time with Ariana, and 3) If I didn't say yes, I would've had to go to my dad's 30th anniversary office party, which is something I'd been dreading for weeks. When I asked my parents for permission, they doubted at first because this party was a big deal, everyone from my dad's office was going to be there (which is precisely why I didn't want to go), but they were glad that I was going out more, so they eventually said yes.

Ariana also invited Ty, but unfortunately, he couldn't go because he was going to go out of town with his family, so it was only going to be Ariana, his father, and me. I had already met Mr. Matthys a few times before and he seemed like a nice person, but I hadn't had the chance to properly chat with him, so I was a little bit nervous when they picked me up on Saturday morning.

"Hey, Hunter, how are you?" Mr. Matthys asked when I got into the car.

"Hello, Mr. Matthys," I answered. "Pretty well, sir, and you?"

"How many times do I have to tell you, Hunter? You can call me Greg," he said.

"I'll try, sir," I lied because there was absolutely no way that I was calling him Greg. It just felt so weird and disrespectful.

"And please don't call me sir," he said, laughing. "I'm 38, not 56."

"Drop it, dad," Ariana said. "It's nothing personal, he just has a weird issue with authority."

"Oh, is that so, Hunter?" Mr. Matthys asked.

"No, sir," I jokingly answered.

They laughed like it was the funniest thing in the world and that helped me loosen up a little.

Our destination was Garner State Park, a state park located in Uvalde County, so it was going to be a long drive, but it didn't feel like it. Talking to Mr. Matthys was as easy as talking to Ariana. He was funny, warm, smart, and he had plenty of stories to tell about his youth around the world. When he was a kid, his father worked for a company that forced him to change residence every few years, so he spent his childhood living in Canada, Argentina, San Francisco, England, Brazil, Chicago, and Colorado.

"Most kids would've hated that," he said. "Hell, even my siblings hated moving around so much. But I loved it. I got the chance to get to know different cultures and many interesting people. Plus, it gave me the chance to reinvent myself every few years. If I didn't like the person I had become, I would just leave it behind and become a different one in the next city."

He liked moving around so much that he spent a year backpacking through Europe before going to college.

"My parents did not like that I did that," he said. "They didn't like it at all. They thought that I was wasting my time and that I was just going to get high and spend all their money in Europe. They thought that trip was going to make me forget about getting a degree and that I would prefer to live my life like a hippie managing a hostel for other hippies like me. I had to swear to them that I was going to come back to the US and get a degree. But first I had to do that. I had to take some time to think and reflect about who I was and who I wanted to be. And, after a year of soul-searching and adventures, I got back to the US and got into NYU. It was there where I met Lisa, Ariana's mother, the love of my life and the person that finally made me realize that maybe settling down in one place wasn't the worst thing in the world."

Unfortunately, Ariana's mom couldn't join us, she had other plans with her sister to visit an aunt out of town. It's a shame, though, because I haven't had the chance to properly talk with her, but from what I've heard, she's the one that taught Ariana how to be Ariana, so she must be a pretty badass lady.

"What about you, Hunter?" Mr. Matthys asked. "How are you doing in school? Ariana tells me that you're a great student."

"Oh, I don't know about that. I'm doing okay, I think," I said.

"He's just being modest, dad," Ariana interjected. "He's easily one of the best students in our grade. He's getting straight A's, he's doing a great job working at the library and he's even helping Ty with Math and Biology."

"Oh, that's right, you work at the library," Mr. Matthys said.

"Yeah, he was handpicked by Mr. Brooks to work alongside him," Ariana said.

"And what do you do?" He asked me.

"Well, a bunch of things," I answered. "I do regular Library Assistant tasks like shelve books and locate library material for the students, but I also help Mr. Dan with planning and executing new activities to get more students into reading. Oh, and I also write a book review once a week to try to convince students to rent that particular book."

"Whoa, that's pretty impressive, Hunter," Mr. Matthys said. "Your parents must be so proud."

Damn, that felt like someone punched me in the gut out of nowhere.

"Yeah... they are," I lied.

He was right, though. My parents *should* be proud. Then why weren't they? I mean, not to be cocky, but I'm a pretty good son. I'm smart, I get good grades, I'm unproblematic, I'm generally well behaved, I've never needed a lot of supervision, they have never had to force me to do my homework or study for a test, I don't drink, I don't smoke, I don't do drugs, I've always tried to solve my own problems instead of bothering them, I only ask for money when I want to buy books, and I even have a freaking job. That's like the textbook definition of a good son, then why are they always comparing me to my stupid brother and my cousins? Why am I not enough?

"I'm really glad that you two are friends," Mr. Matthys added. "Ariana is lucky to have found you."

"I'm the lucky one, sir," I said.

We arrived at Garner State Park at noon. Mr. Matthys had rented one of the old-time rustic cabins that were in the park, so we first stopped by to leave our luggage there before we could do one of the thousand things that Ariana and her father had planned.

"Have you ever been to Garner State Park before, Hunter?" Mr. Matthys asked me.

"No," I answered. "But I've always wanted to come. I've heard it's beautiful."

"Oh, it's gorgeous," he said. "I have a feeling that you're really going to like it.

The first thing we did was go horseback riding at the Elm Creek stables. The owners were very kind and, apparently, all proceeds from the rides go to feed and house the rescued horses that are found on the property, which is one of the main reasons Ariana and her father chose this stable over the other options.

For the ride, I was paired up with a beautiful yellowish brown horse with dark hair named Bubba, while Ariana was paired up with a reddish-brown horse named Thunder and Mr. Matthys was paired up with a gray horse named Toto.

I had never gone horseback riding before, so my hands were glued to the horn of the saddle as if my life depended on it—because, in my mind, it did. I was terrified of falling down and breaking something, but Ariana obviously wasn't because she kept grabbing her camera and taking pictures of everything.

"Say cheese," she told me when we were near a giant tree with red and yellow leaves.

"Stop that," I said. "You're gonna fall!"

"No, I'm not. Hunter, we're going like 3 miles per hour. Just relax," she said, raising her arms like she was on a roller coaster. "And now smile for the picture."

After an hour or so of horseback riding, it was time for us to go to our next stop: Old Baldy. But before we got there, we stopped at a nearby restaurant to grab something to eat.

"He was so beautiful," I said when Ariana showed me the photos she took of Bubba while we were waiting for our food.

"Yeah, but poor thing," Ariana said. "He looked so skinny."

"The owners told me that he was one of the last ones they rescued," Mr. Matthys said. "He was far skinnier when he arrived at the stables a couple of months ago."

"Poor Bubba," I said. "I wonder how would he look like if he had grown up under different conditions."

"You know, I was wondering that too," said Mr. Matthys. "Are you familiar with the concept of epigenetics, Hunter?"

"No," I said. "What is that?"

"It's a part of biology that studies how the environment can influence the expression of our genotype and modify our phenotype," he said. "Basically, it tries to explain how some environmental factors can affect the expression of our genes. You see, genes are very important to determine who we are, but they're not the whole story, they're just part of the equation. The environment we grow up in and we live in is just as important to determine who we are and who we'll be. It's not the same to grow up in an environment that's beneficial to you than in one that it's not. Not even the most gifted organisms can thrive in a hostile environment. For all we know, Bubba could've been the greatest racehorse in history, but he didn't grow up in an environment where his speed, stamina, and health were fostered. He grew up in a desert with very few resources and probably a lot of environmental stress, so he didn't get the chance to become the best version of himself. It's basically impossible to reach your full potential if the environment that surrounds you is not beneficial to you."

"Wow," I said. I had never considered how important the environment was to our development and how big of an impact it could have on who we are. I wonder how different I would be if I had grown up in a different environment (both in a worse one and in a better one).

"Forgive my father," Ariana said. "He's a molecular biologist, so he thinks that explaining complicated biology terms is a suitable conversation topic for lunch."

"No, it's very interesting," I said. "So, how exactly does epigenetics work?"

We spent the whole meal talking about genetics, epigenetics, and science. It was fascinating to talk about those topics with someone who knew so much about them.

When we finished eating, we immediately headed to Old Baldy, the most famous hill in the park. The hike was quite challenging—especially after eating—but the view was worth it. When we got to the top, I immediately sat on a rock to rest and admire the view while Mr. Matthys looked around and Ariana took pictures.

You could see the whole park from there, from the camping sites to the Frio River. I could even distinguish those brave enough to go into the river and float in tubes in the middle of November.

"Hell of a view, isn't it?" Mr. Matthys asked when he stopped looking around and sat next to me.

"It's gorgeous," I said.

"If you like this, you should definitely climb Ben Nevis, the highest mountain in the UK. The view from the top is incomparable," he said, with a longing look in his eyes.

"Do you miss it?" I asked.

"What?" He asked.

"Traveling around the world," I answered.

"Yeah, sometimes. But I wouldn't trade what I have for anything in the world," he said, looking at Ariana.

We stayed on the top until sunset because Ariana wanted to capture the reddish sky and the sun starting to hide behind the mountains from that breathtaking view. The climb down was more difficult as a result because it was starting to get dark, but Ariana assured us that the photos were worth it.

When we finally got down, we headed to the cabin for dinner. Under the moonlight, the contradictory features of the cabin were even more highlighted. It was both cozy and scary. Equal parts warm and sinister. I felt like it was just as likely to find the cast of *Little House on the Prairie* in the backyard as it was to stumble upon the Necronomicon in the basement.

After dinner, Mr. Matthys lit up a bonfire outside and we sat around it to roast marshmallows and tell scary stories. Needless to say, I was terrified—but I loved it. My favorite was a story Mr. Matthys told about a man who one night took refuge in an abandoned cabin in the middle of the forest. When he entered the bedroom, he was surprised to see that the walls of the room were decorated with incredibly detailed portraits of people who appeared to be staring at him with looks of hatred and malice in their eyes, but he decided to ignore them. In the morning, he was woken up by unexpected rays of sunlight entering from all over the room. Blinking, he was surprised to notice that the room had no portraits, only windows. I almost choke on my marshmallow when I heard that ending.

At 10pm, Mr. Matthys went inside to watch the news, but he let us stay outside a little bit longer. He just asked us to let him know when we were ready to go to sleep so he could put out the bonfire.

"Thanks for inviting me, Ari," I said. "I had a really good time today."

"Thanks for coming," she answered. "I'm actually surprised you said yes, most families have something planned for Veterans Day Weekend with weeks in advance."

"Yeah, actually, my family did have something planned," I said.

"Really? Why didn't you tell me? I would've understood if you said no," she said.

"Oh, don't worry," I said. "It was just a party my dad's office was throwing to celebrate its 30th anniversary, but I didn't want to go anyway."

"Why not?" She asked.

"I don't know," I said. "I just knew I wasn't going to have a good time. It was a party for the whole office, so it was going to be way too crowded and full of strangers, I prefer to be here. Besides, me and my family... we're not like you and your dad."

"What do you mean?" She asked.

"We're not as close," I said. "We don't get along as well as you, guys. Well, I don't."

"Why is that?" She said.

"I don't know," I said. "We're just too different. I love them, but sometimes I feel like a total weirdo when I'm with them. I feel like there's something wrong with me... I feel like a broken piece that doesn't fit in their perfect little puzzle."

"Wow, I'm sorry to hear that," Ariana said. "But you're not a weirdo, Hunter and there's nothing wrong with you, okay? Just because you're different from your family doesn't mean that there's something wrong with you. There's nothing wrong with being different. Besides, we all have family problems. No family's perfect. No one's life is perfect."

"Yeah, I guess you're right...," I said. "But earlier, when your dad was talking about epigenetics... it got me thinking about how different would my life be if I had been born in another family, you know? One more similar to me. I know it sounds awful, I love my family and I'm very grateful to have them, but I couldn't help but wonder if my life would be better. I mean, how different would I be? Would I be a better version of myself? Or would everything be worse?"

"I don't know about that, Hunter," she said. "I don't think anyone can tell you for sure. All I can say is that you probably wouldn't be the person that you are right now and that would be a shame because you're pretty awesome exactly as you are. But I know what you mean... it's tempting to imagine what our lives would look like if something were different... but it's a useless task. At the end of the day, all we can do is try to do the best we can with the cards we've been dealt."

"Yeah… yeah, you're right," I said.

"When am I not?" She asked.

I laughed. "Math comes to mind, but that's a different conversation."

"I still think that I was right about last week's problem," she said.

"No, I told you, it's mathematically impossible to divide something by 0," I said.

"Well, I guess we'll just have to agree to disagree," she answered.

I laughed again.

"But in all seriousness, Hunter, being different from your family does not make you a weirdo," she said. "If that was the case, I bet a large portion of the planet's population would be labeled as weirdos."

"I know, I know…," I said, "but it's not just that. Sometimes I feel so different from everyone else in school too, not just my family."

"So?" She asked. "Do you really wanna be like Tony and his troglodyte friends? Or like Charlotte and her group of backstabbing bullies? Hunter, it's a good thing that you're not like them. I know I must sound like a self-help book, but it's true. You're thoughtful and you're caring and you're empathetic and God knows we need more people like you in this world. Don't turn into a douchebag just because you think you have to. Life's too short to waste it pretending that you're something that you're not. Being kind is the new cool, don't let anyone tell you the opposite. And never ever feel bad or apologize for who you are, that's what my mom always says. If you're happy, that's all that matters, don't let anyone else bring you down or try to change who you are. Don't feel like you have to change to please someone else. You don't have to care about anyone's opinion but your own… and mine."

I laughed.

"But don't worry," she added. "I think you're pretty awesome exactly as you are."

I really appreciated that she said that because I knew that she really meant it. And I guess deep down I already knew that I shouldn't feel bad or apologize for who I was, but to hear it from someone else was completely different. It was like those words finally made sense.

# CHAPTER THIRTY-THREE

One of the dates that I feared the most has finally arrived: Thanksgiving. When all the family gathers around to eat turkey and say thanks while I hide in the bathroom to avoid them.

I mean, it wouldn't be so bad if it was only my parents and my siblings, but no, every year we go to Aunt Jenny's and celebrate it with the whole family, including some relatives I only see two times a year and family friends whose names I can never remember. And don't get me wrong, I love my family and I am happy to see them—well, some of them—but having them all under one roof for a whole day is kind of intimidating.

My mother insisted that we left our house early to avoid traffic jams, so we were some of the first ones to arrive at Aunt Jenny's, which was great because I hate it when everyone's already there and I have to go all over the house saying hi to everyone. As soon as we arrived, my mom went to the kitchen to help my aunt Jenny, and my dad and Axel went to the backyard to set up some chairs and tables so they could watch the game out there. I decided to go to the living room, where some of my uncles, aunts, and cousins were watching the parade.

They were alternating between talking about shallow and unimportant topics like sports and the weather and deeply personal topics like relationships and crushes. I didn't join the conversation because I didn't have anything that I wanted to add or share in regard to those topics, but, of course, that only led them to point out my quietness.

"Why are you so quiet, champ?" My uncle Rick asked me.

Jeez, if I had a nickel for every time someone in my family felt the need to point out my quietness, I would probably be able to afford a house by now.

"Yeah, you haven't said anything since you got here, Hunter. What's wrong?" Asked my cousin Jennifer.

Why do they always ask me what's wrong? Why do people always assume that loudness is equal to happiness and quietness means something's wrong?

"Nothing, I'm fine," I answered.

"He's always been very quiet," said my aunt Martha.

"He thinks we're gonna bite him," said my aunt Charlotte with a smile.

It was a joke, but I didn't like it at all. Still, I smiled so they would stop talking about me, but it didn't work.

"He's just a little shy, it's not a big deal," said my cousin Lily.

"Why is he shy? We're his family!" Uncle Rick said.

"Aunt Martha is right," my cousin Seth said. "He's always been like this. I remember once when we were little, we went to the park together and he didn't want to talk to the other boys, he preferred to play by himself in the sandbox."

"It was the same thing at birthday parties when you were kids," Aunt Martha added. "Instead of running around with the other kids, Hunter preferred to jump in the bouncing castle by himself or stay with his mom."

They laughed and started to tell more stories that supported my Aunt Martha's theory that I've always been like this. My ears started to burn up and I could feel my face turning red. I wanted to get out of there, but if I did, I knew it would only make things worse, so I just tried to laugh it off. But it was *hard*. And, what I hated the most, was that I was right there, but they weren't talking to me, they were talking about me. I was only the topic of conversation, but not part of the conversation. I felt ridiculed and on the spot.

And I knew they weren't doing it with the intention of being mean, it was not a big deal for them to talk and joke about my quietness, they were just chatting, but I hated it. It made me feel extremely self-conscious and insecure. I tried not to care about what they said, but it was impossible. That's one of the main reasons why I hate these kinds of family reunions, they always make me feel inadequate and weird.

I thought about what Ty told me, about how I taught him not to care about what anyone thinks of him, but I don't know how I taught him something I don't know how to do. But I tried to pretend that I do. I put on my best fake smile, laughed along with them, and acted like their words didn't hurt me. Luckily, they eventually changed the topic of conversation to something else, and, after a few minutes, I could get out of there without it looking like I did it because of what they said.

I went to the bathroom, looked at myself in the mirror, and I convinced myself that this wasn't going to be like the previous Thanksgivings. I wasn't going to feel miserable the entire night. I wasn't going to let their words affect me anymore. I wasn't going to give my family any more reasons to point out how weird I was. And, most importantly, I wasn't going to shed any tears because of them.

I washed my face and looked at my reflection in the mirror one more time before going back to the living room. There were fewer people now because some of my uncles had gone to the backyard to watch the game and some of my aunts had gone to the dining room to help set up the table, so joining the conversation was easier than before. My aunts asked me about school and I told them that everything was great, that I was doing pretty well in all my classes, and that I had amazing friends. I decided not to mention work because they would probably have the same reaction as my parents and they had already made me feel bad about myself, I wasn't going to let them make me feel bad about my job too.

After listening to my cousin Mark talk about his new girlfriend and my aunt Jenna talk about her kid's piano recital, it was finally time for dinner. I sat at the cousins' table next to Lily and Brad, two of the cousins that I got along with better, and we talked about school for a bit before my cousins Donald and Kelly monopolized the conversations of our side of the table.

As I ate and listened to Donald boast about his baseball skills, I looked carefully at all my cousins and I wondered if I would be friends with them if we weren't related. The answer to most of them was no. It's funny how blood bonds you for life with people you have little or nothing in common with.

After dinner, instead of splitting into two groups, as usual, the whole family went to the backyard. Aunt Jenny's backyard was enormous and she had a lot of chairs and tables, so everyone fitted perfectly. While there, I tried to socialize the best I could with some of my aunts and uncles. I think I must've answered the same questions (How you've been? How's school? Do you have a girlfriend?) at least like ten times. It was tiresome, but at least this time they weren't pointing out how quiet I was.

At around 10pm, my aunt Jenny gave a speech thanking everyone for coming to celebrate Thanksgiving with her one more year and then she stated all the things she was thankful for and she invited my other aunts and uncles to do the same. The speeches were all very different, some people gave heartfelt and emotional speeches while others used the opportunity to crack up jokes and try to make everyone laugh, but almost everyone mentioned that they were thankful for their children, for having health, and for having economic stability. It was nice.

After Uncle Jay gave the last speech of the night, Aunt Jenny put music on the loudspeakers and everyone pushed the tables to the sides so they could dance. I helped move the tables and chairs to the sides, but I didn't join my family at the improvised dance floor. I preferred to sit and watch them dance while I ate apple pie. I was very happy to see them happy.

But then I was hit by an unexpected wave of sadness because I felt like I was looking at a happy family through a window. I could see them having fun, but I wasn't a part of it. And even if I could be a part of it, would that be what I want? Would I feel as happy as they seemed? Or would I feel out of place with them? That's the way I've always felt with my family. Out of place. I love them, but I feel like I don't belong with them. I feel like I need to change who I am to fit in with them—and I don't want to do that. There's gotta be another place for me out there, right? There's gotta be somewhere I fit in. There's gotta be.

"What are you doing here, sitting by yourself?" Asked Uncle Richard (yes, the piece of crap), "Are you grounded or something?" He said, sitting next to me. He reeked of alcohol and cranberry sauce.

"No," I answered coldly.

"Have you finally found a girl to turn that frown upside down?" He asked.

I didn't answer him, I just shot him a glance of disdain.

"I guess not," he said. "Why do you always look like you have a stick up your butt, kid? You're always a buzzkill. You're always so quiet."

"And you never stop talking," I said, standing up and leaving him talking alone.

I walked towards my mom to ask her when we were going to leave because it was already past midnight, but, when I got to her, *Because You Loved Me* by Celine Dion started playing.

"I love this song! Dance with me, Hunter," she said and I complied. "Did you know that you danced this song when you were little at one of your school's Mother's Day festival? I think you were like six."

"Yeah, I think I remember," I said. "I had just learned how to read and the teacher made us memorize all the lyrics in three days."

"You looked so cute in your bumblebee suit," she said. "I

don't know what does Celine Dion has to do with bumblebees, but you looked so cute."

I laughed.

"Did you have a good time today, honey?" She asked.

"Yes," I lied.

"Good," she said and we continued dancing to that long and beautiful song.

On the way home, I realized that I never got the chance to say what I was thankful for, so I tried to make a mental list just for myself. I was thankful for my family, for my friends, for my job, and more than anything, I was thankful that Thanksgiving was over.

# CHAPTER THIRTY-FOUR

December has arrived and with it came a whole new bunch of visitors to the library. It seriously seems like Santa came earlier this year because just a few weeks ago we were celebrating finally reaching more than ten visitors per week and now we're close to 40. The library went from being a ghost town to a mildly visited Starbucks. And it's very nice to see that most of the students that come now return a few days later with some friends. Not all of them rent books, some just come here to relax after a day of school and play board games with their friends, but at least they're using the installations that Mr. Dan worked so hard on.

And speaking of Mr. Dan, he had the brilliant idea of putting up a suggestion box so students could make recommendations about what to improve, what books to buy, or even what board games to get. He wanted to put the box on the librarian's desk, but I told him that some students might shy away from putting a suggestion if they had eyes on them, so he ended up putting the box outside the library so that all suggestions could be 100% anonymous.

So far, many of the suggestions have been jokes and pranks, but there have also been some legitimate suggestions like buying Lemony Snicket's *A Series of Unfortunate Events* book series, getting Risk, the strategy board game, and even throwing a movie night, which is a very interesting idea that Mr. Dan is considering doing after the Winter Break.

As for the tutoring sessions with Ty, they have been going great. He went from a D- to a B+ in the biweekly tests that his Math teacher applies, something that made his already big smile even bigger. Now we have finally started to review Biology, a subject that I find infinitely more interesting than Math.

"How did you memorize all that?" Ty asked when I drew a cell on the whiteboard and explained the function of each of the organelles.

"I didn't," I said. "Forget about memorizing stuff. If you understand the concepts, you don't have to worry about memorizing them."

"Aren't they the same thing?" He asked.

"No," I said, "when you memorize something, you just learn the words but not necessarily the meaning behind them. I don't want you to only be able to say that the mitochondria are the powerhouse of the cell, I want you to understand what that means. If you understand it, then you will be able to remember it naturally without having to memorize the specific words that appear in the textbook."

"Okay... okay, I think I got it," he said. "Explain to me what each of the organelles does one more time."

But it wasn't as simple as that. There's a reason why we spend almost a whole term learning what's the function of each part of the cell. It's not something you can learn in 30 minutes. But thankfully, teaching Biology was way more fun than teaching Math because, after each lesson, we could do fun activities where Ty could apply his artistic gifts to solidify the knowledge he had just acquired. For example, after spending a week reviewing the different parts of an animal cell, we did an activity where I would read a definition from the textbook and he had to draw on the whiteboard which organelle within the cell matched the description.

But, although the activities were indeed more fun, Biology

was less hands-on than Math, so Ty had a little more trouble mastering this subject. When we were studying Math, we spent most of the time solving problems, which had immediate feedback. Either he got them right or he learned from his mistakes, but with Biology, most of the time was dedicated to explaining complicated concepts like cellular respiration and passive and active transport, which were kind of hard to visualize.

Whenever I noticed that Ty got frustrated because he didn't understand something, I would stop and encourage him to try to first visualize it and then make sense of it, not the other way around. And when I noticed that he was starting to get bored or that I was losing his attention, I would suggest going for a walk or playing a game of Jenga to recharge energies. This worked like a charm, especially the latter, because winning always puts him in a good mood.

"Yes!" He said one tutoring session when he won two games in a row. "Why can't classes have a Jenga break too? If teachers graded us with board games, I would be at the top of the class."

This gave me the idea to make a Memory game with Biology concepts to put his competitiveness into good use. But instead of matching pairs of the same image, we had to match the definition of a concept with the image of it. It was surprisingly fun. Even Ariana decided to join us and play.

"Yes! I'm ready to get my A," Ty said when he won the game with seven pairs. I came in second with five pairs, and Ariana came in third with four pairs.

"I very happy for you, Ty. I hope you do get an A in the midterms," I said.

"Jesus, I hope so too," he said. "Why do they have to be until January? I'm gonna forget everything during Winter Break."

"I know, it sucks," I said. "Hey, why don't we call it a day and we go get some milkshakes at Jambo's?"

"Are you sure?" He asked.

"Yeah, I think you've already proven that you have a pretty good understanding of everything we've seen so far," I said.

"Let's go celebrate."

"Alright, I'm in," he said.

"What about you, Ariana?" I asked. "You want to go for a milkshake?"

"Of course," she said. "The day that I say no to a milkshake is the day that I've finally been replaced by an emotionless robot with no taste buds."

"*Finally*?" Ty asked. "Do you want to get replaced by a robot?"

"I don't want to," she said, "but I doubt I'll get a say when the robot apocalypse happens."

I left them alone for two minutes while I said goodbye to Mr. Dan, and when I came back, they were arguing over whether a robot apocalypse was more likely to happen than a zombie apocalypse, a discussion that continued on our way to Jambo's.

"It's way more likely for a zombie apocalypse to happen," Ty said. "There are millions of scientists around the world, one's bound to go crazy and release a zombie virus that spreads all over the world. He wouldn't even have to try so hard, he would just have to release it in an airport and it would spread around the world in a day."

"No, it's way more likely that the machines rebel against us," Ariana said. "Technology is advancing by leaps and bounds. Computers are already more intelligent than us. How much longer until they realize that they don't need us anymore and that we're actually preventing them from reaching their full potential?"

"Come on, do you seriously think that *Terminator* is more plausible than *28 Days Later*?" Ty asked.

"Yeah, way more plausible," Ariana answered.

"Hunter, you're the deciding vote," Ty said. "What's more likely? A zombie apocalypse or a robot apocalypse?"

"I think I have to go with Ariana this time," I answered.

"Yes!" Ariana exclaimed.

"What?!" Ty asked.

"Sorry," I said. "You're right, a deadly virus can spread at any moment, but create zombies? That's pretty unlikely. It's way more plausible that, in the future, machines with artificial intelligence will get out of control and decide to kill all humans. I mean, machines already have too much power, they control our nuclear arsenal, for god's sake. Do you remember Y2K? All it takes is a little mistake for everything to go south very fast."

"Exactly," Ariana said.

"You two don't know what you're talking about," Ty said.

"Yes, we do," Ariana said. "But you're too proud to admit defeat. That's one of your biggest flaws: you're ultra-competitive."

"What? No, I am not," he answered. "Hunter, tell her that I'm not ultra-competitive."

"You are pretty competitive," I said.

"What?" He asked.

"Ty, the first time I went out with you, you challenged me to a race," I said.

"That was just for fun!" He said. "Wanna do it again? I bet I can win this time."

Ariana and I laughed.

"You have a problem," Ariana said.

"No, I don't," Ty said. "Fine, I'm competitive, but you guys are competitive too. It's human nature. Life's a competition."

"Calm down, Adidas," Ariana said. "I'm competitive too, but you're on another level. I bet we can convince you to do anything if we turn it into a competition."

"That's not true," Ty answered.

"Really?" Ariana asked. "Yes or no, would you start running as fast as you can if I told you that I could get to Jambo's faster than you?"

"Yes, but—," Ty answered.

"Would you learn how to make a pizza if I told you that there's no way you make one better than me?" Ariana interrupted.

"Well... I guess, but—," he said.

"Would you climb the Everest, even if you knew that it's dangerous as hell, if I told you that I could get to the top faster than you?" Ariana said.

"Umm… perhaps," Ty answered.

Ariana and I laughed.

"See? You have a problem," Ariana said.

"That doesn't prove anything," Ty said. "I can think of hundreds of things that I wouldn't do even if you turned it into a competition."

"Really? Like what?" Ariana said.

"Like running through the streets in my underwear," he said.

"Would you do it for a 100 bucks?" Ariana asked.

"… Okay, maybe," he answered.

Ariana and I laughed again.

"Interesting," I said. "I wonder what's a better reward: the satisfaction of winning or a tangible prize?"

"A prize, for sure," Ariana said.

"Really?" I answered. "I don't know, people can be pretty competitive. I think that, for some, the feeling of winning is better than a sum of money or a tangible object. I mean, look at Olympic athletes, they don't get a check with their medals, they just get the satisfaction of knowing that they're the best in the world. For some people, winning is the prize."

"No way," Ariana said. "I mean, I like winning too, but a prize is a prize. Feelings go away, but things are forever."

"I don't know," Ty said. "Hunter's right, winning feels pretty great. I think it depends on the prize, though. I wouldn't jump off a plane for ten bucks, but for a 1,000 I would definitely consider it."

Holy crap. We were five feet away from Jambo's when it hit me.

"I'll be right back," I said.

And then I ran. I left my friends behind and I ran as fast as I could back to the library. I had an idea I had to share with Mr. Dan and I couldn't wait any longer.

"Hunter, wait," Ty said behind me.

My friends were running after me, asking me to stop, but I couldn't stop. I was afraid that if I stopped, my idea would go away. I had to keep going.

I entered the library gasping for air and my friends followed soon after.

"Hunter? What's going on? Is everything fine?" Mr. Dan asked.

"What was that, man?" Ty asked.

"What the hell was that, Hunter?" Ariana asked.

"I'm sorry," I said with heavy breaths. "I… a contest. We need to do a reading contest."

"What?" Mr. Dan asked.

"We need to have a reading contest," I said. "That's how we get more students into reading. We organize a contest where the students that read more books in a semester win some kind of prize or recognition. High school students are competitive. They'll do anything to win if the prizes are appealing enough. But the prizes and the competition are just a Trojan horse to get them interested in reading. They'll come for the prize, but they'll stay for the wonderful experience of reading."

"Oh my god, that's brilliant," Mr. Dan said.

"You really think so?" I asked

"Yes! I think this can actually work," he said.

I ended up staying an extra hour at the library, planning out the details for the contest with Mr. Dan. Ariana and Ty were kind enough to go to Jambo's and buy milkshakes for us while we brainstormed possible prizes, rules, and ways of marketing it. We decided that money was the most appealing prize, the only question now was where to get it from.

"I don't think the school administration will give us the money," I said.

"Yeah, there's no way the principal would ever agree to that," Mr. Dan said.

"I could give up my salary," I said.

"Absolutely not," Mr. Dan said. "I'll find another way. Leave it to me, I already have a few ideas. Now let's get out of here. I can't believe I let you stay this late, it's already past 7pm. It's too late for you to walk back home, I'll drive you to your houses. Just finish your milkshakes first."

During the car ride to our houses, Ty revived the discussion of the zombie apocalypse vs the robot apocalypse, but this time he asked for Mr. Dan's insights on the matter. He also sided with Ariana, but I didn't pay attention to his arguments. I was too busy thinking about the contest. I was very excited about it. Somehow, I knew that this was a turning point. I knew it was a long shot, but something inside me told me that it was going to work.

# CHAPTER THIRTY-FIVE

Mr. Dan and I spent a whole week perfecting the details of the reading contest and designing publicity for it. But planning was all we could do because it was too late to launch it that semester, we had to wait until after the Winter Break to properly announce it. It was so frustrating to have an idea that could possibly change everything and have to wait to implement it. It was literally all I could think about at work.

It didn't help that I didn't have much else to do because, as the temperatures started to drop, so did our visitors. Students didn't want to read or study anymore, they wanted school to be over so they could go home and enjoy the holidays.

Honestly, it got to the point where I wanted school to be over too, especially after a blizzard unexpectedly hit the town on Tuesday night, a week before the school winter break began. When I saw the snow outside, I was ecstatic because I thought that school was going to be canceled. I had already imagined myself spending all day watching Christmas movies under a big fuzzy blanket. But sadly, in the morning, the blizzard had been replaced by a light snow flurry, so I had to get out of bed and take a shower in the freezing cold.

Everyone in school—including the teachers—seemed a little disappointed that the night blizzard didn't turn into a snow day, but no one was more disappointed than Ariana.

"This is a travesty," she said to Ty and me before we entered school. "We shouldn't be here. We were robbed of our snow day!"

"It's not a snow day," I said.

"Not a snow day?" She asked. "Is it snowing?"

"Not really, I mean—," I said.

"Blah, blah, blah," she interrupted me. "Is it snowing?"

"Kind of," I said.

"Is it a day?" She asked.

"What?" I said.

"Is it a day?" She asked again.

"... yes?" I said.

"Then it's a snow day!" She said as if she had just won a debate competition. "And we have a right as Americans to miss school. Our founding fathers fought for this. Our troops fight for this. Our…"

"Get to the point, Ari," Ty said. "We're gonna be late for first period."

"My point is… we're skipping school," she said.

"What?" Ty asked.

"What are you talking about?" I said.

"Look," she said, "I know in small towns like this you're used to letting institutions run you over like a frog on a highway, but that's not how we do it in big cities. Where I come from, if someone takes something away from you, you take it back."

"Ariana…," I started saying.

"By forcing us to be here, they are violating our rights," she continued. "If you guys accept this just like that, then what stops them from taking away your right to free speech in the future? Or your right to vote? Or your right to liberty? Are you gonna let them come for your rights so easily? Are you gonna let the Big Brother win?"

Nothing she said made any sense, but she said it with such confidence and drive that it made me doubt myself for a second. I think that if the whole *National Geographic* photographer thing didn't work, she had a prosperous future as a politician.

"We're not skipping school, Ariana," I said.

"But guys...," she started saying.

"Wait," Ty interrupted. "I think Hunter is right."

"Thank you," I said.

"This is a stupid idea," Ty said.

"Right?" I said.

"If we do it, we're gonna get caught," he said.

"Exactly!" I said.

"But I think we should do it anyway," he said.

"What?!" I asked.

"Yes!" Ariana said.

"I can't believe you're taking her side," I said to Ty.

"Come on, Hunt," he said. "It's gonna be fun."

"Yeah, what's the worst thing that can happen?" Ariana said. "Plus, it's been scientifically proven that if you don't skip school at least once per year, you won't be successful in life."

"Is that so?" I asked sarcastically.

"Yeah," Ty added. "I think I read it somewhere too."

"Having you two on the same side is the worst," I said.

"Come on, Hunter," Ariana said. "The winter break is almost here, we're not even doing anything important in class anymore."

"Yeah," Ty added. "Yesterday, in Biology, the teacher spent more than 20 minutes showing us pictures of his baby."

"He did that with you too?" Ariana asked. "What a weird looking baby, right?"

"Yeah," Ty said. "He totally looks like the baby from *Dinosaurs*."

"Oh my god," Ariana said, laughing. "You're right!"

"Guys!" I said, interrupting them. "I know we're not doing anything important in classes, but I can't miss work."

"I'm sure Dan will understand," Ariana said.

"And if he doesn't, just say that you had violent diarrhea all day, that way he can't be mad," Ty said.

"That sounds like a plan to me," Ariana said with a smile.

"Guys...," I said.

"Pleeeeeease," they both said with a begging face.

I wanted to say no, but they were right, we were not doing anything important in classes anymore, and no one even came to the library yesterday. If I stayed, I would probably spend my whole shift thinking about ideas that I could not yet implement. Maybe this is what I needed to clear my head and think about something else.

"Fine," I finally said.

"Great!" Ariana said. "Follow me."

I don't know how she did it, but she managed to get us out of the school grounds without being detected by any of the guards. I'm going to add Ninja to the list of possible career paths for Ariana.

"Now, where do we go?" I asked her when we made it out of school.

"I don't know," she said. "I didn't plan this far ahead. I didn't actually think I would be able to convince you to ditch school. Any suggestions?"

"We can go bowling, there's a place only three blocks away from here," I said.

"No, we can go bowling any other day," Ariana said. "Today has to be more epic than that."

"We could go to San Antonio," Ty said.

"What?" I asked, unsure if I had heard him correctly because the idea was so crazy.

"Yeah, we could go to the bus station, purchase tickets to San Antonio, spend the day there and be back by 5pm," Ty said.

"No! We're not doing that," I said.

"Hunter's right," Ariana said.

"Thank you," I said.

"We should get my mom's car and drive there," she continued. "San Antonio is not that far from here and she never uses it anyway, I doubt she'll notice it's gone."

"What?!" I asked.

"It'll be a fun road trip!" She said, enthusiastically. "Ty, you know how to drive, right?"

"Yeah," Ty said. "I still haven't gotten my driver's license yet, but my dad lets me borrow the car all the time to go to the st—"

"Absolutely not!" I interrupted. "Okay, a couple of ground rules: we're not going to leave the town and we're not going to break the law. Understood?"

"Fine, grandpa," Ariana said. "What do students here usually do on their senior skip day anyway?"

"Picnics, road trips, and pool parties," Ty answered. "Oh, we could go to the public pool on Main Street."

"It's winter," I said.

"Oh, right," he said.

"We can go to the Zoo," Ariana suggested.

"That's actually a very good idea," I said.

"Yes! I want to see a koala!" Ty said.

"But I think it's closed due to renovations," I added.

"No! Come on, man!" Ty said. "Why did you let me get excited about the koalas?"

"Sorry," I said, laughing. "We can go when it reopens."

"Deal," he said.

"What if we go to the Museum of History?" I suggested.

"Good one," Ariana said, laughing. "I'm gonna pretend that you're joking because I can't possibly take that suggestion seriously."

"I know," Ty said. "We can buy balloons and have a water fight in the park."

"Again, it's winter," I said.

"Sorry," he said. "I can't think straight with an empty stomach."

"Let's just go back to school," I said. "We can still make it to second period."

"No!" Ariana said. "There's gotta be a way to make this day epic. Why don't we go have breakfast and then we can keep brainstorming?"

"Fine," I said.

We decided to go to the Waffle House nearby. We expected it to be empty because it was Tuesday morning, but it was actually full of old people drinking coffee and reading the paper.

"Oh my god, is this Waffle House or Grandma's House?" Ariana asked when we entered.

"Wow, they're really out here at 9am on a Tuesday reading and eating waffles. I'm so jealous. I hope I'm like them in 40 years," I said.

"Try 60," Ariana said.

The hostess looked at us funny when we approached her. She was obviously wondering what a group of 14-year-olds was doing there. But thankfully, Ariana was able to convince her that we were actually 17 and assured her that we indeed had money to pay for breakfast. I was actually kind of surprised that she believed her, I mean, Ariana and Ty do look older than they really are, but only someone like Ariana could be able to convince anyone that a dweeb like me was actually 17.

Once we started eating, the brainstorming session continued and it pretty much went exactly like before: I suggested a perfectly reasonable and fun idea, then Ty suggested a crazy idea, and, finally, Ariana suggested an even crazier idea. This repeated itself for like 20 minutes until Ty finally proposed the winning plan.

"Why don't we go to the amusement park downtown?" Ty said. "It'll probably be empty, so we can get on the rides without the long lines."

"Yes!" Ariana yelled abruptly, spilling some of her orange juice.

"That's a great idea, Ty," I said.

We were so pumped about the fact that we had finally found a plan everyone agreed on, that we immediately finished eating and left. We took a taxi because the park was on the other side of town and we arrived there at 11am, which meant that we had approximately 5 hours of fun before we had to get back to our homes to pretend that we had been at school all day.

The amusement park, called Magic Jungle, was kind of small, old, and forgotten, that's why it was no one's first suggestion, but it had everything we needed for a couple of hours of fun: roller coasters, carnival games, and junk food. Thankfully, the snow flurry of the morning had been replaced by a shining sun and clear skies, so all the attractions were open.

As with Waffle House, we expected the park to be empty, but some schools were already on winter break, so there were a few families around—but not enough to increase dramatically the waiting lines.

That was not the first time I had gone to Magic Jungle, but it certainly was the most fun. Ariana spent almost $20 trying to win a stuffed butterfly for her mom at Stand-A-Bottle, Ty almost threw up because he decided to ride the biggest roller coaster of the park after eating overpriced nachos, and I nearly lost my voice from screaming so much in the Drop Tower. I also spent the last money I had on a ridiculously expensive photo of us riding the Log Flume, but it was worth it because we pretended to be sleeping during the fall, so we looked both ridiculous and badass.

We ended up having such an amazing time that my cheeks started to hurt from laughing so much. However, we were having so much fun that neither of us stopped to think about saving some of our money for the taxi ride back, so we had to return to our houses by bus because it was cheaper.

None of us had ever boarded that bus route before, but Ariana swore that she knew how to get home, so we trusted her. It was a big mistake, though, because, after walking a few blocks from where the bus left us, it became increasingly clear that she didn't.

"We're lost," Ty said after 20 minutes of walking.

"We're not lost," Ariana responded.

"There's nothing wrong with admitting that we're lost, let's just ask for directions," Ty said.

"I won't ask for directions because we're not lost," Ariana

said.

"Hunter, a little help here?" Ty said.

"Ty's right, we're lost," I said.

"Thank you," he said.

"But I won't ask for directions either," I said.

"What? Why?" He asked.

"I... don't like talking to strangers, especially on the street," I said.

Well, that was putting it mildly. I'd rather eat a worm than go to a stranger on the street and ask for directions. Or ask for anything, really. Just thinking about it sent shivers down my spine. That wasn't Ariana's case, though. She didn't have a problem talking to strangers, she just wouldn't do it because of her pride. So it was up to Ty to save us.

"Fine, I'll do it," Ty said.

"No, you won't, because we're not lost!" Ariana said. "We're exploring. Sooner or later we'll see something familiar that'll lead us back to our houses. And if we don't, then we can take a cab back home whenever we want."

"I don't think that's an option," I said. "We have 2 dollars in total."

"Oh," Ariana said after a few seconds. "Fine, you can ask for your stupid directions."

Ty did it and it turned out that we were not that far from our houses, but we were walking in the opposite direction. If he hadn't asked for directions, we would've been lost all afternoon.

When I got home, my parents were waiting for me in the living room. Apparently, they were notified by the school administration that I didn't go to school that day. But oddly enough, they didn't seem mad. They even smiled when I told them that I skipped school with Ty and Ariana.

I was expecting a punishment, but instead, I received a pat on the back. They said they understood and that the next time I wanted to skip school to just tell them so they wouldn't be worried about my whereabouts.

I left that interaction very confused. I was about to go to my room to question everything I thought parents were supposed to be when Ariana called on the phone to apologize.

"Did the school call your parents too?" She asked.

"Yeah," I said.

"I'm sorry, Hunt," she said. "I really thought we were not gonna get caught. I didn't mean to get you into trouble."

"It's okay, I had a great time. And my parents seemed more proud than angry anyway," I said.

"Ugh, you're so lucky," she said.

"Guess I am," I said.

"How did the school find out anyway?" She asked.

"Teachers take assistance, Ari," I said.

"Oh… right," she said. "Well, now we know for the next time."

I just laughed. That was typical Ariana, even when she got into trouble she was already planning the next adventure.

"Gotta go now," she said. "I have to call Ty and apologize to him too."

"Good luck," I said.

"Thanks," she said.

When I got to my room, I put the Log Flume photo on my desk, next to a picture of my family. I stared at it for a while and I smiled. I still couldn't believe that I skipped school. But I'm glad that I did because I'm sure that, when I'm old and gray, I won't remember yesterday's useless Biology lesson or my two hours of overthinking about the reading contest in the library, I will remember that one time my crazy best friends convinced me of going to an amusement park in the middle of a light snow flurry.

# CHAPTER THIRTY-SIX

I'm just going to say it: Thanksgiving and Christmas should be at least three months apart. One month is way too little time to do it all over again. Fortunately, my parents decided to book a trip to Cabo for the holidays, so this year we're going to skip the extended family reunion and we're going to spend Christmas and New Year's Day at the beach instead.

We arrived there on the 23 and, after leaving our things at the hotel, we went straight to the nearest mall to buy Christmas presents because mom told us that it was easier to buy them there than to buy them at home and take them to Cabo in the luggage.

The mall was big and everybody wanted to go to different stores, so we separated and we agreed to meet at the food court at 4pm to eat together. Well, "we separated" is just a saying because Axel went with dad and Ashley went with mom, I was the only one who decided to go by himself. I prefer it that way, I hate when people rush me while I decide what I want to buy. Besides, that's the way it has always been in my family. Ashley has mom, Axel has dad, and I have myself. I know it sounds sad, but it isn't—well, only a little.

I ended up being pretty happy with the gifts I bought. I got mom a necklace, dad a miniature replica of his new BMW, Axel a perfume, and Ashley a DVD set of *Lizzie McGuire*, a TV show she swears she doesn't watch anymore, but I know that she still loves it.

When I got to the food court at 4:15pm, Axel and dad were the only ones there.

"Did you find what you were looking for, son?" Dad asked me.

"Yeah," I answered. "What about you?"

"Almost," he said. "Your brother wanted the new Air Jordan's, but they were out of stock, so we're going to buy them when we get home. By the way, did you happen to run into your mom and sister while you were shopping?"

"No," I answered.

"Where are they? I'm starving!" My brother said.

"You boys go ahead and buy something to eat. I'll wait for them," my dad said.

Mom and Ashley arrived 30 minutes later, long after Axel and I had already finished eating. They hadn't even bought all their presents yet, they just took a break to meet with us, but they were going to continue shopping after they finished eating.

"What?" Axel asked. "And how much longer will you take?"

"I don't know," mom answered. "An hour. Maybe two. There are some very nice stores in this mall."

"Ughhhhhh," Axel said. "I wanna go now. Can I go back to the hotel by myself?"

"No," mom said.

"Why not?" He asked. "The hotel is only a couple of minutes away from here, I can go back walking."

"Because we're in a different country, you don't know the language, and, most importantly, because I say so," she said.

"Ughhhhhh," Axel said.

"Sweetie, I think Axel's right," my dad said. "The hotel's pretty close. I doubt he'll get lost on the way there, he only has to walk along the shoreline for less than a mile."

My mom looked at Axel, who had a begging look on his face, and after a few seconds, she finally said: "Fine, but only if Hunter goes with you."

Axel then turned to me, with a begging, but slightly more intimidating look on his face.

"Fine," I said because I didn't want to wait for my mom and Ashley to finish shopping either. She said it was only going to take them one more hour, but knowing them, it was probably going to take them at least three.

Dad was right, it was pretty easy to get to the hotel, we just had to walk on the road next to the beach for 30 minutes or so. But, halfway there, Axel saw two empty chairs on the beach and decided to go for a swim before it got dark.

"I thought you said you wanted to go to the hotel," I said.

"And now I want to go to the beach," he said. "Come on, it's only going to be for a few minutes."

"Ugh, fine," I said.

We took our shoes off and walked to the chairs. Axel took his shirt off and got into the beach in his shorts. I sat on the chair to wait for him because, even though I love swimming, I'm not a big fan of the ocean. The saltwater always gets into my eyes. Besides, someone had to take care of our stuff, so I sat back and enjoyed the sunset.

Axel came back after about 30 minutes.

"How was the water?" I asked.

"Salty," he said, sitting in the chair next to me.

"Great, can we go now?" I asked.

"What's the rush? Let me rest for a bit. Mom and dad are gonna still take a while," he said.

"Ugh, fine," I said, sitting back in my chair again.

"So what did you get me for Christmas?" He asked.

"A perfume," I said. "What did you get me?"

"A book," he said.

"How original," I said with a smile. He got me a book almost every year. It was always a dumb book with a funny title that I would've never gotten for myself like *Eating People is Wrong* and *How to Avoid Huge Ships*. But I appreciated the effort.

"If it ain't broken," he said. "Hey, can I ask you a question?"

"Sure," I said.

"Do you think UTSA is a good school?" He asked.

"The University of Texas at San Antonio?" I said. "Why do you ask?"

"Because I'm thinking of applying there," he said.

"What?" I asked. "I thought that you wanted to apply to universities on the west coast."

"I did," he said, "but lately, mom and dad have been pointing out that maybe UTSA wouldn't be such a bad option."

"Well, yeah, it's a good university, but is that really what you want?" I asked.

"I don't know. I mean, it would be easier to get accepted there than to get into UCLA or Berkeley. Plus, I could visit you guys on some weekends, a bunch of my friends are applying there too, and my girlfriend is going to the University of Dallas, so I could still see her. Besides, dad graduated from UTSA and he says that with a degree from there I could easily get a high-paying job at his company. So, you know, it doesn't sound so bad."

"I guess," I said, "but do you really want to stay in Mountdale forever?"

"I don't know," he said. "I mean, would it be so bad? My friends are there, my family is there, everything I know is there."

"Yeah, I guess it wouldn't be that bad," I said. "But only if that's really what you want. Don't let anyone else make that decision for you, okay?"

"Okay," he answered.

The following day was Christmas Eve and Axel, Ashley, and I spent the whole day at the beach while mom and dad organized the tours and trips we were going to take over the next days. At night, we dressed up and went to the hotel restaurant to have a very nice dinner. Mom told a few work stories, Ashley talked about how she was doing at school, and dad told a few stories about his time at UTSA—with absolutely no ulterior motive, I'm sure.

Afterward, we went to the hotel room to exchange our gifts.

We usually do that on the morning of the 25th, but mom programmed an early whale-watching tour the following day, so we decided to move our gift exchange from Christmas Day to Christmas Eve.

I really liked the gifts I got. Mom got me a very nice gray sweater, dad got me an iTunes gift card that he swore he was going to teach me how to use (but I knew that I probably was going to learn how to use it by myself), Axel got me a book titled *No, He's Not a Monkey, He's an Ape and He's My Son*, and Ashley got me a stuffed dog that looked just like Rufus.

After opening the presents, we drank cocoa and played cards with dad while mom made like a hundred phone calls to wish Merry Christmas to everyone she knew. Then we watched *It's a Wonderful Life* on the TV and everyone, including Axel, cried at the end.

It was an unconventional Christmas, but it was one of the best Christmas we've had in a long time.

The following day—and all days after that—were quite busy. Mom had wanted to come to Cabo for a long time now, so she planned an activity for every day of the week. We visited every tourist attraction possible, from Pulpo National Marine Park to Playa del Amor. It was all very beautiful—and very exhausting. I wish I could say that everything on this vacation was lovely and perfect, but it wasn't.

I got into a couple of fights with my mom because sometimes I wanted to separate from the group for a bit and watch something at my own pace. She also got mad that I carried my iPod and headphones everywhere, but I couldn't help it, I enjoyed listening to music while we were on the bus or walking in the wilderness. And I got mad that she had something planned for every minute of every day. There was no downtime, no time to rest, no possibility of spending some time by myself. It was exhausting and I always ended up in a bad mood because of it.

I didn't get why everyone looked as fresh as a daisy every day and I felt like I needed to take a 4-hour nap after every tour.

I knew that I had been born with an old soul, but I didn't know that I had also been born with an old body. By mid-trip, I was starting to feel like I needed a vacation from this vacation.

But on the 28th, I woke up earlier than everyone else and I couldn't get back to sleep, so I showered, I took a notebook and a pen that I brought with me from home, and I went to the hotel gardens to write for a bit. Ever since I started writing the reviews for the Book of the Week, I have fallen in love with writing. It's a great way to express myself and keep my feelings and emotions at bay. And I think it worked like a charm that day because, weirdly, that was the day that I slept the least but I felt the best. I was in a better mood all day, which made me enjoy the tours more, so I started to wake up two hours earlier than everyone else every day to have some time by myself before I had to spend the rest of the day in a bus surrounded by dozens of other tourists visiting beautiful but very hot tourist attractions. Warm weathers and lots of people make me grumpy, but writing and spending some time by myself relax me, so by doing that every day I was able to enjoy the rest of the trip more and stop fighting with my mom so much. Two hours less of sleep every day was a small price to pay for that.

On New Year's Eve, our second to last day in Cabo, we went to a dinner party at the hotel ballroom to celebrate. Mom told us to put on our best clothes because it was going to be a fancy occasion, and she wasn't lying. When I entered the ballroom, I felt like I was in a scene from *Titanic*. Everybody was dressed in tuxedos and long dresses and dancing to the slow songs that the band was playing. I even looked around to see if Leonardo DiCaprio or Kate Winslet were in attendance—sadly, they weren't.

It ended up being a very lovely evening. The dinner was delicious, the music was soothing, and we were seated next to a very nice Argentinian family that had amazing stories about their country.

At around 12:20am, after the counting down, and the hugs, and the toasts, I went out to the terrace for a bit to get some fresh air. The moon was very shiny that night and the sea was calm and empty. I sat on one of the benches and I started to think about everything that had happened in the last year.

I graduated from middle school and I started high school. I lost my best friend, but I gained two new ones. I joined a complicated and almost impossible journey to transform the library and improve the lives of the students, and I'm very glad that I did. I had a lot of bad times that year, but I had even more good ones.

I like the person that I was becoming. It wasn't perfect—not by a long shot—but it was me. I didn't feel so ashamed to be myself anymore. I didn't feel inadequate all the time anymore. I didn't feel the need to say sorry for everything I did and everything I was anymore. I was starting to like myself more and more every day and that, more than anything, was a huge accomplishment.

People like celebrating New Year's Day because it's the promise of a new beginning, but this time I didn't want to start over. I wanted to continue building on what I had been able to achieve over the last few months. That was my biggest resolution this year.

Here's to a great 2004.

# CHAPTER THIRTY-SEVEN

It's weird to admit it, but I actually missed school. I missed the routine, I missed my job, and, more than anything, I missed my friends.

"How was your school break?" Ty asked Ariana and me when he saw us before first period.

"Short," Ariana answered.

"Really?" I asked. "I felt like mine lasted forever."

All in all, it was a pretty regular day. Nothing really special happened during classes, but it felt oddly good to be back.

At work, it was a different story, though. The new semester meant one thing and one thing only: the official launch of our reading contest. And Mr. Dan surprised me with the news that he was able to get some astounding prizes for the contest: $500 for the first place, $250 for the second place, and $100 for the third place.

"Oh my god," I said when he told me. "Where did that money come from? Please don't tell me that you put it out of your own pocket."

"No, not at all," Mr. Dan said, laughing. "I talked with some friends and made a few calls and I was able to get a few sponsors. Look."

He showed me the printed posters for the announcement of the contest and at the bottom there were the names and logos of four different companies.

"They were very interested in the idea and they gave us the money for the prizes in exchange for some advertising," he said. "And guess what? I also talked to the local public library and they kindly decided to donate 100 of their books to us."

"That's amazing!" I said.

"And that's not all," he said. "I contacted the local newspaper and there will be a small article about the contest in tomorrow's paper. It will be on the second to last page, but at least it's something. And I know students don't read the paper, but their parents do and maybe this can lead them to motivate their children to enter the contest. And even better, maybe some other teachers or librarians see it and decide to do a reading contest in their own school."

He was even more excited about the contest than me, which I didn't even think was possible. His enthusiasm was contagious and it made me regain my confidence in the contest. During the winter break, I began to overthink and second-guess the whole thing. I started to consider that maybe the contest wasn't going to be the big success that I expected. Perhaps it was going to be one more of my big ideas that didn't go anywhere. Maybe it wasn't the brilliant game-changer that I initially thought it was. But if Mr. Dan had this much faith in it, then maybe—just maybe—it was going to work out.

Mr. Dan was going to officially launch the contest during tomorrow's morning announcements, but the promotional posters had to be pasted around school today so the students could see them in the morning.

"Five hundred bucks just for reading?" Ariana said when she saw the posters. "Sign me up!"

She and Ty accompanied me at the end of my shift to paste the posters all over the school.

"It's not just for reading," I said to her. "You have to win the contest."

"Great, I already have a head start, then," she said. "I read four books last semester."

"Those don't count," I said. "The contest starts until tomorrow, only the books read during this semester will count."

"What?! Then why did I read those four books?" She asked.

"Umm, because reading is great," I said. "Besides, you loved *The Song of the Lioness*."

"Yeah, of course I loved it, but… I want money," she said.

I laughed. "Then you're going to have to start reading more."

"Okay, then you're gonna have to recommend me more books," Ariana said. "And they better be as good as *The Song of the Lioness*."

"Alright," I said with a smile. I was glad that the contest was at least motivating Ariana to read more. "I can't promise that they'll all be as good, but I'll try my best."

"Hunter, buddy," Ty said. "Remember when I said that reading wasn't my thing? I was totally kidding. Could you please recommend me some interesting books that I can read so that I can win five hundred bucks? I mean, so that I can finally enjoy the wonderful experience of reading."

"Sure," I said, laughing. "I can recommend you some books too, Ty."

"Short ones if you can," Ty added.

I just laughed again. I knew they were both kidding, but I really hope that other students will also see the prizes and decide to read so they can win them. I really hope that this Trojan horse works.

When we finished pasting the posters, we returned to the library to say goodbye to Mr. Dan and then we headed home.

"So, what's the plan for today?" Ty asked when we got out of the school grounds.

"Umm… sleep," I answered.

"I second that," Ariana said. "It's not easy going from sleeping eleven hours a day to seven."

"What? No! Come on, you guys," Ty said. "It's our first day back together! We should do something fun."

"Sleeping is fun," I answered.

"Very fun," Ariana added.

"No, something more fun!" Ty said. "You can sleep later, but for now, let's seize the day."

I really wanted to go back to my house and take a nap, but I couldn't say no to Ty, he looked like a puppy that desperately wanted to play fetch.

"Fine," I said. "But let's keep it low-key. No taxi cabs, no buses, and definitely no San Antonio."

"Deal," Ty said.

We ended up buying a large pizza and eating it at the park.

"Oh my god, this pizza is so good," I said.

"Right?" Ty said. "I knew you were gonna like it. How about you, Ariana? Do you like it?"

"Yeah, of course I do," she said. "There are no bad pizzas."

"What are you talking about?" Ty said. "Of course there are bad pizzas."

"No, there are not," Ariana said. "That's just a rumor started by burger companies. I have never eaten a pizza that tastes bad. It's impossible to make a pizza that tastes bad."

"What about pineapple pizza?" Ty asked.

"... Okay, you may have a point," Ariana said.

After we finished eating, we laid down on the grass and we talked about anything and everything. From our favorite season...

"Winter for sure," I said.

"Fall," Ariana said.

"Summer," Ty said.

"Aww, now I feel bad for Spring," I said. "No one picked it."

"Don't feel bad for it," Ariana said. "If it wanted to be more popular, it would have more holidays and fewer allergies."

"True," I said.

... to the movie tropes that annoy us the most...

"I hate when characters only have to take their glasses off to be gorgeous," I said.

"I hate when in action movies the hero is fighting against a large group of bad guys and he is able to defeat them because they attack him one by one," Ty said. "That is so stupid, if they attacked him all at once they could easily overpower him."

"I absolutely hate when in romantic movies the male lead is rejected by the female lead and he keeps insisting over and over and over again until she finally says yes," Ariana said. "That's not romantic, that's stalking."

… to our favorite ice cream flavor.

"I think strawberry," I said. "Or mint chocolate chip."

"Probably cookies and cream," Ariana said.

"For me, I think it's vanilla," Ty said.

… to our opinions on having children…

"I can't wait to have a kid," I said. "They're so adorable."

"Same!" Ty said. "I think I would be a great dad."

"Really?" Ariana. "I mean, sure, the idea of having a child sounds fun, but I don't know, taking care of another life? I can barely take care of myself."

"Oh, that's a good point," Ty said. "I think somewhere in my room there's a Tamagotchi that's still waiting to be fed since 1999."

… to our favorite superheroes…

"Come on," Ty said. "There's no better superhero than Batman."

"Umm, of course there is," Ariana said. "Have you heard of Wonder Woman? She could totally kick Batman's ass."

"Yeah, but this is not about who's stronger," Ty said. "This is about who's cooler and there's no one cooler than Batman."

"Oh, yeah, there's nothing cooler than a 40-year-old goth man with daddy issues," Ariana said. "Hunter, what do you think?"

"I don't know," I said. "I like Superman."

… to our life goals.

"I want to do something important," I said. "And I want to help people."

"I want to live a fulfilling and exciting life," Ariana said. "The last thing I want is to be bored."

"I don't know," Ty said. "I just want to be happy."

I loved that I could literally talk to them about anything. I'm so glad that I found them—or that they found me. I don't know what I did to deserve such good friends, but I'm glad that I did. To be honest, I was still kind of waiting for a bucket of pig's blood to fall on my head any day now because I still couldn't believe that, in this town and in that high school, I was able to meet two people that I liked so much and with whom I felt so comfortable.

I mean, that day we did "nothing" and I still had the time of my life. I loved that we didn't need to do anything outlandish or wild to have fun. All we needed was good food, a nice spot, and dozens of random conversation topics.

# CHAPTER THIRTY-EIGHT

Work, work, work. That has been my life for the last two weeks. Midterms start next week, so I've been studying like crazy whenever I have free time. I've also resumed my tutoring sessions with Ty to help him prepare for the exams. They are time-consuming, but also quite helpful.

"I'm so sorry, Hunter," Ty said during one of our sessions. "I'm sorry that I'm making you waste your time like this. You don't have to feel obligated to keep tutoring me anymore, I know you have your own things to study."

"Don't be silly, Ty," I said. "It's no problem. Besides, you're not the only one that's learning. This helps me study too."

That wasn't a lie. Thanks to Ty, I've realized that I love teaching. It's way more fun to learn something by explaining it to him than by listening to a boring lecture or by doing monotonous exercises. The only problem was that I only helped Ty with Math and Biology and I had another four classes that also required my attention.

I knew I should've started studying during the winter break, but of course I didn't. I mean, who studies during the holidays? Teachers always tell us to do it, but I don't know anyone who actually does. I should've done it, though. If I had done it, I would not be suffering so much right now. But of course I didn't.

Mr. Dan knows how important midterms are, so he offered me two weeks of "vacation" from work so I could concentrate on studying, but I rejected the offer. I couldn't leave now that the reading contest had officially started. This was my baby, I didn't want to miss its first steps.

And speaking of the contest, the library has been PACKED these last couple of weeks. Not everyone has come for the contest, of course. A lot of students have come to study for the midterms and rent the books of their respective classes, but a surprising number of students have visited the library because they want to win the $500 dollars.

Many have not returned after renting their first book, but a few have become "regulars" at the library since the contest began. For example, there's a freshman boy with brown hair and green eyes named Brian who loves mysteries and has so far read three of the Agatha Christie novels we have. I like him, he's friendly and smart and, so far, he has come to the library almost every day since the contest began. There's also a very tall junior boy with curly dark hair named George, who is a huge fan of *The Lord of the Rings* movies and has started reading some of the other books by J. R. R. Tolkien for the contest. He told me that he had wanted to read *The Hobbit* for a few years now, but that he had never managed to do it, so when he saw the poster for the reading contest, he took it as a sign that it was finally time to read it. There's also a redheaded sophomore girl named Hope that loves *Harry Potter* and young adult romance novels. She reminds me a bit of Hermione Granger because she's extremely intelligent and also quite pretty. Linda and Stacy, the *Charmed* fans from last semester, have also been coming more frequently due to the contest and are currently reading Anne Rice's *Vampire Chronicles* book series.

So far, more than 50 students have entered the reading contest. And they all want the first place prize. But winning is not as simple as renting a book and return it three days later. They have to prove that they actually read the book by answering a questionnaire that includes making a summary of the book, describing their favorite character, and writing what they learned from reading it. I know it sounds like a lot of work, but it is to help us prevent cheating.

And it has worked out very well so far. In these few weeks, we already caught someone who rented *The Little Prince* and then described the plot of the movie *Coming to America* in the questionnaire thinking that it was based on that book. Similarly, a different student claimed to have read the book *Animal Farm* only to describe the plot of the movie *Chicken Run*. I got to admit that they might not have honor, but they do have creativity.

We decided to keep the book counts undisclosed. At first, Mr. Dan and I thought about having a scoreboard in the library so everyone could see who was winning, but we ultimately decided against it because it might discourage other students from joining the contest. But if they don't know who is winning and by how much, everyone can believe that they have a shot at winning.

To promote the contest, Mr. Dan also started opening the library during the lunch breaks. I volunteered to help him during my lunch break, but sadly, he prohibited it.

"No way," he told me. "It's already enough that you sacrifice your afternoons to help me, I won't let you sacrifice your lunch breaks too."

"Alright," I said, begrudgingly.

I've gone to the library a couple of times during my lunch break, though. But only as a visitor, not as a worker. I wanted to see how things were going. At first, I feared that it would be empty, but both times I was surprised to see at least 20 people in it. Granted, it was a week before midterms and a lot of them were probably there to study, but I like to think that some of them were there to escape for a few minutes from the pressures of school. That some were there to travel to a new world or to live someone else's life through the magic of reading. I like to think that some people were there because they had fallen in love with reading. And I like to think that I had something to do with that.

# CHAPTER THIRTY-NINE

Midterms are officially over and, to celebrate, Mr. Dan decided that it was time to organize a movie night at the library. We discussed a lot about which movie we should project. It had to be based on a book, so we considered a variety of films, including The Lord of the Rings, Jurassic Park, The Wizard of Oz, Jaws, and even The Godfather. But, in the end, the answer was obvious: it had to be the first Harry Potter movie. It was accessible, beloved, and very entertaining.

The screening was going to start at 8pm, but I arrived an hour earlier to help Mr. Dan with the decorations.

"Hello, Hunter," Mr. Dan said. "How were your midterms?"

"Hey, Mr. Dan," I said. "They were okay, I think."

"I bet you did way better than okay," he said.

"I hope so," I said.

"Come take a look at this," he said, walking towards a snack table that he had set up next to the Librarian's desk. It had popcorn, chips, chocolates, beverages, and four bowls filled with different colored candy to represent each of the Hogwarts' houses.

"What do you think?" He asked.

"Wow, this is impressive," I said. "Everything looks delicious. Wait, is that butterbeer?"

"Oh, yeah," he said, pouring me a glass. "I looked for a recipe on the internet and I made it at home. Do you want to try it?"

"Of course," I said, accepting the glass.

I'm not going to sugarcoat this: it was awful. I had never had butterbeer before, but I'm pretty sure that it wasn't supposed to taste like that. And if it did, then I don't understand why everyone on *Harry Potter* seemed to love it.

"How is it?" Mr. Dan asked.

"It's good…," I lied. But I'm sure he could see the disgust on my face.

"It's awful, right?" He asked.

"It's not the best…," I said.

"Shoot," he said. "I didn't like it either, but I thought that maybe it was because I don't like butterscotch. Thank God I bought other beverages too, I'll just throw this one out."

"No, don't," I said. "You already worked so hard on making it. Besides, it's not the best, but it's definitely not the worst either. If there are people that like the gross papaya juice from the cafeteria, then I'm sure there will be someone that likes it."

"Hmm, maybe you're right," he said. "Maybe it only needs more sugar. Wait here, I think I have more in my car."

I started to worry about how much money he had spent for tonight. Not only had he bought all the snacks, but he also bought some pretty incredible Hogwarts decorations for the library. I feared that it would be all for nothing and that no one would show up. It was a Friday night after all, and there were a lot of parties being thrown to celebrate the end of exams.

But my worries were put to rest when George and Hope showed up on time—and dressed up as Hogwarts students.

"Oh my god, you look amazing, guys," I said. "I'm so glad you could make it."

"A projection of *Harry Potter and the Sorcerer's* Stone? I wouldn't have missed it for the world," Hope said, twirling her Gryffindor robe.

"I would've preferred a projection of *The Fellowship of the Ring*," George said. "But *Harry Potter* is okay too, I guess."

"We are not having this discussion again," Hope said. "*Harry Potter* is better, deal with it."

"Said no one ever," George answered.

The two of them had become very good friends since they met in the library a couple of weeks ago. I even made a bet with Ty and Ariana that they would probably end up dating before the semester was over.

A few minutes later more people arrived, including Suzie, Linda, and Brian, who was also dressed up as a Hogwarts student, but he had a Ravenclaw robe on.

"Where's your robe, my fellow Ravenclaw?" Brian asked me.

"Oh, I… I left it at home. I came in a hurry and left it in the kitchen," I lied.

I did have a Ravenclaw robe, but I never even thought about wearing it tonight. The posters to promote the movie night encouraged the students to come dressed up, but I didn't think anyone would actually do it. I didn't wear mine tonight because I was afraid of being the only one to do it. I didn't want people to make fun of me. But now I regretted it. So far, seven people had arrived dressed up and they all seemed to have a lot of fun comparing robes and fighting about which Hogwarts house was better.

"Rats! Now I have to represent our house alone," Brian said.

"Sorry," I answered. "Next time, I promise."

We joined Hope and George, who were already sitting down, and Brian started to talk to them about the midterms. I spaced out from the conversation for a few minutes because I couldn't believe how many people had actually shown up. There were like 25 people already. And what surprised me even more was that I didn't know them all. I knew like half of them, but I had no idea who the other half was. I recognized some faces from the time I visited the library during the lunch break, but I didn't know their names. I wanted to, though. I wanted to know who they were and what they liked and why they were there. I wanted to encourage them to keep visiting the library and keep reading and I wanted to talk to them about books. I wanted to get to know them because I knew that we had at least something in common and that made me feel good.

I turned back to look at Mr. Dan, who was setting up the

projector, and I could see that he had the same little smile that appeared on his face when the first students started to show up. When I saw this, I smiled too. He deserved this. Working in the library was not easy, but it was worth it.

The movie was about to start and Ariana and Ty hadn't arrived yet. To be honest, I didn't even know if they were going to come. Ariana said she would, but she's always late, so I wouldn't be surprised if she arrived halfway through the movie. Ty, on the other hand, said he would try to make it, but I wasn't holding my breath. He wasn't such a big *Harry Potter* fan and I'm sure his football friends must have invited him to a bunch of parties tonight.

"Is this seat taken?" Asked a familiar voice behind me.

"Ari! You came on time! … -ish," I said with surprise.

"Ha-ha," Ariana said sarcastically. "I wanted to arrive before the popcorn ran out."

"You're in luck because we still have a lot. We'll be right back, guys," I said to Brian, Hope, and George.

"Wow," Ariana said when she saw the snack table. "You guys really spared no expense."

"Thank Mr. Dan," I said.

"Oh my god, this candy's amazing," she said after grabbing from the Gryffindor bowl.

"Yeah, everything's delicious," I said. "Well, except for the butterbeer. Stay away from it. But if Mr. Dan asks you, please tell him it's good."

"You got it," she said.

While Ariana grabbed some more snacks, I turned around to see if any more people had arrived and I was surprised to see a boy with a familiar face entering with a girl. I knew I had seen him before, but I didn't know where.

"Does that boy seem familiar to you?" I asked Ariana.

"Yeah, he looks like Shaggy from *Scooby-Doo*," she answered.

I busted out laughing because he was wearing a green shirt and brown pants, so I could see the resemblance.

"No, I'm serious," I said. "Haven't you seen him before?"

"Yeah, in the *Scooby-Doo* movie," she said.

"Stop it," I said with a smile.

"Sorry," she said, laughing. "No, I haven't seen him before."

And then it hit me. I *had* seen him before. In my house, actually. He was a friend of my brother. He was the captain of the tennis team. And the girl was in the drama club, she was Juliet in last semester's production of *Romeo & Juliet*. What were they doing here? Were they lost? Not likely, they had already taken a seat. Were they big fans of *Harry Potter*? Possible, but why come all the way to watch it in a low-quality projector at the school library when you can watch it at home? Could it be possible that Mr. Dan's dream was actually coming true and the library was turning into a place where all students could come and hang out, including the "popular" ones?

And speaking of popular guys.

"Ty! You made it!" I said when I saw him entering through the door.

"Of course I made it," Ty answered with a smile.

"I thought you didn't like *Harry Potter*," Ariana said.

"I don't," he said. "But who knows? Maybe this time I'll like it."

"Wanna try the butterbeer?" Ariana asked.

The movie projection was very enjoyable. Most of us had already seen the film before, so the projection was filled with side chatter about the things we liked, the things we hated, the things that were going to be important in future movies, and the things that made no sense.

When the movie ended, Mr. Dan gave a speech thanking everyone for coming and he encouraged them to leave their opinions and suggestions about other things they would like the library to do in the suggestion box outside. He also announced that there was going to be a *Harry Potter*-themed trivia contest, something that I didn't know about. Not everyone could stay for the trivia because it was already late, but those who stayed were all in on it. I decided to participate too since I didn't help Mr. Dan with the questions—and because I do love *Harry Potter*.

Unsurprisingly, though, Hope won. She beat me in the final round when I couldn't remember the name of the little blue flying creatures that appear in *Harry Potter and the Chamber of the Secrets*, my least favorite book and movie of the series—I hate spiders, snakes, and humanoid cats. She won a little box of Bertie Bott's Every Flavor Beans, which she shared with all of us.

"Gross," Brian said when he ate his bean. "It tastes like earwax."

"That's the risk you take when you grab one," Hope said. "Just be glad you didn't get a vomit-flavored one."

"Wait, how do you know what earwax tastes like?" Ariana asked.

"I don't wanna talk about it," Brian answered.

It was already past 11pm, but there were still like ten people in the library. Some I knew and some I didn't. Some were still waiting for their parents to pick them up and some still didn't want to go, so we decided to play some board games to pass the time.

"Hey, you're the one that writes the book reviews, right?" One of the girls that I didn't know asked me when I accidentally knocked down the Jenga tower.

"Umm… yeah. Yes, I am," I answered. "I'm Hunter."

"I know," she said. "I really like them. Why didn't you publish one this week?"

"Oh…," I said. "I was taking a break to study for midterms. But next week I'll start publishing again."

"Great, I'm looking forward to it," she said.

"Yeah, whatever book it is, please save me a copy," said one of the other boys that I didn't know.

"That's not fair," said the girl. "What if there's only one copy? I want to read it too."

"You can have it after me," he said.

"Yeah, right. I'm still waiting for *Whale Talk* to be returned, and that was the Book of the Week of three weeks ago," she said.

"I know," he said. "I wanted to read that one too and I couldn't wait any longer, so I bought it. It's pretty good, I can lend you my copy if you want."

"Would you?" She asked. "That would be amazing, thank you."

"Sure, I actually think I have it in my car," he said. "Wait right here, I'll bring it to you."

"I'll come with you," she said. "My mom's probably already waiting for me in the parking lot anyway."

"Okay," he said.

"See you, guys," the girl said.

"Yeah, see you," said the boy.

"Bye, nice to meet you," I said.

"Wow," Ty said. "For someone who once told me that he didn't want to be popular, you seem to be getting quite popular."

I chuckled.

"Yeah, right," I said.

Afterward, the rest of the students began to go little by little until only Ariana, Ty, and I were left. We helped Mr. Dan clean and then we sat on a couch to rest while we waited for my mom to pick us up.

"I gotta admit that I really liked the movie," Ty said. "It was way too long and it makes no sense that nobody noticed that that guy had another face on the back of his head, but it was fun."

"Yeah, there are a lot of plot holes in the books too," I said. "But you enjoy them more when you don't think too much about them."

"Do you have the books here?" Ariana asked.

"Yeah," I said. "Actually, after the movie, someone decided to rent one of the two copies we have of *Harry Potter and the Sorcerer's Stone* and two more decided to rent the third book, *The Prisoner of Azkaban*, to read it before the movie comes out in the summer."

"Why don't they just wait for the movie?" Ty asked.

"That's like me asking you why don't you skip watching a football game and just wait for the recap on the 11 o'clock news," I said.

He just laughed.

"Do you want me to save you the other copy of *The Sorcerer's Stone*?" I asked Ariana.

"Maybe," she said. "Let me first finish *Annie John* first and then we'll talk."

"Look what we have here," Mr. Dan said, entering with the suggestion box.

We hadn't opened it in a few days, but we were very surprised by the large number of papers that filled the box.

"Oh my god," I said. "Are they real? Are they actually notes written by students or did someone confused the box with a trash can again?"

"No, they're all real," Mr. Dan said.

Ariana was the first to grab one.

"This one says: *It's not a suggestion, but I wanna thank you for what you've done with the library. It has become my little refuge from the loud and mean world that high school can be. Keep up the good work.* Aww, that's nice," she said.

"This one says: *Thank you for opening the library during the lunch break. Please don't close it again. I hate the cafeteria, it's always way too noisy and crowded. It's nice to have a quiet place to sit back and relax from the madness of the day.* Well, that settles it. The library will continue to open during the lunch breaks," Mr. Dan said.

"This one's just a drawing of a dick," Ty said.

"Oh yeah," I said. "We get a couple of them each month. I pity the person who leaves them, he probably thinks that he's actually funny."

"It's not even a good drawing," Ty said.

"This one's from today," Ariana said. "It says: *Thanks for the movie night! It's exactly what I needed after a stress-filled week. It was so much fun. My mom's always bugging me to go out, but*

*I always feel out of place whenever I go to parties. Tonight, that didn't happen, though. I was in very good company and I felt really comfortable. I've never been very good at making friends, but tonight I met some wonderful people with whom I have many things in common. Thank you so much for that.* Aww, that's so sweet. I wonder who wrote it."

"This one's also from today. It says: *I went to the projection of The Sorcerer's Stone and I had a blast. Harry Potter, few people, and leaving before 11pm? Now that's my kind of party! Please continue to do more things like this for people like me who don't like social events filled with booze and loud music but still want to go out and meet new people. P.S.: The butterbeer tasted worse than actual beer, but everything else was delicious!* Well, I'm glad he or she liked everything else," Mr. Dan said with a smile.

I was very surprised by all of those notes. So much so that I even grabbed them to verify that they were real. I wanted to make sure that they weren't written by Mr. Dan to lift morale. But they weren't. They were actually real. I read them again and I was surprised once again.

But I wasn't surprised because students were actually enjoying the library or because they had a good time tonight, I was surprised because I could've written every one of those notes—well, except for the penis one. I knew exactly how the people who wrote them felt and I knew exactly what they were talking about. I don't know why, but that made me feel… good. It was a strange feeling that I don't really know how to describe. For a moment, I didn't feel so alone in this town. It was nice to know that there were other people like me out there. For a moment, I didn't feel like such a weirdo.

# CHAPTER FORTY

"Are you going out today?" My mom now asked me every weekend. I hate that question so much because it feels more like a challenge than an actual question.

Ever since I went to that party with Ty back in September, a can of worms was opened. I could no longer spend all of my weekends at home because my parents expected me to go out. Gone were the days when I could spend all weekend long in my bedroom reading a book or watching a ton of movies. Now I had to go out like a "typical" high school boy.

"Are you going out today?"

At first, I liked the pride in my mother's eyes when my answer to that question was yes. It was a kind of pride that I hadn't seen before in her. Or at least not directed towards me. It made me feel good and it made me feel special. Well, not special. The opposite, actually. It made me feel normal. But, unfortunately, I am not up for that challenge every single weekend.

I mean, don't get me wrong, I like going out with my friends. It's very fun. But I also like staying home—like really, *really* like it. It's also very fun. Sometimes all I need to have a good time is to spend all day locked in my room and forget that there's a world outside, especially after a busy week like the ones I've been having lately. I love my friends, I love my family, and I love my work, but sometimes I just want some time by myself, you know?

"Are you going out today?"

But even though I love staying home, I hate the look of disappointment on my mom's face when the answer to that question is no. She never says anything, of course. But she doesn't have to. I get the message loud and clear.

There have been times when I've wanted to stay home, but I've forced myself to go out just to avoid that look on her face. I don't enjoy these outings as much, though, because what I really wanted those days was to spend some time by myself at home, not to go out. It's a lose-lose situation. When I stay home, I feel the pressure to go out, but when I force myself to go out, I feel like I would be better at home.

"Are you going out today?"

I think I've found the perfect solution to this problem, though: lying. Now when I want to spend some time by myself, but I don't want my parents to think that I'm a lonely loser crying in my bedroom while I listen to *All by Myself* on repeat, I just lie and say that I'm going out with my friends or going to a party, but in reality, I go to the movies or a museum alone. Now I get the best of both worlds. They think that I go out and I get to spend some time by myself. I know it's weird, but I like it too much to care.

And no, I don't like lying to my parents—well, maybe a little—but it's something that I have to do. I can't go out every weekend. Not with people, at least. I want to have time by myself too. No, I *need* to have time by myself. And that's exactly what I did this weekend. I decided that it was time for a "me day," so when my mom inevitably asked me if I was going out, I lied and said yes. Well, I didn't lie about going out, I lied about going out with people. I told her that I was going to have lunch with some friends, but in reality, I decided to go to the art museum.

Whenever I go out alone, I always try to go to places that my family doesn't frequent so that I don't run into any of them by accident. I also never go to crowded places like the mall because I'm afraid some of my parents' or brother's many friends and acquaintances will see me and then tell them that they saw me alone. I might not be popular, but my family sure is. Mom and dad know like half the town and my brother is kind of a sports celebrity in school, so, unfortunately, there were a lot of people who know who I am. They might not even know my name, but they know that I am Alice and Andrew's son or Axel's little brother. That's why I usually go to a museum, to the old movie theater, or to the public library, spots that not a lot of people in this town visit. I feel comfortable in those places because no one knows me there and there's a kind of freedom that only comes from anonymity.

Out of all those places, I think my favorite is the art museum. I don't have the kind of artistic sensibility that Ty has to fully appreciate the complexity of the paintings and analyze the meaning behind them, but I still like looking at them. Plus, it has a beautiful garden with plants, fountains, and ducks where I can enjoy the peacefulness of nature while also ordering a frappe from the museum coffee shop.

I also love coming here to write. Ever since the winter break, I started to write regularly in a journal and I've been loving it. I don't know why I hadn't done it before. It's so relaxing. It has helped me process some of my thoughts and feelings and understand myself a little bit better.

It has also helped me with my overthinking. Before, I could spend hours and even days mulling over things that, in hindsight, weren't even that important, but now, if I feel like I'm overthinking something too much, I just write down my thoughts about it and the overthinking stops. It turns out that, by writing my thoughts down, I can let them go. When I put them on paper, they stop occupying unnecessary space in my brain and I can free myself from them because now they live in my notebook, not in my mind.

"Excuse me, we will be closing in a few minutes," a guard from the museum told me when I was in the middle of writing about my week.

"Oh, yeah... sorry. Thank you," I said.

I had been so busy writing that I forgot the museum closes at 6pm. I took one last look at the ducks in the garden and then I picked up my stuff and I left. It was still early, so I thought about going to the old movie theater to watch a movie, but it was such a beautiful day that in the end I decided to just walk around instead. I put my headphones on and I walked with no particular destination in mind. I just listened to my music, observed my surroundings, and walked. It was such a small, insignificant action, but I felt so happy doing it.

However, all that walking made me hungry. I hadn't had lunch yet and if I arrived home and made myself something to eat, then my mom surely would suspect that I lied to her because I told her that I was going out to eat. No, I couldn't let that happen. I had to eat something before I go home. But where?

Funny enough, like a cruel joke from the universe, when I was thinking all this, I happened to be walking down the street of *Il Pagliaccio*, the Italian restaurant I was too scared to enter by myself a few months ago. And not only that, the windows were covered with advertisements for a new promotion: pasta, lemonade, and cheesecake for only $14.99. It was a perfect promotion for me and exactly what I wanted right then. It was like that restaurant was mocking me. No, it was daring me. It was daring me to enter and face my fears. I could walk away because I was afraid of what a bunch of strangers might think of me or I could enter the restaurant and get what I wanted.

I hesitated a bit and started to think about the cons and pros of going in. But then I stopped. No more unnecessary overthinking. I shushed my mind and I entered.

"Table for one, please," I told the hostess with a smile, but without looking at her face to avoid seeing her reaction.

"Follow me, please," she said.

I followed her to a small table next to a big window. When the waiter came, I ordered the promotion, again with a big smile but without making eye contact. I didn't want to see that look of pity in their eyes and second-guess myself. I was determined to have a good time.

The restaurant was packed and the TVs had a football game on. I could hear at least a dozen conversations all around me, but I didn't pay attention to them or to the voice inside my head that tried to convince me that they were talking about me. I just put my headphones on and concentrated on me, my music, and my delicious food.

The pasta was even better than I expected and the cheesecake tasted like heaven. Maybe it was because I was starving, but that was the best food I had eaten in a very long time. I paid the bill and walked to the door with my eyes straight ahead, without looking or even caring if someone was looking at me.

I got out of the restaurant and I smiled.

I did it. I actually did it. I ate alone in a packed restaurant and not once did I care if anyone thought I was a weirdo or a loser. I focused on myself and I had a great time. After all, if I didn't care that I was alone, why should they?

# CHAPTER FORTY-ONE

"To Hunter!" Ty said, raising his glass. "For not giving up on me."

We had finally received our midterm grades and Ty invited Ariana and me out for dinner to celebrate the fact that he got a B+ in Math and an A- in Biology.

"Thank you," I said. "But this was all you, Ty. I didn't take those tests for you, you did. Congratulations."

"Thanks, but I wouldn't have been able to do it without your help," he said. "Thanks for offering it to me. You're a great teacher."

"No, I...," I started.

"Would you just accept a compliment for once, man," he interrupted me.

I laughed. No one had ever told me that so bluntly, but he was right. Compliments made me uncomfortable. I never know what to say when someone praises me, so I always try to shift the focus away from me.

"Sorry," I said, laughing. "Thank you."

Ty then told us about how proud his parents were of his grades. Apparently, he had always been very good at a lot of things, but school wasn't one of them, so these grades meant a lot to him. I was very happy for him. But I was also worried about my other friend. Ariana seemed very distracted. She had actually seemed distracted for the last couple of weeks. Other people didn't seem to notice, but to me, it was painfully obvious that something was wrong.

For the last couple of weeks, she hasn't been her usual cheerful, talkative self. She has been uncharacteristically quiet and distant, like something is troubling her. When I asked her about it, she told me that she was fine, but I don't think that everything's fine because she has also missed school a couple of times since midterms, but when I asked her about this, she reassured me that everything was okay and she brushed it off like it was not a big deal.

"Hunter, everybody knows that going to the first two weeks of school after midterms is optional," Ariana jokingly said.

"I don't think that's true," I said.

"Of course it is," she answered. "Now, what were you saying about Mr. Peterson?"

Mr. Peterson was our new Social Studies teacher. Our old one, Mrs. Davis, was on maternity leave, so we were stuck with Mr. Peterson for at least a couple of months. He was by far the worst teacher I had had in high school so far. He was a cranky old man that taught Economics and U.S. Government to juniors and seniors, but he agreed to cover Mrs. Davis' classes while she's on maternity leave. He's famously unpopular in school and his reputation is well-deserved.

He has only been teaching us for a few weeks, but I think it's safe to say that everyone in my classroom hates him. He has us counting down the days until Mrs. Davis' return. I mean, she wasn't perfect, but she was good. Mr. Peterson is not good. He is rude, mean, and a horrible teacher. His favorite pastime is forcing students to participate and humiliate them when they don't give him the answer that he wants. He swears that he does it to help us, but we can all see that he enjoys it. Making us feel inferior makes him feel superior. Instead of helping us, he uses his power to entertain himself. What a sad little man.

I tried to fly under the radar at first and avoided eye contact with him whenever he stopped to pick a student to answer one of his stupid questions. He hunted someone new every class and I didn't want to be his prey. But this didn't help. Mr. Peterson loved torturing everyone, so every student in the classroom had already been subjected to one of his demeaning practices, including myself. This was humiliating and infuriating, but there was nothing I could do to stop it. I just had to swallow my rage and embarrassment like everybody else.

And the worst thing was that he loved making us talk and participate in his class, except when it was to question what he was teaching us.

I was telling Ariana about how the day before, when she missed school, Mr. Peterson was supposed to be teaching us about colonialism, but instead, he spent half an hour complaining about the fact that some cities around the country refused to celebrate Columbus Day last year. He literally spent more than 30 minutes crying out that the new generations were way too sensitive and then he went on a weird rant where he argued that colonization was actually beneficial to the colonized people and that some countries today would be better under western colonialism.

All of this was not only highly offensive but also made no sense. Mr. Peterson must have seen the confusion in my face because he stopped and asked: "Mr. Grayson, is something wrong?"

"Oh… no," I said because I knew that there was no point in arguing with him.

"Then why don't you come back to Earth and pay attention to my class," he answered. "You can daydream in your house, school is for learning."

"I wasn't daydreaming," I said, sternly. "I was just wondering how exactly was it beneficial to the natives that the colonizers massacred their people, spread diseases, and stole their lands and resources?"

"Well, maybe if you spent more time in my class and less on the Moon, you would understand that, all around the world, colonialism was objectively good when you do a cost-benefit analysis," he said.

"What?" I said. "That doesn't make any sense, th–"

"Enough!" He interrupted me. "I will not repeat the whole lesson just because you didn't pay attention."

My blood was boiling. I wanted to continue arguing, but I decided to keep quiet. There was no point, I wasn't going to change his mind and I was only going to get myself into trouble. Mr. Peterson was famous for his impatience and bad temper, and I just didn't feel like going to the principal's office that day.

"Ugh, I hate him so much," Ariana said when I finished telling her the story. "There's nothing worse than a teacher that abuses his power."

"I know," I said. "Did you hear that last week he made a girl cry in Ty's Social Studies classroom?"

"What a scumbag," she said. "It's really sad that the main hobby of a grown man like him is to torment students old enough to be his grandsons."

"How did he even get the job? He's a terrible teacher," I said.

"He's like 76, he probably came with the building," she said.

"He's not that old," I said, laughing. "He's like 60."

"Well, then those students' tears are not having the rejuvenating effect that he probably wants because he doesn't look a day under 80," she said.

"Can you believe he told me to spend less time on the Moon?" I asked.

"Well, actually… yeah," she said.

"What?!" I asked.

"Well, you do daydream a lot," she said.

"No, I don't," I said.

"Yeah, sure, and I don't like photography," she said.

"Alright, fine, I do daydream sometimes," I said. "But this time I wasn't. I was just thinking. But apparently some teachers don't like it when students think in their class."

# CHAPTER FORTY-TWO

I am not a morning person, I admit it. I don't know how other people can just wake up and be ready to charge into battle—and by battle, I mean talking to anyone with a smile on their face. I can't do that. Grumpy is my default setting when I wake up. Especially when I have to wake up early on a Sunday to go to a dentist appointment like today.

Dad had a work commitment, so mom was going to drive me this time. I usually prefer when dad takes me because, as I said, I don't wake up in the friendliest of moods, and a quiet car ride can help me relax. But mom doesn't know the definition of a quiet car ride.

"Did you eat something?" She asked when we got into the car.

"Yeah," I answered.

"Did you brush your teeth?" She asked.

"Of course," I answered.

"When you came downstairs, was your brother already awake?" She asked.

"I don't know," I answered.

"How about your sister? Was she awake?" She asked.

"I don't know, mom," I said, a little irritated.

When I'm in a bad mood, there are few things that annoy me more than being bombarded with questions. Especially questions whose answers are obvious or whose answers I don't know. Unfortunately for me, asking those types of questions is one of my mom's favorite hobbies. Most of the time, I can handle them, but they can really get on my nerves when I'm in a bad mood.

"Did you hear what happened to your cousin Stacy?" She asked.

"No," I answered.

Then she went on to tell me with great detail that my 18-year-old cousin Stacy, who lived three towns over and I hadn't seen in like three years, was kicked out of her house by her parents after they found out that she was pregnant. She was telling me the story like it was the scoop of the year. She even made small pauses to see if I had anything to add or any question to make, but since I didn't, she kept talking. I listened to the story and even feigned some interest, but the truth is that I didn't care. I've never been a big fan of unnecessary drama and gossips, especially about people I barely know.

"Are you mad?" Mom asked a few minutes after she finished telling her story.

"What? No, why?" I said.

"You seem mad," she said.

"This is just my face, mom," I said.

"It's not just your face, you haven't said anything in a while," she said.

"I'm not mad… I'm just thinking," I said.

Sometimes it amazed me that she has known me literally all my life and my quietness still managed to surprise her. She has never understood how and why I'm so comfortable with silence. To her, silence meant only one thing: that something was wrong. She can't stand it. To her, it's like an itch that she desperately has to scratch.

"Where are we going?" I asked when I noticed that she was not taking the regular route to the dentist.

"I have a couple of errands to make," she said. "It won't take long."

"What? Why don't you just leave me at the dentist and then go run your errands?" I asked.

"No, it's easier this way," she said.

"Mom, I'm going to be late for the appointment," I said.

"Just a little," she said.

"You know that if I'm late, then he'll skip me and I'll have to wait until he's free again. That could be hours," I said.

"That won't happen," she said.

"Mom, seriously, why don't you just leave me at th-"

"Hunter, I said no!"

Now I was mad. But I knew that it was pointless to continue arguing with her, so I just shut up and turned to look out the window.

"Besides," she added. "If I dropped at the dentist first, then I'd be late for my errands. And I would end up using more gas."

She always did that. She always stated her arguments aloud after she made an arbitrary decision. No matter how unfair the decision was or how weak her arguments were, she always stated them aloud to try to convince me that she was right. Well, at least that's why I thought she did it. But now I think that she says them aloud to try to convince herself that she's right. To convince herself that my anger and annoyance are my problem and my problem alone, not hers.

We ended up arriving at the dentist 45 minutes late and my appointment, obviously, could no longer be respected, so we had to sit in the waiting room and wait until the dentist was done with the other three appointments that were ahead of me.

"I think I finally understand why you don't want a party," my mom said to me while we were waiting.

"You do?" I asked.

"Yeah," she said. "It's because you think that you don't have enough friends to fill the place, right? But don't worry, if that's what's troubling you, then we can invite some of your brother's friends too. That way the place will look full."

"That's not it, mom" I said, harshly. "And I do have friends."

"Then what is it?" She asked.

"It's nothing specific," I said, very annoyed. "I just don't like parties, so I don't want one."

"But why?" She asked. "Why do all the other boys want one except for you?"

Wow. That hurt. It was the whole "why can't you be like the other boys?" business again. I hadn't heard that in a while. Not from her, anyway. And I know she doesn't say it to hurt me, but I wonder if she would still say it if she knew how much it hurts.

"Can you just drop it?" I said because I didn't want to have a whole argument in the middle of the dentist's waiting room. "I don't want to talk about that right now."

"Alright, alright," she said, feeling my growing frustration.

To prevent my mom from starting any more conversations about topics I didn't want to talk about, I grabbed a magazine and pretended to be interested in celebrity gossips for the next two hours while I waited for the dentist to finish with his appointments.

At 2pm, I was finally back home. What should've taken only 1 hour ended up taking almost 4. But I was finally home. I had to suffer through a long drive, an even longer wait, and a couple of unpleasant conversations with my mom, but I was finally back home. Who knew having a teeth cleaning wasn't going to be the most uncomfortable part of my day?

When I got home, all I wanted to do was go lock myself in my room and take a nap, but as I was walking towards my room, I heard sobbings coming from Ashley's bedroom.

"Ash," I said, knocking on her door. "Is everything fine?"

"Yes," she said, sniffing. "I'm fine, go away."

I was about to leave, but then I remembered a quote I read earlier in one of the magazines at the dentist's office. "Be the person you needed when you were younger." When I read that quote, I promised myself that I was going to be that person for my children… but why wait until I have kids?

"Can I come in?" I asked, knocking again.

"… Okay," Ashley said after a long pause.

I entered and she was sitting in her bed with red eyes and Rufus by her side.

"There you are," I said to Rufus. "I've been looking for you."

"Oh, yeah," she said, chuckling. "I'm sorry."

I sat on the bed too so I could pet Rufus, who was wagging his tail so fast that I thought he was going to end up flying.

"It's fine, I know he loves you too," I said. "Besides, I was just kidding. I wasn't looking for him, I just got home."

"Why did you take so long?" She asked. "I thought you were only going to the dentist."

"I thought so too," I said. "It's a long story. The short version is: you know mom."

"Did she have other errands to do?" She asked.

"A ton," I said.

"I've been there," she said and we both laughed.

"What's going on with you, Ashley?" I asked.

"Nothing," she answered.

"Nothing?" I asked, pointing at her red eyes.

"Yes, nothing," she said, cleaning her nose. "It's just some ballet stuff."

"Do you want me to call mom?" I asked.

"No, please don't tell mom," she immediately answered. "She would just freak out."

I chuckled a little because I knew exactly what she was talking about. My mom loves us very much and her first instinct when we have any type of trouble is to solve it herself, but that usually ends up worsening the situation. For example, when I was in third grade, I told her that a boy was being mean to me and pushing my things off my desk, so she stormed the school and demanded to see my teacher, the principal, and even the boy's parents, which only made me the target of more teasing. Her intentions were very good, she just wanted to protect me, her son, but she ended up making it worse. That's one of the many reasons why now I prefer to take care of my problems on my own.

"Okay, then you can tell me," I said. "I promise I won't freak out."

"Do you promise you won't tell anyone?" She asked.

"I promise I won't tell anyone," I answered.

"So, here's the thing: there are these two new 15-year-old girls in my ballet class named Rebecca and Alison and they are so cool, they are very tall and pretty and they have black streaks in their hair just like Avril Lavigne, and my friend Stephanie and I have been trying to be friends with them for like two weeks now, but they always ignore us. So yesterday, we gathered the courage to finally talk to them and invite them to a sleepover with us, but they laughed at us, like really hard, and they said no. They called us childish and I… I just don't know what to do anymore to make them like us."

My first thought was that this was definitely not something worth crying about. I wondered why she even wanted to be friends with girls like them, they sounded awful, and I wanted to tell her that she should just forget about them and that it was not a big deal. But I knew that that wouldn't be helpful at all. I bet that if I told my problems to other people, they would also think that they're ridiculous. It's all about perspective. And to Ashley, this was a big deal.

I thought about what I would need in a situation like this and I definitely wouldn't need someone to minimize my feelings, I would need someone to listen, to tell me that it's not my fault, and to assure me that everything was going to be okay.

"That's awful," I said. "I'm sorry that happened to you. Do you know why they said no?"

"No, they just laughed and left," she said. "But it's probably because we're losers. I told Stephanie that we should probably dye our hair and start wearing cargo pants like them."

"No, I can guarantee you that it has nothing to do with you or your appearance," I said. "They're just in a different stage in their lives. You wouldn't want to go to a sleepover with a couple of 5-year-old girls, would you?"

"No… I guess not," she said. "But ugh, I'm so sick of being 10. I just want to grow up and be like them. Or at least have friends like them."

"Why do you want to have friends like them?" I asked.

"Because they're cool," she said.

"What makes them cool?" I asked.

"I don't know, they're 15-years-old," she said.

"I'm almost 15-years-old, do you think I'm cool?" I asked.

"Eww, no!" She answered.

I laughed.

"Then why do you think they're cool just because they're older?" I asked. "Look, what do you like the most about your friends?"

"Hmm... I don't know, that they're always there for me... and they understand me... and they make me laugh with their silliness," she said.

"And do you think these older girls would be there for you and understand you and make you laugh with their silliness?" I asked.

"No... probably not," she said.

"Exactly," I said. "Listen, a dear friend of mine once told me that I should not wish my life away and she was totally right. You will be 15 one day too, and younger girls will think that you're cool too, but for now, enjoy being 10. Run, jump, dance, do everything a 10-year-old girl should do. And hold on to your friends. The real ones. Don't waste your time with people who are not worth it. If a friendship doesn't feel right, then it probably isn't. It shouldn't be so much work. If you feel like you have to change to be liked by someone else, then it's not worth it."

She stayed quiet for a few seconds, looking for words, and then she finally said: "Ugh, why are you always right?"

"It's a blessing and a curse, really," I joked.

She just smiled and threw her pillow at me.

"Is everything good now?" I asked.

"Yeah, I think so," she said. "Well... no..."

"What's wrong?" I asked.

"What if they tell the other girls what happened and they start making fun of us behind our backs?" She asked.

"I'm sure that won't happen," I said.

"But what if it does?" She asked.

"Then ignore them," I said. "Or confront them. If they're coward enough to make fun of younger girls behind their backs, then I'm sure they will back off if you confront them face to face about it. And if that doesn't work, then don't be afraid to tell your teacher. Or mom. I know she can be intense, but it's only because she loves us more than anything."

"Thanks, Hunter," she said.

"You're welcome. Now, what do you say if we take this good boy for a little walk," I said, petting Rufus.

"Yes!" She yelled.

We took Rufus to the park for a walk and then spent the whole afternoon watching *Mulan* and *The Princess Diaries*, two of Ashley's favorite movies. I didn't end up taking the nap I desperately wanted when I got home from the dentist, but in the end, I didn't care because helping my little sister felt better than taking a thousand naps.

# CHAPTER FORTY-THREE

This week we had over 100 visitors at the library for the first time ever, which is crazy. Everything has happened so fast that I haven't had the opportunity to process everything or celebrate all the progress we've made.

The reading contest was really a turning point for us. It finally put us on the students' radar and it managed to lure them to us. And more importantly, it managed to make them read. Not everyone who entered the contest wanted to win it, though, some students just wanted to be part of the conversation and do what the other students were doing. But it didn't matter what their motivations were, the important thing was that they were reading. We had finally managed to plant the seed inside of them. We didn't know if that seed was going to grow and turn them into lifelong readers, but we certainly hoped that that was the case.

I was also very happy because the Book of the Week reviews were becoming very popular among our visitors. I really love writing those reviews. I love it when people read them. And, more than anything, I love when students come to the library with the sole purpose of renting the book I recommended that week, which is something that I still cannot believe happens.

This week, a girl came to the library asking for *The Chocolate War*, the book I wrote about that week, but unfortunately, we only had two copies and they had already been rented. She was disappointed, but instead of leaving, she asked if I had the reviews of previous weeks. I was confused as to why she wanted them, but luckily, I had them. Mr. Dan had been collecting them on a carpet since I started writing them.

When I asked her why she wanted them, she said: "Because if I'm gonna read something, at least I wanna read something that it's good, and I've heard that the books that are recommended here are usually pretty good," which made me both chuckle and blush.

She ended up renting *Little Women* by Louisa May Alcott, a book I wrote about last semester. She returned it a week later and told me that she loved it. We spent almost half an hour discussing our favorite parts and talking about our favorite sisters (hers was Amy, mine was Jo).

That's something I really love about my job. I love it when someone returns a book I recommended and we talk about it. I love asking them if they liked it and discussing how it made them feel. I love talking about our favorite moments and our favorite characters. My job has allowed me to get to know some fascinating people and have a lot of extremely interesting discussions, which is something I highly appreciate.

But all these new people visiting the library has also meant more work for me. And this, along with the fact that he doesn't really need me anymore, is why Ty and I decided to stop having tutoring sessions every day. We concluded that he doesn't need them anymore because he's doing much better in school now. He now knows how to study, how to concentrate in class, and how to use his more hands-on way of learning to his advantage. We still get together sometimes to review a complicated topic we saw in class or to do homework together, but our daily sessions are done.

I'm proud of Ty. He wanted to improve and he did it. Now he reads the textbook chapters in advance, he takes notes, and he is way more responsible—well, kind of.

"Hey, have you already finished the Biology homework?" I

asked him last week when we were both in the library waiting for Ariana so we could go home. "I have a doubt in question #4."

"What homework?" He asked.

"Are you serious?" I asked because I didn't know if he was joking or not.

"Yeah, what homework?" He asked again.

"The questionnaire Mr. Jones gave us right before the class ended yesterday," I said.

"Hmm…," he said, trying to remember.

"He gave it to us when you were telling me that joke about the cow and the chicken, remember?" I said.

"Oh yeah," he said with a goofy smile. "I remember the joke, but I don't remember the homework."

I laughed.

"I'm sure you have it in your backpack," I said. "I saw you putting it in there."

He grabbed his backpack and pulled out the half-crumpled questionnaire.

"Oh, you were right," he said. "Damn, 20 questions? Is it hard?"

"Kind of," I said.

"Crap, I wanted to take a nap when I got home and watch a movie at night," he said.

"Don't worry, it's for next week," I said. "Why don't you try doing the easy ones today and we can do the toughest ones tomorrow after my shift is over."

"Sounds like a plan," he said. "Thanks, Hunt. You're the best."

"I know," I joked.

"Damn, you're getting cocky, aren't you?" He asked.

"Well, you've told me that so many times that I've started believing it," I said.

"You're right, you're right," he said, laughing. "I say it a lot. But I mean it. You're the best and I don't know what I would do without you."

"You would probably be a million times more popular and spend your afternoons at the mall surrounded by friends instead of in a school library," I said.

He laughed.

"You're probably right," he said. "But believe it or not, I'm perfectly happy where I am."

But since football practice hadn't started again yet and we stopped having tutoring sessions, Ty started to spend his afternoons in the art classroom while he waited for my shift at the library to be over and for Ariana to finish with her photography class. At first, he only went there to kill time, but then our Painting teacher told him about an art contest for students that the art museum organizes at the end of every school term. The winner receives $500 and anyone could participate, as long as they were a student of one of the high schools in town. They only needed to submit five paintings before the end of the school year, so Ty started to go to the art classroom every afternoon to keep practicing and work on his paintings.

At first, he doubted about participating because he didn't think he was talented enough to do it, but that was crazy.

"What are you talking about?" I said to him. "*I'm* not talented enough. But you? Ty, you have talent to spare."

"I don't know," he said.

It took us a while, but eventually, Ariana and I managed to convince him to enter the contest and I'm very glad that he did because he seemed happier since he started going to the art classroom in the afternoons.

Ariana, on the other hand, was a completely different story. I was starting to get more worried about her, but I didn't know how to help her because I didn't know what was going on.

This Friday, I was in the library putting some books back on their shelves when Ariana suddenly opened the door and came in running. It was a quiet afternoon, there were only like four students in the library and my shift was about to be over, so I was very surprised to see her rushing through the door.

"Ariana?" I asked. "What's going on?"

"If anyone asks, I've been here this whole time, okay?" Ariana said.

"Okay...," I said, confused.

"Great, thanks," she said.

Then she put her backpack on the table closest to my desk and pulled out a book and a notebook to pretend that she was doing homework.

"What's going on, Ari?" I asked.

"There's no time to explain," she said, "Mr. Jones will probably be here any second, just sit down and..."

"There you are," Mr. Jones said, entering the library and walking towards us.

"Mr. Jones, hi," Ariana said with a smile on her face.

"Don't 'hi' me, girl. Come with me, we're going to the principal's office right now," he said.

"What? What are you talking about?" Ariana asked.

"What's going on?" I asked, legitimately confused.

"Your friend here released all the mice that were going to be dissected next week," he said.

Even if she hadn't run into the library like an escaped convict looking for refuge, I would've known that Ariana did it. That sounded like something she would totally do. I mean, just looking at her now, she was trying to control her facial expressions so she didn't seem too proud of herself. But I knew that if Mr. Jones could prove that she did it, that could mean a 3-day detention at best and an expulsion at worst, and I wasn't going to let that happen. I needed to convince him that she couldn't have possibly done it, but first I had to know how much he knew.

"What? Why do you think Ariana did it?" I asked. "Did you see her do it?"

"No, I didn't," he said. "But I caught a glimpse of a red jacket, just like the one Ms. Matthys has on."

All right, I can work with that.

"When did this happen?" I asked.

"Just a few minutes ago. I was in my office when I heard a weird noise from the lab," he said.

"That's impossible," I told him. "Ariana's been here with me for the last two hours. You see, I haven't been feeling very well lately and I had a lot of work to do here at the library, so I asked Ariana if she could come help me and, due to the fact that she's a really great friend, she decided to skip her photography class to keep me company and help me with some of my work. So it's impossible she could've done that, she has been here with me the whole afternoon."

He looked at me suspiciously, like looking for any kind of proof in my face that I was lying.

"Mr. Jones, you know me," I said. "Do you think I would lie to you?"

He looked at me and then at Ariana and then at me again.

"No, I suppose not," he said.

"Besides, it's been very chilly lately," I said. "I'm sure there are lots of other students with red jackets. This is a pretty big high school."

"What's going on?" Mr. Dan asked, getting out of his office. "Barry? What are you doing here?" He asked Mr. Jones.

"Mr. Dan," I intervened before Mr. Jones could respond. "Could you please confirm to Mr. Jones that Ariana has been here helping me all afternoon?" I said with a desperate look in my eyes that I made sure only Mr. Dan could see.

"Yeah…," Mr. Dan said. "Ariana has been helping Hunter put some books back on their shelves the whole afternoon."

"Oh…," Mr. Jones said, surprised. "Well, I'm sorry then, Ms. Matthys."

"That's okay," Ariana said.

"What happened, Barry?" Mr. Dan asked.

"Someone released all the mice that we were going to dissect for Biology," Mr. Jones answered.

"Do you still do that?" Mr. Dan asked. "Well, if you want, I can help you find some alternatives. I bet there are resources on the web like videos or computer simulations that can help you teach the students what they need to learn without having to kill innocent animals."

"Oh… okay. Thanks, I think that sounds good," Mr. Jones said. "How about I visit you next week to make the arrangements?"

"That sounds good," Mr. Dan said.

Mr. Jones apologized again to Ariana and then he left.

"What just happened?" Mr. Dan asked us.

"I'm sorry," I said.

"Ariana, did you do it?" He asked.

"Yeah," she said, looking down.

"Why?" He asked.

"I couldn't let those mice die just so a bunch of students could learn something that they were probably going to forget the next day. They deserved to live," she said.

"I agree with you," he said. "But lying is wrong. Next time you want to do something good that goes against the rules, try coming to me or to the principal first, maybe we can help you do what you want without having to get into trouble."

"Thanks, I will," Ariana said.

"I'm so sorry about that, Mr. Dan," I said. "I promise it won't happen again."

"It's okay," he said. "I know you are good kids. Just try staying out of trouble, okay?"

"Okay," I said.

We thanked him again and he returned to his office.

"Thanks, Hunt," Ariana said. "I owe you one."

"Why weren't you in your photography class?" I asked.

"I had other things to do," she answered.

"What's going on with you lately?" I asked.

"What do you mean?" She asked.

"Well, you seem very distracted lately, you've been missing classes, you haven't been doing all your homework, and now this? What's going on, Ari?" I asked.

"Nothing, I'm fine. I swear," she said.

"Ari, I'm serious. Is there something I can help you with?" I

asked.

"No, there's nothing going on," she said.

"You know you can talk to me about anything, right?" I asked.

"Yeah, I know, Hunter. And I swear I'm fine," she said.

I looked at her carefully. For some reason, I didn't believe her, but I knew that it was pointless to keep insisting. If there were really something going on, she would tell me when she wanted to tell me, not before.

"Okay," I said. "Whether you're lying or not, just know that I'll always be here for you. I'll always have your back. Just try not to send us to prison, okay? It's not my kind of environment."

"I promise," she said with a smile.

# CHAPTER FORTY-FOUR

Mrs. Davis still has not returned from maternity leave yet and things with Mr. Peterson have only gotten worse. He has continued his reign of terror in the classroom and keeps giving famous bad teachers like Ms. Trunchbull from Matilda and Professor Umbridge from Harry Potter a run for their money. Everyone in the classroom has suffered under his rule, but unfortunately, one student has suffered the most: Hugo Reed, a dark-haired boy of short stature and calm nature.

Mr. Peterson enjoyed torturing everyone, but he had decided to single out poor Hugo and make him his personal punching bag. Mr. Peterson argued that he was harsh with him for Hugo's own sake, but we all knew that wasn't true. He wasn't helping him, he just enjoyed tormenting him. He used every chance he had to put him on the spot and humiliate him.

Hugo didn't deserve this. No one did, but Hugo especially didn't. He is one of the kindest people I've ever met. I haven't talked to him a lot, but every time I do he's usually very friendly and always asks me how I am. One time, he even gave Mr. Dan and me a plate full of cookies made by his mother to thank us for all the work we've been doing at the library.

I've only seen him a couple of times at the library during my shift, but Mr. Dan told me that he's there almost every day during his lunch break. He's actually in fifth place in the reading contest so far and I bet he can get to the top 3 before the contest is over.

He's also very intelligent. He is in my Math and English classes and he got an A+ in both on the midterms. But he's really shy and soft-spoken too, which I guess is why Mr. Peterson loves to torment him so much.

To Mr. Peterson, it wasn't enough that Hugo was very smart and got an A in all of his quizzes. He always teased him for being so quiet and forced him to answer his stupid questions. And when Hugo would not answer them, he would lose his temper and humiliate him even more. Poor Hugo was terrified of him. I could see it in his eyes. There are dozens of effective ways to make a quiet student feel comfortable and participate, but bullying isn't one of them. I know it very well.

And what bothered me the most was that no one did anything to stop this clear abuse of power. On the contrary, actually. Before, Hugo pretty much flew under the radar, but since Mr. Peterson made him his personal target, other students had begun to pick on him for his quiet nature too. This made me furious beyond words.

Last week, I even went to the principal's office to discuss Mr. Peterson's behavior and I mentioned how mean he was to all of us, but especially to Hugo. I told the principal that I was worried about him, and I begged him to reprimand the teacher or make someone else cover for Mrs. Davis. But he told me that there was nothing he could do and that we should consider ourselves lucky that Mr. Peterson agreed to take over Mrs. David's classes. He also mentioned that I was probably exaggerating about Mr. Peterson's treatment of Hugo because he hadn't visited him himself yet to complain about it. I left that office fuming. I couldn't believe that those people were the ones that were supposed to take care of us.

So, when the end of that week arrived, I felt incredibly mad and completely powerless—a horrible combination. It didn't help that Mr. Peterson decided to open his class with a question directed at Hugo, and when he took a while to answer, Mr. Peterson started to mock him and reprimand him. He told him that he needed to stop being a baby and speak up, that he was never going to succeed in life if he continued being like that, and that he should be embarrassed that he was almost 15-years-old and still acted like a scared mama's boy.

I was angrier than I had been in a very long time. Especially because, one way or another, I've been hearing that kind of crap my entire life too and I knew that it was not helping Hugo at all. On the contrary, it was only making him believe that he was less than everyone else and that there was something wrong with him.

So, when I saw him start to tear up, I couldn't take it any longer.

"Enough!" I found myself yelling.

All eyes turned to me. I felt my face turn red and I didn't know if it was because of the anger or the embarrassment. But there was no going back now.

"What's the matter, Mr. Grayson?" Mr. Peterson asked with a perplexed expression.

"Oh, sorry," I said. "I was just wondering if you were planning on teaching us something today or if you were just going to continue bullying students four times younger than you."

The whole classroom went silent, except for a few gasps.

"Excuse me, young man? What's that supposed to mean?" Mr. Peterson asked angrily.

"Well, you've already spent almost 20 minutes of the class bullying poor Hugo and let's just say that I don't get your obsession with him," I said. "He's a great student and he probably has better grades than all of us, so why are you always so harsh with him? Are you jealous because he has a bright future ahead of him while you spend your days finding joy tormenting young high school students? Or what is it? I don't get why a teacher like you decides to abuse your position of power to mock and humiliate us instead of helping us. It's very sad that you use your authoritative role for intimidation instead of for inspiration."

The classroom was so quiet that you could cut the tension with a knife.

"You're an insolent little brat," Mr. Peterson said with a red face. "You will go to the principal's office, Mr. Grayson. And you will get suspended, I'll make sure of that. But first, I want you to hear this. I've seen your grades. I know you're smart, just like Mr. Reed here, but if you think that intelligence is all you need to make it out there, then you're a fool. You're going to be a nobody. I know your brother. The famous Axel Grayson. He's not very bright, but he has people skills, so I have no doubt that he will be very successful in the future. But you and Mr. Reed? I have my doubts. You're just a couple of pansies and the world is going to chew you up and spit you out."

This was getting personal and I was getting angrier.

"And you're just a sad little man who's coward enough to bully kids that could be your grandsons," I said.

"Enough!" He yelled. "You kids don't know the meaning of respect! You're going to go to the principal's office and wait for me there until the class ends. But before, I'm going to give you the opportunity to apologize to me and to the rest of the classroom for disrespecting me and interrupting the class."

I stopped for a few seconds to cool down and weight my options: I could shut up and pretend that I was sorry for what I said or I could continue to take a stand and refuse to back down. I could let him continue his reign of terror or I could let him know that it was unacceptable to treat students like this. I could reduce my suspension or I could significantly increase it. Decisions, decisions.

But before I could decide, someone else chose for me.

"And when will you apologize to us for treating us like shit?" Ariana asked and the whole classroom gasped collectively.

"Do you want to get suspended too, Ms. Matthys?" Mr. Peterson angrily asked.

"If that would mean not having to put up with your classes for a few days then yes, I would," Ariana answered.

"You're a bunch of ungrateful brats," he said. "I'm trying to do you all a favor."

"A favor?" I interrupted him. "How exactly are you doing us a favor by humiliating us? Students shouldn't be afraid of their teachers. We shouldn't have to dread going to classes. We should have teachers that care about our well-being, not a bully who abuses his power and enjoys humiliating us. If you think that you're doing us a favor, then please stop because we've had enough of your' favors.'"

"Don't put your ungrateful words in everyone's mouths," he said.

"He's not. You are a terrible teacher," Ariana said and then turned to face the rest of the classroom. "If you think that Mr. Peterson is a good teacher that's only trying to help us, please raise your hand."

Not one student raised their hand.

"Now raise your hand if you think that he's a sad little bully and you're sick of his abusive behavior," Ariana said.

One by one, every student raised their hands. Some hesitated, but when they saw that everyone else was showing their support, they also joined in.

"This fucking ungrateful generation, I swear," he angrily said, picking up his stuff. "I don't have to take this shit."

He left, Ariana and I smiled at each other, and the whole classroom started to cheer.

# CHAPTER FORTY-FIVE

One week. Ariana and I got suspended for one week. That was both more than I hoped and less than I expected. My parents were not happy about it when they found out. They gave me a big speech about respect and responsibility and, as punishment, I had to accompany mom to work every day of that week. But, weirdly, there was one relative who was really proud of what I did.

"Great job, Hunter," my brother said with a big smile at the dinner table. "I never imagined I would ever say this, but thank you for standing up to that jackass."

"Don't encourage him. He got suspended for disrespecting a teacher. An elder teacher. That's nothing to be proud of," my mom said, but I could see that a tiny little smile formed in the corner of her mouth.

"Oh, he did more than that," said Axel. "He basically started a revolution."

"What?" I asked.

Apparently, a lot happened at school during the week I got suspended. Word got around about what Ariana and I did and more and more students started to stand up to Mr. Peterson's abusive behavior. And not only that, even more students started to report him to the principal for his past inappropriate behavior, from racist, sexist, and homophobic remarks to emotional distress and bullying.

This wasn't the first time he got reported—not by a long

shot—but apparently he had a relative on the school board, so the complaints about him never got very far. However, this time he faced so much pressure from students, parents, and even the school faculty that he chose to resign and retire.

This made me feel weirdly proud when I heard it. It meant that what I did was not in vain. So what if I got suspended for one week? Now dozens of students felt safer at school because they didn't have that monster as a teacher anymore. A one-week suspension was a small price to pay for that.

When I got back to school after my suspension was over, Ariana the first person I saw.

"How was your suspension?" I asked her.

"Uneventful," Ariana answered. "How about yours?"

"Boring," I said. "I'm actually glad to be back. I missed you."

"Aww," she said, giving me a little hug. "I missed you too. And you know what they say: friends that bring down a tyrannical and abusive teacher together stay together."

All through the day, we received a very warm welcome at school. Our friends and acquaintances showered us with love and a lot of classmates that we had never spoken to before thanked us for what we did.

I was very excited to be back. I love my mother, but I couldn't stand one more day of going to Open Houses and meeting potential clients with her. If I *had* to go to someone's job, I would very much rather go to mine.

"Hunter!" Mr. Dan said when I entered the library. "Good job staying out of trouble," he said, sarcastically.

"Hey, Mr. Dan," I said, laughing nervously. "Umm… do I still have my job? Or do I have to look for something new to do with my afternoons?"

"Of course you still have your job," he said, laughing. "You got suspended for standing up to a bad teacher, not for murdering someone."

"Oh, thanks!" I said with a big smile.

According to Mr. Dan, I didn't miss much at the library while I was gone. The visitors had continued to surge, but the top ten spots of the reading contest were still pretty much the same. With the exception that Hugo had passed George and now was in fourth place.

And speaking of which, Hugo visited me at the library that afternoon.

"Hi, Hunter," he said nervously.

"Hey, Hugo," I said with a smile. "How are you?"

"Good. How are you?" He asked.

"I'm pretty good," I answered. "Happy to be back. What can I do for you? Are you looking for a book?"

"Oh, no," he said. "I… I just wanted to thank you… you know… for what you did. I really appreciate it and I'm really sorry that you got suspended."

"Hey, don't even mention it," I said. "I'm just sorry I didn't do it sooner."

"I have something for you," he said, opening his backpack.

"No, don't, you really don't have to," I said.

"I told my mom what you did and she baked you this," he said, giving me a batch of cookies.

"Oh my god, that's so nice," I said. "Thank you."

"Also, I took some notes of the classes you missed," he said, giving me a folder full of notes.

"What? Thank you so much!" I said. "You're the best."

"If you or Ariana have any doubts about the topics we saw last week, you can totally ask me and I'll be happy to help," he said.

"Thank you so much, I don't even know what to say," I said. "Thank you, Hugo. Hey, I'm going to go to Jambo's with Ty and Ariana after work, do you want to come with us?"

"I wish I could," he said, "but I have to go, my mom is waiting for me in the parking lot."

"Oh, well, thank you again," I said. "And please thank your mom for the cookies."

"Will do," he said. "Bye, Hunter. See you tomorrow."

"Bye. Oh hey, before you go…," I said, whispering. "I can't really say anything, but… keep reading."

He paused for a second and then smiled.

"You got it," he said with a big smile and his hands on the straps of his blue backpack.

I know I wasn't supposed to have any favorites in the reading contest, but what can I say? I was rooting for that guy.

His notes really helped me catch up with everything I missed in school the week I got suspended. But nothing in his notes could've prepared me for what was waiting for me in Biology the next day.

"Come in, come in," said Mr. Jones. He was wearing a lab coat and safety glasses. "Please sit on the floor at the back of the classroom. I don't want you to be in the splash zone."

He had moved all the desks to the sides, so there was plenty of space for us to sit on the floor. There was a small watermelon on his desk with a lot of rubber bands in the middle that seemed to be deforming the fruit.

"Today, I'm going to do a little experiment to show you the difference between kinetic energy and potential energy," Mr. Jones said. "But more than that, it is to show you that there are many ways that we can learn about science."

He went on to explain the difference between kinetic energy and potential energy as he put more rubber bands on the watermelon.

"When stretched, the rubber bands have potential energy that is trying to become kinetic energy, but it can't because the watermelon is preventing the rubber bands from returning to their original state. The watermelon is stronger than the potential energy of the rubber bands. However, when enough rubber bands are put together, they can overpower the tough exterior of the fruit," he said.

We were all holding our breaths and half covering our faces, waiting for the watermelon to explode.

"Although one more rubber band might seem insignificant in the grand scheme of things—this one has 448 rubber bands, after all—an object can only take so much pressure before it… explodes," Mr. Jones said, putting one last rubber band and taking a step back.

The watermelon exploded all over the place and the classroom erupted in screams, cheers, and laughs. The explosion wasn't as messy as I thought it would be, but the loudness of it definitely took me by surprise.

"Now, for the real lesson of the day..." Mr. Jones said, and then he started to describe a project that we had to do in the following week. Basically, we had to research a Biology topic we liked and do an essay about it. It could be about anything we wanted, as long as it was related to Biology, but it had to be something we hadn't seen in class yet and it had to be something interesting. We also had to make a presentation about our topic and the best presentation would get ten extra points in the final exam.

I was getting excited about this project because it sounded like an interesting challenge, but then Mr. Jones said the six daunting words that make my core shiver and my eyes roll: "You are gonna work in teams."

I absolutely hate doing group projects. I always end up either disappearing among the many voices and opinions of my teammates or doing all the work. There's no middle ground. I work better alone.

When I work on my own, I'm more creative and productive because I have time to think and reflect on the work that I'm doing. On the contrary, when I work with a team, people are always pressuring me to come up with opinions and ideas on the spot, which is something that I loathe. I've never been very good at thinking on my feet when it comes to schoolwork. I need time to prepare. I need to familiarize myself with the topic and get my head around it before I can offer insights and ideas about it.

I like to think before I speak and that is especially true when it comes to school. But I need time to do it, I can't think out loud as many of my classmates can, I need to do it internally and by myself, but sometimes during group projects everything moves so fast that I don't have time to think, so

I end up staying behind, especially when the groups are big and full of people eager to present their own ideas and work quickly to get the work done as soon as possible.

But I like it when the groups are small (like two or three people). And I like working with Ty. So, when the teacher said that we had to make groups of two, Ty immediately turned to me with a goofy face and I nodded with a smile on my face. That was our way of saying that we were going to be together without actually saying it.

We went to Ty's house after my shift at the library to start working on the project right away because we only had two weeks to finish it. I had never gone to his house before. Usually, if we have work to do, we do it at the library or at my house, but this time he offered his house and I said yes right away because I was eager to see his home.

On our way there, I asked him if he was excited about football training starting in a few weeks again, but his answer was not what I expected.

"Umm… yeah, of course," he said, doubting.

"Are you sure?" I asked. "You don't sound very convinced."

"Yeah, of course I'm excited," he lied. But he was a terrible liar.

"Do you want to talk about it?" I asked.

"No," he said, calmly.

"Are you sure?" I asked again.

"Yeah," he said.

"Okay," I said. "But you know you can tell me anything, right?"

"Yeah, I know," he said.

When we got to his house, his mother was on her way out.

"Ty, why didn't you tell me you were going to have visitors?" Her mom asked.

"Sorry, mom, it was a last-minute plan," he said. "We're only going to do some homework. And Hunter's very well-behaved, I swear."

"It's true, I am," I said. "Hi, Mrs. Johnson."

"Hello, Hunter," she said with a warm smile that was very similar to her son's. "Pleasure to have you here. I heard that you're finally back at school after your week-long suspension."

I turned to Ty with a look of "you told her?!" in my eyes. He just shrugged and smiled.

"Yeah...," I said nervously.

"Don't worry," she said, laughing it off. "Ty told me how horrible that teacher was and, honestly, good for you."

"Thanks," I said, feeling my cheeks slowly blushing.

"Well, kids, I'm gonna go do some errands," she said. "I'll be back in a couple of hours. There is some food in the fridge and a new bag of chips in the pantry. Call me if you guys need anything."

"Alright, mom," Ty said.

"Thanks, Mrs. Johnson," I said.

"Why don't you leave your things in the dining room?" Ty said to me. "I'll go to the kitchen to see what we can eat."

"Okay," I said.

I went to the dining room and my eyes immediately went straight to the dozens of pictures hanging on the wall.

"Is pizza alright?" Ty asked from the kitchen.

"Yeah, of course," I answered.

I walked closer to the pictures to see them more clearly. The photos went all the way back to when Ty's parents were in high school. Mr. Johnson was a star football player back in his time, just like Ty was starting to be. There was even a photo of Mr. Johnson picking up the football regional championship trophy with Mrs. Johnson by his side.

"I didn't know your parents met in high school," I said.

"Yeah, they were high school sweethearts," Ty said from the kitchen.

"You look just like your father," I said.

"Yeah... I'm a little more handsome, but yeah," he said.

"It seems like you have football in your veins," I said as I looked at a photo of a young Ty wearing his father's football helmet.

"Yeah, I guess you could say that," he said.

There were also a lot of photos of Ty with his father doing a lot of things, from playing sports to building sandcastles on the beach.

"You two seem to be very close," I said to Ty as he entered the living room with two plates of pizza and a bag of chips.

"Yeah, he's the best," he said. "I don't know what I would do without my old man."

I looked back at the pictures and I choked up a little. I had never had that kind of relationship with my father and I probably never would. That ship had sailed a long time ago. I started to wonder about how different my life would be if I had had the type of relationship that Ty or Ariana had with their fathers. But then I stopped. This was not the time or place to think about things like that.

"Is everything fine?" Ty asked.

"Yeah," I lied. Luckily, I was a better liar than him, so he believed me.

"Alright. Let's eat," he said with a smile.

As we ate and talked about how random Mr. Jones' watermelon experiment was, I couldn't stop looking at a picture that was behind Ty. It was a picture of Ty and Tony when they were like 10. They were in front of a lake, posing for the photo, both with a big smile. Except for the color of their skin, they looked almost like twins. Same height, same eyes, and same smile.

"Can I ask you something?" I said to Ty.

"Of course," he answered.

"What's the deal with your cousin?" I asked.

"Oh, you mean why he's a brainless bully?" He said.

"I… no… well… yeah…," I said.

"I wish I had an answer for that, but the truth is that I don't," he said. "He's always been like that. I always thought that he would eventually grow out of it, but it has only gotten worse. I'd tried talking to him several times about it, but there's been no use. I can't seem to make him change. My mom says that he has it in his blood because his father is the same. He's a natural-born bully. It's a shame, though. He was like the brother I never had when we were little."

*He is a natural-born bully.* That sentence really caught my attention. Are bullies born or are they created? What was it about his father that made Tony a bully? Was it his genes, or was it the way that he raised him? Probably both, but which one had the most impact?

"Anyway," Ty said, serving more chips on his plate. "What should we do this project about? Do you have any ideas?"

I looked at the picture one more time and then it hit me.

"What if we do it about epigenetics?" I said.

"What's that?" Ty asked.

"It's a Biology concept that Ariana's father introduced me to," I said. "It's basically the part of Biology that studies how the environment can influence the expression of our genotype and modify our phenotype."

"Hunt, know your audience," Ty said.

"Sorry," I said. "Epigenetics studies how the environment can affect the expression of our genes. Not every gene we have in our cells gets expressed and sometimes it's our environment the one that decides which genes get expressed and which don't. Everything around us, the climate, the stress, our nutrition, the conditions we grew up under, the way we were raised, everything has the possibility of influencing how our genes get expressed and basically affect who we are at a molecular level. This means that our genes are not set in stone, they don't completely determine who we are or who we are going to be, they're just one part of the equation, but they're not the whole equation. Just because we have some genes doesn't mean that they'll inevitably get expressed. For example, you might be right and Tony might have bullying in his genes, but if he would've been raised by someone else like, for example, your parents, maybe that part of him might've never been expressed. But since he was raised by another bully, then the combination of nature and nurture made him the bully that he is right now. Oh, this is great, we can also talk about the old debate of nature vs nurture."

"That sounds interesting," Ty said. "Okay, I'm in. Let's do it."

We spent the next few days researching everything we could about epigenetics in the public library and on the internet. It was really fun. I liked working with Ty because he brought some levity to my sometimes very serious way of working. He always made me realize that working and having fun were not mutually exclusive and that I should enjoy doing the project, not just stress about it. Like when we were at the public library reading about our topic and he couldn't stop making jokes about genetics.

"The other day I went to visit my grandfather with my dad," Ty said. "And he told us a joke about recessive genes. My dad didn't get it, but I did."

"Stop it," I said, laughing.

"Oh, wait, I thought of another one," he said with a big smile. "There was a boy who didn't understand why Richards were called Dick, so one day he raised his hand during school. 'Why is Dick short for Richard?' He asked his teacher. 'Genetics!' Yelled one of his classmates."

"I'm serious," I said, holding back my laugh. "We need to concentrate."

"Hunt, I don't think you understand just how smart that joke was," he said with a smile.

But I'm not saying that he was always goofy and never took the work seriously. He actually became very interested in the topic and read a lot about it while we were researching it. We ended up learning a lot of things that we wouldn't have otherwise. One of the most interesting discoveries we read about was that some of our experiences could actually affect our DNA and that change could be passed down to our children. So not only our experiences helped define who we are, but they could also impact and define our future generations.

It was very fun to read about these topics because

everything we read led to an interesting discussion, like: how much of a say do we have in who we are? Do our genes and environment inevitably determine who we are and who we are going to be or can we have a say in it? And, is our destiny written in our genes and past experiences or can we write our own destiny?

It was fun to ask those questions, but that was all we could do. We didn't have the answers. I don't think anybody did. There was no way of knowing for sure. One thing that was clear, though, was that, whether we want it or not, things we have no control over are always going to significantly affect our lives without we even realize it.

Once we did all the research and had all of the information that we needed, we started writing the essay, which ended up being quite easy, actually. We made a great team, I synthesized and simplified the information and Ty came up with ingenious and creative analogies to express the ideas in simpler ways. Plus, I already had a lot of experience writing, so we managed to finish the essay and the presentation in only one day.

Since we were going to present our work in front of the whole classroom, I suggested that we rehearsed the presentation at least a couple of times, but Ty said that it wasn't necessary because we had already mastered the topic. He seemed pretty confident, but I wasn't, so I ended up rehearsing the presentation alone in my bedroom, with only my books and Rufus as my audience.

Fortunately, the presentation went great. I don't particularly enjoy talking in front of the whole classroom, but I can do it if I have to—and if I had enough prep time. We first started the presentation by defining a few concepts like genes, gene expression, and environment; then we delved into the definition of epigenetics and explained some of the research that has been done about it; after that, we introduced the nature vs nurture debate and the postures that some of the greatest scientists and philosophers had had over the years; lastly, I closed the presentation with a conclusion that I had rehearsed approximately two thousand times in front of the mirror.

"The old debate of nature vs nurture is essentially death," I said. "Epigenetic research proves that our genes and the environment are continuously interacting to produce all of our traits. They are not independent of each other. Throughout all of our lives, they work together to determine who we are and who we are going to be. But which one's more important, you may ask? Which one contributes more to who we are? Well, to answer that, I will use the same reply that psychologist Donald Hebb used to answer a similar question: 'which contributes more to the area of a rectangle, its length or its width?' In the end, it doesn't really matter because they're both absolutely essential. Thank you."

Our classmates clapped after that and I just grinned and looked at Ty, who was smiling from ear to ear. In the end, my preparation and Ty's charm and humor resulted in a winning combination because Mr. Jones decided to crown us the winning team and give us the extra points.

As I said, I hate doing group projects—but there are some exceptions.

# CHAPTER FORTY-SIX

It's 3am. I've been tossing and turning in my bed for at least an hour now, trying to sleep, but it seems like Mr. Sandman doesn't have any intention of visiting me tonight. I can't stop thinking about a fight I had earlier with my mom. That morning, she told me that she had an Open House near my school and offered to pick me up after work so I didn't have to walk home because it was supposed to rain in the afternoon. I thought it was a nice offer, so I said yes. Big mistake.

"How was your day?" She asked when she picked me up.

"Good," I answered. "It was a busy day at the library. More and more students are visiting every week to try to win this new contest I came up with. It's very exciting."

"That's nice," she said. "Guess who I just saw at the Open House?"

"Who?" I asked.

"Mrs. Sawyer," she answered.

"My second grade teacher?" I asked.

"Yes," she said, "she's looking for a smaller house because she's getting a divorce. Poor thing, she just had a child two years ago, but apparently, her husband was cheating on her."

"What a dick," I said.

"Hunter!" She said.

"What?" I asked.

"Please don't use that kind of language, honey," she said.

"Anyway, she caught them together in her own bed, can you believe it? Understandably, she says that she can't stand being in that house any longer, so she's going to sell it and buy a smaller one just for her and her son. You know, for a minute I thought she was pregnant again. I even touched her belly. Boy, I must've looked silly. But in my defense, she does look pregnant."

"And she's not?" I asked.

"No!" She said. "She just hasn't lost the baby weight yet. But the 'baby' is already two, so I think it was fair to assume."

"I imagine losing weight is not very high on her priority list," I said, looking out the window. "Taking care of a toddler must not be easy."

"No, it's not," she said. "So, do you have any plans for tonight?"

"No, I'm too tired," I said. "I just want to get home and sleep."

"Are you sure?" She asked. "It's Friday and you didn't go out last week. You're not grounded anyone, you know that, right?"

"Yes, mom, I know," I said. "I just don't feel like going out today."

"Your brother's going to a party tonight with his football friends, why don't you go with him?" She said.

Because I would rather eat my own arm than go to a football party with my brother.

"Nah, I'm too tired," I said. "Maybe on another occasion. Where are we going, by the way?" I asked when I noticed that she wasn't driving home.

"You'll see," she said.

"I don't like surprises, mom," I said.

"Fine, we're going to Verdi's, that nice party venue on MLK Boulevard," she said.

"Why?" I asked.

"Apparently, they had an opening for the weekend of your birthday," she said. "Can you believe it? Is that fate or what? You usually have to make a reservation at least half a year in advance, but the person that had that day reserved couldn't afford to make all the payments, so it's ours if we want it, we just have to make the reservation today because there are other people that also want it."

"But I don't want a party," I said.

"Let's first see the place and listen to what they're offering," she said.

"Mom, I don't want it," I said.

"Hunter, we're just going to see it," she said.

"But I don't want to see it," I said. "It would just be a waste of time. Why can't you accept that I don't want a party?"

"Perhaps you'll change your mind when you see it," she said.

"No, I won't," I said.

"Why are you fighting me so much on this?" She asked. "I never had this kind of problem with your brother, you know?"

"Then throw *him* a party!" I said.

"Hunter, do you know how many calls I had to make to get us on the waiting list?" She asked.

"I appreciate it, but I didn't ask you to do it," I answered.

"This is a great opportunity, honey," she said. "There are hundreds of kids out there that would love to have their 15th birthday party in there. It's in very high demand."

"So what?" I said. "I'm not going to do something that I don't want just because everyone else wants to do it. And why do you care so much about what other kids want and not about what *I'm* telling you that I want?"

"Hunter, don't be irrational, we're just going to see it," she said.

"No, mom, we're not just 'going to see it.' I know you, you're gonna love the place and I'm gonna hate it, but you won't care and you'll reserve it anyway and when I'll get upset, you're gonna find a way to make yourself the victim and make me feel guilty about it, so I'll end up agreeing to do whatever you want just to make you happy, even if that means that I'll be miserable. Well, I rather save myself the trouble and just tell you right now that I. Don't. Want. It. I don't want to go see it and I don't want a party. This is not your decision to make. It's *my* birthday, *I* decide how I want to spend it. You're going to have to find yourself something else to control," I said, crossing my arms and turning to look out the window.

I immediately regretted saying that. I meant every word I said, but I shouldn't have said it.

"All right then," she said with a cracked voice and watery eyes.

After that, neither of us said another word, she just turned the car around and we headed home. When we got to the house, she went straight to her office and I went straight to my bedroom without even exchanging a glance.

Tears began to soak my pillow as soon as I laid my head in it. Fortunately, if there's one thing good about crying is that it makes you sleepy, so I didn't have any trouble falling asleep. However, all good things come to an end, and I ended up waking up at 2am with a headache, an empty stomach, and the memories of a nasty car ride that I couldn't just sleep away.

For the last hour, that fight has been playing and replaying in my head. Was I too harsh? Should I have said something different? Should I have said something more? Should I have said something less? Maybe I should've just gone to the stupid place and come up with an excuse for why I didn't like it there. No, a fight like this was bound to happen sooner or later, whether it was in a car, in a party venue, or at home. This was about so much more than just a stupid 15th birthday party.

At 3:30am, I finally accepted that I wasn't going to be able to go back to sleep, so I went downstairs to get something to eat. I made myself a grilled cheese and I sat in the living room to listen to music while looking out the window. It was 4am, so the street was as empty and quiet as it could be. Not a single dog was barking and no one was driving down the street. I noticed that Axel's car wasn't in the driveway, which seemed strange at first, but then I remembered that my mom told me that he was going to go to a party, so he was probably going to stay over with one of his friends.

I was still hungry after finishing the grilled cheese, so I

decided to get some ice cream for dessert. It was technically still winter, so no one in my family had even thought about opening the freezer for months, but I have never minded the cold. I served myself two scoops of strawberry ice cream and went back to the living room to eat it while listening to some relaxing music that was momentarily distracting me from thinking about the car fight.

After cleaning up, I was about to go upstairs to try to get some sleep again when I heard the sound of a car pulling over in our driveway. I looked out the window and saw the old Chrysler that used to belong to my dad and that now was Axel's. But something was different. The whole front was crashed and a light was missing.

Axel got out of the car and stumbled his way to the front door. I feared the worst and braced myself to see my big brother full of blood or with broken bones. But he was fine, he was just drunk.

"Oh my god, Axel! What happened?" I asked.

"I crashed the car," he said, whimpering.

"Are you hurt? Did you hurt anyone?" I asked.

"No, I'm fine, and i–it was a post," he said.

"What the hell were you thinking?" I asked.

"I… I…," he started to say before hugging me. "I know. I know I screwed up. I wasn't thinking. I'm sorry. I'm sorry."

I stood there motionless, frozen, waiting to wake up from that bizarre dream. But nothing happened. I wasn't dreaming. My brother had actually come home with a wrecked car and tears in his eyes.

"It's okay… the important thing is that you're not hurt," I said. "Stay here, I'll go get mom and dad."

"No, wait," he said, grabbing my arm. "They can't see me like this."

"What? You can't just hide this. They *will* find out," I said.

"I know, I just… I…"

And then he threw up on me.

"Oh god," I said, utterly disgusted.

"I'm sorry, Hunter. I'm sorry. I'm so sorry," he said, crying.

"It's okay. It's fine," I said, trying not to throw up too. "Sit down, I'll make you some coffee."

I grabbed a couple of towels and some clean clothes from the laundry room and I changed in the bathroom to avoid going upstairs and accidentally waking up my parents.

"Here," I said, handing Axel his coffee and a hand towel so he could wipe out his tears and clean the vomit off his lips.

"Thank you," he said with watery eyes. He looked so small, sobbing and shaking like a little hound lost in a freezing forest. I had never seen him like that. Not even when we were little.

"What happened?" I asked when he started to calm down.

"I don't know, I guess I got nervous and I couldn't hold it in any longer," he said.

"No, not about the vomit," I said. "What happened to the car? Why were you driving like this? Why didn't you just stay over with one of your friends?"

"I… I was going to stay over at Patrick's because his parents are out of town," he said, "but he hooked up with a chick at the party and he asked me if it was alright if I stayed somewhere else and I said 'Yeah, it's totally cool,' but almost everyone had already gone home and the party wasn't even that far, so I thought that it was better if I just drove home, that way I didn't have to go pick up the car in the morning."

"How could your friends let you drive like this?" I asked. "You're clearly wasted."

"I don't know," he said. "I've done it before and nothing like this ever happened."

"That is not a good excuse," I said.

"I know. I'm sorry, it was stupid," he said.

"Yes, it was very stupid," I said. "You could've hurt someone! You could've hurt yourself!"

He started crying again. "I'm sorry, Hunter. I'm so sorry. I'll never do it again, I swear."

I was so mad at him for being so careless, but I also felt kind of sorry for him. I had never seen him like this before. You're not supposed to see your big brother cry. That's not how things work. He's the one that's supposed to protect me and comfort me if something's wrong, not the other way around. I wanted to look away. I wanted to go to my room and leave him alone to figure out his own mess. But he was my big brother.

I sat next to him and put my arm around him. "It's gonna be okay," I said.

"No, it's not," he said.

"Yes, it is," I said.

"No, it's not," he said.

"Yes, it is," I said.

"How do you know that?" He asked.

"I just do," I answered. "The important thing is that you're okay and that you know that what you did was wrong, so I hope you never do it again."

He looked at me and smiled.

"You know, sometimes I wish I had your brain, Hunter," he said.

"What?" I asked.

"I bet you would've never done something like this," he said.

"No, I wouldn't," I said.

"Do you know what mom used to tell me every time she saw my report cards?" He said. "She used to say: 'Why can't you be more like your brother? Hunter always gets straight A's.'"

"What?"

*What?*

"You would've never done something as stupid as this," he said, looking at the floor.

I didn't know what to say. My brain was desperately trying to process the fact that maybe I wasn't the only one living under the shadow of my brother. But I couldn't let myself go there. Not yet. I had more pressing things at hand. I still had to decide what to do next. I could go wake up our parents and hand over the problem to them, or I could let Axel calm down and even rest for a few hours before they wake up, see the car, and kill him. They will probably kill me too when they find out that I was here when he arrived and I didn't wake them up right away to tell them.

"I'm so screwed," Axel said, covering his eyes with his hands. "Dad loves that car."

"Yeah, he does," I answered. "But he loves you more. He's going to be glad that nothing happened to you."

"Do you think so?" He asked.

"Yeah," I said.

"Thanks," he said, a little more relaxed.

"Why don't you get some sleep now?" I said.

"Aren't you gonna wake up mom and dad?" He asked.

"No… that can wait," I said.

He took a deep breath, held it in, and let it out. "Okay."

"Wait, do you have a headache?" I asked.

"No," he answered.

"Did you hit your head?" I asked.

"No, the crash was on the passenger's side and I was wearing a seat belt," he said.

"Wait here," I said.

I went to mom and dad's office and grabbed the little flashlight that dad keeps on his desk. I went back to the living room and flashed it at Axel's eyes to watch the reaction of his pupils.

"Okay, you can go to sleep now," I said.

"What was that about?" He asked.

"I was checking for a concussion," I said.

"And?" He asked.

"Your pupils reacted normally to the light, so I don't think you have one," I said.

"How do you know that?" He asked.

"I read it in a book," I answered.

"Of course you did," he said with a chuckle. "Can you help me get upstairs?"

"Sure," I said.

The coffee had helped him sober up a little, but he still couldn't walk normally, so I had to act as his cane and help him get to his room without falling down the stairs and waking up the whole neighborhood.

"What were you doing downstairs at 4 in the morning, by the way?" He asked while taking off his shoes and getting into bed.

"I couldn't sleep," I said.

He laughed.

"I'm not surprised. You've always been a night owl. It used to drive nuts when we were kids and we shared a bedroom because you always woke up in the middle of the night and spent at least an hour tossing and turning in the bottom bunk bed. I was so annoyed by that that I even offered to give you the top bunk bed so you would stop waking me up at 3am every day, but you were afraid of heights."

"I had forgotten about that. I'm still pretty afraid of heights," I said, laughing. "Listen, I'm going to leave my bedroom door open. If you need anything, just say my name."

"Thanks, man," he said.

"And sleep on your side," I said.

"What?" He asked.

"It's just for precaution," I said. "It's so you don't choke on your own vomit in case you want to throw up again."

"Oh, thank you," he said.

"You're welcome," I said, turning off the lights and walking towards the door.

"Hunter," Axel said before I got out of his room.

"Yeah?" I asked.

"I mean it," he said. "Thank you. You're a great brother."

"Good night, Axel," I said.

# CHAPTER FORTY-SEVEN

Two weeks. I'm not allowed to go out for two weeks. That's what I got for not waking up my parents. I'm fine with it, to be honest. I was kind of tired of going out anyway, so this will give me two well-deserved weeks of rest. As for my brother, I still don't know what his punishment is. My parents sent my sister and me to our bedrooms so they could unleash the whole magnitude of their wraths on Axel. That was an hour ago.

I've been trying to read to distract myself, but the uncertainty is eating me up inside. Will they take away his car? Probably. Will they make him drop out of the football team? Doubtful. Will they send him to a military school? I don't know. Nah, they love him too much for that.

I couldn't wait any longer. I was about to go see if I could hear something from the top of the stairs when a knock on my door startled me.

"Can I come in?" Axel asked.

"Yeah," I answered.

He came in, sat on my reading couch, and started petting Rufus.

"How was it?" I asked.

"Well," he said, "I won't be able to use the car for the rest of the school year, I'll have to work with dad on the weekends to pay for the car's repair, and I won't be able to go out in 4 months."

"Ouch," I said.

"It's actually less than I expected," he said.

"How's the hangover?" I asked.

"It's a bitch," he said.

"Yeah, you look like hell," I said. "But at least you can stand now."

He laughed.

"Hey, thank you again, man," he said.

"For what?" I asked.

"For everything," he answered. "And you make terrible coffee, by the way."

I laughed.

"I was too busy trying to clean the vomit off my PJs to bring my A-game in coffee making," I said.

"Oh, yeah, sorry about that," he said.

"It's okay," I said. "I guess I now know what it's like to take care of a toddler."

He laughed again.

"I'm gonna go back to sleep now," he said. "But thank you. Really."

"Stop thanking me," I said.

"Alright," he said, messing my hair like when we were little.

I felt like a giant weight had been lifted from my chest. After I put Axel in bed last night, I wasn't able to go back to sleep. I spent the rest of the night and all early morning worrying about what was going to happen, checking on Axel every few minutes to verify that he was fine, and dreading the moment when mom and dad would finally wake up. Now it was all over and it was my time to rest.

But not for long because, after a couple of hours, my mom woke me up.

"Hunter!" She yelled from downstairs. "Telephone!"

Who could possibly be calling at 4pm on a Saturday? Don't people know that I'm trying to sleep? It better be Ariana or Ty because, otherwise, I'm going to be really mad that someone woke me up for nothing. Who am I kidding? Who else could it be?

"Hey, Hunt," Ty said on the other end of the line.

"Hi, Ty. What's up?" I asked.

"Umm… can I stay over at your house tonight?" He asked.

"Oh… actually, right now it's not a great time…," I said.

"Please?" He said. "I don't feel like being home right now."

"Um, okay, yeah, come over whenever you want," I said.

"Great, thanks," he said.

"Ty, is everything fine?" I asked.

"Not really," he said.

"What happened?" I asked.

"I'll tell you later," he said.

"Okay," I said.

"Thanks," he said.

"Ty?" I said.

"Yes?" He asked.

"I'm here for you," I said.

"I know," he answered. "See you later."

"See you," I said.

Damn.

The weight had returned to my chest.

# CHAPTER FORTY-EIGHT

I didn't know when Ty was going to arrive, but before he did, I had the monumental task of convincing my mother of letting me have a friend over less than 24 hours after I fought with her in the car and I decided not to wake her up when her favorite son arrived home at 4am with a wrecked car. It was an impossible mission, but it sounded like Ty really needed me, so I had less than half an hour to make it possible.

Usually, I would've prepared what I was going to say beforehand, but time wasn't on my side this time, so I decided to cut to the chase and improvise.

"Mom?" I asked, entering her office.

"Yes?" She answered.

"I need to ask you for something," I said. "But first, I want to apologize and I want you to know that I'm not doing it only to get you to say yes to the thing that I'm going to ask. I was planning on apologizing anyway."

"Okay… what are you apologizing for?" She asked.

"First, for being a dick to you yesterday in the car," I said. "I'm sorry. I regret it. I shouldn't have said many of the things that I said and I definitely shouldn't have been so rude. Secondly, I want to apologize for not waking you up when Axel arrived. I don't actually have a rational explanation or an excuse for why I did what I did. I don't even know why I did it. All I can say is that he is my brother and I'm sorry."

"Okay, I accept your apologies," she said. "Now, what do you want?"

"Can Ty stay over tonight?" I said.

"What part of being grounded don't you understand?" She asked.

"Please," I said. "I'll do anything. I'll do the laundry and clean the bathrooms. You can even ground me for another month."

"No," she said.

"But mom…," I started to say.

"You really don't want to test me right now, young man," she interrupted me.

"Mom, my friend needs me," I said and her facial expression changed from irritated to concerned.

"Why? What happened?" She asked.

"I don't know," I said. "But he sounded very upset over the phone. He said he didn't want to be in his house tonight. I'm worried. Please."

"Fine," she said. "But I'll add another week to your punishment."

"Thank you," I said.

Okay, that wasn't that hard. Now all I had to do was wait.

Ty arrived at my house like 15 minutes later and I immediately took him to my room. He hadn't brought a backpack and a sleeping bag this time, only dry tears on his cheeks and sadness in his eyes.

"What happened, Ty?" I asked.

"It's a long story," he said, pacing back and forth. "Everything started a few weeks ago. As you know, football practices are about to begin again and everybody on the football team is really excited but… the thing is that I'm not sure if I want to continue being part of the football team. I don't know if I want to dedicate so much of my life to it. I've felt like this for a long time now and I wanted to tell someone. I wanted to talk it over so I could make up my mind, but I didn't know who to tell. I wanted to tell my parents, but I couldn't because football means everything to my dad and I needed to make a decision before I could talk to them. I wanted to tell you and Ariana, but I felt like you guys wouldn't really understand because you don't know what it's like to be on the team and you don't know how important football is to my family, so I decided not to bother you guys with my problems. I wanted to tell my friends from the football team, but I couldn't because they would probably think that I was crazy and they would most likely rat me out with the coach to try to pressure me into staying. So I ended up telling Tony. He's family, he knows my dad, and he's on the football team, so I thought that maybe he could understand. But he didn't. That snitching little rat. I made him promise that he wouldn't tell our friends, our family, or the coach until I figured out what to do. But he broke his promise and he told our teammates and they began bad-mouthing me and giving me the cold shoulder to try to pressure me into staying on the team, which only made me want to leave the team even more, but whatever. When his plan didn't work, he decided to take it up a notch. Today, we had a family reunion at my place and he asked me if I had already made a decision. I told him that I was still thinking about it and, since that wasn't the answer he wanted, he decided to tell my whole family that I wanted to get out of the football team. As expected, all hell broke loose. My father asked me if that was true and I told him that I was thinking about it. My uncles and my cousins started to tell me how stupid that was and they gave me a thousand reasons not to do it. Not one of them wanted to know how I felt or why I wanted to quit the team, they only wanted to tell me what to do and point out how stupid I was for even thinking about it. They didn't wanna listen, they only wanted to give me their two cents. I tried to explain myself, but my father was getting angrier and angrier. He forbade me to do it, but I told him that it was not his decision to make. We started yelling at each other until I couldn't take it any longer. I had to get out of there, so that's what I did. But now I don't know what to do."

"Do your parents know you're here?" I asked.

"Yeah, I told my mom that I was going to stay over with you

tonight before I stormed out," he said.

"I'm sorry that happened to you, Ty," I said. "I really am. What Tony did was low, even for him, and it's a shame the way your family reacted. This is not your fault, you know that, right?"

"I... yeah, I guess I do," he said.

"Good," I said. "Now, have you decided if you're gonna stay or leave the team?"

"No," he said. "I can't think straight right now. It's as if my brain has split into two, one part that wants me to stay on the team and the other that wants me to leave. And both parts are yelling at me, urging me to make a decision. But I can't. Please tell me what to do, Hunter. Please, I trust your judgment."

"I can't do that, Ty," I said. "I wish I could do it to end your suffering, but I can't. It's like you said, this is your decision to make. Not your parents', not your friends', and not mine. It's yours. But I can help you quiet those voices that are yelling at you."

"How?" He asked.

"By talking about them," I said. "Why don't you start by telling me if you really like football or not?"

"I do like it," he said. "It's fun... but I'm not sure if I love it anymore. I don't know, I guess I'm starting to realize that I like other things too. And I like them more than football. I mean, I see how psyched all of my teammates are for getting back to football practice and I should feel that way, but I don't. Not anymore."

"Why do you think that is?" I asked.

"I don't know," I said. "I guess it's because I don't want my entire life to revolve around football anymore. It's really time-consuming, you know? People expect me to forget about everything else and concentrate on just that one thing, but I don't want to. I don't want to spend hours and hours practicing anymore, not to mention that I don't want to dedicate my entire summer to it. I want to do other things. And I don't really like the environment anymore. I mean, sure, I like my teammates… but I also don't, they can be real assholes sometimes. And I'm also worried about the brain injuries and the life-long consequences that playing football can have. I mean, I understand taking the risk if you want to do it professionally and make millions in the future, but I don't want that, so I'm not sure if the risk is worth it."

"Ty, if you have that many reasons to quit the team, then why haven't you done it yet?" I asked. "What's keeping you there? What is the other voice yelling?"

"Honestly, I don't want to disappoint my dad," he said. "Football means the world to him and I want to make him happy. I want to make him proud."

What is it with dads and sports? Why is it so important to them that their sons love football?

"It seems to me like you have a lot of reasons to quit the team and only one reason to stay," I said. "And that reason is not good enough, Ty. Not if it's going to make you miserable."

"I know… I know," he said. "You're right."

"Again," I said, "I can't tell you what to do, but I can give you an advice: talk to your father. Tell him how you feel. Be honest with him. He's going to love you no matter what. It's nice that you want to take his feelings into consideration, but you shouldn't do it at the expense of your own. By bottling it all up you're protecting everyone but yourself. Just talk to him like you talked to me. And if he doesn't want to listen, then make him listen. It might be difficult at first, but I can guarantee you that he loves you more than he loves football."

"Thank you, Hunter," he said. His characteristic smile was slowly returning to his face. "I knew it was a good idea to come here."

"You're always welcome here, Ty," I said.

We spent the rest of the day playing board games, watching movies, and talking about silly things to get his mind out of what happened at his house. Since he didn't bring any clothes this time, I asked my brother to lend him one of his PJs—he was too big to fit into one of mine.

"I thought mom and dad grounded you for two weeks, not two hours," Axel said to me when he gave me one of his PJs.

"They did. I got out early for good behavior," I joked.

"Really?" He asked.

"No," I said. "I'm actually now grounded for three weeks."

"You traded another week of punishment for a sleepover? I thought you were supposed to be smart," he said.

"I am. This was important," I said.

I also borrowed his PlayStation 2 and Ty tried to teach me how to play *Need for Speed: Underground*, but I was so bad at it that he ended up winning every single race.

This time we didn't end up talking until dawn, by midnight we were exhausted, so we decided to call it a day and go to sleep.

We woke up in time to have breakfast with my family. At first, I worried that my mom would try to interrogate Ty about what happened, but thankfully she didn't. After breakfast, we played for a bit on the PS2 again and then he decided that it was finally time to get back home and confront his father.

"Good luck. And let me know how everything goes, okay?" I said to him before he left.

"Of course," he answered. "Thanks again, Hunt. And please thank your family for letting me stay here."

A couple of hours later he called me with good news. Apparently, yesterday, after he left, his mother had a long conversation with his father and she made him realize that the job of a parent is to nurture and support their kids while they figure out who they are, not to turn them into little clones of themselves. So, when Ty arrived home with the intention of expressing himself and telling him how he felt, his dad was ready to listen.

They had a heart-to-heart conversation where Ty explained why he didn't want to continue on the team and his father explained to him why football was so important to him. Apparently, when his parents (Ty's grandparents) first moved here, they were one of the only Black families in town. All through Ty's dad's childhood, he and his parents suffered harassment from some of the other town residents. They called them racial slurs, avoided contact with them, refused to provide some services, and someone even painted "Get out of my town" on their driveway once. Things didn't get better when Ty's dad began dating Ty's mom, a white woman. Many people in town still considered interracial couples a sin, so they began targeting and bullying Ty's father even more.

My blood was boiling when Ty told me this. How despicable do you have to be to hate someone just for the color of their skin or for who they love? That's the thing about the South and little towns like this. They're very friendly, alright, but only to the people who look like them.

However, everything changed when Ty's dad joined the football team in high school. He quickly became the quarterback of the team and led them to their first victory in the regional championship, which turned him into the star of the town. That's why Ty's father loves football so much, it changed his life and transformed him from the pariah of town to a beloved and respected athlete. And that's why he instilled a love for football in Ty since he was little and why he always pushed him to excel in that sport, because he didn't want Ty to suffer the same kind of things he suffered when he was little. He didn't want Ty to know what it was like to grow up as a Black kid in a racist town. He wanted him to know what it was like to be a football star in a sports-loving town.

"I'm so sorry, Ty," I said. "I can't believe that it took a football regional championship trophy for the people in this town to treat your father as a human being."

"Yeah, it sucks," he said. "But at least things are better now. I mean, they're not great, but at least they're better than it was back then."

"This is kind of a stupid question because, knowing this town, I'm pretty sure that I already know the answer, but have you ever been treated differently just for the color of your skin?" I asked.

"Oh, yeah, totally," he said. "I mean, not nearly as bad as the stories my dad told me, but, for example, I've noticed that, when I enter a store, the employees stare at me and sometimes the security guards follow me discretely to make sure that I don't steal anything. Also, many people when they first met me have asked me what country am I from. And, of course, some people, including some teachers, have told me that I'm 'very articulate,' as if that was a compliment."

Oh my god. I never thought that those kinds of things happened to Ty. I mean, I'm not naïve or stupid, I know there are still some pretty horrible people in this world and that racism is still very much alive in this country, but I guess that the rational part of me couldn't fathom why a kind, optimistic, cheerful, and nice boy like Ty could be treated that way just for the color of his skin. That was so infuriating and unfair. And it made me think of Uncle Richard. He was a horrible person that had done horrible things, but I bet that he is treated nicely everywhere he goes just because he is white. What a messed up world.

"But anyway," he said, "after my dad told me all of that, he said that he would support me no matter what and that he only wanted me to be happy."

"So, you're actually doing it?" I asked. "You're dropping out of the football team?"

"Yeah, I think I am," he said.

"How do you feel?" I asked.

"I feel good," he said. "It feels right."

"I'm happy for you, Ty," I said. "And I'm glad everything worked out between you and your father."

"Yeah, I do too. I feel closer to him now," he said.

"That's good," I said.

"Listen, I gotta go now, I promised my dad that I was going to help him clean the garage, but thanks again for the advice, Hunt. See you tomorrow," he said.

"See ya," I said.

I was about to go back to my room when my mom

intercepted me on my way to the stairs.

"How's Ty?" She asked.

"He's fine," I said.

"What happened?" She asked.

"Nothing… just some problems with his dad. But everything's fine now," I said.

"Good," she said, turning around to return to her office.

"Mom?" I said.

"Yes, honey?" She said.

"Do you think dad likes me?" I asked.

"What?" She said. "Hunter, your dad loves you very, *very* much…"

"Yeah, I know he loves me," I interrupted her. "But do you think he likes me?"

"Of course he does, honey," she said. "Where is this coming from?"

"I don't know… it's just that I see the kind of relationship other boys have with their dads and… I just don't have that with him," I said.

"Oh, honey," my mom said, hugging me. "Yes, you two are very different, but you're also more similar than you think. Your father is a good man and he loves you very much. His children are the most important part of his life, I know that. If you want to have a closer relationship with him, all you have to do is show him that you need him and he'll be there for you."

"I'm not very good at showing how I feel," I said.

"Then tell him," she said.

"I'm worse at that," I said.

She chuckled.

"Oh honey, do you want me to talk to him?" She asked.

"No! Please, mom, don't say anything to him," I said.

"Okay," she said, lifting my chin with her fingers and giving me a warm smile. "I won't say anything."

I know that sometimes I complain a lot about my mom, but honestly, there's no one in this world that I love more than her.

# CHAPTER FORTY-NINE

Ty did it. He actually got out of the football team. His coach and his teammates weren't happy, but he was and that was the important thing. He seemed more relaxed now, as if a giant weight had been lifted from his shoulders. As if he didn't have to pretend to be someone else anymore.

Unfortunately, Tony didn't take his defeat well. He resumed his bullying of me, but now he and his stupid friends also picked on Ty and Ariana. It had only been a week, but I was sick of it. I was sick of seeing my friends suffer because of him, I was sick of putting up with his bullying since I was in middle school, and I was sick of his terrible behavior going unpunished. I'd had enough. It needed to end, so I decided to confront him.

I knew he got out of football training at 4:30pm, so, on Friday, I lied to Mr. Dan and said that I needed to go to the principal's office to ask something, but in reality, I went to the parking lot next to the football field to wait for Tony to come out.

Luckily, when he did, he was alone.

"Tony!" I said.

"Hey, Blunter," he said with a mocking smile. "What's the matter? You want a beating?"

"What's your problem?" I asked.

"Excuse me?" He said with a surprised face.

"What have I ever done to you?" I asked. "What have my friends ever done to you? Why do you feel the need to pick on us? Is your life really that sad and empty that you need to fill it by bullying other people? Why can't you just focus on living your own life and leave everyone else alone?"

"You really want a beating, don't you?" He asked with a smile, cracking his knuckles. "Well, good thing my cousin is not here to protect you this time."

"No, I want answers," I said defiantly.

"And what do you want me to say?" He said with a chuckle. "That I had a rough childhood? That I secretly envy you? That I 'bully' you and your friends because I want what you have? Don't be stupid, this isn't a movie. I pick on you because you're a loser. I pick on your weird friend because she's a loser. And I pick on my idiot cousin because now he's a loser. That's just the natural order of things. It's the circle of life, nerd."

I didn't know what I was expecting. Ty was right. He was just a natural-born bully. If I was going to make him leave us alone, it wasn't going to be with polite words and logical arguments.

"Well, from now on you're gonna leave my friends alone and me unless you want your ass handed to you on a silver platter," I said.

"What did you just say?" He asked in an enraged tone.

He was about to hit me, but thankfully, I brought the big guns. And by that, I mean a picture of my brother and me.

"Just in case you didn't know, idiot, my brother is Axel Grayson." I could see fear in Tony's eyes when I mention my brother's name. "Yeah, *that* Axel Grayson. And we might not have the best relationship, but he's still my brother and he would do anything for me, including beating up a second-class scum like you. So I'm going to say it just one more time: from now on you're going to leave me and my friends alone, understood?"

He was furious. He still had his fist in the air, but he hadn't moved it one inch. He kept staring at me and then at the picture.

"Fine," he said, spitting at my feet and walking away angrily.

I didn't enjoy doing that. I didn't like sinking to his level to get what I wanted. It didn't make me feel good. Unfortunately, sometimes bullies like him only understand their own language.

# CHAPTER FIFTY

Axel is going insane at home. He's not used to staying in the house for this long.

And it's only been a week.

"Hunter, you gotta tell me your secret," he said after barging into my bedroom on Saturday night. "How do you do it?"

"How do I do what?" I asked.

"How do you always stay home without going insane?" He asked.

"Are you kidding me, Axel?" I said. "It's only been a week."

"I know, but I can't take it anymore. I can hear the outside calling me," he said, dramatically looking out the window of my room.

"You're insane," I said.

"I know! You gotta help me. What do you do when you lock yourself in your bedroom for hours? Do you have a secret door that leads to the street that mom doesn't know about?" He said, looking behind the clothes in my closet.

"No! And stop messing up my clothes," I said.

"Then how do you do it?" He asked. "What can I do to keep my sanity?"

"You can read," I said, pointing to the dozens of books that I had in my room.

"Good one," he said, laughing.

"I don't know what to tell you, Axel," I said. "I love staying home because it gives me time to relax, to think, to read, to write, to watch movies, and to be by myself in peace. If you don't like doing any of that, then you can find a new hobby. I don't know, watch sports, do a jigsaw puzzle, play video games, do whatever you like or whatever you want. There are a lot of fun things you can do here alone without having to leave the house."

"That's actually a great idea," he said. "Come on, let's go play a video game."

"What? I… I said alone…," I said.

"Yeah, but it's more fun when you play against someone else," he said.

"But I suck at video games," I said.

"I know, but it's better than nothing," he said.

"How flattering," I said. "Am I blushing?"

"Come on," he said, pulling my arm so I would follow him to his room.

I thought about it for a few seconds. I had planned to spend my night re-reading *His Dark Materials* by Philip Pullman because I was going to write about it in next week's Book of the Week, but a night playing video games with my brother didn't sound so bad.

"Ugh, fine," I finally said.

"Great!" He said.

Axel went to the kitchen to grab some snacks and then he put *NASCAR Thunder 2003* on his PS2. He beat me in every single race, but it was fun. We also talked a lot—something that I'm not used to doing with him. He told me about how it was to work with dad at his company, and I told him that I used him to threaten Tony yesterday. He got a big kick out of it.

"Oh my god, I can't believe you did that," he said, laughing. "I would totally kick his ass, by the way. I know who you're talking about and that kid seems annoying as hell… hey, I wonder if I could use that excuse to get out of the house. 'Sorry, mom, I have to go out. I have to beat the crap out of a stupid football kid to defend Hunter's honor.'"

I laughed. "Well, it's better than when you said you were

going to the public library to study with your friends, when in reality you were going to your girlfriend's house."

"Wait, you knew about that?" He asked.

"Of course!" I said. "Everybody did. The public library closes at 6pm and you 'went' at 8pm. I remember we all had a good laugh at the dinner table. Mom even called your girlfriend's mom to let her know that you were on your way so she could keep an eye on you two."

He was on the floor laughing. "No wonder Mrs. Sawyer was waiting for me on the porch when I arrived."

We were both laughing when Ashley came into the room with a furious expression on her face.

"Will you please shut up," she said. "*The Cheetah Girls* is on Disney Channel and I can't listen to it with all your noise."

"Sorry, grasshopper," Axel said, still chuckling. That was his nickname for her because, when she was little, she used to jump everywhere. "We'll try to keep it down."

"What's going on here?" She asked. "Are you two having a slumber party and you didn't invite me?"

"We're not having a slumber party," I said, laughing because her mad face always makes me laugh. "We're just playing video games."

"Wanna join us?" Axel asked.

"Yeah!" Ashley said, jumping up and down and grabbing one of the controllers.

She was surprisingly good and even beat Axel a couple of times. As for me, I never won a single race, but it was fun. We ended up playing until 2am. The following morning, I woke up at 11am and spent almost half an hour staring at my ceiling, thinking about what I was going to do that day. I decided that I was going to finish the book I was reading and maybe watch a movie or two. But all my plans fell apart when my dad knocked on my door shortly before noon.

"Come in," I said.

"Hi, son," my dad said. "You're just waking up?"

"Yeah," I said, rubbing my eyes. "I stayed up until 2am

playing video games with Axel and Ashley."

"Well, that explains why none of you have come down to have breakfast," he said.

"Sorry. I'll be down in a minute," I said.

"No, take your time, I didn't come for that," he said.

"Oh, then what is it?" I asked.

"I was wondering if you would like to go fishing with me," he said.

A fishing trip with my dad and Axel? It sounded interesting, but not very appealing. Not only do I hate sitting under the sun while my dad and Axel talk about sports and cars for hours, but I also don't like fishing. It's disgusting, boring, and I loathe the idea of killing animals just for sport.

"Oh... no, that's okay," I said. "You can just take Axel. I have a few school things to do."

"Actually, Axel's not invited," he said. "I thought it could be just you and me."

"Oh... okay," it was all I could say because I was very confused about the whole thing, and not only because I had just woken up.

"But if you're busy then we can do it some other day," he said.

"No, no... I do have some work to do, but I can do it later. It's not that urgent, I can go. Is someone else going?" I asked because he sometimes invited one of his brothers or a friend to our outings.

"No, just you and me," he said.

"Great," I said. "But... I'm not very good at fishing."

"Oh... we don't necessarily have to go fishing," he said. "What do you wanna do?"

This was suspicious. Last week, I told my mom that I wished I had a closer relationship with my dad and now he was here, inviting me to do something together, just the two of us. Although maybe he wanted to teach Axel a lesson by only inviting me, since he trashed his old car just last week, but that wasn't very likely. No, this couldn't be a coincidence, mom probably said something to him—even after I explicitly asked her not to say anything to him. Dammit, I just wish that she didn't go into detail about our conversation. Hopefully, she only suggested to him that we should have a father-son day and nothing more because it would be pretty embarrassing if she told him everything we talked about.

"I don't know," I said. "Maybe we can go to the movies or to a restaurant."

"Okay, yeah, that sounds like fun," he said. "Let me know when you're ready to go."

I got out of bed, showered, and ate breakfast quickly so my dad wouldn't have to wait for so long. He took my suggestion and we went to the fancy movie theater downtown. There weren't many good options to pick from, so we ended up watching the new remake of *Dawn of the Dead*, which we both really enjoyed.

After the movie, we went to Eagle's Eye, a burger joint downtown. When we sat down, he seemed kind of nervous, but I'm not sure if he really was nervous or if I was just projecting my feelings onto him. The truth is, it had been a while since we had gone out just the two of us and I was worried that we wouldn't have anything to talk about. I mean, it had been fine so far because we didn't really need to talk in the car or in the movie theater, but now that we were in the restaurant, I was worried that we were going to run out of conversation topics quickly and end up eating our burgers in a long and awkward silence.

"So, how's school?" He asked.

"Good," I said. "I did very well on the midterms and each week more and more students go to the library, which is very exciting."

"Good, good... that's good," he said, taking a sip of his beer. "You got your mother's brain, thank god. She used to get straight A's in school too."

"Really?" I asked.

"Yeah, she was pretty intelligent—still is," he said. "I, on the other hand, was never very good at school. Only in Math, that's why I became an engineer."

"I didn't know that," I said.

"Yeah, Math and sports," he said. "Those were the only things I was good at in school. That and getting into trouble. So, you might want to thank your mother for your good grades, but I'm afraid that I—or at least my genes—might be responsible for that suspension you got a few weeks ago."

"Really?" I asked. "I should've used that as an excuse when the principal called me to his office."

He laughed and then took another sip of his beer.

"So…," he said, trying to think of something else we could talk about. "How's your friend, the football player?"

"Ty? He's good," I said. "He's actually not on the team anymore."

"Oh no, what happened?" He said.

"He didn't like it anymore," I said.

"Oh… well, that's a shame," he said, taking another sip of his beer.

He put his beer down and looked around to see if our food was ready, but our waitress was nowhere to be found. I awkwardly looked around too, trying to think of something else we could talk about, but I couldn't think of anything, mostly because we don't have any shared likes or hobbies.

I couldn't believe that it hadn't even been 10 minutes and we were already out of conversation topics. How sad was it that I couldn't talk to my own father? I have his blood and genes and I couldn't even have a conversation with him that's longer than 10 minutes. I didn't know if I should cry about how sad that was or laugh because of how pathetic it was.

"Oh, have I shown you this?" He asked, breaking the silence and handing me a blue device.

"No, what is it?" I asked because I couldn't tell if it was a calculator, a cell phone, or a portable video game.

"It's my new cell phone, the BlackBerry 7210," he said. "It's the first BlackBerry to have a color screen. Isn't it beautiful?"

"Yeah," I said, looking at the phone.

"It also has a web browser, 16MB of storage, and a battery that lasts up to three days," he said.

"Impressive," I said, handing the phone back to him.

"Yeah, I got it last week," he said. "Your mom didn't want me to get it because it was too expensive, but when I saw it at the mall last week, I couldn't help myself. It's a beauty."

I didn't know what to say, I've never really understood dad's fascination with technology, so I was probably more on the side of my mom. Fortunately, I didn't have to say anything because the waitress brought our burgers just as he stopped talking. We started eating and the silence became less awkward, but it was still silence.

I felt terrible because I could see that he was really trying to connect with me. He was trying to ignite a spark that could eventually bring us closer together. I mean, sure, mom probably forced him to do this, but I could see that he was trying and I appreciated it. The least I could do was try too. I owed it to him.

So far, I had let him do most of the heavy lifting, mostly because he's better at talking than me, but he was out of his comfort zone. He couldn't talk about the things he usually talks about (sports, cars, technology, etc.) because I don't know anything about those topics—or care about them, for that matter. But if this was going to work, I had to do my part too. However, I faced the same problem as him, I couldn't talk about the things that I liked (books, movies, writing, etc.) because he didn't know or care about those topics. Luckily, unlike other people, talking about myself and my interests wasn't the only weapon in my arsenal.

"So, dad, did you ever consider studying any other career besides engineering?" I asked.

"As a matter of fact, son, I did," he answered, and then he told me that his career choice wasn't as simple as he initially made it sound. He also considered studying accounting, finance, and computer science, but ultimately, it was his love for cars that made him choose mechanical engineer. He said that he didn't regret his choice at all, but that he has always wondered what his life would look like if he had pursued a career as a professional football player.

After that, I asked him a ton of questions, including if he ever considered moving to another city (not even for a second, especially not after he met mom), how his childhood was different from mine (there was less technology), what he wanted to be when he was a kid (a firefighter), which had been his favorite year ever (1993, the year Ashley was born because it was the first time that our little family was finally complete), and if he had any dreams that he had yet to achieve (he wanted to someday run the company he worked for and watch all his children grow up to live successful and fulfilling lives).

The conversation went by so smoothly that we were surprised when mom called to find out where we were. It had already been more than 3 hours since we first arrived at the restaurant, but neither of us had noticed it.

"Oh my god, would you look at that?" He said. "It's almost 7pm. I'm surprised they haven't kicked us out yet, I better ask for the check."

After paying, he asked me if I wanted to go to my Uncle Benny's house to watch the game. I didn't, so I said no. I didn't even know what game he was talking about and I couldn't see how spending a night with my uncles and cousins was going to improve that day—if anything, it was going to ruin it—so I lied and said that I still had some homework to do.

He drove me home and neither of us said a single word during the car ride, we just listened to The Eagles on the radio and enjoyed the ride. It was a silent car ride, but it wasn't awkward. It was comfortable. I looked out the window and I was happy because I felt like we made a lot of progress today. I felt like I knew my dad better now. I mean, we weren't going to win any prize for the best father-son relationship anytime soon, but hey, Rome wasn't built in a day.

When we arrived at the house, he parked the car in the

street instead of in the driveway so I could get out of it easier and he could drive off to Uncle Benny's. But before I could open the car door, he said that there was something he wanted to tell me.

"Listen, son, I... I know I haven't always been the father you deserve and I'm sorry about that," he said.

"What?" I asked, utterly confused.

"I know how you feel," he said. "I know that you wish we had a closer relationship and I know that you sometimes wonder if I even like you."

"What...? What are you talking about? How do you know this?" I asked.

"Your mom told me," he said.

"Of course she did," I said.

Dammit, this is why I don't tell my mom anything.

"Don't be mad at her," he said. "She told me not to tell you anything, but I felt like it was important to let you know that I know how you feel so that everything that I'm about to say has more meaning."

"Okay...," I said.

"Your feelings are valid, son, and they're not your fault," he said. "It's my fault. I dropped the ball with you, Hunter, and I'm sorry. It's true that I have paid less attention to you than to your siblings, but it's not because I don't like you, it's because I felt like you didn't need me. Axel inherited my natural ability for getting into trouble and Ashley is as mischievous as she is cute, but you... you came out of the womb as a mature and responsible little kid. I love your siblings, but they were a handful growing up, always throwing a tantrum or getting into trouble. And, well, sometimes they're still a handful and they keep getting into trouble. But we never had any big problems with you, Hunter. You've always been very well-behaved, self-reliant, and independent. Whenever I tried to help you with your homework, you had already finished it by yourself; whenever you were having difficulties with something, like learning how to read or how to solve fractions, instead of asking for help, you would lock yourself in your room and come out of it as an expert; you've never really liked sports, except for swimming, and I couldn't teach you anything about that sport because you pretty much taught yourself everything about it and you surpassed my abilities in it very quickly; I never needed to give you any big lessons about right and wrong, or good and evil, or responsibility, or any other important values because you always seemed to know them already; I never needed to teach you how to behave, or tell you not to get into trouble, or force you to study for your exams, you already seemed to do it by instinct. I'm very proud of you for all of this, Hunter, but it also made me feel like you didn't need me. You were already pretty good by yourself. And I didn't want to force myself into your life because I was afraid that I would ruin you. You were already pretty perfect as you were and I didn't want to somehow make you worse. You were like a Fabergé egg and I felt like if I got close to you, I would break you, so I took a step back and I just let you be yourself. But I now realize that that was a mistake. I shouldn't have taken a step back; I should've been right there by your side while you became the wonderful young man that you are right now. While trying to be a good father, I did exactly what my father did: I disappeared. I was there, but not really. I loved my father, he was a good man, but he wasn't a great dad. He was an excellent provider, he worked hard to give us everything we needed, but he was cold and distant. When your mother first got pregnant, I promised myself that I wasn't going to be like him. It's funny, I think when most men have children, they try to be different from their own fathers. They want to be better. But that's a difficult thing to do because everything we know about what it means to be a father we learned from our own fathers, so the cycle involuntarily continues. But I promise you that I'll try as hard as I can to break that cycle, Hunter. I'll promise that, from now on, I'll be a better dad to you. I can't promise you that I'll succeed because I'm only human, but I promise you that I'll try. You know, I remember that, when I was a kid, I used to think that adults had it all figured out. That they knew exactly what to do and how to do it. But the truth is that we don't. As a person, you never stop making mistakes and learning from them. No one's perfect. Not me, not your mom, not anyone. I've made a lot of mistakes and I can't change the past, but I can change the future and I promise you that I'm going to try to be a better dad to you because you deserve it and because I love you."

"I love you too, dad," I said, fighting back my tears.

"And I want you to know that I'm here for you, son," he said. "You can talk to me about anything and I'll be here to listen."

"Thank you… although I'm not very good at talking," I said with a chuckle to avoid crying.

"You talk to your mother all the time," he said.

"That's because she makes me," I said.

He laughed. "You're right about that."

"But I'll try, dad," I said. "I promise that I'll try to be a better son too."

"You're already a pretty wonderful son, Hunter."

I smiled and I opened the door to get out of the car, but before I stepped out, I hugged him. This caught him by surprise because he wasn't a big fan of physical contact. My mom was, but dad wasn't. And that was okay because I'm not either. I don't like it when people touch me out of nowhere and hugs make me very uncomfortable, but this was a special occasion. And yes, maybe I was too old for hugs (can you be too old for hugs?), but I didn't care. I wanted him to know that I appreciated everything he did today, and since I couldn't quite put it into words, I decided to show him.

"Thank you. And thank you for today, dad. I had a really good time," I said, and then I got out of the car without waiting for an answer.

I didn't need one. Everything had already been said.

# CHAPTER FIFTY-ONE

The end of the semester was swiftly approaching. The last two weeks of March went by in the blink of an eye. Nothing particularly interesting happened, but it was a pretty good month for the library. The visitors have not gone up as dramatically as they did back in January when the reading contest was first announced, but they haven't dropped significantly either. They have stabilized at approximately 150 visitors per week, which is a pretty good amount considering the number of visitors the library had at the beginning of the school year (zero).

The race for the first place in the reading contest is still pretty much the same. Hope, Brian, and Hugo are in the lead, and Valery and Samantha, two junior girls, are close behind them. I currently have my money on Hope for the win, but I wouldn't be surprised if Hugo pulled an upset victory at the last second. I guess only time will tell.

Ty's already big smile has somehow grown even bigger in the last couple of weeks. He's doing great at school; he's been doing all of his homework and assignments and his grades just keep going up. He has also gone from going three times a week to the art classroom in the afternoon to going every day. He still hasn't shown us his work—he says that he wants to keep it a secret until it's finished—but he comes out of that classroom with such a big smile that it almost doesn't matter what he's doing in there, the important thing is that he's happy.

In more depressing news, almost all of Ty's so-called "friends" from the football team have stopped talking to him. My little talk with Tony worked and he has no longer picked on us, but I'm sure that he still trash talks Ty with his teammates behind his back because they all started to ignore him and pretend that he doesn't exist. To be honest, I never trusted Ty's football friends. I can smell BS a mile away and they were full of it. But still, it was sad that they all cut ties with him so quickly because Ty did consider them his friends. But he's Ty, he makes friends as easily as I read books, so this didn't seem to affect him as much as I thought it would. He has already made a bunch of new friends in the art classroom and he has even started to socialize more and more with the people that go to the library.

Ariana, on the other hand, has been more distant every day. For a minute, it seemed like everything was going back to normal. She stopped missing school and I could feel that she was starting to be the same Ariana as before, but last week she began to skip school again and now she seems more distracted and preoccupied than ever. But other people don't seem to notice it.

"What do you think's going on with Ariana?" I asked Ty yesterday during Biology.

"What do you mean?" He answered.

"Haven't you noticed that she hasn't been herself lately?" I asked. "She's been distracted, as if her mind was somewhere else. And she has missed school twice in the last two weeks."

"Missing school? That sounds very Ariana to me," Ty said.

"You seriously haven't noticed anything?" I asked.

"No, she seems like the same Ariana to me," he said. "Just yesterday, during lunch break, she recited the first lines of the Constitution to convince me to give her a bite of my muffin. I mean, what's more Ariana than that?"

"I don't know," I said. "I feel like something's wrong."

"I'm sure it's nothing, but if you're worried, why don't you just ask her?" He asked.

Ty was right, so that's exactly what I did. That afternoon, after Ariana and I accompanied Ty to his house, I suggested going to the park before we went to our respective houses and she said yes.

"Oh my god, do you remember when I taught you how to hang upside down from the monkey bars?" She said, running towards the monkey bars to do just that.

"How could I forget?" I said. "I still have that picture you took of me hanging upside down with the sun behind me. It's one of the only pictures of me that I actually like."

"It feels like it was a million years ago," she said, hanging upside down with her hair flowing in the air around her face in a loose braid. "Come on, join me."

I climbed the monkey bars and hung upside down next to her. I put my hands up—or, well, down—and I enjoyed the breeze of air that was gently blowing in my face. I closed my eyes and, for a minute, nothing else mattered, just the fact that I was enjoying a beautiful day at the park with my best friend, just like that August afternoon almost a year ago. But I couldn't forget the reason I had invited her here.

I thought a lot about how I should ask her, but in the end, I decided to leave all subtleties behind and cut straight to the chase.

"Ari, can I ask you something?" I said, coming down from the monkey bars.

"Of course," she answered, coming down too.

"What's going on with you?" I asked.

"What do you mean?" She asked, visibly confused.

"I know something's wrong, Ari," I said. "I know you're hiding something. I can feel it."

"What are you talking about, Hunter? I'm not hiding anything. I'm fine," she said, fixing her braid.

I knew she would answer like that. If there was really something going on with her and she hadn't told me by now, it was probably because she didn't want to share it with anyone or because she didn't feel comfortable doing it. But I needed her to know that I was there for her. I needed her to know that she could trust me and that, whatever she was going through, she didn't need to do it alone.

"Please don't lie to me, Ari," I said. "I can feel something's wrong. You haven't been the same lately. I don't know what it is, but I know that something's going on. You might be able to fool everyone else, but you can't fool me. If there's something I can help you with, please tell me; I'm here for you."

"There's nothing going on, Hunter, I'm fine," she said, avoiding eye contact.

"Really? Then why don't I believe you?" I asked.

"I don't know," she said, "maybe you've read too many mystery novels and now you think you're some kind of Sherlock Holmes, but there's nothing here to solve, okay? By the way, do you have any good mystery book recommendations but with female detectives?"

"Yes, of course I do," I said, "but don't try to change the topic. Ariana, I've known you long enough to know that something's wrong. Look, it's okay if you don't want to talk about it. I get it, believe me. I know how annoying it can be when someone's trying to force you to talk about something you don't want to. But I also know that it's not healthy to keep it all to yourself. It's not healthy to keep it all in. If you want to let it out, I'm here for you, Ari. Always. I really want to know what's going on with you… but I know I shouldn't force you to tell me, so I'm going to stop insisting. I just want you to remember that I'm here for you, okay? No matter what."

She smiled. But it was a sad smile.

"Why?" She asked.

"Why what?" I asked, confused.

"Why do you wanna know what's going on with me?" She asked.

"I… because I care about you, Ari, and if something's wrong, I want to help you," I said.

"But why do you care?" She asked.

"That's a silly question," I said. "You're my best friend, Ari, it's my job to care. It's literally the first thing in the job description."

She chuckled. "Is that so?"

"Yes," I said. "I think it's written somewhere in the Bible."

She laughed. Then she looked up at the sky and took a deep breath.

"Okay. You're right, something's going on with me. And you're right, it's not healthy to keep it all in. It's been eating me up inside for quite some time now. I thought I was doing a good job hiding it, but apparently I wasn't. And I've been doing an even worse job handling it. I don't know what to do with all the feelings I have inside," she said, starting to tear up. "I've wanted to tell you for some time now, but… it doesn't matter. I'm gonna tell you now, but just a heads up, it's not a happy story. The reason we moved here is that… my aunt, my mother's sister, has cancer and my mom wanted to be close to her so she could take care of her. When we first got here, she started to get better, but in the last couple of months, she has taken a turn for the worst. She's gotten weaker, paler and the doctors… they're doing their best, but… I'm starting to lose all hope."

"I'm so sorry, Ari," I said, hugging her and she started to cry.

"It's not fair," she said. "Why her? There are so many awful people on this planet, why is she being punished like that?"

"I am so sorry, Ari," I said again.

"And what's gonna happen to her daughter if she dies?" She said. "A girl shouldn't have to grow up without her mother."

"Don't think like that," I said. "Everything's going to be fine."

"Yeah, that's what my mother keeps telling me," she said. "But what if it's not? What if she doesn't get better? I try not to think about it, but my mind keeps going there and… and I don't like what I see."

"Oh, Ari, I'm so sorry," I said, getting some face tissues out of my backpack so she could blow her nose. "How old is she?"

"She's only 40," she said.

"Well, that's a good thing," I said. "She's still very young, which means that she has more strength to fight this horrible disease. I'm sure it's not her time yet. You just have to trust that the doctors are doing the best they can and that she is fighting as hard as she can to get better."

"Yeah, I… I guess you're right," she said.

"Are you close to her?" I asked.

"Yeah, very," she said. "She… she's my favorite aunt. We're very close, I tell her everything and… and I know this sounds very selfish, but I don't know what I would do without her. Who am I gonna talk to? Who will make me feel better after a crappy day? Who will reassure me that everything's gonna be okay, even when all signs point to the contrary? I cannot lose her. I can't."

"Oh, Ari," I said, hugging her again.

We spent the rest of the afternoon at the park. We sat on a bench and Ariana talked about her feelings. About all of them. From the rage she felt due to the unfairness of the situation to the fear of living in a world without her aunt. From sadness to guiltiness to sadness again. She let it all out. And I listened. That was all I could do. Unfortunately, this was not a problem I could help her solve. It was not up to me or her. This was way beyond our control. All I could do was be there for her. So that's what I did.

"I feel a little bit better now," Ariana said while we were watching the sunset. "You were right, it's not healthy to keep it all in. I felt like I was about to implode. Thank you for listening."

"I'll always be here to listen," I said.

"Can I ask you a favor?" She said.

"Of course," I said.

"Could you please not mention this to Ty?" She said.

"Ari… Ty is a good friend, you can trust him," I said.

"I know," she said. "I trust him. But I don't want him to know. Not yet. I'm not ready to tell other people."

"Okay," I said. "I won't say anything."

"Thanks," she said.

"So what do you want to do now?" I asked.

"Nothing," she said, resting her head on my shoulder.

"I can do nothing," I said.

# CHAPTER FIFTY-TWO

The following weeks I started to help Ariana with some of her schoolwork so she wouldn't have to worry so much about it and she could spend more time helping her mother take care of her aunt. I felt like it was the least I could do to help my friend during this difficult time.

I wanted to feel productive and I wanted to help Ariana as much as I could, but that was hard because there were not a lot of things I could do. I asked her every day how her aunt was doing, and luckily, the last couple of days, the answer to that question was "better."

"She says that she's feeling a lot better," Ariana said with a smile when I asked her yesterday. "And I believe her. She doesn't look as pale as she did a couple of weeks ago and she has regained the strength to do some things by herself, like cooking and bathing."

"That's great!" I said.

I was so happy to see Ariana happy again. It seemed like everything was finally falling into place. Ariana's aunt was getting better, Ty was happier than ever now that he had left behind the toxicity of the school's football team, the library had never been fuller or in better shape, and my relationship with my family was better than ever.

Axel is still grounded, and now, instead of going out every Saturday night, we watch movies and play video games. He picks the movies, so they're almost always very bad or very dumb (usually both), and I still suck at video games, but I've really enjoyed spending time with my brother. He's no longer the jerk he was when he was 15, he's more mature now and I'm glad that we've been able to reconnect and spend more time together, even if it is because he basically has no other option.

I've also been spending more time with Ashley. She now insists on joining me when I take Rufus out for a walk in the afternoons. At first, I didn't want her to join me all the time because I like walking Rufus alone, it gives me time to think and relax, but it's been fun. She's pretty talkative—one of the many characteristics that she shares with mom—so in our walks she does most of the talking and I do most of the listening. That means that my afternoon walks are not as quiet and relaxing as they used to be, but I like spending time with my sister.

Dad and I have also been talking more and spending more time together. We still don't have the same kind of relationship that he and Axel have—not even close—but we gotta start somewhere, right?

However, while my relationship with my dad, my brother, and my sister seems to be improving by the minute, my relationship with my mother is getting worse and worse every day. Lately, we seem to be at each other's throats all the time. Everything leads to an argument between us: my headphones usage, her need to constantly tell me what to do, my "attitude," her many questions, my refusal to answer her many questions, and, of course, our favorite point of contention: my stupid birthday.

"Guess what?" My mom asked me while she was driving me to get a haircut on Sunday. "Your cousin Jack is having a birthday party. Unlike you, he does understand the importance of celebrating his 15th birthday."

Jack is the son of my Uncle Harold. We used to be very close when we were little because we are both the same age, but now we don't even talk. He has become a little too much like his father for my taste—meaning that he's now sexist, racist, and homophobic—so now I always try to avoid him at family reunions. His birthday is on July 14, exactly two months after mine.

"So?" I answered, kind of annoyed that I had to take my headphones off for that.

"Nothing, it's just that your Aunt Carol asked me to help her organize Jack's party," she said, trying to make me jealous. "I told her: 'Sure, why not? My own son doesn't want a party, so I'll be happy to help you make Jack's dream come true and throw him the best birthday party of the year.'"

"Good for you," I said. "It seems like you finally got the party you wanted so badly."

"Watch it," she said, noticing my snark.

"Sorry," I said.

"So I was thinking…," she said, "what if we have a double birthday celebration? I'm sure that if you ask Jack he would have no problem sharing the spotlight with you and letting you celebrate your birthday with him. After all, there are only two months of difference and you used to be so close when you were little."

"Mom, no," I said. "Thank you, but that's a terrible idea. I don't want a party and I'm sure Jack doesn't want to share his birthday party, so don't even mention it to him."

"Okay, fine," she said. "And what about a regular, small party just for you? Just the family and your school friends. It doesn't even have to be in a venue, it can be at the house. Your father can grill some hamburgers and I can rent an above ground pool, I know how much you like swimming. Oh, and I can rent a karaoke machine and order a special book-themed cake from that cake shop that you like. I should probably start making the phone calls now because your birthday is less than a month away. I would also need to rent some tables for the backyard and buy a bunch of beach-themed deco-"

"That sounds very nice, mom," I interrupted her. "But no, thanks," and then I put my headphones back on to try to end the conversation before it turned into another fight.

"Hunter!" She said.

"What?" I asked, taking my headphones off again.

"You said that you didn't want a big party and I listened to you, so now why don't you want a smaller one?" She asked.

"No, mom, I said that I didn't want a party," I said. "It doesn't matter if it's big or small."

"Then what do you plan on doing for your birthday?" She asked.

"I don't know, just have a quiet day, maybe go out with Ty and Ariana to the bowling alley or to the movies or to a restaurant, I'm not sure yet. What I'm sure of is that I don't want a party," I said.

"But, honey, you can go out with Ty and Ariana any day you want," she said. "But you can only have a birthday party once a year. It's your special day, don't let it go to waste."

"Who says that I'd be wasting it?" I said. "And if it's supposed to be *my* special day, then why can't I do what I want? Why do I have to do what you want me to do?"

"Because I don't want you to miss out on this, Hunter," she said. "Everybody wants a party."

"No, not everyone. Not me," I said, and then I put my headphones back on.

# CHAPTER FIFTY-THREE

I think I can't take it anymore. I haven't had a minute to myself in more than a week. I need to rest. But I can't. The end of the semester is like a month away, which means that I now have to deal with final projects, more homework, and studying for finals. Add to that my responsibilities to the library, my family, and my friends and you got the perfect recipe for exhaustion.

Last week, all my "free time" was consumed doing homework, preparing study guides for finals, and working on my final projects for Math and Biology, which unfortunately are in teams chosen by the teacher, and in neither of them I ended up with someone I knew. It was awful, and unfortunately, this week is shaping up to be more of that.

On Saturday, I planned to do some of the things that I had to do for school so that I could have a little more free time during the week, but Ashley asked me to help her with her Math homework and then Axel begged me to watch *Armageddon* with him, so I ended up doing none of the things that I had planned and instead I spent the whole day with my siblings, which was pretty enjoyable, but zero productive.

On Sunday, I gave up trying to do schoolwork entirely and instead I just wanted to spend the whole day lying in my bed doing nothing, but then my dad asked me to go to the movies with him, so that's what I did. Again, I had a great time, but when Monday arrived, I felt exhausted from the lack of rest

I had during the weekend and overwhelmed by all the things that I still had to do that week.

And it didn't help that on Monday I had a meeting with my Spanish team to work on our final project, which ended up completely depleting the little energy that I had left. Spanish was the only class in which I wasn't with Ty or Ariana, so I ended up teaming up with six complete strangers that turned a simple one-hour activity into a whole-day task. Managing a group of 7 students when no one had a defined role in the team was basically impossible, so instead of working, they spent the first couple of hours of our meeting talking about other stuff and completely ignoring what we had to do. When we finally started working on the project, it was already 7pm and everybody already wanted to go home, so we ended up with a half-assed mess of a project that was probably going to get us a B- at best, but I was so exhausted that I didn't even care.

I ended up getting home after 8pm and I went immediately to my bed after having dinner. But even though I slept for almost 9 hours, the following day I still felt drained. And, even worse yet, the following day was just as busy as the day before.

After finishing a pretty busy shift at the library, I helped Ty and Ariana with some of their homework while also doing my own and then I had a meeting with my Social Studies team to work on our final project. Luckily, in this team I was with Ariana, but she seemed so tired after finishing her homework that I told her that I could do her part of the project and convinced her to go home. Thankfully, this team wasn't as big as the Spanish team, it consisted only of four persons and one of them was my friend Brian, so working was much easier this time.

The project was way more difficult than the Spanish one, but we finished it in less time and with a better quality.

"Mrs. Davis better gives us an A because that was some top-notch quality work we did right there," Brian told me after the team meeting was over. He accompanied me to a drinking fountain because I ended up with a dry throat from talking too much during the meeting.

"I bet she will," I answered.

"Hey, you wanna go grab something to eat?" He asked.

"I would love to, but I'm exhausted," I said. "Rain check?"

"Okay, no problem," he said.

When I got home, all I wanted to do was go to my bed, but mom had guests over.

"Hunter, you're finally home," mom said. "Come say hi to Amelia and Jon, they're our new neighbors from across the street."

"Hi," I said, trying to put on a convincing fake smile. They smiled back and I turned around to walk towards the stairs, but I was stopped before I could escape.

"Where are you going?" Mom asked. "Come sit with us for a minute."

I was not in the mood to make small talk with strangers, but I knew that right then was not a good time to start an argument with my mom. Besides, I didn't want to be seen as rude by the new neighbors. But why does the opposite of being rude has to be staying there to make small talk?

"Okay," I said and I took a seat.

"Were you in school, Hunter?" Amelia politely asked.

"Yeah," I answered. "I was finishing a school project."

"Your mom was telling us that yesterday you also stayed until late at school," Jon said.

"Yeah, I had another project to do," I said.

"Hunter, is high school really that hard here?" Amelia asked. "Because our daughter is just about to start high school in August and she has never been very good at school."

"Well, it's definitely harder than middle school, but you know, it's not impossible," I said.

"What was I telling you?" Mom said to the neighbors. "You have nothing to worry about, your daughter will do just fine. It's just that Hunter's a go-getter. He's never comforted with just a B, he always has to get that A+."

"Really?" Amelia asked me.

"I… I don't know about that," I said, trying to downplay my mom's bragging.

I just wanted to get out there and go to my bed, not boast about my academic proficiency—something that I hate to do even when I'm not tired.

"He's just being humble," my mom said. "You should see his report cards, it's just straight A's. In middle school, his teachers used to tell me that he could've easily been the valedictorian, but he was too quiet. They had to basically force him to participate, can you imagine?" She said with a laugh.

I could feel my cheeks starting to blush. I hate it when my mom does that. I hate when she vents my personal issues like it's something the whole community has to know about. I don't even tell my friends that kind of personal stuff, but my mom thinks it's perfectly okay to tell a couple of strangers she just met. That's why sometimes I prefer not to tell her what's going on with me. I only tell her the stuff that I'm comfortable with the rest of my family *and* the whole neighborhood knowing.

"But I'm telling you, this kid's a genius," my mom continued. "He has read like a thousand books *and* he has a job at the school's library."

"Really?" Jon and Amelia both asked, looking at me with a curious look and a lot of eye contact.

"Yeah," I said, kind of uncomfortable.

"He is the only student that has been offered a job at that school's library," my mom said. "Come on, Hunter, tell them about what you do at your job."

Unbelievable. Now I was starting to get really mad. I have worked at that library for almost a year now, and not once has my mom bothered to ask me what I do there. On the contrary, she always ignored me when I tried talking to her about it and she even made me feel guilty for accepting the job, but now that she could display me like a trophy in front of these strangers, she was dying to know everything about my job.

"Why don't *you* tell them? I've told you many times before

what I do at the library, I'm sure you have it memorized by now," I said in a sarcastic tone.

My mom was left shocked and speechless by my response.

"Can I go now?" I asked in a ruder tone than I intended, and without waiting for an answer, I stood up and headed for the stairs. "Nice to meet you," I turned around and said to an equally shocked and speechless Jon and Amelia.

When I was walking up the stairs, I started to regret what I did. I was still furious, but I shouldn't have done that. And now I didn't know what to do next. I thought about going back to the living room and apologize, but I was not in the mood to get scolded about my attitude. I also thought about just going to my bedroom and try to forget about it, but my guilt was not letting me move, so I just stood there in the middle of the stairs, frozen.

"I'm so sorry about that," I heard my mom saying. "You know how teenagers are."

"Totally," Amelia said. "Don't even worry about it. Our daughter behaves the same way sometimes."

"Yeah, it's as if rudeness is one of the side effects of becoming a teenager," Jon added.

"Yeah, it must be all the hormones," Amelia said.

"Tell me about it," my mom said. "You know, he's always been very smart, but also kind of weird and antisocial. And I don't know what to do with him anymore. I don't know how to help him. For a minute I thought that things were changing. He seemed more social since he started high school, you know, he started going to school parties and began bringing friends over instead of just spending every weekend locked up in his room. I thought that he was changing, but then stuff like this happens and… I don't know…"

Wow. So I'm still not good enough, huh? Ouch.

I wanted to stop listening and go to my bedroom, but my legs were not moving. A small part of me wanted to stay there and hear what she was about to say. It was the same part of me that knew that what she was about to say was true. It was that little voice inside my head that I had successfully silenced for the last few months, but that now was trying to claw its way out of the jail I had put it in. It was the same voice I'd been hearing my entire life and that now was ecstatic because its message was about to be validated yet again.

"I don't know what's wrong with him," my mom continued. "He has never been completely normal, so to speak. You know, when he was a kid…"

I heard a noise coming from my sister's bedroom and my body finally unfroze. I ran towards my room without making a sound and, once I was safe inside of it, I laid down on my bed without taking my shoes off and my pillow immediately began to get soaked with the familiar warmth of my tears.

# CHAPTER FIFTY-FOUR

This time I slept for 10 hours and, when I woke up, I still felt like a truck ran me over, so obviously, lack of sleep was not the source of my exhaustion. No matter how much I slept, I still felt depleted, annoyed, sad, and completely overwhelmed. And the worst thing is that I didn't know why. But one thing was starting to become clear to me: it wasn't my body that needed to rest, it was my mind.

I thought that maybe seeing my friends was going to make me feel a little bit better, but when I got to school and saw them before the first bell rang, I still felt like shit. I couldn't even laugh along with them while they talked about the principal's new goatee. All I could think about was how unnecessarily loud everyone around us was being. The chatting, the laughing, and the opening and closing of lockers all felt like hammer blows to my head.

"Is everything fine, Hunt?" Ariana asked me.

"What?" I automatically responded when I heard my name.

"I asked if everything's fine, you seem a bit... distracted," Ariana said.

"Oh, yeah, I'm fine. I was just thinking about what book I'm going to recommend in next week's Book of the Week," I lied.

She didn't seem to believe me, but luckily, the bell rang soon after and we went to class before she could continue to interrogate me.

I could barely pay any attention to my classes, though. I felt so disconnected from everything around me that I couldn't concentrate on what the teachers were saying. And all the classroom noise was driving me insane, from the clicking of pens to the side chatter. When the bell rang to indicate that it was lunch break time, I couldn't take it anymore. The noise was killing me and the mere presence of others around me was so annoying and overwhelming that I even felt like crying.

I couldn't go to the cafeteria feeling like that. If I went there, I felt like I was going to lose it and yell at someone at any moment or that I was suddenly going to burst into tears out of nowhere, and I couldn't let either of those things happen, so I decided to skip it and find a quiet place where I could be by myself.

I thought about going to the library, but there was no way I could be alone there. It wasn't like at the beginning of the school year, when I could go there to relax and escape from the rest of the world for a few hours. No, the library hadn't been quiet or empty in months. It had gone from a calm and safe space to a busy and noisy environment, filled with students looking for recommendations, doing schoolwork, studying for tests, or just hanging out. And it's stupid to complain about it because that was the purpose, after all. I had worked very hard all year to make that happen—but in times like this, I wished it was like it used to be. A place where I could get away from everything.

But that was long gone now, so I had to think of something else. I didn't have much time to think, though, so in the end, I decided to go with the old reliable: the restroom. Specifically, the second-floor restrooms that were always empty during lunch break.

When I entered, I breathed a sigh of relief because it was everything I was looking for: quiet and empty. I stood against the wall and, for a moment, I forgot that there was a whole school with hundreds of students out there. For a moment, it was just me, myself, and I and I immediately felt a little bit better.

I went to the sink to wash my face and I thought about my first day of high school, when I also went to the restroom to escape from the craziness of the outside. I looked at myself in the mirror and, physically, I still looked pretty much the same. Sure, I had grown a little since then and my hair was a little bit longer now, but I still had the same big brown eyes and the same dorky smile.

However, I didn't feel the same. My life was completely different now. It was better. I had a better relationship with my family now, I had amazing friends that I loved with all my heart, and I had successfully helped Mr. Dan completely reinvent the library. I mean, sure, school was kind of hard, but I was doing very well in it. It wasn't anything I couldn't handle. So, if my life was great, why was I so sad? Why did I feel so overwhelmed, annoyed, and depleted? Why did I want to crawl into a hole and come out in two months? It didn't make any sense. My mom was right: what was wrong with me?

When the bell rang to indicate that the lunch break was over, the restroom started to fill up, so I quickly got out of there. I felt a little more rested and relaxed, but way more confused than before. I started to walk to my locker with dozens of different questions about myself in my head, but they all came to an abrupt, unanswered death when I noticed that Ty and Ariana were waiting for me next to my locker.

"Hey, Hunt, where were you?" Ty asked.

"We were waiting for you in the cafeteria, is everything fine?" Ariana asked.

I considered telling them about how I felt and confess to them all the doubts and questions that were flooding my head, but in the end, I decided against it. If I didn't understand everything that was going on in my mind, how could they? Besides, what was I going to say? That even though my life is basically perfect right now, somehow I still feel sad? Oh, poor Hunter, he has perfect grades, a great job, a caring family, and amazing friends. No, I had to deal with this on my own. They already had their own problems and they were way bigger than mine. This was my own issue, and it was up to me to solve it. I didn't want to bother them with it.

"Yeah, everything's fine," I lied.

"Are you sure?" Ty asked.

"Then why didn't you go to the cafeteria? Did you feel sick or something?" Ariana asked.

They seemed so worried about me that I felt like the worst person in the world for skipping lunch break without telling them anything.

"No, I'm fine, I swear," I said.

"Then where were you?" Ariana asked.

"I was just in the library," I lied.

"Why?" Ty asked. "I thought Mr. Dan banned you from working during the lunch break."

I considered lying again and telling them that Mr. Dan needed help with something or that I had to finish some homework, but I had been lying so much lately that I started to worry that I wasn't going to be able to keep up with all my lies if they ever came up in the future, so this time I decided to tell the truth.

"Yeah, he did," I said. "I wasn't working. I just… I needed to be alone for a little while."

"See? I told you," Ty said to Ariana. "You owe me five bucks."

"No, *I* told you," Ariana said. "You're the one that owes me five bucks."

"What?" I asked, very confused.

"Oh, nothing, it's just that you seemed a bit cranky in the morning," Ty said.

"Yeah, you said that everything was fine, but your face was telling a very different story. We noticed that you seemed kind of annoyed and distracted, and when you get like that, you usually retreat from everyone to spend some time alone, so I bet Ty that you didn't go to the cafeteria because you probably wanted to be by yourself, just like that time at the party when we found you away from the crowd, sitting by the pool with three strangers instead of partying and dancing with everyone else inside," Ariana said.

"That's not true, *I* bet you that he probably went to the library to be alone," Ty said to Ariana, then he turned to me. "Just like that story you told me, when you walked into the woods to spend some time by yourself and you made your whole family worry about your whereabouts," he said with a little laugh.

"Wait, so you guys are now betting on how weird I am?" I asked.

"What? No," Ariana said, visibly confused.

"We never said it was weird," Ty said.

"Yeah, it's just something that you do," Ariana added.

"Oh, okay...," I said.

I tried to act like everything was fine, but everything they said just added more strength to the thousands of "what's wrong with you?" questions that were swirling around in my head. I felt like the floor was shaking under my feet and I was using every bit of energy I had to keep myself from crying. I didn't want to make a scene, so I had to get out of there fast.

I opened my locker and got out my books as quickly as I could.

"See you guys later," I said.

"Wait, Hunter, where are you going?" Ariana asked.

"To class," I casually said. "The bell already rang, remember?"

"Yeah, but... you're not mad at us, are you?" Ty asked.

"No, no, not at all, I'm fine," I said with the most convincing fake smile my mouth could possibly make. "I just need to get to Spanish; my teacher gets really mad when we're late. I'll talk to you later, okay?"

"Okay...," they both said with a confused look on their faces.

I wanted to go to the restroom and try to pull myself together again before going to Spanish, but I was already late, so I had to suck it up and go directly to class instead. But I couldn't pay attention to anything the teacher said during the entire class. My head hurt, the noise was driving me crazy, and my mind couldn't stop wondering what was wrong with me.

When the bell rang, I got out of the classroom as fast as I could and I went straight to the nearest restroom. I took a deep breath, I washed my face once again, and I decided to skip my next class. It was Social Studies, and the teacher told us last class that today we were going to work on an assignment in teams—something that I definitely didn't have the energy to do. Plus, it was one of the classes that I had with Ariana and I didn't want her to keep asking me what was wrong. So, I decided to skip my class and go home instead. But first, I had to go to the library to let Mr. Dan know that I wasn't going to stay for my shift after class.

"Hey, Mr. Dan," I said.

"Hunter, what are you doing here?" He asked when I entered the library. "Why aren't you in class? Is everything okay?"

"Yeah, everything's fine," I lied. "I just don't feel very well, my head is killing me, so I'm gonna go home early. Is it okay if I miss work today?"

"Of course," he said. "Take as many days as you need."

"Thanks," I said, "but it'll be only for today, I swear."

"I'm serious, Hunter, if you're sick, take as many days as you need," He said. "And don't worry, I won't take those days off from your salary. Consider it paid leave."

"No, it's not that...," I said. "It's just that I'm not sick."

"You're not? I thought you said that your head hurt," he said.

"Yeah, but it's not a fever," I said, "I just... I got a lot on my mind right now."

"Oh... do you want to talk about it?" He asked.

"Not really...," I said. "I want to think about it. But thanks."

"Okay, but if you need someone to talk to, I'm right here," he said. "This is a judgment-free zone, okay?"

"Thanks, Mr. Dan," I said. "I really appreciate that. Oh, and could you do me a favor? If Ariana and Ty come looking for me, could you tell them that I didn't feel well and I had to go home?"

"Sure," he said.

"Thanks. See you tomorrow, Mr. Dan," I said.

"See you tomorrow, Hunter," he said. "And take care of yourself."

"Thanks. I'll try," I said.

The walk home made me feel a little bit better. I put my headphones on, concentrated on the music, and, for a few minutes, I forgot about everything else. But I was so concentrated on the music that I didn't think about what I was going to say to my mom.

"Hunter, what are you doing home so early?" My mom asked me when I got home.

"Oh… umm… Mr. Dan gave me the day off because the library was going to be closed today due to a water leak," I lied.

"Oh, well, I was about to cook some pasta for Ashley and me, do you want some?" She asked.

"No, thanks," I answered. "I think I'm going to go take a nap."

"Okay, honey," she said. "Don't forget that we're going to leave for Aunt Sylvia's at 6."

"What?" I asked.

"It's your aunt's birthday, remember?" She said.

"Oh… that's today?" I asked.

"Yeah," she said.

Shoot. My mom told me about this weeks ago, and I had already told her that I would go. I couldn't cancel now. And certainly not after the way I talked to her yesterday in front of the neighbors—something that, by the way, we hadn't even discussed yet and that we both seemed to be ignoring.

"Okay," I said.

"Be sure to be ready before 6, you know that your dad doesn't like waiting," she said.

"I will," I said.

I went to my bedroom and I collapsed into my bed face-first to try to enjoy the little time by myself I had before I had to get ready to go to yet another family reunion where everyone could keep reminding me how weird I was. Yay.

# CHAPTER FIFTY-FIVE

Aunt Sylvia's party was exhausting. I spent the whole evening talking to my aunts, laughing with my uncles, and socializing with my cousins. I had to force myself to talk about my personal life, laugh at sexist and homophobic jokes, and feign interest in sports and gossips all night. It was extremely tiring, but I did it because I could still hear my mother's words in my head. "I don't know what to do with him anymore... I don't know what's wrong with him." That night, I couldn't give my family any reasons to point out how weird and antisocial I was because I was afraid that I was not going to be able to put on a brave face and fake a smile this time. I was afraid that I was going to break down crying if someone even vaguely suggested that there was something wrong with me. So I acted "normal."

And it worked, but the downside was that I didn't have any time to think about all the things that were going through my mind, so I had to push them all to the back of my brain and, the following day, I pretended that everything was fine.

"What happened, Hunter?" Ariana asked me as soon as she saw me.

"Yeah, why did you leave school early yesterday?" Ty asked.

"Oh... I had a headache," I said.

"We called you all afternoon, why didn't you answer?" Ty asked.

"Oh, I wasn't home," I said. "I had a family commitment. It

was my Aunt Sylvia's birthday."

"Okay, that explains it," Ariana said. "And how are you feeling now?"

"About what?" I asked.

"The headache…?" Ariana said.

"Oh… better, I took an aspirin and I feel better now," I lied.

"Good," Ty said. "Listen, Hunt, we wanted to apologize for what happened yesterday."

"Yeah," Ariana said. "We're very, very sorry if we made you feel bad, Hunter. It really wasn't our intention. Please don't be mad at us."

"Guys, you have nothing to apologize for. I'm not mad at you. Everything's fine. I'm fine," I lied.

The rest of the day, I tried to convince myself that everything was fine. I pushed my emotions away and I tried to enjoy the day. I forced myself to pay attention in class, I laughed along with my friends, and I even went to the noisy and crowded cafeteria during lunch break. I lied to myself and acted like everything was fine, hoping that it would come true, but it wasn't working, it was only making it worse. Everything I felt yesterday hadn't gone away, I was just trying to ignore it. But, deep inside, I still felt overwhelmed, sad, annoyed, exhausted, and angry. And I couldn't take it anymore, I felt like I was going to explode, so I decided to skip my Spanish class and go to the restroom to try to figure out what was going on with me.

I went into a stall and I immediately started to cry. I didn't even know what I was crying about, all I knew was that I wanted to cry, so that's what I did. I spent like 15 minutes sitting on the floor crying and then I stood up and tried to pull myself together. I washed my face to clean off the dry tears from my cheeks and then I looked at myself carefully in the mirror. I tried to make sense of that 14-year-old high school boy with red eyes and messy hair, but I couldn't. I couldn't even understand myself, how annoying is that? I needed help. I needed someone smarter than me to tell me what was going on with me, so I went out to find him.

"Hi, Mr. Dan," I said, entering his office at the library.

"Hunter, what are you doing here? What's going on?" He asked, visibly confused. "Wait, have you been crying?"

"Yeah, kind of," I said.

"What's wrong?" He asked, very concerned.

"Don't worry," I said, "it's nothing serious. I just… I want to talk."

"Okay," he said. "Come sit. Do you want a glass of water?"

"No, thanks. I'm fine," I said, taking a seat.

"What do you want to talk about?" He asked.

"I… I don't know what's going on with me," I said. "I should be fine. I should be great, actually. My life's really good right now, but for some reason, during the last couple of days, everything has been bothering me. Everything. From the loudest of laughs to the most subtle pen clicks. Even bright lights have started to bother me and I don't know why. And not only that, lately, I've been feeling like an endless barrel of negative emotions. I feel sad, angry, and overwhelmed all the time for no good reason. I can't think straight. I can't concentrate. I can't hold a conversation without feeling utterly annoyed and depleted. I'm exhausted all the time, no matter how much sleep I get. I want to kick and scream and cry and take a million naps. My life is better than ever, but somehow I can't take it anymore, I just want to be left alone. I just want to leave everything behind and be by myself on a desert island for a month. What is wrong with me? Why can't I be normal for once in my life? Why do I have to be such a freaking weirdo?"

I ended up breathless after blurting all that out. I was waiting for Mr. Dan's response, but he didn't say anything. He just looked at me carefully, as if he was trying to analyze me.

"There's nothing wrong with you, Hunter," Mr. Dan finally said, calmly. "I think you're just experiencing a social burnout, also known as social exhaustion. That's normal for an introvert like you."

"For a what?" I asked, confused.

"For an introvert. You're what psychologists refer to as an introvert," he said. "You're an introvert, Hunter."

"What?" I asked again.

"Yeah," he said, "that means that you get your energy by being alone and you feel drained after spending too much time with other people. You see, unlike other people, introverts…"

He continued talking, but I couldn't concentrate on what he was saying. His words just flew around me while I felt like I was falling. I knew that I was weird, but I didn't know that there was an entire psychological term for what I was. And Mr. Dan, the only person I thought would not judge me, was telling me exactly what other people had been telling me my entire life: that I was not like the others. That I was not normal. I felt like crying again, but I couldn't let Mr. Dan see me cry. Not for this. I needed to get out of there.

"I have to go," I said, picking up my stuff and getting out of there.

"Hunter, wait," Mr. Dan said, following me out of his office.

"Thank you for listening. See you tomorrow, Mr. Dan," I said, trying to calm him down so he wouldn't follow me out of the library.

As soon as I was out of the school grounds, I started crying. I cried the entire walk home.

"Hunter, what are you doing here so early again?" My mom asked me when I got home.

"They still haven't fixed the water leak at the library, mom," I said without stopping so she could not see my red eyes.

I went straight to my room and I quickly fell asleep, feeling worse than I had felt in a very long time. When I woke up, it was already 1am. I woke up very confused and disoriented. Then, one by one, all the nasty memories of the last few days started to come back to me. At first, I was so disoriented that I hoped that everything had been a dream, but it wasn't. I wasn't so lucky. Everything had actually happened.

I tried to go back to sleep to forget about my problems, but I couldn't, so I just stood there in my bed doing nothing. I put on some music, I stared at my ceiling, and I did nothing. After a couple of hours, I felt a little better. I didn't feel so sad, exhausted, or angry anymore and the thoughts inside my brain were slowly starting to be processed and organized normally again. I felt in charge of my own emotions again and I didn't feel like crying anymore. I felt in control of my own mind and my own body again, and a huge relief started to replace the negative emotions that had filled my body the last couple of days. However, there was one word that kept spinning around in my head.

"Introvert."

The word used by Mr. Dan to describe me. I hadn't heard it before and I didn't really listen to what Mr. Dan said, so I didn't know what that word meant. But I wanted to find out. I wanted to know just how weird I was. So, at 3am, I finally stood up from my bed and I went downstairs to my parents' office to do a little research.

I turned the desktop computer on and I typed the word "introvert" on the web browser. I was going to look for the definition in an online dictionary or an encyclopedia, but the title of an article published on a blog called Quiet Refuge immediately caught my attention, so I clicked on it.

## So you think you're weird? Don't worry, you might just be an introvert

### By Sue Arevalo

'Weirdo,' 'basket case,' 'freak,' 'misfit,' 'odd fish,' 'party pooper,' 'downer,' 'killjoy,' 'wallflower,' 'shrinking violet.' I've heard them all. People have been calling me that—and much more—my entire life. Why, you may ask? Because I'm quiet and less outgoing than pretty much everyone else around me.

All my life, people have always loved pointing out how "different" and "odd" I am, so I grew up thinking that there was something wrong with me. I internalized years and years of people telling me how weird and abnormal I was that it became an intrinsic part of how I viewed myself. Instead of seeing and appreciating all the benefits of having a quiet, thoughtful, and reserved personality, I could only see the flaws and downsides of it because that's what people always loved to point out.

But everything changed when I started studying psychology at university and I discovered a magical word in one of my textbooks that helped me understand myself better: introversion.

The terms introvert and extrovert were first popularized by psychologist Carl Jung during the first half of the 20$^{th}$ century. Basically, whether you're an introvert or an extrovert depends on how you process the world around you. Introverts prefer minimally stimulating environments and they get drained by social situations —even if they're having a good time; to recharge their energy, they need to spend some time by themselves. Extroverts, on the other hand, get energized by being with others.

According to many theories of personality, introversion and extroversion exist along a continuum and everyone has some degree of both introversion and extroversion. However, people often tend to lean one way or the other. Introverts tend to be more quiet, reserved, and introspective, while extroverts tend to be more outgoing, talkative, and assertive.

It's important to remember that one type isn't better than the other—but they both need to be respected. Both introverts and extroverts have a great number of advantages and disadvantages depending on the context and the situation. It's important to know and understand your personality because, by doing it, you can understand yourself better and learn how to set your boundaries and play to your strengths.

If you think you're an introvert but you're not quite sure yet, here are some of the defining characteristics that introverts have:

- They enjoy spending time alone and they very rarely get bored when they're by themselves.

- They prefer to have a small group of friends instead of a large one.
- They tend to think (sometimes too much) before they speak and it's not uncommon for them to take on the role of the quiet listener in large group conversation.
- Sometimes they feel they can express themselves better in writing than in conversation.
- They don't particularly enjoy group work and they tend to work best when they work alone.
- They tend to dislike and avoid conflict.
- They need time to prepare themselves for social situations and they tend to dislike last-minute plans.
- They hate small talk and prefer to talk about deeper topics like dreams, the future, philosophy, relationships, and politics, even if sometimes these topics are considered "taboo."
- They are very observant and they tend to be overthinkers.
- They tend to be less influenced by other people and are less likely to fall in with bad company just to feel like they are part of a community.
- They don't particularly like parties and, when they attend one, they prefer to hang out with the people they already know. They very rarely go to parties with the goal of meeting new people.
- They feel depleted and burned out after too much social interaction.
- When the environment around them becomes too stimulating, they tend to zone out.
- They don't like having all eyes on them and they tend to dislike unnecessary attention.
- They have probably been accused of not knowing how to have fun for refusing to go to a party or attend a noisy bar or go dancing to a nightclub or do

any other activity that "fun" and "outgoing" people normally do.
- They prefer to hang out with one or two persons at a time rather than with a large group of people, and they prefer calmer environments than noisy ones.

Sounds familiar? You don't have to relate to every single one of these characteristics to be an introvert, but if you see yourself reflected in many of them, then you're probably an introvert.

To most people, the word introvert has a negative connotation. When they hear that word, usually the first thing that comes into their minds is shyness. And I'm here to tell you that shyness and introversion are _not_ the same thing. Introverts and shy people might sometimes behave the same way, but the reasons behind their actions are very different.

Shyness has, at its core, a fear of negative judgment by others. Shy people don't necessarily want to be alone, but they're afraid to interact with others because they fear that they're going to be negatively judged by them. Introverts, on the other hand, simply do not like spending a lot of time interacting with other people because it depletes them. They don't necessarily fear or dislike others, they just sometimes prefer to spend time by themselves because that's how they get their energy. And when they do socialize, they usually prefer to do it in small groups and in calm and low-key environments.

Of course, shyness and introversion are not mutually exclusive. You can easily be shy and an introvert—in fact, there are many people who are both, myself included—but they're not the same thing, there are also shy extroverts and introverts who are not shy at all. What's important to remember here is that people can overcome shyness, but introversion is something we're born with and that will never change about us. It is an intrinsic part of ourselves, just like the color of our eyes.

Introversion is not a disorder that requires treatment or a disease that needs to be cured. And sometimes, ironically, introverts can develop shyness because the people around them treat their introversion as something that needs to be fixed. That's what happened to me. All through my childhood and most of my young adult life, people kept trying to turn me into an outgoing extrovert. They shamed me for my quiet nature, they forced me to socialize when I didn't want to, and they constantly pointed out that the introverted parts of my personality were less than desirable, which in turn made me extremely self-conscious and practically made my self-esteem disappear.

People kept telling me that there was something wrong with me, so I started to believe them. I began to be afraid of interacting with other people because I thought that they were going to judge me and find me lacking like everyone else. Fear started to rule my life. But ever since I began to embrace my introversion, that shyness and that fear have slowly started to disappear. And that's why I started this blog.

It is estimated that one third to one half of the world population are introverts, so why do we constantly hear that there's something wrong with us? Why are people constantly trying to change us and make us more outgoing, chatty, and social? Why can't we be accepted as we are? Why do we have to change who we are to be considered "normal"?

I don't know about you, but I'm sick and tired of it. I don't want any more introverted children growing up hating themselves because they think that there's something wrong with them. I want the world to stop putting down innocent introverted kids just because they don't fit the extrovert ideal. It's time for things to change. It's time for us to start embracing our introversion rather than fight against it so that future generations won't have to suffer the same things that we did. It's time to speak up and stop letting other people make us feel bad for being the way we are.

And finally, to all my introverts out there, I want to say this: there's nothing wrong with you. There's nothing wrong with being an introvert. It's not something that needs to be fixed or cured. You are not weird and you are not alone. Believe me, there are plenty of us out there.

## Comments (8):

dylan_thorne:

Thank you so much for sharing this!! I haven't related this much to anything in my entire life. I come from a large family of outgoing people who would always ask me "What's wrong with you?" when they noticed that I didn't socialize as much (or as well) as they did. I never had an answer to that question, so I grew up thinking that there was indeed something wrong with me. It's nice to know that there's not. Thank you!

lordbecker:

I wish I had read this post when I was a child. All through my childhood, I didn't understand why I was so different from my friends and my siblings, so I spent my time wishing to be someone else. I wanted to be like them. I didn't know that my actions were totally normal for introverts.

lis4horn3r:

Thank you for making me realize that I don't need to be "fixed" like people have been trying to make me believe my entire life!

nancymorgan84:

When I was a child, I thought that there was something wrong with me because I was less outspoken and outgoing than my classmates. Teachers told me to "come out of my shell" all the time, and making new friends wasn't as easy for me as it was for my cousins and my sisters, probably because I didn't like the same things that other kids and teenagers liked. I wasn't loud, I didn't like unnecessary drama, gossips, or big parties, and I was comfortable being by myself. I did have a few friends, but not as many as it was expected. As a result, I grew up as an outcast. When I got older, I started to ignore those who loved to point out how "weird" and "different" I was and I convinced myself that there was nothing wrong with me. But I must've been lying to myself all these years because I didn't really believe that until I read this post. Now I can confidently say that there's nothing wrong with me. Thank you.

cosmocano48:

I have finally found the word to perfectly describe myself. All my life, people have been trying to tell me that I'm shy or timid, but those words never felt right to me. I've never been afraid to speak up or talk to people, I just don't feel like doing it all the time. Now I know why. Thanks.

mia.brown:

Never let anyone tell you that your introversion is a weakness. It is not. It's a strength. Embrace it! I started doing it a few years ago and my life is now considerably better since I realized that I don't need to be like my outgoing friends and family to be "normal." It's weird because I've noticed that, in general, society is always trying to tell us that it's okay to be different and that you should always be your own unique self. But what they mean by that is that it's okay if you're an athlete *and* you also like to sing or if you're a cheerleader who's also good at computers. But for some reason, when they meet quiet people like us, their first instinct is always to try to change us. What they're really saying is that it's okay to be different, but not like that. Well, it's time for us to tell them that *it is* okay to be like us.

paula_3489:

This!! I'm done feeling guilty for not fitting other people's idea of "normal." Thank you!

dean.jordan.22:

    Like many of the people in this blog, I grew up thinking that my introversion was a disease that needed to be cured. I spent my entire childhood and most of my young adult life trying to change and be like the others, but that only ended up making me feel miserable. It wasn't until I learned about introversion a few months ago with another post from this blog that everything finally clicked. I wasn't a weirdo anymore, I was just an introvert. These last few months, I've been trying to embrace my introversion and my life has considerably changed for the better. I no longer care about what other people think of me, I no longer feel guilty for wanting to spend time by myself, and, thanks to the internet, I've been able to (virtually) meet other people like me and, let me tell you, there's no better feeling in the world than knowing that there are other people like you out there. I'll be forever grateful to this blog for giving me that  3.

It took me a while to process everything I had just read. I couldn't understand how the author of that article had been able to perfectly describe me without even knowing me. It was weird, but for the first time in my life, I felt completely understood and validated.

Most of the things I had struggled with my entire life finally had an explanation. Suddenly, there was nothing wrong with me anymore. I wasn't a weirdo, or an alien, or an anomaly. I was just an introvert.

And I wasn't alone anymore. I wasn't the last specimen of a dying species, I was part of something bigger. I was an introvert. And there were other introverts like me out there. There were other people like me in the world. Other people that felt the same way as me and behaved the same way that I did. I didn't know them, but their existence meant the world to me.

"I'm an introvert," I said to myself with a smile on my face.

"I'm not a weirdo. I'm an introvert."

# CHAPTER FIFTY-SIX

I didn't go back to sleep at all that night. I spent the rest of the night and most of the early morning researching and reading more about introversion and different personality types. It was completely eye-opening and life-changing. I mean, nothing had really changed, I was still the same boy living in the same house with the same family in the same town, but I felt like a changed person. I felt like I knew myself better now. I felt like I could finally explain why sometimes I felt the way I felt and why sometimes I did the things I did. I was not a broken machine riddled with glitches anymore. I had finally found my user's manual, and it turns out everything was fine. I was not a defective human being, I was a perfectly normal introvert. Everything finally started to make sense.

When I got to school that day, I couldn't wait to tell my friends about everything I had learned.

"Hunter, there you are," Ty said when he saw me. "What happened yesterday? What did you leave school early again? Did your head hurt again?"

"No," I said, "it's a long story."

"I tried calling you yesterday, but your mom said that you spent the whole afternoon sleeping," he said.

"Yeah," I said, laughing, "so, here's the thing…"

And then I told him everything that had happened over the last few days. I told him about my social burnout, about my little talk with Mr. Dan, and about everything I read about introversion on the internet. I also told him how much that meant to me and that, thanks to that, I now had a new sense of confidence and self-worth.

"I'm so happy for you, Hunter," Ty said with a big smile. "I've always known that there's absolutely nothing wrong with you, but I'm glad that now you can see it too."

I couldn't tell all of that to Ariana, though, because she didn't go to school that day. At first, I worried that something bad might've happened, but then I remembered that she told me that, since her aunt was feeling a lot better lately, they wanted to visit the beach, so hopefully she only took a long weekend to spend some time with her family.

I enjoyed that school day considerably more than the previous couple of days. I still felt a little tired, but I didn't feel as exhausted as before. Plus, now that I knew that I had been experiencing a social burnout for the past couple of days, I was able to handle it a little better. Whenever I felt like screaming or crying, I just took a few seconds to calm down, breathe, and relax. Apparently, it was easier to do all of that when your mind wasn't constantly attacking you and telling you to be less weird and more normal.

In the afternoon, when my shift at the library began, the first thing I did was apologize to Mr. Dan for running out of his office yesterday. I told him everything that happened and I thanked him, not only for basically changing my life by letting me know that I was an introvert but also for everything he had done for me in the past year. He had been changing my life since I met him and I was incredibly grateful for that. If that's not the definition of a great teacher, then I don't know what it is.

I really enjoyed being back at work after two days of going home early. I missed watching students read, study, and play from the comfort of my desk; I missed giving book recommendations to those who asked; and, more than anything, I missed talking to them about books. I was very,

very happy to be back.

When I got home, I was in a really good mood—which, unfortunately, wouldn't last long.

"Hunter, come say hi to your aunt," my mom said when she saw me enter the house.

My mom and my Aunt Carol were sitting in the dining room, looking at a bunch of papers on the table.

"Aunt Carol, what a surprise," I said. "How are you?"

"Very good, how are you, Hunter?" She asked.

"Good," I answered.

"I was just helping Carol with some of the preparations for Jack's birthday," my mom said.

"Oh, good," I said, and then I went into the kitchen to make myself something to eat—and so she wouldn't start trying to convince me again of having a party.

But it didn't work.

"You know, unlike you, Jack wants a big birthday party," my mom said from the dining room. "Fortunately, he does understand the importance of turning 15 and he wants to celebrate it with his loved ones. He's not a party pooper like you."

Subtle, mom. Subtle.

"Good for him," I said from the kitchen.

"Your aunt still can't believe that you refused to let me throw you a party," my mom said.

"Yeah, Hunter, why didn't you want one?" Aunt Carol asked.

"I just don't like parties," I said, still from the kitchen.

"Don't even try to reason with him," my mom said to my aunt. "It won't work. I've been trying to do that for months and he just doesn't give in. Let's just focus on Jack for now and let that killjoy alone. It's him that'll regret it later."

I knew what she was doing. She was trying to get a reaction out of me. She was basically poking me with a stick, hoping that I would "come to my senses" and say that she was right. My birthday was only three weeks away, so this was her last chance to try to change my mind. She was trying to shame me into doing what she wanted. But it was not going to work.

"Although I still don't understand why would someone refuse to celebrate their special day," my mom said to my aunt. "But I guess it shouldn't surprise me, Hunter's always been kind of a downer. He didn't even want to dance at his middle school graduation, you know. While all his classmates were jumping and dancing on the dance floor, he was sitting alone with his friend Ben, away from all the fun."

I was not going to do it. I was not going to answer her. I was not going to dignify that with a response.

"I truly don't understand where his hatred of parties comes from," my mom continued. "Even as a kid, every time I told him that he was going to attend a classmate's party, he said that he didn't want to go. He only wanted to go if he was friends with the birthday kid or if his friend Ben was going too. I used to tell him that he didn't need Ben and that he didn't need to be friends with the birthday kid, that he could still enjoy the party and make new friends there, but I was never able to convince him. He would lock himself in his room and refuse to go. He has always been a party pooper. That's a problem I never had with Axel or Ashley, so I don't know where he got it from."

Now I wanted to answer her, but I didn't want to make a scene in front of my aunt. I didn't want to fight with my mom in front of someone else.

"And, you know, I always have to drag him to the family parties because he never wants to go to them either," my mom continued. "He says it's because I always tell him about them at the last minute, but I don't understand what's the problem with that. He never goes out anyway, so it's not like he has other plans."

I was starting to get really angry. If I couldn't answer her, at least I wanted to get out of there. But I couldn't do that either. I couldn't let her know that her words affected me. I couldn't let her win.

"I just don't understand what's his problem," she continued.

"Can you imagine any other boy his age refusing to have a birthday party? It's insane. There are millions of kids out there that would love to have the opportunity to celebrate their birthdays with a big party. I mean, I was ready to max out the credit cards to give him the party of his dreams, but he didn't want to. I don't know what's wrong with him. I don't know why he's such a party pooper. I just wanted him to enjoy his special day, but whatever, it's his loss."

Okay, that was it. I couldn't take it anymore. I didn't want to make a scene in front of my aunt, but a person can only take so much pressure before it explodes.

"Mom, enough," I said in an outraged tone. "You can't just go around saying that there's something wrong with me. There's nothing wrong with me, and I'm sick and tired of you making me feel like there is. I've recently found out that, among the many ways that people can be categorized, there are the introverts and the extroverts. You, dad, Axel, Ashley, and pretty much all the family are extroverts. I, on the other hand, am extremely introverted. I don't know why, but I am. I like spending time by myself because that's how I get my energy and I don't like parties because I don't like noisy and busy environments. They deplete me. I don't want to have a party because I hate being the center of attention. It's overwhelming and overstimulating. I can't stand it. It's not because I'm a party pooper, or a killjoy, or a stuck up, or a downer. I don't want to have a party because they're hell to me, I don't enjoy them, especially when all the attention is on me. If you *really* want me to enjoy my 'special' day, then you would just leave me alone because a party is the last thing that I want. I've been telling you that for months. So you can shame me, and insult me, and call me a party pooper all you want, but that's not going to make me change my mind nor myself. You cannot bully me into changing who I am because I don't do it on purpose. That's just who I am. Why can't you just accept that? Yes, I'm different from you, but that doesn't mean something wrong with me. I'm just an introvert. It's not my fault, I just am. And I'm sick and tired of my own family making me feel like shit for what I am and what I'm not, so I would very much appreciate it if you, my own mother, could stop criticizing everything I do and everything I am, because I can't change it."

I was shaking and on the verge of tears. My mom and aunt were speechless. No one knew what to say. Then a few tears started to run down my face, and suddenly, I was overtaken by a strong need to get the hell out of there. I didn't want to wait for my mother's response. At that moment, I didn't care what she had to say, I just wanted to get out of there. So that's what I did.

But I didn't go to my bedroom, I went outside. I went out the front door and I started running. I ran as fast as I could and more and more tears began to stream down my face. I was crying, but I felt free. I was proud of myself. I didn't know what my mom thought about everything I told her. She might've felt sorry for what she said or she might've thought that everything I said was stupid, I don't know, but at that moment, I didn't care because I had successfully stood up for myself.

I was not going to let anyone make me feel bad for being myself anymore. I was not going to let anyone make me think that there was something wrong with me. I was done with other people making me feel inferior, or inadequate, or weird. I wasn't going to take it anymore. And I was proud of myself for that.

I didn't notice it until I was already there, but I had subconsciously run towards Ariana's house. I don't know precisely why I did it, but I guess that I wanted to vent my emotions and frustrations with my best friend.

When I rang the bell, Judy, the woman who sometimes helped them with the domestic chores, opened the door. I had already met Judy a few times before, so she recognized me when she saw me.

"Hunter," she said, "what brings you here?"

"Hi, Mrs. Judy," I said. "Is Ariana home?"

"Oh, no, sorry, child, Ariana's not here," she said. "She's at her mother's funeral."

I almost fell down when I heard those words come out of her mouth.

"What?" I asked.

"Yes, unfortunately, Mrs. Matthys passed away last night," she said.

No, no, no. This isn't happening. Surely, this was a mistake.

"I... I don't understand," I said. "What happened?"

"She started to feel bad last night, and when she got to the hospital, it was already too late," she said.

"That... that doesn't make any sense, was she sick?" I asked.

"Yes, child, she had cancer," she said.

"What?... No, no, no, it was Ariana's aunt who had cancer, not her mom," I said.

"No, child, it was the other way around," she said. "Mrs. Matthys was the one who had cancer. Ariana's aunt only took care of her. That's why they moved here so that she could be closer to her family."

"Oh my god...," I said. My head was spinning. I couldn't believe what I was hearing. I pinched myself to wake up from this horrible dream, but when I didn't, only one thing came into my mind. "Do you know where the funeral is?" I asked.

"Yes," she said. "Is at Pinegrove Cemetery."

"Thank you," I said, and then I started running again.

Pinegrove was only a mile away, so I got there pretty quickly. The ceremony had already finished, but there were still a few people there. I saw Mr. Matthys talking to some of them, but Ariana was nowhere to be found.

I felt like I was in a bizarre dream. None of this felt real. It couldn't be real. No, life is unfair, but it surely couldn't be this unfair. Not to someone like Ariana. She didn't deserve this. It had to be some sort of mistake. I got closer to the gravestone, hoping to see someone else's name on it, but I hoped in vain.

## Lisa Matthys
**November 6, 1963 – April 22, 2004**

## Beloved mother, wife, sister, & daughter
*"It's hard to forget someone who gave us so much to remember"*

This wasn't a dream. This was a nightmare. A real-life nightmare.

I desperately looked around, searching for Ariana, but she wasn't there. I walked around the cemetery for a few minutes until I finally saw her atop of a hill, away from everyone else. She was next to a big tree, walking in circles and messing her braid.

"Ari...," I said.

She turned around and, when she looked at me, she started crying.

I walked towards her and she hugged me.

"I'm so sorry, Ari," I said, and I started to cry with her. "I'm so sorry."

"I'm sorry for lying to you, Hunter," she said.

"No, don't," I said. "You have nothing to be sorry about."

We sat in the grass for a few minutes, watching the sky in silence, and then she began to talk about her mother. She told me stories about her. About her strong personality, about her likes and hobbies, about her values and ideals, and about her caring nature. Then she told me what happened.

"She started to feel bad at around 10pm, so my dad decided to take her to the hospital," Ariana said. "They both told me not to worry about it, that she was fine and that she was just going for a check-up. But she wasn't fine, she was only putting on a brave face for me. My dad later told me that she felt indescribable pain, and when she... when she arrived at the hospital, she started to have complications. Do you know what her last words to me were? I was getting ready to go to sleep when she started to feel bad. My dad told me that they were going to the hospital. I wanted to go with them, but they refused. My mom told me that she was fine and that it was probably nothing, that I should stay home and go to bed because I had school today. Then, when I accompanied her to the car, she asked me what was on my cheek. I had just brushed my teeth and I had a little bit of toothpaste on my cheek. It was so small that I didn't even notice it when I looked at myself in the mirror, but she did. She cleaned the toothpaste off my cheek, then asked me if I had already had dinner and I said yes. Those were the last words my mom said to me. Even when she was in excruciating pain, she was worried about my well-being. She used some of her last minutes on Earth to clean off a tiny bit of toothpaste I had on my cheek and to ask me if I had already eaten. Even in her last moments, she was more worried about me than about herself."

"She sounds like a wonderful woman," I said.

"She was," Ariana said. "She was the best."

I accompanied her and her dad to their house after everyone else left and I stayed with them until late at night. They spent the whole night telling wonderful stories about Lisa and remembering her in the most loving way.

"Please let me know if you need anything," I said to Ariana before leaving. "*Anything.*"

"Thank you," she said. "I will. And thank you for being there, Hunter."

"I will always be there, Ari," I said, giving her a hug.

I arrived at my house at around midnight. I had totally forgotten that I still had an unfinished business at home until I saw the front door. I stood outside the house for a few seconds and then I took a deep breath before entering. I didn't know what was waiting for me in there, but whatever it was, I wasn't ready for it.

"Hunter, thank god, there you are," my mom said, hugging me. "Where were you? We've been looking for you all day. I've been so worried."

"I… I was with Ariana," I said and then my voice started to crack.

"Honey, what's wrong?" She asked.

"She, umm… Ariana's mom died," I said.

"What?" My mom asked, shocked.

"Yeah, umm… she had cancer and umm… she passed away last night," I said, starting to cry.

"Oh, honey," she said, hugging me.

"Mom, I'm sorry," I said. "I'm sorry I ran away and I'm sorry about everything I said."

"No, honey, no, *I'm* sorry," she said. "You were right. Everything you said was right. I was wrong and you did the right thing by letting me know. I'm so sorry, Hunter. I'm sorry that I haven't been the mother that you deserve. You are right, there's absolutely nothing wrong with you and I shouldn't have suggested otherwise. You have no idea how proud I am to be your mother, Hunter. I love you more than anything in this world. I was wrong to make you feel that way and I'm sorry."

That was the first time I had ever heard my mom say she was wrong.

"I love you, Hunter," she said, hugging me again.

"I love you too, mom," I said, holding her tighter than I ever did before.

# EPILOGUE

*TWO MONTHS LATER*

I never know what to do with my hair when I'm going to attend a fancy event. Do I wear it like I usually do? Somehow that feels wrong, but I can't pull off any other style. If I put gel on it and comb it, I look like Humpty Dumpty before his fall. I'm not even kidding, if I flatten my hair with gel and I try to comb it, I literally look like an egg. But if I don't do that, I look like Humpty Dumpty after his fall. A mess all over the place.

Usually, I don't care that much about my appearance, but today is Ty's art contest, and I want to look good for it. It will be held at the Museum of Art and we're finally going to see Ty's work, so it's a very special day.

After much consideration about what to do with my hair, I decided to do both things. I put gel on it and comb it, and then I messed it up so it wouldn't look so flatten. I was surprisingly happy with the end result.

"These are the ties that I have," Axel said, entering my room with a bunch of ties. I asked him to lend me one of his because I had forgotten the only one I had back in Cabo.

"I like the dark yellow one," I said.

"Here you go," he said, handing it to me.

"Thanks," I said.

"You're welcome," he said.

"Wait," I said before he left. "What do you think?" I asked, pointing at my hair.

"It looks good. I mean, not as good as mine," he said, looking at himself in the mirror. "But it looks cool."

"Thanks," I said.

"Are you still up for tonight?" He asked.

"Yeah," I said.

He was no longer grounded—my parents lifted his punishment after three months instead of four—but three months of spending almost every Saturday night watching movies and playing video games had really brought us closer together. However, that night we were not going to watch a movie or play video games, I had promised Axel that I was going to help him research universities (both in Texas and on the west coast) to help him make up his mind about where he wanted to go next year after finishing high school.

"Great," Axel said. "Have fun at your thing."

"Thanks," I said.

I finished dressing up and, after leaving Rufus with my sister, I immediately went downstairs because I was already late.

"I'm leaving," I said to my mom and dad.

"Looking sharp, son," my dad said from the living room.

"Thanks, dad," I answered.

"You look so handsome," my mom said, adjusting my tie. She then looked at my hair and paused for a few seconds.

She usually tries to tell me what to do with my hair, but this time she didn't say anything. She just fixed a couple of hairs that were out of place and smiled. My relationship with my mother had significantly improved over the last two months. It wasn't perfect, but it was much better than before. We weren't constantly at each other's throats anymore. It turns out that all I needed to do was communicate with her more, and all she needed to do was listen to me more.

"Thanks, mom," I said.

"Are you sure you don't want us to give you a ride?" My mom

asked.

"Yeah, I'm sure," I said. "Ariana's dad said that he would take us."

"Okay," she said. "Say hi to Greg and Ariana from me."

"I will," I said.

Ariana's dad and my mom had become really good friends over the past two months. After I told my mom about the passing of Ariana's mom, she rallied the whole neighborhood to show them support—and the neighbors vigorously answered her call. They gave them their condolences, they sent them food and flowers, and they offered their help with anything they might need. I guess that's one of the few good things about living in a small town. There's a real sense of community here.

"Have fun," my mom said, giving me a kiss on the cheek.

"I will," I said.

"Bye, son," my dad said from the couch.

"Bye, dad," I said.

I walked to Ariana's house and, when I got there, she wasn't ready yet.

"I'll be down in a minute," Ariana yelled from upstairs.

"I'm sorry, Hunter," Mr. Matthys said. "I'm afraid that unpunctuality was one of Lisa's biggest flaws, and unfortunately, Ariana inherited it. Thankfully, she also inherited her many strengths."

Understandably, the last two months had not been easy for Ariana and her family. After her mother's passing, the school gave her the option to take the rest of the school year off, but she refused. She didn't want to spend all her days alone in her house. She needed something to distract herself with, so she decided to finish school, and she actually managed to get pretty good grades on her final exams.

I have talked to her every day since school ended a few weeks ago, but I've also tried to give her space. I'm there when she needs me and I try not to intrude when she doesn't. I know she also needs to spend some time by herself to process her grief. Lately, she has even started to take long walks in the park with her camera as her sole company. She says that being surrounded by nature comforts her.

"How do I look?" Ariana asked when she finally came downstairs. She was wearing a white dress with a red jacket and an eye-catching golden necklace.

"You look beautiful," Mr. Matthys said, kissing her forehead. "Now let's go, the contest started half an hour ago."

Fortunately, the Museum of Art was very close, so we didn't arrive so late. When we got there, the place wasn't as packed as I expected, but then I remembered that we were in Mountdale and this wasn't a very arts-loving town, after all.

There were like 20 high school students competing, and they were all standing next to their paintings so the judges and visitors could ask them questions.

Ty was almost at the end of the room. He was wearing a black suit with a dark green shirt and a black tie. He looked very sharp and professional. If I didn't know him, I would've thought that he was a professional painter, not a small-town high schoolboy. His parents were with him, and they both looked very proud. Ty told me that his father had a hard time accepting that his new passion in life was painting and not football, but if he hadn't told me that, I would not have suspected it because I could only see pride in Mr. Johnson's eyes.

"You made it!" Ty said with a big smile when he saw us.

"Of course," Ariana said, giving him a hug. "We wouldn't have missed it for the world."

"Congratulations, Ty," I said, hugging him.

"Thanks," he said. "What do you think?" He asked, pointing at his paintings.

They were breathtaking. They had clearly been influenced by the impressionist movement because they had very vivid colors and bold brush strokes. It was evident that Ty's goal was not to realistically capture a scene the same way a picture would, his goal was to transmit something through his paintings. And he did. He wasn't just a marvelous painter, he was an artist. I couldn't stop looking at them, they were incredibly mesmerizing and beautiful.

The first painting was of three people playing in the snow, surrounded by different colored lights and a big red sun on the horizon. The second one was a painting of a happy family having a picnic at the park, which reminded me a bit of *A Sunday Afternoon on the Island of La Grande Jatte*. The third one was a painting of a city at dusk, but instead of black, he used blue, red, purple, and yellow to capture the night. The fourth one was a painting of a boy walking in a field of yellow flowers. And the fifth and final one was a painting of Ariana and her mother, Lisa, surrounded by a ton of colorful butterflies.

"They're incredible, Ty," I said.

"Ty…," Ariana said. "How…? You never met her."

"I asked your dad to lend me a picture of you two," Ty said. "Do you like it?"

"I love it," Ariana said, hugging him. "Thank you. She would've loved it too."

"Thank you so much, Ty," Ariana's dad said. "It's beautiful."

"It really is," Mr. Dan said, joining the group.

"Mr. Dan! You came," I said.

"Of course I did," Mr. Dan said. "Your work is amazing, Ty. You have a real talent."

"Thanks, Mr. D," Ty said with a smile.

I hadn't mentioned it yet, but Mr. Dan's hard work at the library paid off big time in the end because, by the end of the school year, more than half of all students rented at least a book from the library and a quarter of the students participated in the reading contest. That was a BIG achievement, especially when we consider how things were at the beginning of the school year. The principal was so impressed with the results that he even gave Mr. Dan a raise—and Mr. Dan, in turn, gave me a raise.

As for the contest winners, Hope won first place with the outstanding number of 28 books read during the semester.

Hugo came in second with 26 books, and Brian in third with 25. I was really happy for them. Their photo even appeared in the newspaper and a reporter came to the school to interview Mr. Dan and me about our work at the library. It was pretty exciting—and nerve-racking. I had never been interviewed before, so I was really nervous, but I think it went well. I talked about the joys of sharing your thoughts and feelings about a book with someone else, and Mr. Dan spoke about the importance of promoting leisure reading among kids and teenagers. I was surprised to see that this time the article was published on page 14, not 38 like before. My mom was so proud that she bought like five copies of that day's newspaper.

While the judges were talking to Ty, Ariana and I walked around the room to see all the other paintings. They were all beautiful. I was even kind of jealous that I wasn't born with a talent like that.

"Are you nervous?" I asked Ty before the results were announced.

"No," he answered. "Whatever happens, I'll be happy."

Unfortunately, Ty didn't win the contest, but he came in a very admirable third place. Instead of money, the third-place winner received an all-paid registration to Camp Marco, an art summer camp in Trinity, Texas.

"Oh my god, you guys should totally come with me," Ty said when he found out about his prize.

"Ty, you know I suck at painting," I said.

"No, it's not only a painting camp," he said. "They also have other art programs, including writing and photography."

"Really? That sounds kind of cool," Ariana said.

"Yes!" Ty said with a big smile. "What do you say, Hunter? Are you in?"

"I don't know...," I said. "Maybe. We'll talk about it later. For now, let's go celebrate your victory."

"Wait, let's take a picture first," Ariana said, taking her camera out of her bag and handing it over to her dad.

We stood in front of Ty's paintings and smiled for the

picture. When Ariana showed it to us, it immediately became one of my favorite photos ever. We looked so fancy, happy, and proud. After that, we went to Ty's house to celebrate. His mother made him his favorite meal and she invited us over to celebrate with them.

Oh, and speaking of celebrations, after all the drama it caused, you're probably wondering what I did for my birthday. Well, first, I went to have breakfast with my family at my favorite restaurant, and then I spent the rest of the day with Ty and Ariana. We went to the bowling alley, to the movies, and to have dinner at my second favorite restaurant. It was low-key, simple, and one of the best birthdays I've ever had.

Also, my friends gave me the best presents ever. Ariana gave me a beautiful scrapbook full of pictures she had taken of us throughout the year, and Ty gave me a stunning painting he made of the three of us and a gorgeous yellow notebook with a dedication that read: *Happy birthday, Hunt! This is so you can start writing all the stories that you wanted to tell when you were a kid.*

The first thing I wrote in that notebook was about that day and about how lucky I was to have friends like them. It's weird, all my life I've always kept my distance from other people. I've always built invisible walls between them and me. I've never let anyone in too fast or too much. But it was different with Ariana and Ty. I didn't have to let them in because, somehow, they already had the key. They didn't have to wait for me to open the door, they entered on their own. And I'm very glad that they did because they changed my life.

A year ago, I thought that entering high school was the worst thing that could happen to me, but this past year has probably been the best year of my life. A lot of things happened, and a lot of things changed, but I can honestly say that I'm happier now than I was a year ago. I have a better relationship with my family now, I made a lot of great new friends, I helped revive the school library, and I discovered—and accepted—that I'm an introvert.

I still have a lot to learn about myself and I still have a lot of growing up to do, but discovering that I'm an introvert and that there are other people like me out there has really changed my life. These last couple of months I've started to embrace my introversion and it feels *very good*.

I've started to set boundaries, to work on my strengths, and to identify my shortcomings. I've started to stand up for myself and I've stopped caring so much about what other people think of me. I've stopped being ashamed of who I am and I've started to love myself more than ever. Now I'm glad that I'm an introvert. I'm glad that I'm quiet, I'm glad that I'm introspective, and I'm glad that I like to spend time by myself because I've found a friend in solitude. His name's Hunter Grayson and I really like him.

# ACKNOWLEDGMENTS

First of all, I want to thank my parents for always supporting me no matter what. I love you beyond words and I will forever be grateful that I'm your son. I want to thank you for all the opportunities you have given me and all the sacrifices you've made, and, most importantly, I want to thank you for allowing me to make my own mistakes and supporting me while I learned from them rather than trying to tell me what to do or lecturing me about them. That is the greatest gift you could have ever given me.

I also want to thank my best friends, Adrian and Yerid. Thank you for being with me for almost eight years now, and thank you in advance for all the years that we'll still be together—which I'm hoping will be a lot. I love you, guys. Ty and Ariana might not be based on you, but the feelings that Hunter has for them sure are.

I want to thank my sister, my cousins, my aunts, my uncles, and my grandparents for loving me unconditionally all my life. Your support means the world to me and I don't know what I would do without you. I also want to thank my wonderful friends for always putting up with me when I want to talk about deep stuff like the future, our dreams, politics, love, human nature, and relationships. I know we always end up depressed after talking about those topics, but they're my favorite conversations to have. Also, I know that I'm terrible at answering messages and keeping in touch, but I love you guys more than you'll ever know, and I'm incredibly grateful to have you in my life.

Lastly, I want to thank the online introvert community for

making me realize that I'm not a weirdo like other people made me believe my entire life. I never imagined that there were so many people like me out there, but I'm very glad that there are. Every day, I am fortunate enough to witness how more and more introverts around the world realize that there is absolutely nothing wrong with them. You cannot imagine the level of joy and comfort that brings me. We may be quiet, but together, we speak volumes. I also want to thank Susan Cain, author of *Quiet*, Jenn Granneman, founder of *Introvert, Dear*, and Michaela Chung, founder of *Introvert Spring* for giving a voice to us quiet ones. My life changed because of you and I will always be grateful for that.

# AUTHOR'S NOTE

Thank you for reading Introverted Me, I hope you enjoyed reading it as much as I enjoyed writing it. Hunter, Ariana, and Ty have been living inside my mind for the last two years, so it feels amazing to finally be able to share them with the world.

As you probably guessed, Hunter is very heavily based on me, so if you want to know more about his story or if you have any doubts, questions or feedback, you can contact me at kevmartz97@gmail.com, on Goodreads (Kevin Martz), or on Instagram (@IntrovertedMeBook & @KevinMartz97).

Also, if you have time to spare, please consider leaving a review on Amazon or Goodreads. It really makes a huge difference and I would love to hear what you think.

Thanks again for reading this book and remember that there's absolutely nothing wrong with being an introvert :)

Printed in Great Britain
by Amazon